Producer & International Distributor
eBookPro Publishing
www.ebook-pro.com

The Resistance Lily
Dana Levy Elgrod

Copyright © 2022 Dana Levy Elgrod

All rights reserved; No parts of this book may be reproduced or transmitted in any form or by any means, electronic or mechanical, including photocopying, recording, taping, or by any information retrieval system, without the permission, in writing, of the author.

Translation: Translated from the Hebrew by Noël Canin

Contact: dana.elgrod@gmail.com
ISBN 9798411097085

THE RESISTANCE LILY

DANA LEVY ELGROD

PROLOGUE

In times of liberty, freedom and peace, each of us has a dream.

Sometimes we fail to define the dream before we are robbed of it, and our hope of realizing it.

In times of war, exciting dreams vanish, to be replaced by one simple dream. Survive.

Driven by an animal instinct, we tread along a winding path, littered with potholes. Some of us lose our way, others stray into dark alleys, but unique individuals see the way clearly. They know that ultimately a light will shine upon us, restoring our ability to dream.

I resolutely fought to reach it.

I gave up the exciting dreams, and discovered that even in the darkest hours we, as human beings, have an instinct that is stronger than survival.

Love. Unconditional, infinite love.

CHAPTER ONE

Smoke rises to the vaulted ceiling of the hall and I squint to prevent the spreading, burning sensation in my eyes. I look around. There doesn't appear to be a single person in the hall that didn't have a cigarette between his fingers. Cigarettes seemed to have become an inseparable part of hands. Deep inhalation and rapid exhalation. Another inhalation, another exhalation. The smoke, thickening and stinging.

Talking animatedly, men in tuxedos and formal uniforms are standing in small groups. Women, in elegant dresses, are standing among them, smiling, giggling, occasionally managing to join in the conversation. But not even the broadest smiles can hide the prevailing fear. In a flash, a smile vanishes, replaced by beseeching words. Occasionally, a single word is enough to evoke a suspicious look, followed by a scribble in a notebook. Once noted, you will never manage to fake another smile.

Round tables are scattered along the walls, each covered in white with colorful vases of flowers set in the middle. The black and white floor tiles seem like a huge chess board. When I tilt my head, I can imagine those in uniform on one side of the board and, on the other, frightened men in tuxedos and women in their finery, holding glasses of champagne. They continue to giggle and laugh until their cheeks collapse with the effort.

I imagine moving the pieces on the board, one step at a time, but time after time my king fails to avoid the looming threat, and I am defeated. I've never been any good at this game. My father claimed I wasn't focused and was shamelessly reckless. I'm not surprised by the fierce burning in my heart I am feeling now. The longing for my parents is always there, unrelenting, even in my dreams. Dreams that yearn to take me back to the past, but inevitably toss me into the gray present and uncertain future.

I pull a cigarette out of the pack, slightly raising one hand. Not three seconds go by before a man in a tie, holding a gold lighter, lights it. I am forced to assume a polite smile and nod my head in gratitude.

He opens his mouth and I imagine he wants to introduce himself. Quickly, I turn my head and lean towards Odette. His shadow moves away and I sigh with relief.

"He actually looks rather nice," Odette chuckles and takes a sip of her wine.

"So why didn't you introduce yourself?" I say, stubbing out the cigarette in the ashtray. "Nice boys no longer excite me," she says, arranging her gold curls on her shoulders and scanning the hall. "And I *really* need to be excited."

"Well, have you found anything exciting?" I look down as an officer in a gray uniform goes past.

"You know I have." She grumbles. "But he simply refuses to acknowledge my existence."

Looking up, I follow her glance in the direction of the bar. Her bright eyes are fixed on a massive figure in a tailored suit, and her teeth bite gently into her lower lip.

"Do you understand, Josephine?" She murmurs without looking at me. "That man excites me."

"No, quite honestly, I don't understand." I pour myself a glass of wine, examining the man she longs for. His soot-black hair is brushed ceremoniously to one side. His eyelashes are long so it's impossible to tell whether he is asleep on his feet, or simply bored to death. His upper lip is trembling slightly, spoiling the aesthetics of his perfect face with its rough, chiseled masculinity. He nods at a German officer facing him, and an unpleasant shiver goes through my spine. In a moment, anger burns as well. "How in God's name can you be excited by a man who collaborates with that scum?"

"Shshsh…" She turns her head towards me in alarm. "Someone might hear you." A fake smile stretches across her lips, and she flutters her eyelashes at a group of men standing nearby. "Smile!" She orders me, without moving her lips.

I clench my fists under the table and smile. The men continue to talk amongst themselves and Odette stands up.

"How can he not notice my flirting, it's unacceptable." She smooths down her long, blue, velvet dress with her hands. "No man has ever ignored me, and he will not be the first." She winks at me and strides to the bar, swaying her hips scattering smiles in all directions. The artificial smile is wiped off my face. I'm supposed to feel fortunate. Supposed to thank my hosts for enabling me to get through this terrible period without experiencing the hardship of the French people. I'm also supposed to feel anxiety looking at the soldiers of the occupying army, perhaps even fear, but the only thing I feel is shame. Intense shame at sitting here in this hall, full of food and dressed up to the nines while my friends, acquaintances and neighbors are fighting every single day for their right to exist with dignity.

Crumpling the edge of the tablecloth between my fingers, I sigh. I really don't want to be here. I really shouldn't be here. A proud French girl at a ball for cowardly collaborators and loathsome German officers who have devastated our country. I'd be willing to be in any other place in the world, except this damned place.

My eyes burn with cigarette smoke, but it doesn't stop me from pulling another cigarette out of the pack. I place it between my lips and again, like magic, a male hand pops up holding a lighter, and once again smoke spirals upward.

"Thank you," I filter through my teeth without raising my head to face the man in the black suit.

"Smile." The command comes from a familiar male voice and I nod and smile.

The chair beside me is pulled back and Claude tranquilly sits down.

"I'm assuming you don't really want to be here." He pours wine into my glass and smiles his calm smile.

I don't respond.

"You know, the day you chose to move in with us, we chose to relate to you as one of the family."

It wasn't a question, but I nod in agreement.

"I'm sure you'd prefer to be with your parents in New York, but…"

"You're wrong," I whisper and take a sip of wine. "I prefer to be here, in France. In my home. It's just that some of the French have forgotten that this is their home, and behave like cowards. They flatter these Germans as if they were our masters."

"Josephine, be careful of what you say," his tone hardens. "We lost the war and now we are struggling to survive with dignity."

"What dignity are you talking about?" I smile with bitterness and stub out my cigarette in the ashtray. "Every week you host traitors who collaborate with the enemy. And if that weren't bad enough, we also have to smile at the enemy."

"Smile!" He commands quietly, standing up to shake the hand of a German officer in a black uniform who has come to thank him for his hospitality. The German bows and holds out his hand. I shake it, smile deviously and introduce myself with only my first name. The moment he releases my hand, I wipe it on my dress. "Is this beauty also your daughter?" The officer asks in French with a foreign accent.

"Josephine is a family friend, she's been living with us for several years." Claude continues to stand, holding onto the back of my chair. "Her parents moved to the United States before the war and she stayed with us to finish her schooling."

"The United States?" The officer asks without taking his eyes off me.

"They moved a year before war broke out." I can hear the tension in

Claude's voice. "Her father was a highly respected engineer in France and he decided that…"

"He's still a highly respected engineer in France," I burst out. "It's just that now, he prefers…" I feel Claude's hand pressing down hard on my shoulder.

"His wife isn't well," Claude says hurriedly. "So he wants to help her recover and will then return to help in the important effort we are all making, that all Europeans are making." He emphasizes the last words.

The officer continues to stare strangely at me and I realize I should have kept quiet. My hands are trembling and sweating and I rub them on my lap.

"Do you manage to stay in touch with him?" He asks coolly, putting his hand in his pocket.

I shake my head. "We haven't been in touch for several years now," I tell the painful truth but it doesn't seem to calm him.

Please God, don't let him take out his notebook. It seems to me that if his bright eyes continue to scan me, he'll be able to read my thoughts, and I won't leave this hall in the same elegant way I came in. I repeat the desperate prayer in my heart and recover. I fumble for my pack of cigarettes and quickly take one out.

Two lighters flame and for a moment I close my eyes and lean over the officer's elegant lighter. He lights my cigarette and I nod in thanks.

"Claude is right." I shrug and fake a chuckle. "I'm really sorry my father is missing my host's successful balls. I'm sure he'd prefer to be here, enjoying your company."

The frozen face of the German softens but he still stares intently at me.

"Forgive me, but all this talk of politics and war just bores me." I shrug my shoulders and flutter my eyelashes at him. "Women shouldn't discuss things like that, we need to deal with what is really important." I take a small mirror out of my bag and look at myself. "We must make sure we look good so that you can continue to enjoy our company." I pinch my cheek and titter.

"I'd be very glad to spend more time in your company." The German takes his hand out of his trouser pocket and I sigh with relief. "Maybe you'd like to dance with me." He gestures to the dance floor.

"I'll be glad to accept your invitation after I've freshened up a little," I stand up, holding my handbag. His eyes move coarsely over my body. "We French women, you know." I titter again.

"We're always equipped with a make-up and perfume kit in case we meet a charming man like you."

His smile broadens and I turn away before he notices the expression of revulsion on my face.

I quickly cross the dance floor. Adrenalin washes through my body and my heart is beating at a dizzying pace. The long black chiffon gown rustles with each step and I glance in the direction of the bar. Odette is chatting cheerfully with two men. One of them was the commander of a Paris police station years before war broke out. He refused to move to Vichy after the invasion, but very quickly returned to his position, proving himself to be yet another wretched and spineless collaborator. The other man is a young French policeman I'd seen a few times before, one of Odette's enthusiastic beaus. She notices me and smiles, shrugging ruefully. I realize that yet again she hasn't managed to capture the attention of her traitor.

For one brief moment I was able to understand her frustration. Good French men had become a rare commodity in Paris, almost like good coffee, which people at the ball were drinking in abundance. Those who weren't incarcerated in POW camps or hadn't volunteered to help the Germans, were taken to work in factories in Germany. The few who are still around aren't really eligible for the "good men" group. They enjoy their freedom, thanks to family connections with the occupying army and, as far as I'm concerned, they are no better than those wearing gray or black uniforms.

I consider escaping to the stairs that lead up to the residential floor and locking myself in the bedroom. They were only a few steps away. But I notice a crowd of women around Brigitte and know that she would stop me, make me introduce myself and smile at her traitorous friends. She is wearing the purple dress I sewed for her, playing with the top button of her décolleté while one of the women touches and examines the embroidery on the belt on her hips. I love Brigitte with all my heart. She took me into the heart of her family, treating me like another daughter and I will always be grateful to her. But this game is too much for me right now and I stride towards the glass door.

The alarmed glances of the women standing at the door make me turn my head towards the lobby. Three men in brown coats enter with an arrogant stride. Their faces are cold and they stop at the first table. One of them tosses his hat onto the table and everyone sitting there stands tensely to attention. Three officers in gray uniforms quickly leave their chairs, and even those in black uniforms click their heels and nod reverently.

Claude signals to waiters to approach and walks over to greet the honored guests.

The hierarchy of evil. I roll my eyes in scorn. Military officers fear SS officers and everyone, without exception, is terrified of the secret police. Strange how they define it as the secret police when there is nothing secret about the sickening figures who have just turned the ball into a survival arena for all participants.

Fear prevails in every corner of the hall. If the smell of smoke wasn't so dominant, I'm sure I could have smelled the fear. This game is far too much for me. I rub my nose and turn again towards the glass door. Opening the door, I peep out. Not a soul there. The garden is deserted. Walking over in my high heels, I lean my elbows on the low stone wall. The cold freezes my bones but I prefer turning into a block of ice than being warm in that terrible hall.

"Smile," I murmur tiredly to myself. "Smile even when you feel like vomiting. Smile even when you want to scream, even when you feel like wiping out all those German bastards with a machine gun."

"You don't have to smile for me."

The deep male voice stops my breath. Stressed, I bow my head. In a flash, my body stiffens and I realize the terrible implications of my murmurs.

"No, no, I didn't mean…" I stutter, refusing to look at the man standing beside me. "Maybe I had a little to drink and you know French women… alcohol…"

"I most certainly know French women." He sounded amused. "But I haven't yet met a French woman who can indulge in a warm hall but prefers to go out into the cold.

Are things that bad in there?"

I frown in an attempt to identify his accent. Fear spreads through my body, eclipsing the sensation of cold, and I realize that this time I really am in trouble. My fingers are trembling on the clasp of my handbag and, finally, I open it and take out the pack of cigarettes. Playing with a cigarette, I place it between my lips, cautiously raising my head towards the offered flame of the lighter and choke. His upper lip is raised in a slight playful smile on his strong face. His long eyelashes hide the color of his eyes, and I cannot make out whether his smile is real or not. My anxiety increases.

"Thank you," coughing, I take a step back.

"Gabriel Augustine." He holds out his hand and, for a moment, I examine the long, thick fingers, trying to repress the thought of them closing around my neck and suffocating me. "And you, do you have a name?"

"Yes," I whisper, inhaling the nicotine into my lungs.

"And your name is?" The tone of his voice is still amused. I wipe away the cold sweat on my forehead. Pull yourself together! I scold myself. You've managed to get yourself out of worse situations. It's only a survival game.

"Josephine." I cough and toss my cigarette onto the rough tiles. "Josephine Portier." I hold out my hand and he takes it, his thumb sliding over it and then he shakes his head and quickly removes his jacket.

"Forgive my bad manners." He approaches and I step back in alarm. "Your hand is freezing and while I'm talking to you, you could catch pneumonia." He closes the gap between us and drapes the jacket over my bare shoulders. His gentlemanly behavior is hardly surprising, but I'm unable to recover from the anxiety enveloping me. I stare at his white buttoned shirt that perfectly matches his upper body. His shoulders are enormous and his prominent muscles are visible through the thin cotton, easily able to help him viciously grip my neck or break vital bones in my body. Unfortunately, I've seen this happen more than once. Too often in recent years.

"Would you like me to accompany you inside?"

I shake my head.

"Well, if you have no objection, I'll keep you company out here." He leans forward, placing his elbows on the wall. For a moment, he looks like an ordinary man. A tall, impressive man. What a pity he's probably the one who will make me pay for my big mouth.

"I didn't mean what I said." I approach the wall, pulling the jacket more tightly around my body. "When I drink too much, I talk nonsense, like a little girl."

"What are you doing here?" He asks, ignoring my beseeching comment.

"I live here." Another slip of the tongue. Maybe I shouldn't have told him. I may have gotten my beloved hosts into trouble now.

"You can't possibly be Claude's daughter." He glances at me, then turns his gaze back to the garden. "They're blond and blue-eyed and your exotic appearance is hard to miss."

Is my assassin trying to compliment me now?

"I'm not his daughter. I've spent the last few years with them. They're actually my second family."

"And where is your first family?"

Half-closing my eyes, I try and work out what he's staring at with such concentration, but the garden is dark and apart from the row of trees I can't see a thing. Maybe he's focusing on the quickest way to eliminate me.

"They moved to New York. I stayed to complete my studies. I was supposed to complete my fashion design course but when the Germans bombed…" I fall silent. Relative to someone who is supposed to be begging for her life and expressing trust in the new government, I'm not doing very well. "In any case, I didn't complete my studies and I help Claude and Brigitte at their garment factory."

"I'm sorry to hear that your plans have been disrupted by the war."

The sincerity of his words confuses me, but I recover myself. It's a test. He's testing me.

"Compromises must be made to aid the war effort," I recite one of Claude's speeches. "All Europeans must mobilize to help the Reich."

"Of course," he says indifferently.

"Your accent isn't Parisian but neither is it German." I hurriedly change the subject.

"Because I am neither one nor the other." He moves away from the wall, and I am forced to straighten up and raise my head to look at him. "I'm a Swiss diamond dealer and I've been staying in the city for the past few months."

"You're Swiss?" I ask in an attempt to gain some time to work out whether he's leading me astray or not.

"Yes." Again he smiles, a small smile that makes his eyes close even more. "And as you probably know, we're a neutral country so we've decided not to force anyone to smile against their wishes."

My lips stretch into a smile. This very natural action seems strange to me and I rub my cheeks to see if I'm smiling a real smile.

"When a woman isn't forced to smile, her smile is so much lovelier." He winks at me and his other eye opens slightly. Just before it closes again, I notice that it's a dark green color. The sensation of heavy cold disintegrates into a warm tingling down my spine, and the smile is wiped off my face.

It's a test. It has to be a test. I'd seen how my brave friends had spoken out in the past and been attacked by someone posing as a suitor. I'd heard about torture, humiliation and severe punishment meted out to their families. It was a game of survival and I couldn't allow myself to lose.

"Thank you for the jacket." I take it off and hand it to him. "Nobody forces me to smile." I arrange my black wavy hair on my shoulders and raise my chin. "I smile because I'm happy. I'm proud of the German Reich's decision to save the European peoples from failing leadership, and unite us under a strong leadership that will provide economic and social stability."

Gabriel's face remains expressionless and I put on my fake smile and enter the warm hall that has never felt so cold to me.

CHAPTER TWO

Lying in bed, I leaf through an old fashion magazine, absorbed in impressive designs of the elegant evening dresses worn by models, my fingers traveling over the perfect finish of the high collars. My course in fashion design was abruptly and brutally disrupted in June, 1940. I will never forget that cursed day when the Germans invaded Paris. The memory of their grandiose parade makes me shiver. "Invaded Paris," is not an accurate way to define it. Our army was defeated, and German soldiers simply strolled into the streets of the city. No-one tried to prevent them and no-one believed that three years later these cursed invaders would still be here.

In my naiveté, I believed it was just a bump along the way, that our great leaders would join forces with the British. Stroking the edge of the worn page, I laugh contemptuously. The flag with its swastika was hung at the front of the building and the classrooms were confiscated and turned into Nazis' offices, but this was only the beginning. When I was told that several of our brilliant lecturers had been accused of communist ideology and disappeared one by one, I still hopped over the bumps and maintained cautious optimism.

During this period, we were still meeting once a week at Nita's house. She was a friend from the course who kindly agreed to host us. We'd sit in the spacious drawing room, drinking wine, laughing, comforting and being comforted and, from time to time, one of our lecturers would join us and give us a precious hour of intensive study.

I skip a few pages to the picture of a model in a long yellow skirt and shudder. I'd always loved the color yellow. I begged Claude to find me some yellow fabrics. It was such a summery, optimistic color. I loved it until the evening I arrived for a meeting at Nita's and found her wearing a patch in that color on the lapel of her blouse. I was so busy feeling sorry for myself about the way in which my life had changed and the shattering of my dream to complete my studies and open my own boutique, that I hadn't really listened during dinner to Claude's explanations of the sensitive situation of certain groups in the French population. I lived in my own melancholy bubble, completely indifferent to the plight of others. Even during that gathering, I didn't grasp the meaning of the patch, none of the students asked her about it and Nita didn't volunteer information.

At the meeting a week later, only half the girls came and the guest table was laid with relatively modest food in comparison to previous meetings. This time, Nita spoke. She told us that her father had lost his job as a chemistry lecturer at the university, and her mother, who had never worked a day in her life, had started working in a friend's bakery on the corner of the street. She apologized for being unable to continue hosting us and asked if we could hold the meetings at one of our houses.

I remember with shame how the girls squirmed uncomfortably in their seats and how, one by one, with weak excuses, left. Out of a group of twenty proud and smiling girls, four were left. Not really proud or smiling. That evening, we didn't discuss design, studies or dreams, but the hardships that had sprung up in our lives since that damned invasion. It was only then I began to realize I was living in a bubble. Each one shared the difficulty of making a living and when it was my turn I told them about the foreign and oppressive presence in Claude's factory. How in one day, all the soft, colorful fabrics vanished, and the prestigious factory became a production center for gray and black uniforms.

Simone shuddered and censured me for cooperating with the Germans, and Natalie rolled her eyes and cursed. Nita was the only one who said nothing but I will never forget the look of disappointment on her face.

And so, that evening, a few months after the invasion, the season of meetings came to an end for me, and the season of shame began.

I throw the magazine onto the dresser and burrow into my soft, pampering duvet. My thoughts drift to the dining room on the ground floor, to the small family dinner, three years previously, when Claude told us he faced two possibilities. Turn the clothing factory into a factory for the production of uniforms, in exchange for a fair price from the Germans, or part with it with nothing.

Brigitte burst into tears, and while Claude attempted to comfort her, Odette made an impassioned speech about our being an occupied nation, and how history has proved that whoever cooperates with the occupier, manages to survive the hardship of the times.

Given that she had never taken any interest in history lessons and the only thing that mattered to her were her many suitors, her speech managed to impress me. I found myself nodding in agreement, and so the die was cast, formally turning us all into collaborators.

The door to my room opens and, flushed and smiling, Odette bursts in. She takes a step forward, spins round and leans back against the door with a dreamy expression.

"I'm a genius," she declares, giggling. "The dress you sewed for me, simply doesn't allow any man to remain indifferent."

Reluctantly, I sit up and look at my new artistic creation. I had undoubtedly succeeded with a stylish finish on the delicate, velvet fabric, and Odette is the perfect model for this special gown. The truth is that she is the perfect model for any gown, but the blue color blends with her eyes and her gold curls give her a look of nobility.

"Did you succeed in getting the attention of the man who excites you?" I'm surprised that my question about him makes me uneasy.

"Which one?" She giggles again and turns her back to me.

Standing up, I unzip her gown.

"Uh, you mean the man who accompanied you from the garden into the hall?" Stripping off the dress, she tosses it onto the back of the chair.

"No, he didn't accompany me, he only…" I stammer with embarrassment.

"Stop being so serious," she scolded me affectionately, stretching down on my bed in her transparent slip. "If there's a man who prefers you to me, I'm willing to accept defeat."

I stare appreciatively at her perfect figure, inadvertently sliding my hands over my hips. She is taller and more slender than I am, but every time I compliment her, she firmly maintains that she'd sell her soul to the devil for my full, round curves.

"He's not at all my style." I grumble. "Vile collaborators don't excite me." I open my closet door, toss her a nightdress and lie down beside her.

"Shshsh…" she hushes me in alarm. "The cleaners are still here. They mustn't hear you, you know none of them can be trusted." She gives me a hard look, and deftly puts on the nightdress. Indifferently, I roll my eyes.

"Father told me he's one of the most successful diamond dealers in Europe." She pulls the fine pins out of her hair. "He says that during the war, only a few dealers managed to build up their businesses."

"I've told you…I don't care if he's French, Italian or Swiss, he's still a traitor!" I whisper in her ear.

"You're incorrigible." She digs her elbow into me, and turns on her side to look at me. "In any case, tonight I finally met a man who excites me, and I think I excite him too."

"Who's the lucky man this time?" Covering my mouth with my hand, I yawn.

"He's an intelligence officer." She bites her bottom lip. "He only arrived in Paris two weeks ago, and is considered a rising star in this war."

"A German?" I shriek.

"You say that as if they aren't human beings." Her glance hardens. "There are two sides in every war. One side wins and the other side loses. That doesn't make the losing side inhuman."

"Do you hear yourself?" I move away to the edge of the bed. "They aren't only a winning side. They are scum who exploit their victory in order to brutally trample anything standing in their way. They…"

"Shshsh…" Odette silences me, frowning with annoyance. "I told you, the cleaners are still here. And in any case, you're talking nonsense. If we, the French, had won the war, do you think we'd behave any differently?"

"There is no doubt about it." I get off the bed and move to the armchair near the window.

"So how do you explain the fact that so many honest, decent French people collaborate with them?" She scrabbles in my handbag on the dresser, takes out a cigarette and a lighter and gestures to me to open the window.

I open it and shiver with the cold breeze coming in.

"The honest and decent don't collaborate with them." I sigh and hug myself. "The honest and decent don't spend time with them at balls, don't make a living from their filthy money, and don't smile at them as if they'd come here to save us. The honest and decent are lying in bed and dying from hunger."

"You and your disgusting judgements." Rising, she goes over to the window. "Have you forgotten that you are here, well fed and satisfied, because of our ability, as your hosts, to live in peace with the occupiers?" Throwing the cigarette out of the window, she stares at me. "We patiently accept to your righteous outbursts, but you refuse to acknowledge that you put us all in danger."

"I can't continue to live like this!" I shriek. "I can't continue to smile and giggle and eat excellent meat, while our friends pay outrageous prices on the black market for a rotten egg. I'd rather fight them for our existence and finally rid myself of this terrible shame that is consuming my soul."

Odette closes the window and looks fearfully at the closed door. Tensely, I anticipate a counterattack but she bows her head, and when she looks at me her eyes are full of tears.

"Josephine, I'm just as proud a Frenchwoman as you are." Taking my hand, she strokes it. "Ever since the beginning of the war, I've seen my people wither away. I've seen people drinking cheap coffee in a café one day, and disappear off the earth the very next. One neighbor informs on another, women fight to the death in line for food rations, men, who desert their women and children so they won't be sent to Drancy." She sniffs. "I'm not sure there is any French pride left."

"But there are others." I squeeze her hand. "There are those who hang on to their humanity, who help their neighbors, join the underground and hide people who are wanted."

"All that heroism isn't for me." Her shoulders droop in defeat. "I've never been courageous, I've always chosen to keep my sanity, wear rose-colored glasses and repress all the evil in the world. My little war is not to allow them to break my spirit, and when the day comes for them to leave…" she leans over and whispers in my ear: "I will take off my rose-colored glasses and will have to live with the shame that you are feeling now. Until then…" She straightens up and stretches her neck. "Until then, I will go on living a lie and fantasizing about that man who managed to excite me." Dropping my hand, she leaves the room.

Opening the window, I fill my lungs with cold air and dream about uniting with my parents. Allow myself to fantasize about my father's loving hug and my mother's comforting smile. Her serious illness distanced her from me for such a long time that I can't remember when I last spent time with her. My father tried to compensate in every possible way, and I never felt anything was missing. Apart from mother. Mother is missing all the time. I supported his decision to travel with her to New York to try the new treatment. I prayed that when they return I'd finally have my mother back. The only thing that comforts me now is that they are safe there, not here with me, ashamed.

Going back to bed, I pray that we meet again soon, in a time when pride is restored to France.

CHAPTER THREE

The young boy standing in the entrance holding the huge bouquet of flowers, looks thin and pale.

"Don't stand there like a scarecrow, come in and close the door after you," Odette shrieks at the cold blast of air.

The boy takes a hesitant step forward, closing the door behind him. He looks wonderingly at the magnificent entrance, reverently examining the works of art hanging on the walls, the antique mahogany dresser and the massive carpet covering the floor. That expression isn't unfamiliar to me. Visitors coming to our sumptuous apartment always pause in the entrance, impressed by Brigitte's unique design.

The four of us stand in front of him, waiting tensely for Lucille, the housekeeper, to take the bouquet of flowers from him. The knocks on the door were heard exactly two minutes after we sat down to the evening meal, and although we had never feared uninvited guests before, these days, no-one in Paris wants to hear knocking at the door.

"It's so exciting to receive a bouquet of flowers." Odette breaks the heavy silence. "I can't remember the last time I received such a bouquet." She gestures to Lucille to bring her the bouquet.

The boy remains standing but sways on his feet. The smell of roast from the dining room is so strong I seem to hear his belly constricting again and again. My sense of shame is overwhelming.

"Would you like to join us for dinner?" I ask, to the astonishment of the other three.

"No, mademoiselle. Thank you for your generous invitation but I have several more deliveries." The boy bows and rubs his belly.

Lucille opens the door and I look wretchedly at Brigitte.

"Wait." She smiles at me and nods. "Lucille, make him something small for the way."

The boy's face lights up in gratitude, and Lucille closes the door, muttering grudgingly to herself. She goes into the kitchen, followed by Brigitte.

Odette holds the bouquet in her arms and removes a small envelope.

"Wait until the boy leaves," orders Claude quietly and she grumbles.

Brigitte returns and hands the boy an oblong box wrapped in a paper bag. He doesn't peep inside, merely nods and eagerly thanks her. He quickly leaves the house; if he were to remain, someone might regret it and take the treasure away from him.

I continue to look at the closed door, my heart contracting inside me.

"Papa, may I please open the letter now?" Odette wrinkles her nose pleadingly and Claude nods, caressing her head.

She removes the note from the envelope and her enthusiastic expression changes to one of open disappointment. She hands me the bouquet.

"For me?" I take a step back without taking the bouquet from her.

"Maybe you didn't tell me everything that happened yesterday in the garden between the two of you." She winks at me and waves the note.

"Nothing happened." I still refuse to take the bouquet from her. Going back into the dining room, I sit down at the table and wait for them to join me.

I can't believe that this collaborator thinks he can win me over with a bunch of flowers. He must have heard my traitorous words. He is probably trying to approach me to see if I am part of something larger. Maybe he even believes I'm a member of the Resistance and participate in activities against the occupation. I smile bitterly to myself. What underground would accept the services of a spoiled young woman who lives with collaborators?

"I repeatedly tap my fork on the edge of the table, and when I look up, the three of them are seated looking at me quietly.

"He wrote that he'll come and fetch you at seven o'clock." Odette puts the note on the table. "Father, the suitor is the diamond dealer you told me about."

"He's a good fellow," said Claude quietly and seemed thoughtful.

"Josephine, you should go and get ready." Brigitte glanced at the clock on the wall. "You can leave your meal. I believe that if he's coming to fetch you at this hour, he'll take you to a restaurant."

"I have no intention of going anywhere with him." I stick my fork into a piece juicy roast and thrust it into my mouth.

"You can't refuse the invitation of such a man so rudely," she insisted. "He has connections with high ranking people and we shouldn't make enemies at a time like this."

"And I shouldn't accept his invitation if I'm not interested in spending time with him," I say with my mouth full. "I won't go out to dinner with traitors."

"Shshsh…" the rebuke comes from all three together, and Brigitte looks anxiously in the direction of the kitchen.

"Go out with him tonight and explain gently that you aren't interested in a relationship right now," Odette joins in her mother's attempts at persuasion.

"That isn't good enough." Thoughtfully, Brigitte rubs her forehead. "Tell him you have a longstanding relationship with a French soldier in a POW camp."

"Or that quite simply, I won't go out with him." I smile maliciously at her.

"You will go out with him and you will tell him what Brigitte has suggested." Claude concludes, standing up to pour wine into everyone's glasses but mine. "Now go and get ready."

I want to go on protesting but know that the battle is lost. Despite the attempts of my adoptive family to present family decisions as democratic, Claude always has the last word, and none of us dare protest.

"I also have a date this evening," Odette jumps up from her chair and pulls me to my feet. "He's a nice young man I met yesterday at the ball and I didn't want to rudely refuse his invitation." Not waiting for her parents' reaction, she hurries out of the dining room.

"Liar," I scold her when she comes into my room with several dresses over her arm.

"It's not really a lie." She tries on a black dress, shakes her head and takes it off. "He really is a nice young man and I can't refuse the invitation of an intelligence officer, they know that, too. I simply prefer not to worry them, so I didn't tell them he's German."

"But you don't want to refuse the invitation." I help her zip up the long wine-colored gown and, looking in the mirror, she nods to herself in approval.

"True. I don't want to refuse. I'm tired of sitting at home bored and waiting for the next ball. Why should you be the only one to go out and enjoy yourself?"

I briefly consider sharing my indiscretion in the garden and my uneasiness at the real reason for his invitation, but she has turned to the dressing table and seemed so calm and happy. Sighing, I choose a long, buttoned down, dark blue gown with a modest neckline.

"Odette, do you remember what happened to Monique?"

"How could I forget?" She shuddered. "Unfortunate girl."

"Don't say that. She isn't unfortunate, she's a heroine."

"She was unfortunate because in the end she was hanged," Odette said through clenched teeth. "And they forced her family to witness her terrible end, and immediately afterwards they disappeared. So with all due respect for your definition of a heroine, I prefer to call her unfortunate."

"Her only mistake was to accept the invitation of a German officer." I refuse to drop the subject. "And I'm certain there was a logical reason for a member of the underground to choose to spend time with an officer who ultimately betrayed her."

"And that is precisely why I don't get involved in unnecessary adventures." Standing up, she helped me with all the buttons, then sat down again.

"And maybe that's exactly why we shouldn't be going out tonight with men we don't know."

"Don't talk nonsense." She waved her hand dismissively. "The only thing they can discover about us is how bored we are." She giggles. "But more importantly," her tone becomes serious. "You do know you can't hide your body in that dress." She arranges the pins in her hair and peeps at me in the mirror. "It's a known fact that men are more attracted to women who hide their treasures." Rubbing rouge into her lips, she smiles to herself.

"So maybe you should try it for once," I tease her and sigh again.

"I like low necklines. I might not have a great deal to show, but what I do have, I show with pride."

Vacating the chair for me in front of the dressing table, she brushes my hair. "We are two complete opposites." She coils several black strands of hair, fixing them with clips to the side of my head. "You look like a mature woman and I still look like a girl." Turning the chair, she skillfully applies make-up to my face. "Your eyes are huge and black while mine are small and blue. Your face is oval with high cheek bones and mine is round. My skin is white, almost transparent, and yours is a natural, blush pink." She lightly powders my cheeks and hands me a red lipstick. "At least I have luscious lips like yours." She sets a red kiss on the mirror.

"You're beautiful." I replace the red lipstick and choose a more delicate pink one.

"I know." She puts on a hat, tilting it to one side. The lace decoration on it slightly covers her eyes. "We're only twenty-six. There is still plenty of time to be a woman."

"Odette, aren't you afraid you'll say something that might compromise you?" I ask quietly, settling the wool cloak around my shoulders.

"I've learned to talk a lot without saying anything." She chooses a mink coat for herself, puts it over her arm and takes one more look at herself in the mirror. "In any case, the Germans are convinced that French women don't have any brains. All we have to do is compliment them and remember to smile." She smiles her perfect smile but I can't smile back at her.

"Sometimes I can't help it." I put a packet of cigarettes and the lipstick into my handbag. "Sometimes I feel like standing in front of them and screaming at them to get out and go back to their own stinking country."

"Let's make a sisterly pact." She stands in front of me, holding out her hands. I take them. "On the day they leave and France is ours once more, we will stand together under the arc de triumph. We'll hold hands just as we're doing now and we'll scream all the curses we've accumulated inside us."

"Let's do it now." I pull her in the direction of the door and she bursts out laughing. Her lilting laughter always sounds to me like music and now, too, manages to lighten my fear a little.

She pauses at the door to put on her shoes and I go out and put my hand on the banister. The sounds of conversation from the ground floor toss me back into wretched reality, and I go downstairs, repeating to myself the rules of tonight's entertainment. Smile a lot, talk less. Answer only what he asks you, and don't forget the tears when telling him about your invented lover.

I'm standing motionless on the last step when I see the man who insists I go out with him standing in the entrance. He is kissing Brigitte's hand and shaking hands with Claude. Gabriel is much taller than Claude and his shoulders almost touch the door frames. His masculinity overpowers the air and when he raises his eyes to mine and smiles a little, a strange tranquility washes over me.

"Good evening, Josephine." His deep voice rouses me from my daydream. "I hope I haven't spoiled any entertainment plans you had for this evening."

"Josephine never goes anywhere." Odette declared from behind, forcing me to descend the last step. "I suspect the neighbors already believe we treat her like a servant."

"I'm sure everyone appreciates your fine hospitality," he responds politely, and when she approaches, he kisses her hand. She examines him for a few seconds and then recovers herself and peeps behind his back.

It's difficult to ignore the fact that Gabriel is scrutinizing her at length. The relaxed expression on his face has disappeared and his jaws are locked tight.

"Are you going out this evening?" He moves, blocking her view of the street.

"Yes." She puts on her coat. "I also deserve to enjoy the night life of this city."

"You can't go out tonight." His hard tone makes me shudder and I notice him glancing in Claude's direction.

"If Josephine can go out this evening, then so can I," she answers Gabriel impatiently, and I find it hard to understand why he thinks it is appropriate to address her so commandingly and impolitely.

His upper lip quivers and Brigitte and Claud exchange confused glances. Claude opens his mouth but at that moment, Odette manages to slip past Gabriel and skip down the steps leading to the access path, "Papa, the young man I agreed to meet has arrived." She calls. "I don't want to keep him waiting but don't worry, I'll be back before curfew."

I hear the sound of her running and stare at the three of them standing with their backs to me, looking at the street. The sound of the car driving away reawakens the throbbing tension in my belly. When they turn around to face me, Gabriel seems to look through me at some mysterious point behind me.

"We need to go now." He bows his head to me and then approaches and kisses my hand with an ostensibly mechanical gesture. He doesn't look at me. The tension in the air could be cut with a knife.

"I'll try and arrange it," Gabriel murmurs quietly, pressing Claude's hand.

My eyes are fixed on his long fingers and I could swear I saw a note passing between their hands.

Claude puts his hands in his trouser pockets and the note vanishes.

"Try and enjoy the evening." Brigitte caresses the fabric of my cloak and her eyes dart restlessly back and forth.

"Yes, have a delightful evening." Claude nods and returns his gaze to the dark street as if expecting to see Odette come skipping back.

I want to distance myself from the arm held out to me. I want to ask what the hell just happened here and why everyone is looking terrified, but Gabriel taps lightly on my lower back and my feet move forward.

"We don't have much time." He urges me and I descend the steps with him.

We cross the access path and stop opposite a white Citroën. Tiny drops of rain fall on my face, and Gabriel looks up at the sky and hurries to open the door for me. Only after I am seated does he close the door and approach the driver's seat.

"Tell me where she went and with whom," he demands and I look at him uncomprehendingly. "Josephine, where did she go?"

"Uh…um…" I stammer in order to gain time, meanwhile debating if I'm supposed to share personal information about my best friend.

"I don't have the time to explain to you why this information is important now." He tries to soften his voice. "I simply need you to trust me."

Trust him? I don't even know him.

Glancing at the house I see that the entrance door is still open. What is going on here?

"Josephine, I need to know now!"

"I don't know where she went." I stammer in confusion. "She went out with a man she met yesterday at the ball."

"What man?" He drums his fingers on the steering wheel.

"An intelligence officer."

"A German?" He shouts and I nod shrinking against the window.

"Then there's a chance we'll find them at one of the restaurants on the Grand Boulevard," he concludes to himself, and starts the car. I glance at the house again and see that the door is still open.

The wheels of the car sail along the wet road, and the silence inside the small space blends with that outside. I want to ask him why he appears so stressed and whether it wouldn't be better to take me home where I could sink into my warm, safe bed. I want to ask him what was written in the note and why the hell we have to find Odette and her German officer. I want to ask so many questions but his eyes are fixed on the road, as if he prefers to ignore my presence. I remain silent and practice my false smiles.

The gloomy view from the window fits my distress perfectly. I'm not used to being out in the evening and now I understand that I am not the only one. Two German soldiers are marching along the sidewalk and a boy is riding his bicycle at the side of the road. Lights shine in the windows of several buildings but all the curtains are drawn. People once lived in apartments that are now completely dark. They have been standing empty for several years. Since the invasion, so many families have escaped to the south and many were forced to do so.

I sigh heavily when I remember walks with my father on hot summer nights. The streets bustled with life. Full of colors, smells and the sound of children's laughter. Now, even laughter has become a rare commodity.

The car turns left and we pass a small café. The rain intensifies and drops drum on the three tables standing on the sidewalk. Apart from one man inside, reading a newspaper, not a soul is to be seen. The deserted streets continue to accompany us and my distress increases. I debate whether this would be a good time to tell my strange suitor about my invented relationship, but the car turns left again and I choke when I see three men in wool coats and hats pushing a man in pajamas into a black car while he tries to protect his head.

I glance at Gabriel but he doesn't take his eyes of the road. He seems not to have noticed what happened a second ago.

"We'll see if they're here," he says without looking at me and parks the car next to the sidewalk. I hold my cloak tightly around me and thank him with a nod when he opens the door for me. He waits for me to straighten the folds of my dress and offers his arm to me in the most natural way. I have no interest in this intimate gesture but the distress refuses to abate, and I'm longing to end the evening. I slip my arm in his and we enter the restaurant.

"A world within a world," I murmur as we stop in front of the hostess. The opulent restaurant is full of people. The round tables, scattered about the wide space, are laden with good food, laughter is heard from all sides and French blends with German.

"I don't see them here." He turns his head right and left and I do the same. He apologizes to the smiling hostess and we go back out into the street.

Gabriel holds the steering wheel and looks at his gold watch. "Stupid girl," he says angrily and beats his fists on the steering wheel.

I don't know if this is directed at me or at Odette, but I no longer care about this man's rude behavior. As far as I'm concerned, every passing minute brings me closer to the end of this evening. I clench my teeth and stay silent.

The car continues to sail along the asphalt and I hold my handbag close.

"Will you tell me why we're looking for them?" I ask in a small voice.

"You don't need to know the details," he answers brusquely. "When we find them the only thing you need to do is persuade her to go home."

"Why?" I insist, and see the tremor returning to his upper lip,

"Because she must be at home tonight."

"If you're upset because she went out with another man, why didn't you invite her to go out with you? She tried to flirt with you so often, I don't believe you could have missed it."

He rolls his eyes scornfully and stops the car outside another restaurant. A flag with a swastika waves next to a sign with large printed letters of the name 'Soldiers' House.'

Now it's my turn to roll my eyes. I pray we find them there, suppressing the most logical possibility that she will refuse to return home with me.

He opens the glass door for me and it seems as if we've entered the same restaurant. The very same abundance, luxury and even the laughter sounds the same. However, this restaurant has two floors, and in the corner of the ground floor are broad leather sofas.

"She's here," says Gabriel quietly, turning his head to me and smiling. I know it isn't a real smile and I respond with one of my own fake smiles.

He asks the waitress for a quiet place for two and she leads us to a side table.

"I'll go and call her." I rock back and forth impatiently.

"Sit down!"

If until now I thought him rude and strange, now I suspect a far more serious problem. He pulls out the chair for me, waits until I'm seated and sits down opposite me.

I turn my head in the direction he is gazing and notice Odette. She is sipping wine, giggling and explaining something to those around her with exaggerated motions. For one brief moment, when I realize how happy she is, my smile is real.

"Go to her in exactly two minutes," Gabriel requests in his deep voice.

"Explain to her that you aren't feeling well and ask her to go home with you."

"Will you tell me what the hell is happening here?" I whisper, ignoring the waitress who is pouring wine into our glasses.

"No," he says shortly and stands up when a German officer in a black uniform stops before us. He shakes his hand warmly and exchanges a few sentences with him in fluent German but with a different accent from those in uniform. When he introduces me he speaks in French again and I hold out my hand so that the German can press his foul lips there and kiss it. The officer scrutinizes me at length then nods approval to Gabriel and thumps him on the back. Gabriel sits down and glances at his watch.

"Go to her now." His tone is firm and I rub my neck in despair. If he has forgotten the basic rules of politeness, there is no reason for me to behave politely.

"If that's what will shorten this nightmare of a date, I'll do so with pleasure." I push my glass of wine into the center of the table and stand up.

It should be a simple task, I tell myself soothingly, hesitantly walking over to Odette's table. The arm of the tall, fair German sitting next to her lies casually on the back of the sofa behind her back, and he is looking at her with enjoyment while she motions to him to fill her glass with wine. She giggles incessantly, bouncing up and down on her backside.

At Claude's balls, she was allowed to drink one glass of champagne and didn't dare have any more. Here, surrounded by German officers, there is nobody to keep her in check. The task will be more challenging than I'd hoped. I take another step forward and she notices me.

"Josephine," she calls out and jumps up. "What a lovely surprise!" She waves her arms, beckoning me to join them. "Franz, this is Josephine, my best friend in the whole world." She picks up her glass from the table and sips at length. The German stands, bows his head and shakes my hand. His friends bunch together on the sofa, making room for me.

"I can't join you," I say apologetically. "I'm not feeling very well and I'd be glad if Odette could come with me to the cloakroom."

"Oh, my poor girl." Odette takes another sip of her wine then clumsily makes her way between the sofa and the table. "Of course I'll come with you."

Setting her glass down on the table, she blows Franz a kiss and links her arm in mine. Leading her to the cloakroom, I have to urge her to go inside. Her eyes are glassy and she doesn't stop giggling; I realize I must choose my words carefully. Checking the cubicles, I heave a sigh of relief when I see they are all empty.

Leaning against the sinks, she arranges her curls on her shoulders.

"Odette, I have a terrible headache. I'd be glad if you could come home with me." Standing beside her, I pucker my face in distress.

"I have aspirin in my bag." She waves a finger in the direction of the restaurant and hiccups.

"I don't think it will help."

"And I don't believe you really have a headache. You're probably disappointed in your beau." Giggling, she places her hand on her mouth when another hiccup appears. "It seemed strange to me too that he actually insisted I shouldn't go out this evening. If it was me he was interested in all the time, I don't understand what strange game he's playing." She pinches her cheeks.

"That's really not the point." Grasping her elbow, I make her look at me. "I honestly don't feel well and I'd appreciate it if my best friend would accompany me home."

"I'm sure Gabriel is a gentleman." She shakes her arm free of my grasp. "Ask him to take you home and Mama will take care of you."

"But I'd prefer you to come home with me."

"Josephine, don't be a baby." She sways angrily at the door. "I'm sorry your suitor is behaving strangely because of me, but I'm really enjoying myself with my suitor. There's no chance I'll end the evening now."

The door slams behind her and I realize I've failed in my mission.

I continue to stare at the closed door and her words filter down to me. What game is he playing? Why did he invite me to spend the evening with him if he desires her? Is all this unfairness to me the result of jealousy?

The volley of commands he fired at me from the moment we left the house echo in my mind, and anger overcomes me. The time has come to restore the self-respect he took from me.

Returning with resolute steps to the restaurant, I angrily sit down opposite him, pointedly ignoring the steak on an ornate plate in front of me.

"I don't wish to be here," I whisper between clenched teeth, lowering my head. "I've had a partner for seven years. He fought proudly for his country and, unfortunately, he's imprisoned in a POW camp. I intend to wait for him to return to me and so I'm not emotionally available for a relationship. There is no point in continuing this evening."

Slowly, I look up and see that he isn't even looking at me. His eyes are fixed on Odette's table and his finger is rhythmically tapping on the wine glass.

"Did you hear what I told you?"

"Yes." He glances at his watch and brushes his hair aside. "I understand that you have failed." His green eyes flash with anger.

"I tried." I shrug, twisting the diamond earring in my earlobe. "I said exactly what you asked of me, but she prefers to remain here. I suspect she is already drunk and I won't manage to appeal to her logic."

"It seems you didn't try hard enough." A broad smile spread over his lips as he bowed to a man in a tailored suit who was passing by. Leaning forwards, he takes my hands. This intimate gesture makes me uncomfortable and I jerk back. "Josephine, come closer," He tilts his head and his eyes bore into mine.

I straighten up and he presses my hands, signaling me to lean forwards. My head is close to his and he presses his lips to my ear.

"You didn't try hard enough!" His forceful whisper makes me swallow and turn pale. "You have exactly five minutes to make your friend leave the restaurant and go home with you."

Pulling back my hands, I stand up. They're sweating and I wipe them on my skirt.

Picking up his knife and fork, Gabriel smiles as he cuts a piece of his meat.

I no longer care about the reason for his bizarre demand. I have to leave this restaurant. With or without her, but primarily without him. I have no choice but to try another tactic. Glass in hand and smiling in all directions, I slowly walk over to Odette's noisy table and stand beside her.

"Josephine, have you decided to join us?" She receives me enthusiastically and to my relief doesn't mention our argument.

"I think I'm really drunk." The giggle coming from my throat sounds really embarrassing.

"This is precisely the place to be when you're drunk." One of the officers laughs and thumps the place next to him.

"I think I'm about to vomit." I cover my mouth and he moves away in alarm.

"I thought you knew how to drink like a man." Odette stands up unsteadily on her heels. "Your beau has given you too much to drink, apparently he has no intention of being a gentleman this evening."

Everyone around bursts out laughing and when I turn my head to Gabriel, his harsh expression is fixed on me. His insulting commands add to the disgusting laughter of the Germans, and holding Odette's hand, I collapse into her arms. "You have to come home with me right now. Please, Odette. Come home with me now."

Pushing me away, she gazes intently at me. For a moment I mistakenly think she is focused, but her eyes cloud again and she scowls in anger.

"Has your honorable beau insulted you?" Folding her arms on her chest, she thrusts out her chin. "Tell me right now if he's behaved disrespectfully to you. I'm sure Franz will put him in his place. Won't you, Franz?"

The officer jumps to his feet and salutes her. His friends burst out laughing and she collapses onto the sofa, joining in with her lilting laugh.

I've failed again.

Tears of insult and despair fill my eyes but I refuse to give up. "Odette, get up and come home with me!" I shout, stamping my feet.

The sounds of laughter stop, and I anxiously realize that not only the Germans are staring at me, but all the diners in the restaurant. My cheeks turn hot and I freeze.

"She's gone mad…" Odette murmurs, evading my glance.

"I just…I just want to go home…" A tear rolls down my cheek and I don't even try to wipe it away. I feel so humiliated.

"Go away." Franz waves his hand. "You're bothering us."

"Please, Odette. Come home with me." Tears sting my eyes. Turning her body towards Franz, she pointedly ignores my presence.

I jump in alarm when huge arms close round my belly and a large body holds me from behind. I can barely breathe.

"Forgive her," the deep voice booms over my head. "She's a little disappointed in how our date is progressing."

Odette glances suspiciously at me. The Germans gaze at him with complete indifference.

"Josephine, my dear, the evening isn't over yet and I promise you will not leave here disappointed." He turns me to him, leans forward and kisses me on the cheek.

"What are you doing?" I whisper, my throat suffocated.

"Shshsh…" He caresses my head and straightens up. "I suggest you stay because in a moment her tears of sadness will turn to joy." He places his hand on my back and leads me back to our table. I collapse onto the chair.

"I failed," I murmur, taking a large sip of wine.

"Do you believe that you tried your best?" He puts his hand on mine, gently caressing it.

"I think so." I wipe away my tears and sniff. The extreme change in his mood confuses me even more.

"You tried several times." He leans forwards and wipes a tear from my upper lip with his thumb. "It seems that no matter what you said, or how often you tried, she would have chosen to stay here."

I nod, finding strange comfort in the rough thumb gently moving over my cheek.

"Good. I need you to remember that." He smiles a small smile and this time it seems real. "And now I must ask you to trust me."

"I don't know you." I stare into the green eyes flashing under the long lashes.

"I don't know you either but nonetheless I'm taking a chance on you." He holds my chin in his palm and I frown uncomprehendingly. "It's too late for her. For them." He seems momentarily pensive, and then his hand leaves my chin and he takes a gold ring set with tiny diamonds from his little finger.

"What are you doing?"

"I'm saving you."

Standing up he whistles loudly. Silence prevails in the restaurant.

Gabriel smiles at me and goes down on one knee in front of me.

"What are you doing?" My shoulders tremble and I stare at him in horror,

"Josephine Portier, will you marry me?"

CHAPTER FOUR

Silence.

My heart beats wildly and the walls of the restaurant close in.

This strange man is on one knee in front of me, presenting me with a ring that until a moment ago was on his finger. His smile is broad and there is no tension in his face.

Could I be dreaming?

"Look at me," he whispers without moving his lips, his eyes not leaving mine.

The anxiety is so strong that I can't breathe. I realize I am conscious and surrounded by strangers who are waiting with bated breath for my response, but his response, which still echoes in my mind, prevents me from escaping from this place. I am saving you…I am saving you…

"Josephine." Gabriel takes my hand and kisses it. "Will you consent to be my wife?"

He nods slowly, hinting to me to do the same, and my neck tilts forwards as I imitate his movement just once.

Pandemonium.

The ring is slipped on my finger and I am swept into the air and whirled around in his arms. Clapping and happy cries in German and French are heard from all sides, and a crowd presses in around us. His large hands hold my cheeks and his fleshy lips are pressed to mine in a powerful kiss.

I barely have time to recover when I'm back on my feet and pressed to his large body. I hear Gabriel thanking everyone for their congratulations. My back trembles with cold.

"What the hell is going on here?" Odette's agitated voice jerks me back to reality. I am forcefully removed from the protective wall of his body. Her blue eyes stare at me in amazement.

"I…I…" Words escape me and my eyes fill with tears.

"I assume this has caught you unawares." Gabriel smiles at her, putting his arm around my shoulders and drawing me back to him. "I preferred to keep it a secret so that no-one would spoil her surprise."

"But you don't even know each other." Her glance darts from me to him and she sways on her feet.

"We didn't want to make our relationship public until we were sure it was the real thing." Gabriel sounds so sure of himself that for a moment even I believe him. "To tell the truth, I knew the first time I laid eyes on her, but Josephine hesitated." Tossing me into the air again, he laughs in pleasure.

"It's impossible." Odette scratches her head and tries to focus her attention. "I'd have noticed something. Only yesterday evening she called you a traitor."

I open my eyes in horror and again Gabriel laughs.

"Women…" This time he turns to Franz, and only now do I realize that he is standing beside her. "One little argument and you're called names."

Franz smiles and nods in understanding.

"Is it true?" Odette refuses to be persuaded. "It isn't just a joke? Because I think I've had a glass too many."

The only thing I can do is nod my head.

"I don't know whether to shout at you or hug you," Odette stammers.

"Better hug me." I burst into tears and hug her. Stress threatens to paralyze me again, and only when she wraps her slender arms around me do I manage to sniff and breathe in some air.

"Congratulations," she whispers and I am grateful she's so intoxicated she doesn't continue to interrogate me.

"We have to tell mother and father." She pushes me backwards, her eyes shining with excitement, "They'll be astonished!" She bursts out laughing. "Let's all four of us go home and continue the celebration." She turns to Franz, her eyes pleading. He nods assent and she claps her hands in joy. "You can tell us about your secret relationship. It's so exciting!" Running back to her table, she fetches her bag and fur coat.

"With your permission, I'll drink another glass with my future wife." Gabriel pulls back my chair and gestures to me to sit down. "We'll join you in a few minutes." He senses that I'm delaying and presses my shoulder, forcing me to bend my knees and sit down.

"Don't be too long." Odette links arms with Franz. "I'm not sure that in my condition I will be able to keep your secret." She frowns as she examines me, and then allows Franz to lead her outside.

I stare at the ring and my fingers tremble. My breathing sounds like a groan. Gabriel's large hand caresses my own, but the trembling doesn't stop.

"I suggest you have a little wine, you have a difficult evening ahead of you."

I take two large sips, pleading for the red liquid to calm my storm of emotions. When I am about to take another sip, Gabriel gently takes the glass from me.

"Not too much, you will need to stay focused."

I nod.

He continues to eat in a leisurely manner, stopping occasionally to thank people who come up to congratulate us. I press the knife to the meat but it falls when the trembling of my fingers increases. I put down the fork and twist the new ring on my finger. I can't think of even one thing he could say now that would soothe me. I look right, staring at the Germans dining at their pleasure, look left and then return to look at the man opposite me. Did he really make me an offer of marriage? Did I really consent?

I let out a dry laugh, but it breaks off the moment Gabriel's eyes are fixed on me.

He looks at his watch, sighs and signals to the waitress to approach. He asks for the bill and after she congratulates us both with exaggerated enthusiasm, the restaurant owner approaches, warmly shakes Gabriel's hand and refuses to take any money from him.

The way to the exit door seems to take forever. Gabriel's arm is around my shoulders and he stops at every table to be congratulated. When the glass door slams behind us I rub my burning cheeks. I didn't even notice that my lips were constantly stretched in a false smile.

I sit down in the front seat and the moment he starts the car I open my mouth to take a deep breath. "Gabriel, please tell me what is going on." I look tensely at him, removing the ring and placing it on his knee.

"Put it back on your finger immediately!"

Confused, I take it and put it on again.

"Do not take it off again." His commanding tone softens and he glances at me. "There are things it would be better for you not to know yet. All you need is to continue to trust me."

"Maybe if you told me what is going on, I might calm down a little." I open the window and close it again when rain drops splutter in. "I understand that…"

"You don't understand anything."

The car turns right and turns again. The streets are deserted and the gloomy weather makes the landscape even more dismal and gray.

In a few minutes I will be home, I comfort myself. I'll reach my safe and protective bubble. I'll tell Claude and Brigitte about the awful evening I had to endure, and they will calm me down. Every time I returned upset, they'd manage to calm me. This time too they'll do it, I'm certain.

The car stopped three buildings before the house.

"Move forward a little," I say impatiently, having to fight the urge to open the door and run home. The ring is like a handcuff pressing on my finger, I long for the moment I will be able to take it off.

"Shshsh…" He silences me, fixing his gaze on the street ahead.

A black car is parked behind Claude's Citroën, another in front of it. I assume that one of the cars belongs to Franz, but don't understand whom the second belongs to. The last thing I feel like doing now is smiling politely at unwanted guests.

Gabriel taps twice on the steering wheel and then looks at his watch.

"Well, why aren't we getting out?"

"Shshsh…" Again he taps on the steering wheel and I shake my head, putting my hand on the door handle. "Not yet!" He presses my thigh and I look anxiously at him. "Look." Continuing to press my thigh, he nods towards the house door.

The door is open. My eyes open in terror when I see Claude being dragged out by the police station commander. His young aide is urging Brigitte to descend the steps and she hugs her handbag. I can't hear the voices but see Odette waving her hands and trying to pull her father to her. Franz is standing behind, his arms folded, doing nothing.

"Dear God, we have to help them," I shout and pull the door handle downward.

"You can't help them." Gabriel leans forward and his upper body holds me in place. "But if you act correctly, you might be able to save yourself."

"Are you mad?" I try to push him away. "Let me out so I can help them." Panic leaves no room for logic. "Why are they taking them away? Where are they taking them? In any case it doesn't matter, I have to go with them."

"Control yourself." The harsh command shocks me and I try and push him away once more. "Josephine, this is no longer a game. This is about your life. Everything you do from now on will determine whether you save yourself or whether you will meet the same fate they do."

"You can help them." I gasp when his shoulder presses on my lungs. "You can certainly help them. You have friends in the police, I'm sure you have friends in…"

"I have tried to help them." He draws back a little, and again I'm forced to look into his worried eyes. "You also tried, don't forget that. But now your fate is tied to mine, and anything you do will have direct implications on me. Don't make me regret saving you."

"I don't understand what is happening here." Tears blur my vision. "I have to try and help them."

"We should try and help ourselves now." He sighs and gets out of the car. My door opens and he holds out his hand. I take it and don't let go even when he starts walking towards my beloved, adopted family. My knees knock against each other, I am extremely dizzy. The closer we get, the louder the pleadings of the humiliating images.

"Please, leave my wife and daughter alone." Claude holds onto the door of the car and refuses to get in. "Please, take me and leave my family alone, they know nothing. They have nothing to do with it."

"Father, where are they taking us?" Odette is weeping hysterically and the stunned Brigitte is caressing her head.

"Good evening." Gabriel stops in front of them on the other side of the car. "Pierre, why are you arresting them?" He addresses the police commander by name.

"I have an immediate warrant for their arrest," the police commander answers sternly, looking embarrassed.

"On what grounds?"

"I can't tell you that."

Again sounds of pleading and weeping and I sway on my feet. I look from Claude to Brigitte to Odette. For the first time I see my host weeping. Real tears down his cheeks, and he sobs aloud.

I pull my hand from Gabriel's and run around the car. I hug Claude murmuring words of comfort. I don't know what I'm saying, don't know if he responds, but my heart is weeping and all I want is for this strong man who has become my second father, to straighten up and reassure me that this is all a nightmare.

"Mademoiselle, I have to take you as well." The commander's authoritative voice makes me choke and I step back in alarm. "I've received instructions to take the whole family."

Terror. Terrible anxiety. This time I can actually smell the fear, it bursts out of me, overcoming any other scent.

"Josephine is not a member of the family." Gabriel walks round the car and pulls me to him, distancing me from my dear ones who are looking so lost.

"But she lives with them and I believe that…"

"I asked her to marry me this evening." Gabriel maintains a calm manner, showing the policeman my engagement finger with the ring. No-one but the commander seems to notice this declaration. The family are huddled in an embrace, attempting to comfort one another.

"Congratulations." The commander scratches his head. "But in any case she lives with them, and I think I have to take her as well."

"There is no clause in your warrant that instructs you to think" Gabriel's tone hardens. "Only family members are written there and my fiancée is not a member of their family but of mine."

The commander exchanges a glance with his aide and then stares fearfully at Franz who is lounging against the fence in his spotless gray uniform.

My beating heart threatens to burst out of my chest, and without noticing, I link my fingers in Gabriel's, feeling as if this is the only thing keeping me upright.

The screech of a car on the wet asphalt breaks the awful silence. It stops next to the police car and two men in brown coats dart out without switching off the engine.

"You're taking your time." The man in spectacles vindictively addresses the police commander.

"We were waiting for the girl," stammered the commander and, without any preparation, the men pass the police car and drag Claude away with them. Odette's screams shatter the air around me.

"Dear God…" I murmur, trying to rush forward and stop them. Gabriel's fingers release mine, his strong arm surrounds my waist and I am pulled back.

"Don't say a word!" He whispers into my ear and I sob quietly.

The men don't have to drag Brigitte and Odette. They both hurry into the car and sit close to Claude. Again sounds of weeping and pleading and my sobs turn into prayers.

Odette peeps out with weeping eyes. "Josephine, save us," she begs, and the door slams in her face.

I can't breathe.

The spectacled man sits in the driver's seat and the other man leans against the door, arranging his hat on his head and looking directly at us.

"Are those the only family members?" He asks the police commander without taking his eyes off us.

The police commander opens and closes his mouth. It seems to me that this moment of silence is the longest second of my life. My sobs cease and pictures of a dark cellar and cruel torture race through my mind.

"Those are the only family members," responds the police commander firmly.

I choke back a sigh of relief.

The man doesn't seem satisfied by the answer he'd received. "So who are those two?"

"You've probably heard of Gabriel Augustine," answered the commander in a placating tone. "Everyone at your headquarters knows the Swiss diamond dealer. Thanks to him, the Fuhrer manages to purchase more equipment for the war."

Gabriel bows his head and the other man responds with the same motion of the head, then fixes his eyes on me.

"This is my fiancée." This time, Gabriel precedes the police commander and his arm shifts from my waist to my shoulders.

"I was present at the proposal." The surprising intervention comes from the fence. Franz smiles and lights a cigarette. "And with your permission, I will return to the bar to celebrate your successful operation." He gets into his car without another glance at the secret police car.

"We should also go and celebrate our engagement." Gabriel says, caressing my head.

"Wonderful. Everyone is celebrating and only we have to go to work." The man shrugs his shoulders and gets into his car.

Before I can blink, the car shoots forward and disappears at the end of the street.

I continue to stare at the steam left by the exhaust and anguish engulfs me. I wait to feel the moisture of tears but my eyes remain dry. I open my mouth to let out a scream of terror but nothing comes out.

"I hope to be among those invited to the wedding," the police commander shouts as Gabriel crosses the street with me, leading me to the car.

"Of course," Gabriel shouts back, opening the door for me.

The car travels slowly. Turning my head, I look at the open door. Lucille, the housekeeper, is standing smiling in front of the police commander and his aide. I'm not imagining that. She really is smiling. Her smug smile scars my heart.

"I have to stay and look after the house…" I rest my head against the window. "I have to go back there, I have to…"

"You can't go back there." Gabriel puts his hand gently on my thigh. "Not now and not any time soon."

"But…" I open the window, feeling suffocated.

"I'm sorry." He sighs.

Drops of rain land on my face like tears, instead of those that refuse to trickle from my eyes. Taking a packet of cigarettes and a lighter out of my bag, I place a cigarette between my lips and try to light it. My lips are trembling and contorted and the cigarette falls into my lap. I try again and let out a jarring sob when the cigarette falls again.

Gabriel turns the steering wheel left and picks up the cigarette; he takes a lighter out of his jacket pocket and lights it for me.

I breathe in the smoke, rain continuing to wet my face.

"It's just a mistake," I whisper, staring at the cloud of smoke whirling out of my mouth into the gray street. "It has to be a mistake. They know Claude, they come to his balls, use his factory. They like him. He always cooperates with them."

"It isn't a mistake."

"It's a mistake." I blink and inhale again. "Turn the car round and take me to the interrogation offices. I'll explain to them. Remind them…"

"It isn't a mistake!"

All the emotions combine in a ball of rage in my belly.

"It's a mistake!" I scream and throw my cigarette out of the window. "You don't know them at all, I know them. You could have done something but you chose to do nothing. You were at their balls, you ate their food and now, when they've been arrested because of some mistake, you behaved like a coward and didn't say a word!"

He doesn't respond, just continues looking at the road.

"Turn around! You have to take me back. I know it's a mistake and I have to testify in their favor. I have to try and help them."

"Nobody can help them now."

The car turns again and I don't recognize the area. I wipe my face with my cloak and close the window. The rage refuses to abate, coupling with a sense of unbearable helplessness.

"I should have gone with them." My voice trembles and I sniff when the tears finally come. "I should have gone with them to testify in their favor. Even if it wouldn't have helped, at least I'd know I tried and didn't abandon them like a miserable coward."

Twisting the ring on my finger, I lean back in exhaustion.

"It really wouldn't help them." Gabriel stops the car in front of a tall residential building. "And it wouldn't help you."

What will I do now?" I wrap the cloak around me and look at him. "Maybe I could go to friends of my father in the south. Maybe one of my old friends would agree to take me in. Maybe I'll try…"

"You're coming to live with me. And tomorrow you will formally become my wife."

CHAPTER FIVE

I stand in the hallway leading into the drawing room, and cannot get a word out of my mouth.

He makes a joke. It was undoubtedly a sick joke. A direct continuation of the previous, nightmarish hours.

I lean against the entrance door and quickly scan the space. Luxurious carpets cover the floor. Brown leather sofas that look almost new, an enormous gold chandelier is suspended from the ceiling, heavy wooden furniture that give the place a warm home-like feeling. It's not what I would expect from the apartment of a European bachelor, who is temporarily living in Paris.

Hugging myself, I sigh heavily. I really don't want to be here now. I want to be in the warm drawing room at home, receiving my dear ones after those Mafiosi in brown coats understand they've made a terrible mistake and return them to me. The first thing I will do is slap Lucille's face for daring to smile despite her employers' terrible humiliation. Employers who had treated her with respect for twenty years. I clench my fist and imagine how that slap will wipe the smile from her face.

"Stinking traitor," I say between my teeth.

Gabriel comes in from the hallway; beside him walks an elderly woman, her gray hair caught in an untidy bun at her neck. She is wearing a white apron and holding a bottle of red wine and two glasses. Her round face is deeply wrinkled but, despite her advanced age, she moves with the grace of a young girl. She smiles at me as she puts the glasses on the table, but doesn't introduce herself. She doesn't seem surprised by the presence of a woman in the apartment at this hour.

"Thank you, Marie." Gabriel takes the bottle from her and pours wine into the glasses. "You should go home now before the curfew."

"Monsieur Augustine." She nods and turns to the door. "I've heated the bath water and lit the fire." She is wearing a long wool coat and glances briefly at me. "Don't you want me to prepare something to eat?"

"There's no need." Opening the door for her, he leans against the frame. "We had dinner at a restaurant."

I put my hand on my belly. Although I hadn't managed to taste the food this evening, the last thing I wanted was eat.

Gabriel takes a bundle of notes out of his pocket and hands it to her. She looks at the notes and frowns uncomprehendingly.

"Mademoiselle Portier is moving in with me."

She opens her eyes in surprise.

"I asked her to marry me this evening and, to my joy, she agreed." His tone is as dry as if he were describing the quality of the steak he had ordered in the restaurant.

"Oh, congratulations!" Marie smiles excitedly and fervently embraces him. I expect to see some degree of embarrassment in the two at the intimacy of her blessing, but both merely smile affectionately at each other.

"I need you to buy her some clothes tomorrow and…" he scratches his head. "And everything else that women need."

She looks at the notes and then at me, examines me from top to toe and walks away from the door. Walking towards me with her energetic step, before I can avoid her, she presses me to her in a warm embrace.

"I'm happy for him and for you." She pats my back. I'm unable to return her embrace. "It will be so nice to have another woman in the apartment."

"Thank you," I murmur, and sigh when the realization that this nightmare is indeed real hits me again.

"Do you wish me to bring you anything special?"

I want to scream that I want my life back again. I want her to walk with her light steps to the Gestapo cellars and bring back the people I love. Tell me that this entire evening is just a wretched mistake and tomorrow everything will be all right. But I just step away from her and shake my head.

"It's high time we had good news." She nods to herself in satisfaction and leaves the apartment.

What good news is she talking about? Stressed, I turn the earring in my ear and look around me. She didn't ask why I'd come here without a suitcase, or how come she'd never seen me before. She hadn't asked a thing. Just blessed, nodded and left. And now, here I am, alone with a strange man in a strange apartment, having to cope alone with my new reality.

Hugging my bag, I go to the window, part the curtain and look out into the quiet street.

Marie is walking with small, energetic steps. For a moment it seems to me that she's dancing, as if the old Paris still exists and she has nothing to worry about. A few minutes later, she disappears into the misty darkness.

Hands are laid on my shoulders and I jump.

"Your cloak is wet and you're trembling." His deep voice is calm, I continue to look out at the street as he takes it off me. "Here, this will warm you." He hands me a glass of wine and stands next to the fireplace.

The only lamp in the street flickers twice and goes out. My thoughts take me back to the restaurant. I can hear Odette's lilting laugh. Again I feel the humiliation at the sniggers of the Germans and my helplessness when she refused to go home with me. That feeling is like a fist to the belly. Unconsciously, I twist the ring on my finger and ponder Gabriel's strange marriage proposal, unable to comprehend why I'd agreed, consented to it. Then my thoughts thrust me back to that cursed sidewalk. The pleading and weeping; Odette asking me to save them, my adoptive family had really been arrested by the Gestapo.

Choking, I place my hand over my heart. Claude, Brigitte and Odette are now being interrogated. My breathing grows heavy. I'm in a strange apartment with a strange man. I'm utterly alone. If only it were a nightmare, I'd have woken from the sharp pain splitting my heart.

I'm awake. And it did all really happen. "I can't stay here." Slowly, I turn my head, closing my eyes as the sense of heavy tiredness assails me. "Could I use your telephone, I'm sure I can think of someone who would agree to host me. Someone I know."

Opening my eyes, I see him looking at me. He isn't smiling, but neither does he look as distressed as I am.

"Josephine, please sit down." He gestures to the sofa.

"I don't wish to sit down. I wish to go." Putting the glass of wine on the dresser, I hug my bag. The only object remaining in my possession.

"Josephine, please sit down."

Sighing, I go over to the sofa and erectly and stiffly sit down on the edge.

He goes to the dresser, takes my glass of wine, and sets it down in front of me. Only after I take a small sip does he go back to the fireplace and light a cigarette.

"I realize that this new situation is uncomfortable for you, but the moment I decided to save you, I linked my fate with yours. Now both of us must cope with the discomfort."

"I didn't ask you to save me." I take out my pack of cigarettes, frowning when I find it to be empty. He gives me his cigarette and I nod in thanks and rub my forehead. "I don't really understand what you saved me from. I haven't done anything, apart from thinking thoughts that could be construed as betrayal, and if you didn't inform on me when I said what I did in the garden during the ball, then nothing happened. I'm rather sure those bastards don't yet know how to read thoughts."

"It's a lot more complicated that you think." He lights another cigarette, slightly loosening the tie around his neck.

"Explain it to me."

"Better not. The less you know the safer you are."

"Safer?" I take two long sips and frustration erupts in me like a burning wave. "Safer?" I shout and throw the glass into the fireplace. It shatters and the red liquid stains the brown tiles.

"They arrested my adopted family, I have nowhere to live and am with a strange man who decided arbitrarily that he wants to marry me. What safety are you talking about?"

"I don't *want* to marry you, I *have* to marry you." Taking the ashtray from the fireplace cornice, he sets it on the table in front of me, seemingly indifferent to my outburst and the shards of glass crackling under the sole of his shoe.

"You don't *have* to marry me." I drum the cigarette on the ashtray, finding it hard to quieten the storm raging inside me. "If you don't explain to me at this very moment, exactly what happened tonight, I will leave and go directly to the Gestapo offices. There, I will explain that this dreadful arrest is just an embarrassing mistake and that's all."

He is silent.

"If so, then I'm going now!" I get up. "What was I thinking when I agreed to come here with you? Why didn't I insist on following them? I could have spoken." I twist the ring on my finger until it seems to cut into my skin. "I can still speak. I will testify in their favor and fix the injustice done to them." I turn towards the door and a hand grasps my arm.

"Sit down!"

"No!" I try and wrench my arm away.

"Josephine, please sit down. When we have finished talking, if you still wish to leave, I won't stop you."

I send a longing look in the direction of the door, but the need for answers is stronger and, grumbling, I sit down.

"What do you know about your adopted family?" Gabriel asks, sitting down in the armchair to my right.

"Everything I need to know."

"What needs to be known?" He stretches back, inhaling his cigarette.

"Is this an interrogation? Am I being interrogated now?" Irritably, I stub out the cigarette.

"Try and answer."

"I know they took me in with open arms. I know they're good people. I know they agreed to change their factory production line to produce

German uniforms. I know they organize successful balls." I roll my eyes scornfully. "I know everyone likes their parties. The French, Germans and, as it turns out, even Swiss collaborators. I know they surrendered to the occupation and cooperated completely with the occupiers."

"What do you know about the score of telephone conversations between Claude and a British Intelligence agent?"

"What?" The bag falls from my hand and I stare at him in confusion.

"Do you still wish to go to the Gestapo offices?" Gabriel leans forward, setting his glass down in front of me. Frowning, I sip hurriedly.

"That's impossible. I'd have noticed something. He was always so cautious. Always asked me to treat our guests with respect, always spoke about the need to accept defeat with humility until…"

"Until what?"

"Until…" I swallow the rest of the wine, and rub my forehead.

"You don't really wish to be interrogated by our pleasant friends in the secret police." Gabriel stands up, massaging his neck.

"Did you know something?" I grope for the bottle. "Did you inform on him?"

"With your permission, I won't answer the first question. And the second question is unnecessary since you are sitting here now." He removes his tie and throws it onto the sofa. "You can use the bathroom now. I'll wait for you to finish and then I'll go in."

I raise my head to look at him. My neck stretches and my mouth opens. I have so many questions and no idea where to begin.

"Only yesterday, before the ball, we were getting ready and I…" I murmur and stand up. "Well, I'll go and wash my face."

The bathroom is very wide and in the middle stands a white bath with metal feet. I go over to the sink and splash water on my face. The Germans believe he's a traitor? Could Claude really be collaborating with the British? While I was grumbling and complaining, was he actually putting himself in danger? Looking in the round mirror, I rub my eyes. And I told him I was ashamed of him. Not directly, but that's what could have been inferred from my words. I hurled harsh words and insults at him and he never said a word in his defense.

My shame overwhelms me. How could I not have noticed something? Brigitte and Odette knew and hid it from me? I'm trembling. No-one emerges innocent from Gestapo interrogations. The realization that I have been saved is of no comfort to me right now.

I dry my face and look sadly at the tears reflected back from the mirror. It looks as if I have grown up in the last few hours. I don't recognize the spoiled girl who yesterday lay in bed, grumbling about her bitter fate. I see grief and fear in my eyes. This time, it isn't fear of the occupier, it is fear I won't manage to prove myself worthy of being saved.

Returning to the passage, I hear voices in conversation.

Had they returned? Had the men in brown coats returned to take me away?

My belly constricts and I quail. A terrible anxiety paralyzes me. Holding my belly, I straighten up. If this is my fate, I will accept it. I will go without pleading and weeping.

I take one step after another; small, measured steps; and suddenly, I seem to hear laughing. A flash of hope ignites in me. Could it be Odette? Maybe they released her and she's come to find me? But as quickly as it is ignited, so it is extinguished. Not even she would laugh in such a situation.

Long, straight, bronze-colored hair. This is the first thing my eyes absorb.

"Gabriel, I'm not wearing anything under this coat." The woman with long slender legs smooths her hands over her hips.

"Marion, this is not the right time," He responds firmly.

"What the hell could be more important to you that stripping me right now?" She approaches him, raising her head to kiss his chin.

I hesitate whether to return to the bathroom, but Gabriel looks away and his eyes catch mine.

"It's not the right time." He gently moves her aside and continues to look at me.

The lithe body turns and feline eyes look at me in astonishment. In front of me is a beautiful, groomed woman, a decade older than me.

"Are you hosting a relative?" She examines me suspiciously.

"No," he responds briefly, the situation clearly an uncomfortable one for him.

"So who is she and what the hell is she doing in your apartment at this hour?"

Her vitriolic tone and the way she poses the question confirms to me that she is no random visitor. They have a relationship and if I don't regain my presence of mind, she might suspect me.

Gabriel doesn't answer. I twist the ring he gave me. Despite the enormous pain of my shattered world, I feel pain at having to crack hers.

"Pleased to meet you, my name is Josephine." Holding out my hand, I turn it so she cannot miss the ring. "His fiancée."

"His fiancée," she mimics my serious tone and bursts out laughing. "Gabriel, where did you find this funny child?"

Gabriel releases the top button of his shirt and briefly bows his head. When he raises it, his long lashes stand out and his dark green eyes flash at me with acceptance.

"Marion, I should have found the right time to tell you about Josephine, before you met her in the apartment." He walks around the astonished woman to stand beside me. "We are indeed engaged, and will marry tomorrow."

"This is impossible." She shakes her head. "I come here almost every evening, you..."

"I'm sorry." He bows his head and I notice no discomfort in his voice.

"You're sorry," she murmurs, her eyes awash in tears. "Is that all you have to say to me?" I thought you were happy with me. I thought our separation was temporary, that after the war you'd stay with me. I thought there'd be something real between us."

"There was and it was over a long time ago," Gabriel responds briefly. I stop staring at the poor woman and try to discover sadness or distress on his face. Nothing. His face is blank. He opens the door to the apartment. "It has always been and will always be Josephine. Our relationship was over a long time ago. I'm sorry if I have done anything to make you think differently, but you'd do well to come to terms with it so we can go back to being good friends."

"Go back to being friends?" She blurts out scornfully and hurries to the exit. "I will never be your friend, but Josephine…" She turns her gaze on me and smiles spitefully. "Don't get too comfortable. He was mine in the past and will be mine in the future. I know this man and his needs well, and I know that what I am capable of giving him a child like you could never give him." She slams the door after her and I hug myself in embarrassment.

"I apologize." My feet carry me to the table and I pour myself a glass of wine. "I should have given you privacy and waited for you to tell her."

"You did well," he responded coolly, pouring himself a small glass of liqueur. "If you'd delayed, Marion would have been suspicious, which would have put us at risk."

"In any case, it isn't a pleasant situation for a woman. I wouldn't want to be in her shoes."

"Do you think she'd want to be in yours?" He didn't wait for a response and tapped on his glass. "You need to take into account that the moment she recovers from the shock, she'll be back. She lives in this building on the first floor and she'll be waiting for an opportunity to find you alone in order to interrogate you. She's no fool and she has connections with all the people who are problematic for us."

"Brigitte would say that there is nothing more dangerous than a revengeful woman." I finish the wine and lay my head on the back of the sofa.

"A clever woman." He puts the empty glass down on the bar. "In any case, you are not yet completely safe and Marion is not our main problem at the moment. If your name comes up during interrogation, they might burst in here tonight and it won't look good if on our engagement night I am asleep on the sofa. You will have to sleep with me in the bedroom." He gestures to the closed door on the left side of the drawing room.

I nod in complete indifference.

"I'm going into the bathroom, in the meantime, feel free to clear up the mess you've made here." Shaking off the shards of glass from his shoes, he vanishes into the corridor.

In the service cupboard, I find cleaning materials and collect the fragments. Waves of pain wash over me, forcing me to stop every few seconds to hold my belly. I'd never have believed that emotional pain could become physical.

Placing the bucket next to the wall, I look at the chess board on a rectangular table next to the fireplace. The carved, ivory pieces are on either side of the board, ready for the game. I sit down on the chair in front of the white pieces, put my elbows on the table, my face between my hands. Staring at my pieces, I stroke the king's head.

Josie, I'm giving you the advantage, make your first move, I hear my father's amused voice. I choose a pawn and advance two steps forward.

Always so reckless. He shakes his head in disappointment.

Papa, I hate this game! Knocking over the pawn, I cause the pieces around it to fall.

My darling child, this isn't just any game. I imagine his fingers rearranging the pieces on the board. *It's a magical, special world that teaches you how to think and develop a strategy.*

I will never be able to understand it. I sigh.

Imagine that these are real people and this is a real war and you have to threaten my king.

I don't want to imagine war. It's ridiculous. After all, you fought in the Great War and said it was terrible. I hope you will never need to fight again.

Who knows! Leaning forward, he caresses my cheek.

Closing my eyes, I stroke my cheek.

"Papa, if you'd only suspected what was about to happen, I'm certain you wouldn't have agreed to my staying here without you," I murmur, drying the tears trickling down my cheeks as I stand up. If only I'd listened and learned, maybe I'd be able to understand what move to make in this cursed war.

Again I knock over all the white pieces and sniff.

Damned game.

Walking to the closed door, I enter the bedroom. An enormous four-poster bed stands in the middle of the room, on either side of which are two massive wooden chests. Crimson velvet curtains are tightly drawn. Behind an armchair in the same color is an opening into a walk-in closet without a door. Flickering light bulbs make me look up at the ornate chandelier, followed by another flicker and then darkness.

The room is completely dark and so is the drawing room. I'm accustomed to electricity power failures, at home I learned to enjoy them. But in this strange apartment, I have no idea where Gabriel keeps candles and the darkness is threatening.

Taking off my shoes, I sit on the edge of the mattress. Exhaustion takes over and I yawn and tremble. I stare as if in a dream at the strong, masculine face entering the room. The candle emphasizes his harsh features and the special, calming shade of his eyes. Not exactly how I imagined my guardian angel as a child, but apparently we discover what he looks like only when he is the only one left to save us.

"Electricity power failure," he says what I already know, setting the candle down on the chest beside me. He is wearing only flannel pants and I make myself stare at the flickering candle and not at his naked, upper body. "I can wear a shirt if it bothers you."

"It doesn't matter to me." I sit on the mattress, drawing my knees up to my chest.

"You can't sleep in that dress." He sighs. "Nobody will believe that a girl who has just gotten engaged gets into bed fully dressed."

"I don't have a nightgown." I'm horrified by the idea of lying naked next to him.

"Stay in your slip." He holds out a hand and I roll my eyes in despair but stand up. He waits for me to brush my hair to one side and gently undoes the buttons. When the dress falls to my feet I hide my face in my hands and sigh. "It's as uncomfortable for me as it is for you." He steps back and waits for me to get into bed and cover myself with the blanket. The mattress sinks as he lies down beside me.

"I don't want to think about my discomfort at the moment." I turn my back and the suffocation in my throat makes me cough.

"They're probably enduring a terrible interrogation in some dark, cold cellar now, and I am lying in this bed, unable to do anything to help them." My voice breaks and I burst into tears.

"I am truly sorry I couldn't help them." The sincerity in his voice makes me cry even harder. "But now all we can do is pray that your name doesn't come up in the interrogation and that I will be able to take you to a safe place."

I continue to sob into the pillow. Pictures of this evening's events rush through my mind like a fast-forward film. Gabriel's demand that Odette remain at home, the way in which he again and again looked at his watch, his angry commands to persuade her to return home.

I choke when the terrible realization arises in my mind.

"Would they have escaped without me?" I turn and lean on my elbow. He is lying on his back and gazing at the ceiling. "Gabriel, if Odette hadn't gone out to that restaurant this evening, would they have escaped without me?"

He is silent.

"That note you gave him was actually information that he was about to be exposed." I put my hand over my heart in a desperate attempt to moderate my heart beats. "If Odette had stayed home they'd have had enough time to escape. But how?"

For a moment, he closes his eyes, and when he opens them he remains silent.

The pictures come back to my mind but chronologically this time. I'm not sure I want to understand what they're telling me.

"When you realized she intended to go out, you tried to stop her. When you failed, you asked me to try and take her back. If I'd succeeded, they'd have escaped, but…" I frown. "But if they'd escaped, I'd have come home to an empty house and they'd only have found me. They'd have taken me for interrogation and I'd have no information to give them."

"Correct."

"But why wasn't I included in the escape plan?" Lying on my back, I cover my mouth with my hand in alarm when I realize the harsh answer.

He moves and leans on his elbow to look at me. I find no consolation in the calming expression reflected to me.

"The plan was perfect." He sighs. "At least it was supposed to be. Saving three at the price of sacrificing one."

I remove my hand from my mouth and pull the blanket up to my neck.

"Are you sure you want to hear this?"

Clenching my jaws, I nod.

"The note I gave Claude had information about the exact time of the raid. They were waiting for him to carry out another conversation in code, after which they planned to come and arrest all of them. They intended to escape through a hidden door in the kitchen, join someone from the underground who would provide them with papers, a fake identity and transit permits to get to the villages and from there they'd make sure of a safe passage for them to Switzerland."

I gaze at him with wide open eyes.

"I've told you a lot more than you should know." He falls silent and I grasp his arm and press it.

"I want to understand why I wasn't included in the escape plan."

He shakes his head.

"Gabriel, please. I deserve to know why they decided to leave me behind."

"It wasn't an easy decision." His eyes are fixed on mine. "It is never an easy decision to leave someone behind. But if they discovered you at home, they'd assume you knew how and where they'd gone, and the hours the Gestapo would waste on interrogating you would give Claude and his family the valuable time they needed to escape."

"I can understand that." The tears burst forth and I wipe them on the edge of the blanket. "Three for one, it's logical after all." But the sense of outrage is so strong that no logic can dim it. "I just don't understand why you insisted that I return with her. After all, if I had managed to make her return, they'd have had to take me with them, wouldn't they?"

"No." He lies on his back again. "We'd have taken Odette home and I'd have found some excuse to take you back to the restaurant or join me in a walk through the street. In any case, we'd have sacrificed you to save them."

"I understand." My throat is choking and I refuse to allow the tears to fall again.

"You don't really understand. Nobody can comprehend abandonment. But ultimately you were clever enough to enable me to save you when I realized that it was too late for them."

"What would have happened to me if your plan had succeeded?"

"You'd have been interrogated for several hours. They'd have thought you were refusing to cooperate. The family would have been saved but they'd have hanged you to make an example of a traitor."

The laconic way in which he presented the shocking scenario brings back the trembling.

"And what will happen to them now?" The trembling is so strong that my teeth chatter.

"They will not be returning home in the near future." Gabriel stands up and goes to the closets. He returns with a woolen blanket and covers me with it.

"You don't even know me, so why did you risk saving me."

"At the ball, when you smiled at me in the garden, not your fake smile I saw you presenting to Claude's guests, but your real smile, I felt for a moment that we'd beaten them. It's been too long since I felt the taste of victory." He lies down with his back to me.

His answer confuses me even more.

"But in the same breath, you say you would have sacrificed me."

"Yes."

"And you're only a Swiss diamond dealer…"

"Only a Swiss diamond dealer."

CHAPTER SIX

I sit up in bed and look around the room.

Where am I?

In a flash, the events of the previous night return to me and I feel extremely nauseous. I try to recall the precise moment I realized that my bubble had burst. The precise moment I was still enveloped by protective walls, a warm, embracing family and then, suddenly, it was cruelly taken from me.

Rubbing my eyes, I yawn. For hours I tossed and turned in bed. Every time sleep engulfed me, my heart began to pound. I was certain I could hear those cursed footsteps and the door being kicked open. I sat up in the silence, trying to understand whether the hard steps passing in the street were stopping at the entrance. I waited breathlessly for shouts and pandemonium, but the quiet returned, and only my heart continued to pound.

I'm quite sure that at some point I didn't know if I were dreaming or awake. After every choking came a caress or soothing words from the strange man who had saved me. But I found no consolation in them. My heart bled and the sadness was unbearable. And even at this very moment it is still hard to contain.

Holding onto the edge of the blanket I shudder. From now on I am utterly alone. I have no protective, adoptive family, no friends or acquaintance to rely on. I have only myself and this unrelenting anguish.

Drawing the curtains, I look out at the gray street. It doesn't really matter if the day is sunny or raining, the walls of the buildings are charred and Paris is gray. Not even sunrays are willing to illuminate it.

My dress is laid out over the back of the chair and folded on the chest of drawers is another dress in a light blue color. When I pick it up I see the price tag. A white packet is lying next to it and I take out underwear, a white slip and stockings.

It would appear that I am not completely alone in my sad new reality. In it is a strange man who sends his housekeeper to buy me all the things a woman is supposed to insist on buying for herself. I shrug indifferently and get dressed. The dress is insipid and two sizes too big for me.

I manage to imagine Odette standing in the corner of the room, letting out a noisy shriek that I simply cannot leave the room in that rag. How I would love to hear that shriek now. I would give everything I have to hear her scornful laughter. I would give everything I had because, now, I have nothing left.

Leaving the bedroom, I cross the drawing room. Sounds of conversation are coming from the direction of the dining room, but I continue directly to the bathroom. A floral, square box is on the dresser under the sink, and when I open it I find a hairbrush, a new toothbrush, a make-up kit and perfume. I have no doubt that Marie started her shopping spree in a perfume store. A fundamental, almost existential commodity for any French woman.

With the occupation, the Germans took our expensive wine, tobacco and even our pride, but they didn't realize that in order to finally break us, they needed to take away our perfumes. They still hope, apparently, that artificial scents will blur the stink of their presence.

I laugh bitterly as I wash my face and spray myself liberally with the perfume. Its scent is too sweet. Brigitte would probably fake a cough and scold me for overusing the spray. "Perfume should attract men to you, not flies." She'd click her tongue and send me back to the bathroom.

I remove the pins from my hair and brush it; it's difficult to look at myself in the mirror without being overwhelmed by waves of shame at not attempting to help them. The only thing that consoles me a little is that nobody came to take me away for interrogation during the night. This morning, gray though it may be, I am still a free woman.

I make myself look in the mirror again, focusing this time and examining every feature in my pale and sunken face. This freedom was given me by grace and not by right. If their plan had worked out as they'd expected, it is probable that I would now be facing a firing squad.

My life is a gift and I have no idea what to do with this gift. The only thing I know for certain is that I can't sit idle. Maybe I am here on borrowed time, which I will use to prove to myself that I am worthy of it.

I nod to myself with the remnants of confidence I manage to recruit, and walk from the bathroom into the dining room.

Gabriel is sitting at the table in a pressed, three-piece suit, reading the newspaper and sipping his coffee. Marie places a breakfast tray in front of him. When he notices me, he puts down the paper and stands up.

"Bonjour, Mademoiselle Josephine." Marie's face lights up and Gabriel pulls out a chair for me.

"Good morning," I respond and immediately regret it. There is nothing good about this morning.

"It's a big day." She smiles with pleasure as I sit down. "An exciting day for you. I will make sure you eat a breakfast fit for a princess."

"Have they been released?" I ask excitedly, my hand over my heart.

Gabriel shakes his head and his eyes widen in warning. I realize he doesn't want me to discuss them in front of Marie, and my shoulders droop with disappointment.

"Well, what is so exciting about today?" I ask, sipping the glass of coffee she pours for me.

"You have chosen a bride with a healthy sense of humor." Marie laughs, kindly patting my shoulder. "A woman with a sense of humor is very important in a relationship."

"Bride?" I look at him in confusion.

"I've found a priest who will marry us this afternoon." He picks up the newspaper and continues reading.

"Are you serious? Are we really going to do it? I thought it might be enough if we were just engaged."

Panic fills me and I ignore the exasperated look he gives me.

"All women are tense on their wedding day." Marie takes my hand with a motherly look. "I remember my own wedding day as if forty-five years hadn't gone by. I was so tense, wept all morning. I wanted to lock myself in the bedroom and never go to the wedding." Smiling, she closes her eyes. "The only moment I knew I was doing the right thing was when I stood in front of my Marcel and he took my hand and kissed it. He's been gone ten years now, and I can still feel that kiss." Sighing, she opens her eyes. "You've won a very special man, and if he's chosen you, I have no doubt that you are special too. Try and be happy today. We haven't had that many reasons to be happy since those bastards arrived." She falls silent and steals a glance at Gabriel. His upper lip is trembling and he frowns in anger. She winks at me and shrugs. "I'm too old to be afraid of that scum."

"I really love you now." My lips curve in a broad smile. "I'm willing to marry you today."

Marie bursts out laughing and pats my cheek.

"Your smile makes you beautiful. I understand why he has fallen in love with you."

Touching my cheek in surprise, I realize she has made me smile a real smile, and I look at Gabriel. Briefly raising his eyes from the newspaper, he gives me a small smile that makes me blush with embarrassment.

"His smile is also special." Marie sighs. "It's a pity I don't get to see much of him. I hope that now you're here we will both be seeing more of him." She sighs again, but a moment later her enthusiastic smile brightens her face. "How can I spoil you on this exciting morning? Even if it's no longer morning…" She looks at the round clock hanging on the wall. "We've rushed to buy you everything to make you feel at home, so I can prepare fish or meat."

I look at all the abundance set before me on the table and instead of feeling fortunate I only feel shame again.

"Marie, if I had to exist on food rations, what would I be eating now?'

"What a strange question." She folds a napkin and places it next to my plate. "Why should you bother your head with thoughts like that when you can have whatever you wish to eat?"

"I want to know."

Fidgeting with discomfort, she picks up the napkin, shakes it out and refolds it. "Well, you certainly wouldn't eat eggs," she mutters, and Gabriel briefly looks up from his newspaper and then continues reading. "You also wouldn't eat meat or fish or those cheeses."

"Then what would I eat?"

"If you manage to get there really early, I think you'd eat bread and maybe a little butter."

"That's all?" I shriek.

"People have learned to make do with what there is, and find ways of getting other foodstuff."

"How?"

"Those with relatives in the villages receive packages from them, and those who don't, barter on the black market with whatever they have, so they won't starve to death."

I recall the few times I went down into the cellar at home to fetch a bottle of wine and had to maneuver my way among scores of food crates. I'd never given any thought to that abundance. Hadn't tried to understand where the crates came from or how Claude got hold of them. I knew there was a shortage; I'd seen women struggling in lines to get their rations and was ashamed. Now that I understand what they were struggling for, the shame is greater.

"I will make do with bread and butter. Thank you."

"Don't talk nonsense." Marie waves her hand disparagingly. "It's an important day and you must eat well."

"Just bread and butter. Thank you."

"Gabriel?" she addresses him with frustration.

"Serve her what she wants," he concludes dispassionately.

I hear her angry mutters as she goes into the kitchen. Returning, she places in front of me two thick slices of bread and a small plate of butter.

"Thank you." I put the napkin on my lap and generously spread butter on the bread.

"You can be very sure that they don't spread that amount of butter on their bread." She rolls her eyes. "They spread it thinly, *Cherie*."

Unmoved by her scorn, I remove the top layer of butter.

She leaves us and I eat quietly, looking at the headlines on the front page of *"Die Pariser Zeitung."* A photograph of the Fuhrer with his hand raised; a dense caption in German; and another photograph of a military parade.

"Have the stalls run out of all the French newspapers?" I have difficulty hiding my anger.

"Does it really matter in which language you read their propaganda?"

"I'd prefer to read this garbage in a language I understand."

"You must be careful with what you say," Gabriel says without taking his eyes off the newspaper. "Marie is reliable and would never do anything to hurt me, but you can't take a risk with other people, even those you're sure are your friends."

"I don't really have any friends left." I nibble at the bread, chewing it in boredom. "Since Claude chose to present himself as a collaborator, they all disappeared. Evaporated in the wind."

"We've found you a wedding dress." He changes the subject sharply and stands up. "This afternoon, we will have the ceremony in church and then it will be easier for me to get you permits." He waits for me to wipe my lips with the napkin, and when he realizes that I am deliberately delaying, he gestures to me to join him. We pass into the drawing room and he points to a fabric bag hanging on the coat stand.

"Are you certain this ceremony is necessary?" I walk away from the stand.

"I'm certain."

I inhale with frustration and remove the hanger from the stand. Opening the long zipper of the bag, I take out a long white dress with pink pearls sewn around the neck.

"I can't believe this is happening to me." All the difficult emotions I've managed to repress all morning drain into uncontainable sadness, and I collapse onto the sofa and burst into tears.

"I apologize if this is not what you hoped to receive." Gabriel approaches and kneels down. "I know you would have preferred to choose your own dress."

"It has nothing to do with the dress." I sniff and he takes a white handkerchief from his jacket pocket and hands it to me. "I lost everything yesterday. Everything that was important to me. And now I have to act this delusional part and marry a man I don't even know. Without family and friends beside me. Just you and me and the ugliest dress I've ever seen in my life."

"I thought it had nothing to do with the dress." A small comforting smile appears on his lips, his eyes convey warmth but it doesn't pierce the wall of sadness.

"It doesn't, not really." I wipe my nose with the handkerchief, giving him a wretched look. "I think I believed I could manage to get through these times in peace and quiet. Under the radar. That I would continue to complain and grumble and feel bad about myself without it really touching me. But now everything touches me in the most painful places." I put my hand over my heart. "I try and persuade myself that this happened for a reason, that I need to wake up and actively join the resistance, but everything is happening so fast and I can't overcome the pain and think logically."

"You don't need to join any resistance." His hand caresses my arm. "We will have a modest ceremony, get permits for you and you can continue to complain and grumble without it really touching you."

"It has already touched me!" Angrily, I shake off his hand. "It has already touched and scarred me. I will never be able to go back to my foolish innocence, but I will play the game until I've had enough time to know what to do with myself."

He is silent for a few moments then finally pats my thigh. "I've invited a few friends and a photographer so we'll have documentation of the ceremony." He stands up and straightens his jacket. "I must ask you to invite a friend so that it will look authentic."

"I've told you, I don't have any friends left. Maybe you can ask your friends at the Gestapo to release Odette and let her spend the day with me?" I know my request is impossible but nonetheless I look up at him beseechingly.

"Find another friend. You have until four o'clock." Looking at his watch he turned to the door. I feel my heart break again. He puts on his coat and I listen listlessly to his explanations about how the ceremony will take place at the Église de la Madeleine in the eighth district of Paris.

"We want people to believe that I am part of this joy, don't we?"

"Of course." He stops and turns round to me.

"So how the hell is a bride supposed to wear such a large and strange dress?"

"It's the best I could find. There aren't any wedding dress boutiques now."

"Organize a sewing machine for me."

"Josephine, I have a lot of important things to do, I can't worry about nonsense now."

"I can help with that," Marie calls enthusiastically, her steps can be heard at the end of the corridor and she puts her cleaning materials down on the floor. "I have a sewing machine at home. It may be old, but my granddaughter manages to sew very nice dresses with it."

Fortunately, she didn't hear the start of the conversation. Gabriel again looks at his watch and rolls his eyes.

"If that is what will make my bride happy, she will have the sewing machine." His forced smile doesn't really bother me.

"You can keep it." Marie sits down beside me and tightly embraces me. "I was so frustrated that I couldn't think of the right wedding gift. If this will make you happy, I will give it to you."

"It will certainly make me happy." I pat her back while thinking that the word "happy" isn't really an apt word at this moment.

"He can't worry about nonsense now…" She mutters, shaking her head. "I thought you had more sense," she scolds Gabriel, taking her handbag down from the stand. "From now on, you have to relate seriously to any of Josephine's requests, as if they were the most important thing in your world. It's the only way to have a happy marriage."

"I apologize, you're right." Stifling a smile, he helps her on with her coat. "Josephine, can I make any other wish come true?"

I ignore his tone of sarcasm. "Yes. I want flowers."

"You shall have them."

"Not just any flowers." Bending over the dress, I examine the seams. "I want a bouquet of yellow roses."

"Your wish is my command." He smiles and leaves the apartment with Marie.

At the dining room table, I diligently undo the stitching of the dress, until the fabric is stretched and ready to be cut. I straighten up. He'd asked me to invite a friend to the wedding but I have no idea whom to call.

Going into the drawing room, I pick up the receiver and put it back again. The period when I was surrounded by friends ended several years ago. Some were taken, others disappeared and most had simply chosen to distance themselves from those marked as collaborators. We were marked with a blinding spotlight.

I pick up the receiver, this time with purpose, and ask the operator to put me through. After several rings, a man answers; he sounds particularly tired. I introduce myself, ask to talk to Natalie, and wait.

"Josephine?" She sounds surprised and hard as well.

"Natalie, my dear, it's so good to hear you."

"To what do I owe the honor?"

I consider continuing with ordinary conversation in order to soften her a little, but can't think of anything ordinary to say.

"I'm getting married today. I'd be glad if you'd honor me with your presence."

"Married? Today? Who is he?"

"It's a long story, I'll be glad to tell you sometime. I just thought that if you agree to come, I'd have at least one friend to accompany me."

"What's happened to Odette?" The spite is evident in her voice. "You're like Siamese twins, has a black cat crossed your path?"

"She…she had to leave." I cough to hide the tremor in my voice.

"What happened? Was she tired of enjoying herself with…?" She falls silent, and I realize she's remembered that the operator is listening to our conversation.

"Perhaps it was a mistake to call. I apologize and wish you a pleasant day." I take the receiver from my ear and a moment before I ring off, she seems to say something more.

"Josephine, I'll come." She repeats it loudly.

"Thank you very much, Natalie." I cough again when tears fill my eyes. "I appreciate it very much."

She repeats the place and the hour twice and then rings off.

Heavily, I replace the receiver, refusing to sink back into self-pity. Natalie was the right choice. For years I'd listened with respect to Odette's gossip about several of our past friends' irresponsibility in choosing to join the Resistance. Natalie's name often came up. If Odette had only known what her revered father was doing.

The door opens and a flushed Marie comes in. She is excitedly holding a sewing machine that looks as if it's from the previous century.

"This is my treasure." She strokes the black metal. "It belonged to my grandmother, passed on to my mother and then to me. And now it is yours." She hands it to me and continues to hold on until she is sure it is safely in my arms.

"I will treat it as if it has passed down the generations of my own family." I smile at her.

"Gabriel is like a member of my family." She says, accompanying me into the dining room. "We've been together for ten years and he's like a son, so I will love you like a daughter."

"Ten years?" I set the machine down on the table and look at her in confusion. "He's only been here for a few months."

"Ten years." She nods and examines the white fabric spread out on the table. "He comes for a few months every now and again and then leaves. But he always comes back to me." She chuckles.

"And where is your family? Children and grandchildren?"

The smile is erased from her face and her good eyes grow sad. "After the occupation, they moved to Vichy. It was the right thing to do."

"Why didn't you go with them?" I hand her the edge of the fabric and concentrate on cutting it.

"Paris is my home," she responds in an angry tone. "Those German bastards might think they have occupied my home, but they're wrong. They're only unwanted guests who will ultimately leave in shame."

"Amen…" I murmur and hand her the other side of the fabric.

"And apart from that, who will take care of my Gabriel?" She winks at me.

"He doesn't strike me as someone who needs taking care of."

"Everyone needs someone to take care of them." She helps me stretch the fabric on the table and I settle it under the needle of the sewing machine. "Now you must also take care of him." Her rebuke is gentle but firm. "Learn something from an old woman who has known great love in her life; If a woman wants to be loved unconditionally, she needs to give her man unconditional love."

"There isn't much love left in this world." I try and concentrate on my sewing without letting her sense my discomfort at this conversation.

"That's where you're wrong." She rubs my back and sighs. "Love is the only thing they will never be able to take from us and, thanks to that, we will win."

CHAPTER SEVEN

I'm standing in a small side room of the church dressed in my bridal gown. In one arm, I hold the bouquet of yellow roses and Marie holds my other hand in hers. I thought I could repeat to myself that this is just a game and repress the fear, but nothing has prepared me for the hysteria that is overwhelming me. Breathing heavily, my palms are sweating and I can't respond to Marie's words of encouragement.

"You are so beautiful." She presses my hand and I merely nod my head. "Who'd have thought you'd manage to turn that dress into this wonderful gown." She strokes the pink pearls that now decorate my hips. "I told him he mustn't see you before the ceremony, it brings bad luck."

I nod, closing my mouth and praying the nausea will pass.

"Your friend has arrived and is sitting in the hall."

I nod.

"Maybe I'll bring you a glass of water? You are so pale."

I shake my head, terrified by the thought that she'll let go of my hand.

"That's the sign for you to enter." She declares with excitement as the sounds of the organ burst into the adjacent room.

"Don't let go of my hand." I manage to whisper and blink fiercely. It's just a game, I repeat to myself again and again as my feet move involuntarily and, suddenly, I find myself standing at the entrance to the hall.

Raising my head in an attempt to breathe a little air, I stare dazedly at the impressive arches and ornate columns. My gaze passes over a row of columns until my body seems to petrify and become part of it.

In the hall are rows of empty chairs and, at the end, near the last row, stands Natalie. In front of her are three men in black SS uniforms and a young man holding a camera.

As I try to regulate my breaths, Marie urges me forward. With each step, my vision blurs; I try to focus only on the figures standing in front of me; a priest in a long, black cassock and, beside him, the stranger who is supposed to make me his wife.

"I can't move." My voice squeaks.

"*Cherie*, only a few more steps." Marie links her arm in mine and walks resolutely forward.

We reach the last row of chairs and the men in black uniforms fan out their arms in salute. My knees lock and I turn my head quickly towards Natalie. She isn't smiling and is as white as a sheet.

What the hell am I doing here?"

I turn my head towards the exit and Marie's bony arm separates from mine and the bouquet of roses is taken from me. I manage to imagine myself spreading out my arms and floating above the chairs. Escaping from this church, a free woman. But a male arm is linked in mine, holding me close to a body in a black suit.

"You're beautiful." Gabriel whispers in my ear and walks forward with me.

The priest smiles at me, bowing his head and the realization that this ceremony is being performed by a real priest increases my hysteria. When Gabriel moves to stand in front of me, my chest heaves with breaths that sound like anguished groans.

My glance passes from the priest to the pale Natalie and from her to the smiling Marie, finally resting on the SS soldiers.

"Look at me!" Gabriel's command makes me shake my head and fix my eyes on the small smile on his face. He holds my hands firmly and silence prevails in the hall.

I hear the priest's baritone voice but can't understand what he is saying. I hear my heavy breathing and my heart beats and I don't dare take my eyes off the calm smile of the man standing in front of me.

Gabriel's lips move in response to the priest's question and then I hear applause. I feel my hand being pressed, Gabriel signaling that it is now my turn.

I look at him wonderingly, trying to understand what I'm supposed to say. Gabriel's smile broadens and he nods at me. "Ah, yes, of course," I murmur, and again there is applause and enthusiastic cries in German and French.

Gabriel removes my engagement ring, transferring it to the finger on my other hand. He replaces it with a ring set with the largest diamond I'd ever seen in my life. I don't have a moment to blink when my body is lifted, swept into the air and he kisses my lips to the sound of our guests' cheering.

"That's it? We're finished?" I ask in confusion when he sets me back on my feet and caresses my head.

"Almost." He laughs. "Look at the camera."

His arm is around my shoulders and I raise an artificial smile just as the photographer takes his place in front of us. He takes photograph after photograph and starts giving instructions to the guests. A group photograph; a photograph with the couple and the soldiers; a photograph of the bride with the women; with the bouquet of flowers…I continue to stand there, a smile glued to my face, while only those beside me change.

Gabriel hands glasses to everyone and pours the wine. The SS officers appear calm and at ease in Gabriel's company, and Marie stands beside him like a bodyguard. She sips her wine slowly, fixing them with a suspicious stare. Natalie, on the other hand, looks like a prisoner waiting impatiently for her release. Maintaining a safe distance, she rocks restlessly on her feet.

"I must get home." She puts on her coat and hesitantly approaches me. "It was a charming ceremony."

"Wait." Putting my glass of wine on a chair, I approach her.

"I really can't stay." She glances in the direction of the Germans.

"I'll accompany you to the exit." Linking my arm in hers, I press her to me. When I'm sure nobody can hear us, I stop and embrace her. "Thank you for coming."

"If I'd known that they would be your guests, I wouldn't have come." She grits her teeth and looks furiously at me.

"If I'd have known that they would be my guests, neither would I." I snort scornfully.

"I understand your hosts have been arrested." She whispers, glancing again in the direction of the front of the church. "Now I understand why they didn't arrest you too." She takes another step towards the exit. "In any case, I wish you a happy life with your collaborator."

"It's not what you think." Striding forward, I stop her. "It's thanks to him I was not arrested. But I invited you here because I know what you do."

"Are you trying to trap me?" She asks in horror.

"No!" I shriek and then whisper again. "I want to join. The time has come for me to join you."

"It's not for you," she responds coolly, buttoning up her coat. "Go on enjoying yourself with that scum and take care of yourself."

"Natalie, please." I tug at her arm, making her look at me. "I know I've woken up late but I'm certain I can help. I don't know how exactly, I only know that I have to do something so I won't go mad; so I can stop living in shame."

Removing my hand, she straightens her coat sleeve. "If this is a dirty trick, it will be the end of you." Her eyes are wide and threatening.

"When my end comes, I'd prefer it to be meaningful." I put my hand over my heart.

She massages her neck nervously but finally gives me a sad smile. "Do you remember Louis' little bar on Rue de Montmorency?"

"Yes, of course."

"Be there tomorrow evening. And when the barman asks you what you want to drink, ask for Fleur-de-Lis."

"The Lily flower…" I murmur excitedly, bowing my head in gratitude.

"Don't thank me yet." Straightening up she brushes back her long, black hair. 'You should think about this seriously. Many who thanked me in the past are no longer with us, and not by choice." Taking a rose from my bouquet she smells it. "You always had a strange affinity for this color." She turns her back and walks erectly to the exit.

Voices and steps behind me grow louder and embracing the bouquet, I turn my head.

"We will hold a suitable celebration in a few days' time." Gabriel shakes the hand of one of the officers and then presses me to him. "Now I will go and celebrate my marriage in private with my wife."

"You have chosen a very beautiful woman," the German says with a heavy accent. "Tonight you will celebrate with her and tomorrow we'll be glad if you'll join us at that pleasant guest house you introduced us to on Rue *Godot de* Mauroy."

I know exactly what pleasant guest house he is referring to, and can't make the connection between this man who saved me and the wild night life taking place there. Inadvertently, I raise my head and look at him.

He smiles his small, confident smile at the German and, to my surprise, shakes his head.

"Herr Zemel, now that I'm a married man, I prefer to give up these pastimes." Bending his head, he winks at me.

His little gesture, the fact that he protected my honor, makes me squirm with discomfort. I'm accustomed to the arrogance and vulgarity of those in black uniforms. I'd encountered it at Claude's balls, but didn't think I'd ever see someone refuse them.

"You'll be back to celebrate with us!" The German dismisses his refusal with a salute and laughs. The other two officers respond with a grin, and I realize that I will never be able to suppress my hatred of them. They click their shining heels and with an arrogant step, leave the church.

"Bastards," Marie says furiously through her teeth and embraces me. "Don't worry about them. They're motivated by their need to humiliate us. It's become a fuel for them. This is your special day, don't let them spoil it for you." She straightens up and smiles proudly at Gabriel. "Come on, let's go home and I'll prepare you a meal fit for kings."

"Marie, *Cherie*." He caresses her head affectionately. "Thank you for your loyal accompaniment today, but you can leave us alone this evening. I'm sure we'll find something to eat."

"Of course." She chuckles. "The young couple has no need for accompaniment on their wedding night."

I find myself blushing and nodding.

We leave the church together and although I entered the same way, only now do I stop for a moment to wonder, as always, at this magnificent building. This place always makes me feel so small and insignificant in comparison to the city's magnificent history.

When my father brought me here for the first time, he told me with his typical enthusiasm that the building of the church took eighty five years. Napoleon had intended the building as a tribute to the *Grande Armée*, the French army under his command. I sigh and carefully descend the steps. If our national hero could see the German officers saluting in this building he'd turn in his grave.

Wehrmacht soldiers strolling in the square point at me and shout congratulations in German and broken French. Several French women approach to congratulate me. All I want is to escape to the car. Marie parts from us and Gabriel opens the door of the car for me.

"Thank you for protecting my honor and refusing their invitation," I say when the car starts moving.

"It would have looked strange if I hadn't refused," Gabriel responds coolly. "I had to make up for the fact that my bride looked as if she'd been forcibly dragged to church."

The extent of the hurt I feel surprises me. "I really apologize for not being a good enough actress." Pressing my head to the window I gaze at the pedestrians. "If you'd invited other guests it would have been easier for me to cope with being forced into the wedding."

"It was calculated, like everything else I do. When you're in a war for survival there is no place for emotion, only logic."

"It's impossible to detach oneself from emotions." I roll my eyes.

"It is possible. And you must learn to do it. You have no other option."

I want to answer that I will never detach myself from the fierce hatred I feel for his guests, but find there's no point in continuing such an oppressive discussion.

"Take me to Rue de Rosiers."

"What for?"

"I feel like enjoying a pleasant stroll with my new husband." I try to hide the anger in my voice.

"We'll go to the apartment, change your dress and I'll take you to a nicer area."

"No." I clench my teeth and then turn my head to him with a broad smile. "Now that we're married you should regard any of my requests as a wish from the heart."

He smiles his small smile. "You will attract a lot of attention, a woman wandering about in a wedding dress is not a common sight these days."

"I thought that was the whole point of this idiotic game. Everyone would see that we are married."

His eyes narrow with suspicion but he continues to smile. "Your wish is my command." He turns the steering wheel. A few moments later we arrive in the quiet street and he parks the car.

Opening the door for me, he holds out a hand and I straighten up and arrange the train that hides my shoes. Gabriel glances briefly at the street, scratches his head as if he were trying to understand why I've chosen this particular place but doesn't say a word. He waits for me to take his arm and in my other arm I hold the bouquet of flowers. A woman standing in her garden and scolding her toddler, opens her mouth in surprise. I bow my head in greeting and start walking slowly along the sidewalk.

"It's too cold for strolling in this weather." Gabriel takes off his jacket and places it round my shoulders.

"I'm not cold," I murmur, stopping at the house that once belonged to Nita's parents. The white swastika on the gray wall near the door has faded in time, and the pale light behind the curtains indicates that the house has new tenants.

I didn't say a word when she and her family were deported. I didn't cry for them. And now I want to cry out so that everyone will hear, know that I remember and am ashamed. Nita, I remember you and will never forget, I say wordlessly, taking another step forwards and dropping a yellow rose in front of the house.

"Do you want to tell me why this particular street?"

"No special reason." I continue walking. "I used to walk here with my father."

I recognize the faded mark of the swastika on another house and turn to look at Gabriel." Aren't there any streets like that in your country? Streets that remind you of better days?"

He frowns thoughtfully, I drop another rose.

"There are places. Not streets." He pulls me to him to allow a cyclist to pass us and, staring at me in surprise, the latter almost crashes into us. "There's a small patisserie I often used to visit, a bicycle repair store…" He falls silent when two Wehrmacht soldiers stop in front of us and click their heels.

"Congratulations," they say to us and go on their way.

We continue walking until I recognized the house of Dr. Blum, our family doctor. I lean against the stone wall, examining the faded sign. A flag with the swastika waves proudly over the door. "I remember smells." Another rose drops on the ground and I replace my arm in Gabriel's and distance him from the house. "I remember special cooking smells in this street." I hurry across the street to the opposite sidewalk. "And I remember sounds." I drop another rose beside the wall of a marked house. "Sounds of children laughing, shouting, sounds of happiness, anger…" I have to slow down when my walk seems to turn into a run in the despairing need to reach the next marked house, and only sigh with relief when I drop a rose at the entrance. "Sounds of life."

"You're trembling." Gabriel turns me to him and rubs my arms."

The sound of steps hurrying behind us makes me lean against Gabriel and I look in terror at the young Wehrmacht soldier who is holding a small bouquet of yellow roses.

"Madame." The soldier stops in front of us and gazes at me, mesmerized. "I believe these are yours." He hands me the bouquet and, paling, I press them to the remaining roses in my hand. "When I noticed the first near that house." He points at Nita's apartment. "I thought to keep it for myself." He smiles and flushes. "But I saw more roses next to other houses, like a magical path leading me to you." His French isn't perfect but neither does it sound broken and harsh like that of the other Germans. "At first I thought I was dreaming when I saw a beautiful bride in this of all streets." Laughing he bows his head to Gabriel. Tension swirls in my belly and I have difficulty breathing. "I was supposed to marry just before war broke out, so we decided to wait." His expression becomes sad. "Now I only hope she is healthy and well and waiting for me to return. I haven't heard from her for a long time now."

"I'm sure she's waiting for you." Gabriel kindly pats his shoulder.

"I hope so." He shrugs and smiles at me. "I chose to spend my leave here. Our Fuhrer has made sure that every soldier has a chance to visit your beautiful city at least once." He looks back at the waving flag there. "Our beautiful city." He corrects himself.

I clench my teeth and command myself not to say anything.

"I wish you a peaceful and happy married life." He bows his head and hurries to the opposite sidewalk.

Gabriel doesn't say a word, and I don't protest when he leads me back to the car.

He says nothing on the way back. I notice the tremor in his upper lip and realize that he is angry. Even my small act of remembrance has failed. We arrive at his residence and he forcefully holds my elbow and leads me hurriedly up the steps.

The apartment door opens and instead of leaving me, he lets out an angry growl and pulls me into the bedroom. My feet trip on the dress and I fall onto the bed. Gabriel is still holding me fiercely by the arm and I manage to sit up and look at him in terror.

"What are you doing?" I whimper and try to shake off his grasp. "Please don't force yourself on me, please…"

"What the hell are you talking about?" He drops my arm and takes a step back. Pressing the light switch, his expression conveys shock. "Josephine, I would never do such a thing."

"Then why drag me into the bedroom?" I rub my arm and wipe my eyes.

"To make sure nobody hears what I'm about to tell you." He lights a cigarette and brushes his hair to the side with his fingers. Walking to the window, he closes the curtains and looks at me with an expression I can't fathom.

"Your name came up in interrogation."

"Without any preparation he tosses the bombshell, and in a second, my body freezes and I look at him in fear.

"Several hours before the ceremony, an acquaintance of mine in the SS sent me information that your friend is talking."

"Odette?"

Gabriel nods.

"But…what could she have to say about me?" I rub my arm again and again.

"You have to understand that when people find themselves in the interrogation cellars of the Gestapo, they will say anything to save themselves and their families."

"But what could she say about me?"

"She said they were being interrogated by mistake, and if someone should be interrogated, it was you. She insisted that the only person who would undermine the occupation was you." He hands me his cigarette and I try to control the trembling of my fingers to hold it. "She said that you revere the Resistance and they should have handed you over before you entangled them."

"Dear God," I murmur, stubbing out the cigarette in the ashtray on the dresser. Fear prevents me from thinking logically and I hit my forehead with my fists. "I have to get ready, they're probably on their way her to take me. They'll be here any minute and I'm still in this damned dress." I try and rip the fabric off my body and my nails scratch my neck. "I have to change clothes." The fabric refuses to tear and I scream with frustration.

"Calm down." Coming towards me, he holds my hands. "They won't come. I've taken care of it."

"How? How did you take care of it?" Dizzy with panic, I try and release myself from his hold.

"I went to them."

"To the offices of the Gestapo?"

He nods.

"And what did you tell them? What did they say to you?"

Putting my hands on my thighs, he gets up and leans against the door frame.

"I know one of the interrogators personally. I brought a bottle of very expensive and excellent cognac with me and, after several glasses, my story sounded plausible." He lights another cigarette. "I told him that our relationship has deepened in the past few months and that you told me about your suspicions regarding your hosts. I added that since you have a highly developed imagination, I thought you are making it up and so didn't find it necessary to warn anyone."

"No." I burst into tears. "You shouldn't have done that. Claude would have managed to persuade them of his innocence, but now you've put the rope around his neck. We have to go there together and…"

"Josephine, the rope was already wound about his neck before he was arrested. They have solid evidence against him, and I did what I had to in order to isolate you from the accusations against them."

"What will happen to him now? What will happen to them?"

"You know what will happen to him." Gabriel sighs. "And tomorrow morning, they will transfer Brigitte and Odette to a camp outside Paris."

"Can I go and say goodbye?" Tears sting my face.

He shakes his head.

"You have to understand that what you did today puts you at risk. Puts us at risk." His tone becomes more severe. "We don't know if they're following you, we don't know if you are out of danger, and all these childish gestures can set off the alarm and then our fate will be no different than theirs. You must not be so reckless."

"You brought SS soldiers to make the Nazi salute at our wedding ceremony," I say with a suffocated throat.

"I had no choice."

"Neither did I have a choice," I raise my voice.

For a moment, he closes his eyes, and when he looks at me again I can see no anger in them.

I stand up and my heart sends waves of pain to every part of my body. I take several steps forward, stopping in front of him.

"Thank you for saving me again." I drop my eyes to his chest and put my arms around his waist. Tears burst from my eyes and I allow myself to digest the bitter news and mourn my hosts.

He doesn't embrace me, but his hand rests on my head, gently caressing it. The sobs turn to breaths and when the tears stop, my eyes are dry and burning. A numbness surrounds me. Sniffing, I straighten up.

"That's it. I'm done weeping," I murmur exhaustedly and turn my back. I undo my hair and let it fall to my shoulders and he undoes the zipper of my dress. I shake it off and it drops to the floor.

"Tomorrow I will get you transit permits and I'll get you out of here."

Silently, I get into bed.

"Do you want anything to eat?"

I pull the blanket up over my head. After a few moments, I hear the bedroom door close. Now, on my own, the tears return and there isn't anyone in the world who can comfort me. I come to terms with the horrifying fact that I will never get my life back.

CHAPTER EIGHT

I put on the robe which was lying over the chair next to the bed, and rub my eyes. I didn't feel Gabriel coming into the bedroom at night, nor did I feel him getting out of bed in the morning. The only times I realized I wasn't alone in the bed during the night were when I woke, drenched in sweat, and heard whispered words of comfort.

Now, it seems to me that I have woken in someone else's body. Fear is no longer gnawing at my bones. As if I'd used up my quota of fear and it had been replaced by a strange apathy. The realization that I'd lost everyone who'd been important to me here, hits me forcefully, and I find no point in fearing for myself.

Going into the bathroom, I wash my face. Dark smudges mark my eyelids and my black hair accentuates my pallor. I don't linger in front of the mirror but go into the corridor.

"Good afternoon to the beautiful bride," declares Marie with pleasure. "Are you joining Gabriel in the dining room?" She shows me a tray laden with food and shrugging apathetically, I trail after her into the room.

Gabriel raises his head from a black velvet tray on which lie a score of diamond rings. Standing up, he pulls out a chair for me and I tie the robe belt more tightly around my waist and look at his pressed suit. If I hadn't seen him in his pajamas on my first night here, I'd have been sure that his luxurious suit was an inseparable part of his body.

"Put your work aside," Marie rebukes him. "When your wife joins you,

you must give her all your attention."

"Of course." He scribbles something in his diary and covers the jewelry tray.

Marie enters and leaves frequently, setting food on the table. Taking a piece of bread I spread on it a meagre layer of butter. In the corner of the table are two newspapers, one in German and the other, *"Le Matin,"* in French. Pulling the French newspaper towards me, I give Gabriel a nod of thanks.

"I got your permits this morning," he says, putting food on his plate.

"Permits for what?" Listlessly, I nibble at the slice of bread.

He examines my face. "I've told you twice already. Transit permits. We'll leave Paris tomorrow morning in the direction of Switzerland. I'll leave you with good friends of mine, and when things get better, I will return to take care of our marriage annulment."

The bread sticks in my throat and I cough.

"I'm not leaving Paris."

"You don't have a choice," he says calmly, but I notice the tremor in his upper lip and realize he is angry.

"I'm not leaving Paris." Folding the newspaper, I lay it on the table.

"Josephine, you really aren't safe here, and the best way to make sure you are safe is to get you out of France."

"I told you, I'm not leaving," I raise my voice, "and it's not up for debate."

"Marie, please pour Josephine a glass of coffee." He smiles at the embarrassed figure standing in the doorway. Running to the kitchen, she returns with a jug and a cup. "And now, I'd be grateful if you'd leave us alone." He smiles at her again and his upper lip trembles again.

She leaves and I look determinedly at him. "You can't force me to leave."

"I can't permit myself to continue worrying about you." His eyes are fixed on mine, flashing with resentment. "I have more important things to do."

"I didn't ask you to worry about me."

"You have to understand that I'm dealing with very sensitive issues here." He tries to moderate the irritation in his voice.

"I have to be focused and I can't be if you continue to be my responsibility."

"Do you intend dragging me forcefully to the train station?"

"No."

"Do you intend pushing me into the boot of your car?"

"No."

"Then you had better come to terms with the fact that I'm staying here. I realize that you aren't comfortable hosting me, so by the end of the day, I will find a friend who will agree to have me."

"That's unacceptable to me." He bangs his fist on the table. I shrink but make myself continue to look at him. "I have joined my fate with yours, I cannot allow myself to get into trouble because of your recklessness."

"I. Am. Not. Leaving. Paris." I quickly stand up and run out of the room.

Going into the walk-in closet, I take my meagre possessions off the hangers, throw the clothes onto the bed and look for a bag in the drawers of the dresser.

"Sit down!" His voice is firm and he points at the armchair.

Raising my chin defiantly, I fold my arms.

"I asked you to sit down!"

Grumbling out loud, I sit on the edge of the chair.

"Until now, have I done anything that could be interpreted as disrespectful?" His voice is quiet but threatening. I shake my head.

"So what right do you have to walk out in the middle of a discussion and treat me with disrespect?"

"It wasn't really a discussion."

He rubs his thumb along his upper lip and his body stiffens. "Until now, have I done anything to make you stop trusting me?"

I shake my head.

"Then when I explain to you that you need to leave, are you capable of understanding that I'm doing so for your own good?"

I nod.

"Well then, are we agreed that you will leave with me tomorrow morning?"

"No."

I watch him clenching his fists and attempting to calm down.

"Gabriel." I stand and put my palms together beseechingly. "I promise to leave your apartment and you won't hear from me again. I promise not to interfere in your business, no matter what happens, and I will never mention your name. But I can't leave. I have lost so much, I simply cannot leave my poor defeated city."

"And what exactly will you do here if I let you stay?"

"I'll find a friend who will take me in, I…"

"It's impossible." He interrupts me. "Everyone knows we are married, I've changed your name to mine. It will look suspicious if you leave my apartment."

"Then I'll stay here." I take a step towards him and he steps back. "I promise you won't know I'm here. I don't need anything from you. I'll take care of myself."

"Josephine, I can take you somewhere safe, distance you from all the terrible events you've had experienced. I can make sure you have an opportunity to start over and try to forget…"

"I don't want to start over." This time, I interrupt him. "And I will never forget."

He is silent for a long time and I place my hand over my heart. "Gabriel, please let me stay here, I promise to behave perfectly."

He rolls his eyes and the small smile I so wished to see appears on his face. "You must understand that if we don't go away on a make-believe honeymoon, we'll have to hold an event for show with several people you don't really want to meet."

"I will behave impeccably."

He sighs. "Why do I have the feeling I will regret it?"

"I promise you won't regret it." I quickly put on the large blue dress and my high heeled shoes. "I'll go out now so I won't disturb you."

He fidgets uncomfortably and lights a cigarette. When I emerge from the bedroom, he follows me into the dining room and when I sit down, he continues to stand, looking troubled.

"I must go to the office." He puts the tray of diamonds into his suitcase. "What are your plans today?"

I shrug and spread butter on another piece of bread.

"In any case, from now on you must always have your new papers on you." He places an envelope in front of me and a sheet of paper with a photograph of me from the wedding stuck to it with my new surname. I move my finger over the black print. Madame Josephine Augustine. For the first time in my life, I don't have my father's surname, and it's not a good feeling. In just two days, I'd lost those dear to me and my identity.

"I have another request," Gabriel says and I look up at him. "It is a necessary condition of your staying here."

"Anything." I nod vigorously.

"For the period we present ourselves as a married couple and live under one roof, I swear I won't lie to you and you need to swear that you will always tell me the truth."

"I swear."

My swift, unequivocal response doesn't make him look less worried. I look down, glancing once more at my new surname. The ceremony had been real, the priest had been real, and so had the witnesses who accompanied us. Turning the ring on my finger, I examine the government seal on the document. "How do you plan to persuade them to annul our marriage once the situation has calmed down?" I whisper, glancing at the door. "A real priest married us and, as far as I know, they don't annul marriages that quickly."

"Well, it would appear that you are stuck with me." He grinned.

"No. No," I shriek. "You said it was only pretense, that we can annul it as soon as the situation is quiet."

"Calm down." He rolls his eyes. "A marriage has to be consummated and we have no intention of consummating it." He winks at me and I blush when I realize the act of consummation he means. "We'll meet this evening." He says and the doorway is immediately blocked by Marie. He turns round, bends and briefly kisses my cheek. "Is there anything I can do to make my wife happy?" He says monotonously.

I shake my head and then, regretting it, vigorously nod my head. "I'd like to receive a wedding gift."

"Of course. What would you like, a chain, a bracelet?"

"A bicycle."

"You have a modest bride." Marie laughs and pats his back.

"Your wish is my command." He chuckles and disappears down the corridor.

The moment I hear the house door close, I stand up and grab my new identity papers. Inside the envelope are several notes, and even though it doesn't seem right to use his money, I realize that it's better to put that aside and buy myself some comfortable walking shoes.

"Do you need a companion?" Marie walks after me to the door.

"No, thank you. I'm only going out for a short walk." Wrapping my cloak around me, I leave the house. My heels are hard on the tiles and I hold onto the banister and carefully go downstairs.

The door to the flat on the first floor opens and Marion comes out in a red silk robe. Her lipstick is the same color; she has rollers in her hair and the sweet smell of perfume envelopes her.

I nod hello to her and she steps forward, blocking my way.

"Congratulations are in order," she says, examining me from top to toe.

"Thank you." I try to move to the right and she moves with me.

"Less than twenty-four hours after the wedding and he's already left your bed?"

"He had to go to work." I move to the left and she moves with me.

"Gabriel is his own master. He can always postpone his work if there is a good enough reason. He postponed it often enough for me."

"I have no interest in disturbing his work."

"Would you perhaps join me for coffee and we can have a little chat?" She gestures to the door. "Since I am your only neighbor, we should get to know each other."

"Another time." I move past her and skip hurriedly down the stairs.

Only when I reach the last stair do I let myself pause and catch my breath.

That woman knows him better than I do. She feels, justifiably, I suppose, that I have stolen her man. I have no doubt that she suspects something is wrong, and now that he has agreed that I stay with him, I have to improve my acting skills not to put him at risk.

I blush again when I recall how he'd explained quite simply the reason for the annulment of the marriage. "Josephine Augustine…" I murmur to myself, frowning in discomfort.

Going out into the street, I tighten my cloak around me. It is freezing cold. Listlessly, I scan the gray buildings, their gray appearance had never bothered me or spoiled the beauty of this special city for me. But now, with swastikas waving everywhere, I really need to make an effort to discover its beauty.

I walk along street after street until I reach the commercial area. Clothing stores are empty. Two women pass with vigorous steps and German soldiers patrol the sidewalk, stopping every now and again to look into store windows. They are everywhere! Soldiers in gray and black uniforms, wandering the city with their arrogant walk, impressed by the Paris monuments as if they were a gift whose worth they were estimating. I'm surprised by the ferocity of my hatred for them.

Two soldiers stop in front me, greeting me, and I force a smile. When they have gone, I curse and spit on the ground.

In the shoe store, an elderly woman is sitting, knitting a scarf. When I enter, she greets me, continuing to knit. I quickly choose black shoes with a flat, rubber sole, walking about in them inside the little store.

"I'll take them." I hand her the note and she raises her eyebrows in wonder.

"I don't have any change for this sum."

I look at the wretched shoes, refusing to wear my heels again.

"Perhaps I could offer you something else?" She points at the shelves.

I scan the meagre supply and see nothing I need; finally I see a long piece of velvet fabric the color of lilac, carelessly lying over the back of a wooden chair. I point to it and the woman nods enthusiastically.

"A few years ago, I couldn't even stand in this store, it was so crowded."

She complains as she wraps the fabric in a bag. "This street was full of life, and now look at us…praying for someone like you to come in. And when it finally happens, I can't even give you change." She frowns with frustration. "Our best clients are the Germans."

"It's only a bad time, it will change." I try and encourage her.

"Doesn't look like it. With all their marches and occupations. Every country is collapsing before them like dominoes. As if they weren't human beings, but unconquerable machines".

A noise outside makes her stop talking, and we both rush to the window overlooking the street. "I didn't mean what I said," the stressed salesperson mutters. "They may have installed microphones here." She walks away from the window, looking anxiously around her. "Maybe you're spying for them? Maybe…"

"They're not here for you." I step back and lean against the wall. "They're taking random people in the street. It's better they don't see us." I point at the shutter and she nods, shutting it, leaving only a tiny chink through which we can peep out.

Commands in German. Alarmed shouts in French and several women are pushed into the middle of the street. All the shutters of the stores opposite are closed and my eyes dart about in fear.

The "Resistance." The salesperson whispers. "I heard they put a bomb outside the offices of the Gestapo last night and one of their officers was killed."

"The Germans will retaliate." I shudder.

"They won't retaliate," she corrects me, "they are doing so at this very moment. I read in the newspaper that the Fuhrer demands ten of us for every one of theirs."

"There are only eight women there." I turn my head to look at the tiny store, checking to see if there is a way out. There isn't. We are trapped here.

In a flash my complacency vanishes and fear flows through my veins. I am afraid for myself and helplessness makes my heart pound wildly.

Two SS soldiers in black uniforms knock with their batons on a store on the other side of the street, and when the shutter remains closed, they fire a deafening burst of gunfire.

"Dear God," mutters the salesperson, grasping my hand.

The shutter opens and a young man with a slight limp comes out, his hands in the air. An old woman runs after him and I can't look anymore.

"They'll come to us now." The salesperson spins round, muttering hysterically.

"Sit with me." I tug at her elbow and make her sit beside me, our backs to the street. She is weeping and I hold her hand and whisper our anthem.

Arise, children of the Fatherland, the day of glory has arrived!

Against us tyranny's bloody flag is raised!

One shot and I choke. Another shot and I hum again.

In the countryside, do you hear, the roaring of these fierce soldiers?

A burst of firing that seems never to end makes me stop breathing and, weeping, we hold each other.

The salesperson starts to hum with me,

They come right into our arms,

to cut the throats of our sons, our friends!

Quiet. Silence.

It seems to me that we continue humming the anthem, but I might be imagining it.

I continue to sit embracing this woman who is a stranger to me, and sadness turns into anger and hatred that consumes any other emotion. I don't know how long we sit there in silence, each one withdrawn into herself in a comfortless hug, but when she gets up and cautiously opens the shutter, the street is quiet again.

Several pedestrians are walking along the sidewalks, close to the wall, trying to become invisible. They openly ignore the red stain on the street and are careful not to bump into each other.

"It's starting to get dark," the salesperson says in an anguished tone, taking a loaf of bread, some butter and a tomato out of a small cupboard. "I think you saved my life." She looks into the store window. "I'd be glad to share my evening meal with you." She spreads a floral cloth on the counter. "I don't have much to share but if you're hungry, I'll give it all to you. I got the tomato this morning." She presents it proudly and my belly constricts. This time in shame.

"I didn't save your life." I wave my hand and retreat to the door of the store. "Fortunately for us, they simply decided to go to another store." I pick up the bag with my heeled shoes and the fabric. "Better you share that tomato with your family."

"I don't have anyone to share it with." She sighs. "Both my sons fought at the front and now they've been taken to work in the factories of those bastards in Germany."

"At least they're alive." I smile sadly at her.

"What kind of a life is this?" She blazes. "They were supposed to return as heroes, and now they are serving our new masters."

I can find nothing comforting to say in response and so am silent.

She cuts the tomato in two halves and hands one to me wrapped in paper. "Take it. This way, I can pretend I'm not eating my dinner alone."

"Thank you." I take it and put it in the bag. I'm hypnotized by the sight of this elderly woman cutting a slice of bread and weighing the butter on a tiny scale in order to use the exact amount allocated for this meal. She is so focused on the precise spread of butter on the bread, smiling to herself when she glances at the half tomato she has left. I feel she has given me a treasure I will never know how to appreciate as she does. Groping in my bag, I take out the remaining notes and put them on the counter next to the tomato.

"What are you doing? I can't take that," she shrieks, but I wave my hand in dismissal and run outside, turning quickly in the opposite direction to the area where the massacre took place.

My heart doesn't calm down, not even when I'm several streets away from there, and I glance back every time I think I hear firing. After about an hour, I stop at the entrance to the government building. Two flags with swastikas are flying from the balcony on the top floor. I arrange my cloak on my shoulders and go up to the office on the first floor. A sleepy French clerk receives me with indifference.

"I've come to get my coupons." Sitting down in front of him, I present my new papers.

"Ah, Monsieur Augustine's new wife." He is roused from his torpor and seems surprised. "Why do you need coupons? The diamond business in crisis?" He grins as if at a joke.

"I'm a French citizen." My tone hardens. "I've come to get what's due to me."

"Your papers provide benefits." He places several documents in front of me. "You should be glad you are counted among the friends of the Reich. Not even the curfew hour applies to you."

"I want to receive exactly what my French brothers and sisters receive." I quickly sign the documents and push them towards him.

He shrugs indifferently and stamps the papers. Within quarter of an hour I am standing outside the building and proudly examining my food coupons. It's the first time since war broke out that I really feel part of my people. Claude enveloped us in protective walls, isolating us from the survival hardships that were the common lot. Now that this bubble has burst in my face, I am determined to prove to myself that the gift of my life was no random gift, and I resolve to prove that I am worthy of it.

The sun has set. The street is quiet and I walk along the sidewalks. My thoughts give me no peace and I hug my bag and walk quietly along one street after another, staying close to the gray walls of the buildings.

Raising my eyes, I gaze with confusion at the steps leading to Claude and Brigitte's house. My legs have simply brought me here, and when I see the Nazi flag flying at the side of the door, my heart breaks and I burst into tears.

I have no idea what is happening to them now. Are they still being interrogated? Have they been convicted? Do they expect me to do something to help them?

I long to run up the steps and open the door. Gather up all their personal possessions and pictures, keep their treasures with me so our enemies can't contaminate them. And more than anything, I want to slap Lucille. Scream at her that she's a foul traitor and I will never forgive her.

Stroking the stone wall, I sniff. For the first time in my life I realize that hatred can turn to an urge for revenge. I want to avenge my dear friends, my motherland, but as yet, I don't know how.

Walking away from the wall, I continue along the sidewalk. The sounds of firing echo relentlessly in my mind. One shot, and another, and then an endless volley, brutally putting an end to the lives of innocent people. The lives of people who were once free and proud of their country and now, all that is left for those who loved them, is a painful memory.

When I reach the entrance to the building where I now live, I finally allow my mind to digest what I'd experienced in the street. My body feels old and tired. How can one contain the fact that with the same randomness as they were chosen, by the same token, they could have chosen me?

"Josephine, where have you been?" Gabriel slams down the telephone receiver and approaches me, his body trembling with nerves.

"I've been telephoning every contact I have for the past hour and…"

Raising an exhausted hand, I wordlessly ask him to stop. Hugging the bag I collapse on the sofa.

"You can't just vanish like that." He still sounds angry but now, he is acutely examining me.

"I didn't vanish, I went to buy comfortable walking shoes." I sigh heavily.

"You've been held up until now because of some stupid shopping? Haven't you heard about the act of retaliation the Germans carried out a few hours ago? I don't understand how you can be so irresponsible."

"I heard about it." Taking out the half tomato, I put it on my chest. "I heard one shot and another and then a whole volley of shots. I thought it would never end."

"You were there?" He sat down on the table in front of me and looked anxiously at me.

"All I did was go shopping for shoes and then there was shouting and pleading, and then they knocked on the door of the store on the opposite side of the street and then…" I fall silent and show him the half tomato. "And then I received this treasure as a sign of gratitude from the nice salesperson whose sons are in Germany."

"You're in shock. You aren't making any sense." He leans forward to caress my head and the gesture threatens to overwhelm me, but I mustn't allow this to happen.

"I'm not in shock." I shake my head. "I'm sad. Angry. Full of hatred. But I'm not in shock."

"All right." Still looking at me with concern, he straightens his tie and sits up. "We'll have dinner now and then we'll have a serious conversation about the precautions you need to take."

Glancing at the clock on the wall, I realize that I'm running out of time. I'm supposed to be meeting Natalie and now there is no chance that he will let me go out.

"We also need to talk about our wedding ball." He rubs his neck and doesn't appear to notice my restlessness.

"Gabriel," I address him cautiously, "have you by any chance managed to buy the bicycle I wanted?"

"It's in the lobby, behind the staircase." He takes off his jacket and hangs it on the coat rack in the entrance. "White, with a basket decorated with yellow roses." He winks at me and I open my eyes in surprise. The small smile that appears on his face makes my heart contract and expand in the same breath, It seems to me that I'm truly seeing this man for the first time, and now he appears to be the best thing that could have happened to me under these terrible circumstances.

I return a small smile, wishing this rare feeling of the security and comfort he radiates could continue forever.

A knock at the door.

Gabriel briefly closes his eyes and when he opens them again, he no longer looks at me but turns to the door.

"*Mon Cheri,* my dear," Marion enters in a white robe and wet hair. She seems to be the only woman in the world who makes sure her make-up is perfect even when she's taking a shower. "The bulb in my bedroom has burnt out and I really need help, is there any chance you'd agree to come to my apartment and change it for me?"

"I was just sitting down to dinner," he responds apologetically, and I realize this is precisely the opportunity I'd prayed for.

"Gabriel." I pretend to be shocked. "What kind of gentleman refuses to help a lady in distress?"

He narrows his eyes in confusion and even Marion seems surprised.

"Dinner will wait. I've promised a friend I'd pop over to see her. Her mother is ill." I explain without being asked. "She takes care of her day and night, so it's important I keep my promise."

Slipping between them, I leave the apartment.

"Josephine, better wait for me here." He follows me out and grasps my elbow.

"My dear husband," I turn to him. "I'll be back before you have time to miss me." Standing on the tips of my toes, I kiss him softly on the lips.

He opens his mouth to protest again, but Marion doesn't disappoint.

"Let her go." She hangs on his arm. "You can wait with me until she gets back."

I skip quickly down the stairs and wheel the bicycle out into the street. I don't remember ever being so excited by a gift I'd received. In my childhood, my father spoiled me with whatever my heart desired and when I grew up, the gifts became more expensive and continued to come from one suitor after another. With some of them I enjoyed a romance that seemed serious at the time. I smile to myself, stroking the basket decorated with yellow roses. Going to nightclubs, films and parks that ended in white nights, when Odette and I would regale each other with every tiny detail of what had happened in the course of the evening.

The searing sensation in my heart returns, together with the painful longing for the period of my innocence. I don't feel the slightest anger towards her for her attempt to implicate me during the interrogation. At another time, I'd have been angry or disappointed, but now I understand. Three in exchange for one. I sigh. Even Odette had to understand this at some point.

The ride is easy and quick. The streets and sidewalks are empty and I'm able to pass through the streets without having to maneuver between pedestrians or cars. I slow down only when I notice three Wehrmacht soldiers entering a building at the end of the street, and then pick up speed again.

Rue de Montmorency is completely deserted. Both bars at the beginning of the street are closed. On one is the faded sign of the swastika and the window of the other is sprayed with graffiti in French. It isn't hard to guess who the owners of the bar were before the occupation. If my ignorant French brothers had been aware of the destructive propaganda ingrained in their minds when they still believed that our occupiers had our welfare at heart, they'd probably have scrubbed off these terrible slogans until their hands bled.

A faint light is coming from Louis's bar. I take my bicycle inside and lean it against the wall.

There are customers seated at only one table. Two shabby, unshaven men in berets are sharing a jug of tea and talking in low voices. The place looks filthy and neglected, bearing no resemblance to its golden days when Louis would organize poetry reading evenings, standing at the entrance and personally welcoming each of the guests.

Louis left Paris several years ago, and standing behind the bar is a young man who examines me with curiosity. Behind him are shelves of empty wine bottles; again and again, he bounces a coin on the counter.

I scan the place, waiting to see if Natalie would pop out of some hidden door to welcome me, and I recall the code words she asked me to tell the barman. I arrange the folds of my dress and sit down on a bar stool in front of him.

"Good evening, Madame." He continues to bounce the coin. "What can I offer you to drink tonight? I have coffee made from a unique blend of leaves." He grins. "The finest vintage wine from 1940." Again he grins. "And maybe you'll make do with a glass of tea?"

"Fleur-de-Lis," I whisper excitedly.

"Fleur-de-Lis?" He repeats aloud.

I nod, looking around fearfully.

"What the hell is Fleur-de-Lis? Some strange European cocktail?"

"No…" I open my eyes wide as if to share a secret with him. "You know. Fleur. De. Lis." I emphasize each word.

"Listen, Madame, if this cocktail isn't made of a blend of muddy coffee and a cheap imitation of red wine, I don't think I can help you."

The coin rolls along the counter and I catch it and tap it in frustration on the counter. Natalie has deceived me. She probably thinks I'm collaborating with the Germans, otherwise what justification would there be for their presence at my wedding? She doesn't know my true story, and now she probably won't ever know. I bounce the coin on the counter and the barman catches it and shrugs apologetically.

I can't blame her. I wouldn't take a chance on me if I were in her shoes.

"Thank you." I murmur disappointedly and return to the street with my bicycle. I tuck up my dress to sit on it and the two men from the bar stand on either side of me.

"I don't have any money." I cry out in alarm. "My bag is empty. You can see for yourselves."

"Fleur-de-Lis," one of them whispers, nodding to me to accompany him.

"What did you say?" I ask looking tensely on all sides.

"You heard me." He arranges his hat on his head and strides towards the bushes.

The excitement returns with a rush of adrenaline. Passing through the bushes, I push my bicycle into the rear yard of the bar. The other man takes it from me and puts his mouth close to the door. "Fleur-de-Lis," he whispers hoarsely, and two seconds later, the door opens and a young boy peeps out.

The men push me into the dark entrance and once the door is closed and locked my bicycle joins a row of other bicycles. The boy continues to stand with his back to the door and the two men go down steep stairs with me behind them.

I blink to get used to the strong light and find myself standing at the entrance to a bar-like cellar. Long tables are placed along it, around which are seated about twenty men and women. A bearded man, standing in front of them on a chair, making an impassioned speech, falls silent when he notices me. Suddenly, all heads turn to me and I flush with embarrassment.

"Maurice, this is the friend I told you about." Natalie jumps up from her place at the table on the left, and eagerly approaches me. "Don't look so alarmed. Everyone here is a friend."

Nodding, I allow her to lead me to her table.

"Friends," she shouts, although everyone is still quiet. "Josephine asked to join us and we welcome any new friend. She is an old acquaintance of mine and I can guarantee her."

"Welcome." Calls are heard from all sides and Natalie pours me a glass of wine.

Maurice bows his head to me and continues his impassioned speech. He speaks about the successful operation that led to the assassination of the Gestapo officer, and when his friends cheer, he waves a hand and they fall silent. He removes his hat and sadly recalls the Germans' act of retaliation. I'm chilled by the realization that he is referring to the shocking event I'd witnessed. Maurice goes on to talk about the weapons the British are parachuting into the villages, and the network for smuggling out wanted people. My eyes open wide with surprise when he concludes his speech by praising Claude and his courageous choice to sacrifice himself and his family for the sake of the French people.

He asks everyone to raise glasses while he continues to praise Claude's courage, and I bow my head and carefully wipe away my tears.

Natalie strokes my back and I am distressed by the knowledge that I didn't know him at all. I loved him with all my heart but didn't know the heroic figure and it seems I won't have that privilege in the future.

Wine is poured into the glasses and the discussions grow heated. One of the young women feels they should lie low for a time and the shabby man who had accompanied me argues that this is the right time for escalation. They argue fiercely about every issue Maurice raises and after an hour he sums up the decisions. I didn't participate in the discussions and don't understand their implications in depth.

Suddenly, Natalie gets up and whistles. She points at her wristwatch and everyone hurries to the stairs.

"We meet here every evening." She moves close to Maurice and smiles at me. "Today was a bit messy, but by the next time you come, we will have decided which group you'll be in."

"Thank you." Looking at the deserted tables, I sigh. Maurice's praise of Claude is still on my mind.

"Do you want us to accompany you home?" Maurice asks.

"No need," I answer at once, grimacing in pain. "I want you to know that I thought he was a traitor. A collaborator."

"Claude?" Natalie asks, nodding.

"If that's what you thought, good." Maurice smiles at me, stroking his wild beard. "It means he was protecting you and now you can continue on his path."

"Josephine, are you sure you want to do this?" Natalie asks assertively. "You don't have to. You've sacrificed enough, and you've only just gotten married."

"I do want to." I answer firmly. "I need it more than I want it."

"Then you're accepted." Maurice pats me on the shoulder.

"Maybe it's important to tell you that I don't know how to do anything except sew." I smile in embarrassment.

"We'll teach you everything you need to know." He conveys so much confidence that for a moment it seems to me he could single-handedly beat the German army.

Natalie taps on her watch and Maurice nods and motions to me to go up before them. About five men are still standing at the entrance; they leave in pairs every few seconds. When it is my turn, I hug Natalie goodbye and mount my bicycle.

I didn't notice time passing while I was sitting there, which is to my detriment. In less than an hour the curfew will begin and I really don't wish to discover the benefits of my new papers if I'm found in the streets after the allotted time. I pedal fast, passing through street after deserted street, constantly having to assess the way to avoid any encounter with patrolling groups of soldiers.

Panting and flushed, I reach our building with five minutes to spare before curfew. Leaning my bicycle against the wall, I go up the stairs. When I reach the door, I settle my breathing, sighing with relief when I pull the door handle and find it unlocked.

Gabriel is sitting at the chess table in his flannel trousers and a white vest. There is no doubt that his tailored suits don't show off the figure hiding underneath them. I stare at the muscles in his arms and remember how, at our first encounter, I imagined how he'd use them to strangle me. Now, I allow myself to imagine those arms comforting and taking care of me, but the small grimace of his upper lip thrusts me back into reality.

He is so concentrated on the pieces in front of him that for a moment it seems I can slip past him into the room, unnoticed.

"Do you know the game?" He suddenly asks without raising his head.

"Yes."

"Come and sit with me."

I sit down on the chair in front of him. He stares in concentration at the board. It doesn't look as if he intends to move any of the pieces.

"Feel free to make the first move whenever you're ready."

I sit there tensely. The last thing I feel like doing now is playing this stupid game. Rolling my eyes, I choose a pawn and move it two places forward.

"So reckless…"

I try and move the pawn back to its place but Gabriel puts his hand over mine, not allowing me to move it. "Once you have made a move, you can't undo it."

"It's just a silly game." I complain. I wait for him to explode at me and disperse the anticipated tension.

Leaning back, he massages his neck. "Why don't you think about your move before you make it?"

"I did."

"I don't believe you thought about it in depth." His long lashes lift slightly and there is no mistake. He is angry. Very angry. "There are two traps here." He points to the board. "One is yours and one is the enemy's. Do you understand that?"

I nod. I have no doubt, he isn't really talking about the game.

"Before you made your first move, we were in the same position of strength."

Again I nod.

"Now I'm already thinking several moves ahead and know for certain I will defeat you."

"I told you that I know the game, but I didn't say I'm good at it."

"In this game, you don't have the privilege of being defeated." He clenches his jaws. "You have to survive."

"I don't just want to survive, I want to fight back."

"Fight back." He repeats scornfully. "And how the hell do you intend to fight back when the other side knows the game better than you do? The other side is patient, smart, cunning, and you can't even consider your first move!"

"I hate this game!"

"You don't have to love it, but if you choose to play you must excel at it."

He stands and I lean my elbows on the board, considering his words.

"Come and have dinner." He holds out his hand to me and I weigh up whether to refuse and go to bed, but can't remember the last time I ate. I don't know whether my exhaustion stems from chronic heartache or the irresponsible way I've spent the past few days.

We sit down in the dining room and I'm surprised to find that he hasn't touched his plate. He's been waiting for me all this time.

"Do you want to tell me who you've been with this evening? Actually, I already know, but maybe you'd like to tell me about it." He asks casually, pouring me a glass of wine.

"I seem to remember my wife sending me to change a light bulb in the neighbor's house, which I managed to do. It took exactly five minutes and since then I've been waiting for her to return and have dinner with me."

I know that he isn't lying about dinner, but my frustration at his laconic use of my title makes my chest tingle strangely.

"You meant, to change the light bulb in your lover's apartment." I cut a slice of bread and spread a little butter on it.

"My ex-lover." He squeezes lemon over his fish and the smell makes my belly contract.

"You don't owe me an explanation. I apologize, I shouldn't have raised the subject at all." I close my eyes, breathe in the smell rising from his plate, and nibble at my bread again.

"Just as I expect you to treat me with respect and maintain my reputation, I will do the same for you."

I put my slice of bread on my plate and look at him. His eyes show no sign of cynicism or mockery, and I know he is telling me the truth.

"You can't go on existing on bread and butter." He pushes my plate of fish towards me.

"I haven't yet earned it." I push it back to the center of the table.

"I've earned it." His tone hardens. "You're living with me now and I will share everything I have with you."

"I'm grateful to you for that. I really am." I put my hand over my heart. "But in recent years I have lived like a leech on the back of good people. It's time I learned to take care of myself." Getting up, I leave the room and return with half of the tomato. "I think I've honestly earned this." I smile sadly at him. "I will gladly share it with you." I cut the tomato in small pieces and offer him the plate; he nods his thanks and takes one piece. I put the rest on the slice of bread and close my eyes to enjoy it juiciness.

"You have to stop blaming yourself."

"I'll learn in time," I respond, shaking my head when he offers me a glass of wine. "And I think you're right. I need to learn the rules of the game because I didn't understand anything today." He doesn't ask me to explain myself but my urge to share is stronger than I am.

"I was with the Resistance," I say cautiously.

"I know."

I don't ask how he knows. It doesn't even surprise me.

"I got to the meeting and everyone there seemed so mature and serious. Unafraid, resolute." I take a sip of water and sigh. "It just made me ask myself a lot of questions. Where have I been all this time? Why has it taken me so long? Why did I have to experience this crisis in order to wake up?"

"Josephine." He leans forward and puts his hand on mine. "I understand and respect your need to take part in the Resistance, but it is too risky for you, and directly impacts me. You have to understand that when you put me at risk, you are sabotaging things greater than some Resistance operation."

"They do very important things."

"I'm not saying they don't. But right now you cannot understand the big picture and therefore it is better you leave it."

I don't respond.

"Do you understand what I'm telling you?"

I nod.

"So can I trust you to put this adventure aside?"

I don't respond.

"I'm waiting for your answer."

"I'm not answering so I won't have to lie to you!"

I leave the dining room and lock myself in the bathroom. While washing my face, thoughts thrust me back into the events of the day. I understand his concern but can't allow it to penetrate. This evening, I felt I was in the right place; I felt a flicker of pride and can't allow him to take that away from me.

Entering the bedroom, I see Gabriel sitting in the armchair, smoking a cigarette. Without saying a word, he goes into the bathroom.

Curling up under the blanket, I close my eyes. A few minutes later, the light in the room goes out and the mattress beside me sags. Hugging the pillow, I pray he won't decide to open the subject again.

He doesn't say anything. His breathing grows heavy and again I'm alone with my cursed thoughts. Oddly enough, I find comfort in his being so close to me. Although I know nothing about him, I already feel he isn't a stranger, on the contrary, being close to him makes me feel secure. Cautiously, I move over to his side and am soothed only when his warm arm lightly touches mine. If I could manage to ignore my embarrassment for a moment, I'd lift his arm and put it around me, escape from these terrible hours of loneliness. But the voice of reason reminds me that for him I am only a guest. Just a strange girl he has decided to adopt out of the goodness of his heart.

The cigarette smoke in the cellar stings my eyes. The questions put to me in German aren't clear to me and I murmur pleading words. A large hand slaps me and my cheek burns, when I raise my arm to cover my head I find I am wounded.

"Tell me about him!" Now the command is given in French and I shake my head. Another slap and I swallow saliva mixed with blood. "Tell me everything you know about him!"

The physical pain is so great. My arm is almost ripped out and I open my mouth and sob. I'm not sobbing because of the pain but because I realize that I'm talking. Telling them. Telling them about him.

"Gabriel, wake up." I shake him in alarm and rub my arm. "Please, wake up."

"What's wrong?" He switches on the light and looks worriedly at the door.

"They tortured me. I was in their cellar and they beat me, threatened me and…"

"Have you had a nightmare?" Sitting up he leans against the headboard.

"It was so real. I could actually smell the mold on the peeling walls, and my eyes stung from their cigarette smoke." I'm trembling, but when he pulls me to him, I shake him off and wind the blanket around me. "I didn't want to tell them about you but they hurt me and in the end I did tell them." Bowing my head, I fight the tears threatening to burst out.

He switches off the light and I breathe heavily. His arm closed around me. I don't try to move away. His touch stops the trembling and slightly soothes the storm inside me.

"What did you tell them?" He asks, stroking my head.

"I told them your full name."

"And what else?"

"I told them you're from Switzerland."

His body slides down with me in his arms and now my head is on his chest. His heart beats slowly and mine quickens. "I told them you're a diamond dealer from Switzerland."

"And were they satisfied with that?" He chuckles.

"I don't know. I don't think so, but I couldn't think of anything else I know about you."

"Grave indeed." He suppresses his laughter and, shocked, I raise my head to look at him. "Grave indeed that those are the only details a wife can provide about her husband." He kisses the tip of my nose in the way an older brother might kiss his sister, and I shrink in confusion. "We'll start working on that tomorrow so that no-one suspects our charade." He yawns and settles the pillow underneath his head. "Until then, try and dream more optimistic dreams, because I have no intention of allowing the Gestapo to spend a night with you in their stinking cellar."

I finally manage a smile and instead of moving away from him, I put my head back on his chest. Strange that I feel so safe wrapped in this man's arms, but right now he is all I have, and suddenly that seems like a lot.

CHAPTER NINE

I'm brushing my teeth in the bathroom when Marie enters with several bags, a crafty look on her face.

"I'm just finishing in here." I gargle and spit into the sink.

"You should stay here with me." She closes the door and leans against it.

"Why?"

"I've just met Marion, your sweet neighbor from the first floor."

It wasn't a question but I nod and grimace.

"I'm an old woman now." She chuckles. "But there are a few things I can tell you as a result of my age."

"Let me guess, some hints relating to my married life."

"Yes." She nods eagerly, and for a moment her wrinkles seem to disappear and a young and energetic girl stands in front of me.

"Everything's fine with us, you don't need to worry."

"Everything's fine? That's the reply of a woman who's been married for at least twenty years and you've only been married a few days."

"Marie, you really have nothing to worry about." I avoid her glance and brush my hair.

"*Cherie*," she walks in and folds the towel lying on the counter. "There aren't many decent men in Paris these days, and there are too many single women."

I continue to brush my hair, trying to appear indifferent, but understand where she's heading.

"Single French women are dangerous," she adds quietly. "They're women who are used to dressing up, enjoying themselves, feeling courted and now they long to feel the comfort and security a man can give them."

"I understand, but what does that have to do with me?"

"Your husband is a rare and sought after commodity. A very handsome, wealthy man who has connections with high ranking people. Your neighbor was under the illusion that their relationship was one of true love. Illusions are a dangerous thing."

"He's married now. She doesn't have a choice but to sober up." I respond, surprised by my tone of anger.

"She won't sober up as long as you behave like a peacock that hasn't discovered its own feathers."

"I don't understand what exactly you expect me to do." Putting down the brush, I turn round to face her.

"I expect you to stop wandering around with that miserable expression on your face, and start showing the world your beautiful feathers. Show our neighbor that you are a proud young woman who is happy in her relationship and won't hesitate to show her claws if she senses danger."

"It's so childish." I smooth out an imaginary crease in my dress. "To bother with external appearance and worry about my neighbor's flirting. As if we don't have more important things to do."

"What's more important than looking after your man at home?" She folds her arms on her chest. "What's more important than making him proud of his choice, and knowing that you are proud of him and will do anything to keep lone she-wolves away from him?"

"So what you're actually saying is that if I don't start dressing up, he will hop into other women's beds." I shake my head despondently. "Is he that shallow?"

"Shallow?" She shrieks. "My Gabriel is certainly not shallow. He's a unique man, and so many women see this, except for one woman, and she's the most important of all."

"I do see it! I simply don't think it's really important to him."

"You're probably right." She sighs. "I tend to interfere in things that don't concern me. I apologize if I've annoyed you." She rubs her hands on the gray apron. "Anyway, I thought you'd want to change that blue dress and let me wash it. So I spent the morning buying you a few things." She points at the bags and leaves the room.

Grumbling, I turn back to the mirror. If she knew the marriage was fake, she wouldn't waste her time making these comments. Husband and wife…I snort scornfully. He did something heroic and saved me. This is where his responsibility ends. He doesn't look at me in the way a man looks at a woman, certainly not after sampling a real woman like our sensuous neighbor. I rub the end of my nose, remembering the snatched kiss last night. Like a brother kissing his sister. I shouldn't embroil myself in an unnecessary adventure, especially when the situation between us is so clear.

So why are her words like a blow to my belly?

I spread out the contents of the bags on the counter, examining with interest an elegant long dress. It is a pale gray color with a V-neckline. And this time, Marie got my size right.

Until a few days ago, I'd paid attention to my dress. I'd scrupulously matched items and gone to work for Claude groomed from head to toe. Now it seems idiotic to me. Who cares how I dress when at any given moment they could catch me in a random retaliation operation, and eliminate me with a single bullet.

Marie's words echo in my mind and now they anger me even more. But the anger doesn't come from her interference, but from the insolence of our neighbor. She doesn't know that our relationship isn't real but, nonetheless, is trying to come between us.

Before the occupation, I was confident in my femininity. I wasn't lacking in suitors and was never too shy to flirt with a young man I liked. Since these loathsome Germans arrived, they made me feel less of a woman and more of an object intended to satisfy their needs. So I left the game. I refused to participate in it. I cleared the arena for any single French woman who didn't care if they trampled her honor.

Gabriel was something else. He didn't look upon me either as an object or as a woman. I respect that, but not the insolence of our neighbor.

I quickly strip off the blue dress and throw it into the laundry basket. I put on the gray dress, make-up, and tie a velvet ribbon in my hair. A last glance in the mirror takes me back to the last ball. For a moment I can hear Odette's giggles and see Brigitte's approving look. I smell Claude's cologne and catch my breath when he scolds Odette and tells her to behave herself.

I turn the heart-shaped diamond earrings in my ear; he'd given them to me last Christmas. If only I'd had time to tell him how proud I am of him.

Going into the dining room, I bow my head to Marie.

"Wonderful, the peacock is showing its feathers." She claps her hands and sets two plates of scrambled eggs on the table.

Gabriel comes in. He tightens his tie around his neck and a small smile appears on his face.

"You are indeed a beauty." He kisses my cheek and sits down.

The compliment should have made me happy, but the way he said it again proves that he doesn't see me as a woman. I reprove myself when my heart contracts in disappointment and I sit down.

Gabriel hands me the French newspaper and when I see the small picture on the front page, everything goes black around me.

My breathing grows heavy and I open my mouth for air but can't breathe. My eyes dart across the picture and my finger strokes the image looking back at me with wide open, expressionless eyes. I hear the scream that leaves my throat and the newspaper is snatched from me.

"Josephine, I apologize." Gabriel tosses the newspaper to the floor and pulls my chair back. "I didn't look at the newspaper. If I'd known that picture was there I'd never have given it to you."

I continue to choke. The terrible picture of Claude hanging from a lamp post still flickers in front of my eyes.

"I am so sorry." Gabriel's voice is anguished. He kneels in front of me stroking my arms.

"Traitor," I murmur. "The headline was – traitor."

"Hero," he says fiercely. "Now all French citizens will know who he truly was."

"It's *Le Matin*, a French newspaper," I shout. "It's a newspaper with French editors and articles and they chose the headline. Miserable cowards!" I stand up resolutely, refusing to allow grief to overwhelm me again.

"And you," I round on him, "what exactly are you? You saved me and your role is over? Neutral Switzerland." I exhale with scorn. "Here within the walls of your home you can say that the Germans are terrible, but you still do everything to protect your business interests. You go to their balls, sit with them in restaurants and talk to them in their revolting language. But Switzerland won't stay neutral forever. The day will come when they have no other place to invade and they will come after you, and all the diamonds in the world won't help you when that happens!"

My eyes are burning with fury and I clench my hands until my nails cut into the flesh.

Gabriel gazes at me blankly, and closes his arms around me. "I'm sorry you had to see it. I promise I will be more careful in future."

"You don't have to protect me like a little girl." I try and push him away but his embrace tightens around me. "I can cope with this terrible reality. I refuse to continue to live in a bubble, and I will do anything to stop his sacrifice from being in vain." He presses my head to his chest without yielding, but I don't want his comfort now. I don't need it. And I don't want the tears gathering in my eyes to turn into weeping. I want to be strong. Not thanks to him, but thanks to me. I exhale. "I'm all right now, you can let me go."

He steps back and I see Marie standing in the doorway with tear-filled eyes. They both pity me, but I don't need their pity. I have to hang on to the anger inside me, keep the hatred searing my belly so I won't forget why I must join the Resistance.

"I have to go."

"Have breakfast with me and I'll drive you." Gabriel sits down and gestures to me to sit.

"I'm going to get my own food, like any other French citizen."

"You need food coupons." Marie intervenes.

"I have them."

"At this hour you won't find anything." Looking at the clock, she shakes her head. "And there is no reason for Gabriel Augustine's wife to stand in line for food when she has everything here."

Gabriel motions to her to be quiet. "You can use the money I gave you yesterday for food." He spreads the German newspaper on the table.

"I gave it to someone who needed it more I did."

I anticipate a harsh response but it doesn't come. He just stands up and takes several notes out of his trouser pocket.

"I don't want your money! I want to get my food by myself."

Returning the notes to his pocket, he goes back to the newspaper.

"Take the money," Marie scolds me. "At this hour nothing is left. Maybe you can pay someone ahead of you in line…"

"No. I'll get my own food," I say and leave the room.

The long line of people, women, men and children, winds like a snake to the end of the street. I tighten the cloak around me, feeling that my elegant dress is unnecessary. The other people look shabby and exhausted.

"It's useless standing here." The young woman in front addresses me with frustration. "I don't know what I was thinking when I volunteered to take my brother to school this morning, it's clear there will be nothing left. We'll barely get the leftovers."

"But the line is so long," I tell her, "how can we all be standing here for nothing." I turn my head and see that I'm no longer the last in line. A boy passes, holding a bag tightly to his chest. He looks tense and disappears down a side street, and three boys leave the line and run after him.

"Three against one." The young woman smiles bitterly. "What's your bet?"

"They're chasing him for the food?" I'm shocked.

"As if it were the first time."

"Where are the police?" I look around.

"It looks as if you're here for the first time." She laughs.

I droop as time passes. Crowding, shouting and the line just grows longer. I no longer see the young woman who was before me, now there is a man holding the hand of a freckled boy. I try to understand where the young woman has disappeared to, and when I move sideways slightly, I'm tripped up and fall to the ground.

"Why did you do that?" I angrily ask the tall woman who is now standing in my place.

She doesn't look at me.

"I asked you why you pushed me." I try to push back into my place and am rudely pushed not by her but by the women standing behind her.

"You left the line, you lost your place!" One of them shouts at me.

"I didn't leave, I was pushed," I say irritably between my teeth and forcefully push back in. I stand tensely, expecting resistance, but nothing happens. Another hour goes by, then another and another, and when I finally see the window of the nearby building, the line is pushed back and the iron door slammed shut.

"What's happening now?" I ask, mystified.

No-one answers me. Exhausted, heads down, backs bowed, each one walks away.

I stand alone on the sidewalk in front of the closed door, food coupons in hand, trying to decide what to do.

"Pssst…" The whisper comes from the alley. "Come on." The female voice sounds familiar.

Going into the alley, the young woman who'd been ahead of me in line is smiling victoriously. "You need to be more assertive." She shows me a paper bag. "I got bread and a nice lump of butter."

"I'm glad for you."

"It's not a lot, but it will take the edge off the hunger." She hugs the bag. "If I had any jewelry, I'd eat a lot better, but I used them to buy goods on the black market."

"I'll try again tomorrow." Unthinkingly, I push my hair behind my ears, not believing I'll have to go back to the apartment defeated and hungry.

Her eyes are fixed on my ear lobes. "If your diamond earrings are real, I know a place where you'll get a good price for them."

"They're not for sale." Hurriedly, I hide my ears under my hair.

"You're strange." She emerges from the alley and I walk next to her. "Those earrings will buy you food for a whole week. Maybe more. You can't eat diamonds."

My belly rumbles and even bread and butter seem like a feast, but my defeat is even harder to bear. The earrings are all I have left of Claude. Can I really part from them?

I remember the horrifying picture in the newspaper and hold my belly in pain.

"Whoever gave them to you would understand," she says quietly. "They're just objects. Whoever gave them to you would want you use them to survive."

The dreadful picture from the newspaper fades and I can imagine Claude standing in front of me, smiling in agreement. But my heart doesn't stop aching. I can't continue to live at the expense of others. "You're right, they're just objects. It's what's in my heart that matters."

"Now you're talking like a survivor." She smiles at me." I'll take you to the paradise of the hungry. I only want you to share something small with me in return."

"You'll have it."

We walk along, street after street, until it seems we'll walk forever. On the way, the young woman, Francine, tells me about her fiancé who had gone off to war and not returned; about her constant worry for her elderly parents; the abundance when her father had run a women's clinic; about her older brothers who had gone to Vichy and left her to take care of her younger siblings. She talks ceaselessly, without asking me a single question about my story. It seems I'm not the only one who feels alone. When we reach the fifth district, the sun is starting to set.

"Getting food is a full time occupation." I lick my dry lips.

"It's not that bad." She winks at me and enters a corner building. We go up the stairs, and when I enter the apartment on the third floor, I realize what paradise she was talking about.

After half an hour of tough negotiation undertaken by Francine, we return to the staircase without the earrings but with three bags full of treasure.

"Thank you, Claude," I murmur to myself, rubbing my earlobes sadly.

I insist that Francine take one bag and she insists on accompanying me home. That walk through the quiet streets had never seemed so frightening. We held fast to the bags, walking close to each other whenever we heard steps. For the first time, my fear didn't stem from an encounter with the Germans but from my fellow French citizens.

The sound of bicycle wheels approaches and again, we stop, standing close together. A pair of bicycles stop beside us and then another, two boys exchange evil looks and come up to us.

"Go away!" Francine shouts, but they aren't deterred. One of them jumps off his bicycle and the bag drops from my arms.

"Go away!" Francine screams again, standing in front of me.

The sound of heels tapping the sidewalk, and the boy retreats in alarm. He gets on his bicycle and in a second the three disappear.

"Madame." The German soldier bows to me and smiles at Francine. "Is everything all right?" He asks in French. We both nod vigorously.

"Don't forget your bag." He picks up the bag from the sidewalk.

"Merci." I nod, and he bows his head again and crosses the street.

"Who would have thought I'd be glad to see a German soldier." Francine spits on the ground and we both laugh, walking on quickly.

I part from her with an embrace at the entrance to the building, and suggest she borrow my bicycle. I suddenly realize I am leaving her alone on the battle ground.

She refuses, showing me her bony arm. "I've learned to fight for what belongs to me." She laughs. "And I really hope we meet again."

I watch her as she walks away, again feeling my earlobe without its earring. All the time we were walking, I'd managed to distance that terrible picture, but now it hits me harder than ever. I hadn't had time to part from him; tell him I'm proud of him; thank him. It is over. He is no longer with us. And I have no idea where Brigitte and Odette are.

Going up the stairs, I sigh. My pride in the success of my operation doesn't dim the pain. I hear sounds of laughter coming from the apartment, and I roll my eyes tiredly, realizing whom I'll meet inside.

"Good evening." I say with a fake smile as I go inside.

Gabriel is sitting in the armchair and, opposite, smoking a long cigarette, Marion sprawls on the sofa.

"Good evening." Gabriel stands up and approaches. Kissing my cheek, he takes the bags from me.

"You look terrible." Marion sits up and grimaces with pretended concern. "You look so tired. Why don't you send your maid to do your shopping?"

"You look beautiful." Gabriel moves, hiding her from me.

I know she's right and that in his polite way, he is trying to encourage me, and I give him a genuine smile.

"I have food," I whisper proudly. "And this time, if you'll permit me, I'd be glad to invite you to dinner."

"It would be an honor" he responds, giving me his small, special smile.

He turns to Marion and she continues looking at me, but this time her glance is particularly malevolent.

"We want to get ready for dinner." Gabriel addresses her. "We can continue our conversation at another time."

"She inhales her cigarette and wrinkles her nose in distress. "I'd be glad to join you. Promise I won't bother you."

"Not tonight," I answer instead. "We've planned a romantic dinner, just the two of us."

"Well, maybe tomorrow." She gets up, her sweater revealing her shoulder.

He doesn't respond and this time I am keep quiet.

She stands close to him, kisses him on both cheeks and then blows me a kiss.

I remind myself that she was here before me, that I took her man and, but I can't find the graciousness to respect this. I can't bear her presence, and am nonetheless surprised by the sigh of relief that bursts out of me once the door closes behind her.

"A romantic dinner, that's wonderful." Marie declares from the corridor. "And I see you have brought surprises." She takes the bags from Gabriel and smiles at me in satisfaction. "I have heated the water. You can indulge in a bath and in the meantime I will prepare the meal." Going into the corridor, she adds, "you can enjoy it together."

I pale and avoid his glance.

"That woman just has to poke her nose into everything." Gabriel grins.

"I heard you," she shouts, laughing.

"Josephine, I have to make a call." He ignores my embarrassment. "You go in first." He takes off his tie and tosses it onto the sofa.

Hurrying into the bathroom, I strip off my dress, lie in the bath and stare at the wall opposite me. Quietly I muse over the harsh events of the past days, and pray I'll find a way to contain and live with the pain.

I notice a new robe hanging on the rail and shudder. My new hosts do everything they can to make me feel at home, and I haven't shown them a moment's gratitude.

I dry myself, trying to understand what caused my outburst at Gabriel this morning, accusing him so venomously. He behaves respectfully towards me; he has given up his privacy and comfort, even his lover, and I've never even thanked him properly.

My belly is rumbling awkwardly. Passing into the dining room, I examine the ornaments on the dressers. I have no understanding of art, or ever pretend to, but each object here has been chosen with care. Nonetheless, this apartment, opulent though it may be, isn't anything like the home of my previous hosts. What is lacking here is the touch of a woman.

"Josephine has managed to find treats," Marie calls out and, when I turn round, I see Gabriel seated at the head of the table. He looks so masculine and comfortable in his flannel trousers and vest, so I can understand why Marion refuses to accept her defeat. For a moment I regret not being a true rival.

"How did you manage to get hold of all this without money?" He examines the table with interest.

"It isn't polite to ask a lady questions like that." I smile, inadvertently rubbing my earlobes. When I look at him, his glance is fixed on my fingers, and I quickly drop them.

"Your earrings," he murmurs to himself.

"The diamond earrings?" Marie shrieks. "You bartered with your diamond earrings, well, you didn't get enough for them!"

"I received more than what I brought back here." This conversation is disconcerting for me. "I shared what I received with the young woman who helped me."

Marie opens her mouth but Gabriel motions to her to be quiet.

"Josephine, it's an excellent meal and thank you for sharing it with me."

"It's the least I could do, and I think I should apologize for my outburst this morning."

"No need." Picking up the bottle I'd bought, he murmurs to himself. "I shouldn't have let you read the newspaper without going through it before giving it to you."

I want to protest his intention of censoring, but my belly doesn't stop rumbling and I swoop down on my first meal in several days. This time I don't refuse wine, nodding acceptance whenever he offers to fill my glass.

Marie refuses our invitation to join us and goes home. We continue to sit in the dining room for a long time. Gabriel proves to be a worthy partner in my affection for Cabernet Sauvignon and I sigh regretfully when I find the bottle is empty.

"This time, with your permission, I will invite you." He smiles at me and takes a new bottle out of the glass cupboard.

"I won't ask you how you earned that," I say cynically, but don't protest when he fills my glass.

"In exactly the same way that you got your treasures." He winks at me. "Diamonds…"

"I didn't have an easy day." I sip the wine, feeling a need to confide in him. "It was even horrifying. You can't imagine what is happening out there." I take another sip and he lights a cigarette and looks silently at me. "The line starts at the allocation point and ends at the end of the street and if I hadn't fought for my place, nobody would have said a word in my defense."

"Did they hurt you?" He asks with concern, passing the cigarette to me.

"No. But it could easily have come to that. Everyone is so intent on getting the meager food rations they allocate there, they aren't deterred by anything. As if they've forgotten basic manners and mutual help." I inhale deeply and return the cigarette to him.

"And those who managed to get their meager goods had to escape fast because of thieves." I take several sips and sigh. "On the way back here, two boys tried to grab the bags and I froze. I should have protected what was mine, but I froze in fear. It was pathetic." I shake my head in embarrassment, "just the thought of being saved by a Wehrmacht soldier."

"It won't happen again." Gabriel stands and picks up the plates. "There is no reason to put yourself at risk when you have everything you need right here."

"I have no intention of living at your expense." I finish my glass of wine and pick up the glasses. "When my supply is finished, I will simply go earlier to stand in line."

"I didn't forbid your adventure today, but I refuse to let it happen again. It doesn't look good for Madame Augustine to be standing in line for food." He leaves the room.

"I don't care how it looks." I run after him with the glasses. "Even if I were really your wife, I'd want the right to be independent."

Putting the dishes in the sink, he goes into the bathroom. I lean against the door, and the moment he comes out I face him, ready for battle. He nods at me to go in and resentfully, I obey. Washing my face and brushing my teeth, I recite to myself all the arguments I will present to him. The light bulb flickers twice and the room goes dark.

Damned electricity cuts.

I find my way to the bedroom, and Gabriel meets me at the end of the corridor with a candle in his hand. In the bedroom, he hands me a new nightgown and turns his back so I can remove the robe and put it on. He waits for me to get into bed and then, blowing out the candle, he lies down beside me. He says nothing and I realize this is his way of allowing me the last word.

But I still haven't said my piece.

"What does Marion do to make a living?" I ask, fidgeting with the blanket.

"She occasionally appears in performances at the Moulin Rouge."

"And she earns enough to live so ostentatiously?"

"I help her."

"Financially?"

"Yes."

His answer so infuriates me that I rub my earlobes and murmur with irritation.

"If you have something to say, say it loud and clear."

'If a woman sleeps with a man for financial gain, it makes her a prostitute, doesn't it?"

"I told you, we used to have a relationship, but I no longer see her in that way."

His dry responses don't allay my anger, merely increase it.

"What you are saying is that you no longer sleep with her but still support her. So it seems she has exactly the same status as I do, just that she does it voluntarily whereas it is imposed on me."

"Do you want me to stop helping her? Would it make you feel better if she has to struggle for her food?" He asks, sitting up.

For a moment, I imagine her in her long silk dress, fighting off the mean women who shouted at me this morning, and I burst out laughing. I cover my mouth with my hand as his eyes open in wonder, but I can't stop.

"I'm sorry." I cough. "That was really childish of me. Of course not. You are doing something good and I have no idea why it makes me so angry."

His small smile spreads over his face and he pulls me to him, his arm around my shoulders.

"It's absurd and ridiculous that I can't stand her. I don't even know her, and I can only imagine how I'd feel in her place if I lost my man to a woman who suddenly appears in his life. I'd feel broken and crushed."

"Your man will come back. And I'm sure not a day goes by that he doesn't think of the beautiful woman waiting for him at home."

"What man?" I turn and look at him.

"The soldier." He frowns. "The one in a POW camp."

"Ah. That one." I avoid his glance and go pale. "Well…" I slide down on the mattress and turn my back to him.

"I thought you weren't even listening to me in the restaurant and maybe this is a good time to tell you I was lying to you. I thought you liked me and were really courting me, so I made up the story to keep you away."

"I see." He sounds pensive. He moves away to the edge of the mattress. "If that's what you thought, you weren't entirely wrong."

Now my eyes are open in surprise.

CHAPTER TEN

As I page through the newspaper, I roll my eyes every time I discover yet another page torn out.

"You really don't have to do this." I grumble. "There's no point in censoring the news. I'll discover it all in the end."

"I need you to be in a good mood today." He sipped his coffee.

"Why? What are we celebrating? Have the British and the Americans entered Lyons? Will Charles de Gaulle come to Paris at the head of a victory march?" I fake a broad smile.

Raising his eyes from the newspaper, he laughs and his deep laugh sounds like the most romantic chanson I'd ever heard.

"I promise you that when that happens, I won't have to worry about you being in a good mood." He caresses my shoulder.

"This evening you will have to appear to be in a good mood at our bridal party."

The smile is wiped off my face.

"I've booked the restaurant at the Ritz Hotel for our guests. We'll treat them to dinner, drinks, dancing and once the evening is over you can go back to hating them without my interference."

"Does this mean that your German friends will be there?" I push my plate away.

"Yes."

"Then you'd better take Marion with you. I have a feeling she'd play the role of a happy wife much better than I will."

"But I didn't marry Marion, I married you." Standing up, he put on his jacket. "I've left money for you on the mantelpiece in the drawing room, use it to buy a dress and anything else you need."

I groan aloud.

"I'll pick you up at six-thirty, and you can of course invite friends."

The realization that I might miss another meeting of the Resistance distresses me. I missed yesterday's meeting and can't afford to miss another. "I'll meet you there."

"I don't think that's a good idea."

"I promise not to be late and when I arrive, I'll make you proud of me." I place my hand over my heart.

"The event starts at seven, and I insist you be there on time." He shakes his head despairingly and goes to the door. A moment before disappearing down the corridor, he turns back. "I forgot to ask, is there anything I can do to make you happy?"

Again the same monotonous tone.

Looking up at the ceiling, I think about it. "Actually, there is something that would make me happy, but it might be too big a request."

"Try me."

"I'd like a record player and some records so things won't be so quiet here."

"Your wish is my command." He gives me his special smile and leaves the apartment.

I'm relieved that he didn't ask me about my plans, and I work out the times in my head. Wearing a dress and smiling is not a difficult task. I did it at all of Claude's balls and this evening I will manage to fake amiability too, if I'm focused. It will complete the saga of my fake marriage, and I'll be able to completely devote myself to my new calling.

I take the lilac velvet fabric I bought from the salesperson in the boulevard, out of the bag and nod. For a moment I'd been worried that I'd have nothing to do until the evening but now I know exactly how to pass the time.

I look up at the clock on the wall. I hadn't noticed the hours passing and I don't even remember Marie setting a lunch tray on the table.

I look at my creation with pride, and nod with satisfaction. Sewing the lace onto a strip of remaining fabric, I make a matching ribbon for my hair. "*C'est tout*, I'm done!" I call out enthusiastically, and run to the bathroom.

I get dressed, put on make-up and tie the ribbon around my head. Even if this were a real bridal party, I couldn't have dreamed up a worthier gown. The velvet clings to the upper part of my body and flares below the belt, the sleeves are long and widen at the elbow. It reaches my ankles and the black, high-heeled shoes add just the right degree of elegance.

Leaving the room, I gasp at Marie's cry of wonder.

"*Oh la la.*" She walks around me in excitement. "The peacock isn't only spreading its feathers, it is showing them off!"

"The dress is a success." I stroke the fabric and smile at her.

"Success to say the least. It is superb."

"Thank you very much, Marie." I hug her, go into the drawing room, put on the black cloak, and tuck the money Gabriel left me into my handbag.

"It's still early," she says uncomprehendingly. "Gabriel told me the event won't start for another two hours."

"I have an errand to run before that." I open the door and kiss her cheek.

"Don't be late for him." She wags an admonishing finger at me. "Very important people will be there this evening."

"I know." I pout.

"Make him proud of you. He deserves a little gratification." She sighs, and I nod and run to the staircase.

"*Merde,*" I whisper when I see the door to Marion's apartment wide open. My heels are so noisy, she must have heard them and, indeed, within seconds the red silk robe flows out, followed by the rest of her body.

"*Cherie*, you look very nice." She blows smoke from her cigarette straight into my face. "Aren't you a little early? The event only starts at seven. And where is Gabriel?"

"I have an errand to do before that," I say impatiently and pass by.

"So, we'll meet there," she calls after me.

"I'll be waiting," I shout, feeling a sting of anger. Why the hell did he have to invite her? Maybe I should have insisted he stop helping her. At that moment, I wouldn't have minded seeing her fighting for a place in line to get a wretched food ration.

I cross two streets in my heels, realizing that if I want to get there and leave on time, I have no choice but to take a taxi. However, the only passing taxis were rickshaws, drawn by bicycles. I wait to see if an ordinary taxi passes but in the end I wave a cyclist to stop.

Almost half an hour is wasted on a slow journey and I ask him to stop two streets away from the meeting place. He seems surprised by the note I hand him, and I waste a few more minutes persuading him not to wait for me.

An hour and a half. That's all the time I have to get there on time. An hour for the meeting and half an hour for the ride to the hotel. Walking fast and looking fearfully around me, I force myself not to run. Running could be interpreted as running away, and I don't need anyone to stop me and ask unnecessary questions.

The door to the cellar is closed. Locked. I lean against it in disappointment. How the hell do I get in?

I knock once on the door, then again, approaching the door, I whisper "Fleur-de-Lis."

The door opens slightly, and the thin boy gestures to me to come in quickly. I go down the stairs and the same spectacle meets my eyes. Maurice standing on the stage, making a speech, but this time only about ten men and women are sitting in front of him.

"Josephine, come and sit beside me," Natalie calls and I hurry towards her.

"Your dress is ravishing," she whispers, stroking my back. "Wear something a little less noticeable next time."

"I have to go to a party," I respond in embarrassment, and we turn our gaze to the improvised stage.

This time, there are no drinks on the tables. Everyone is listening tensely to Maurice, and when he refers to two rare Fleurs-de-Lis, glances wander to a young woman of about my age. She is beautiful and delicate with blond hair and a sprinkle of freckles across her nose. Beside her sits a pale, terrified girl with the same color hair.

"We want to take you to a safe house," Maurice says. "But our contact can only receive the message tomorrow evening."

"Can't they stay here in the cellar?" Asks one of the women.

"No, too dangerous. Two members were arrested several hours ago. We can't be sure that this address won't come up in the interrogation and so, from tomorrow, we will hold our meetings elsewhere."

A brown-skinned girl stands up. "I'll take them home with me."

"No." Maurice gestures to her to sit down. "Each member here is marked. Names will come up in interrogation, our descriptions, maybe even our addresses. We must all think about where to sleep in the coming days."

"So, what do you suggest?" Natalie walks over to the frightened girl and strokes her head.

Two women start arguing and very soon everyone seems to be arguing. Minutes pass and when I look at the clock I see with anxiety that almost an hour has gone by.

Maurice whistles and everyone shuts up. "We're all burned. We have to think of an acquaintance who is honest enough to agree to look after them until tomorrow evening."

"What about Josephine?" Natalie points at me and I go pale. "She's only been at one meeting, no-one will mention her name in interrogation."

I shake my head in alarm, and Maurice strokes his beard and looks at me.

"I have to go to my bridal party," I mutter in embarrassment. "There will be problematic guests there, and my husband won't accept it with understanding and…"

"Josephine, why are you here?" He asks quietly, and apart from the accelerated beating of my heart, I can't hear a thing.

"To help."

"And how exactly did you think you could help?"

"I don't know. I waited for instructions."

"It's time for your trial by fire."

Standing up, he asks everyone to leave. Within one minute, the cellar empties and only he, Natalie, and the two girls, whom he called Fleurs-de-Lis, remain.

"You have a chance to participate in the most important aspect of our national Resistance," Maurice says with a meaningful expression. "To help save two souls. It is an enormous privilege."

I nod and swallow the lump in my throat.

"No-one could identify them as Jewish sisters. They will go with you to the party and you will say that they're your cousins, come from the village to celebrate with you."

"I don't know if I can do that." I look at the beautiful older sister and she bows her head.

"If you fail, their fate will be a cruel one." Natalie intervenes. "If you're lucky, they'll be sent to a labor camp and if not, they'll…" She is silent and when the girl raises her head, she gives her a furious look. I realize she is trying to protect her young sister. "If not, you will live with the knowledge that you have sent them to their death." Natalie refuses to censor her harsh words. The young girl bursts into tears, and I rush to hug her.

"The problem is that my husband knows I have no family here. I honestly think I will put them even more at risk."

"You're the best chance they have." Maurice shrugs. "Look carefully at them. Their names are Miriam and Sarah. And you don't have the privilege of failing."

I move away from the girl. "Stand up, please," I request quietly and both stand. "This evening your name is Nita," I turn to the younger sister and arrange the crumpled collar of her dress. "And you are Michelle." I stroke the older sister's head. "You are the daughters of my mother's sister and you've come especially to celebrate."

They nod.

"And we're late…" I glance at the clock in frustration and walk to the stairs. "I promise to do my best." I call to Maurice and Natalie and go up the stairs. My heart is beating wildly and anxiety and the weight of responsibility threatens to paralyze me.

They walk along the street with me, looking fearfully about them.

"Please don't look so fearful." I admonish them. "You're French women who have come to celebrate with their cousin. Smile and make brief, polite responses if anyone who asks and I'll try and end the evening as quickly as possible."

I curse when I find no taxi in the next street as well, and carry on walking quickly with the girls following. At the end of the street I see the boy with the bicycle and rickshaw who had brought me here.

"Thank God." I start to run and they run beside me.

"I decided to wait for you anyway." The boy smiles at me and looks admiringly at the beautiful girl.

"I promise you an extra note if you manage to take us swiftly to *Place Vendôme. Hôtel Ritz.*"

"Done!" He salutes me and the moment we are seated, he pedals off with all his strength.

"Josephine, we are grateful beyond words," the older sister whispers, pressing my hand.

"Don't thank me yet." I exhale with difficulty. "I have no idea if we can even get through this evening."

"I'm Miriam and my sister is Sarah." She presses my hand again, smiling at me and my anxiety increases.

"This evening we will be Nita and Michelle. We won't disappoint you." She looks severely at her little sister.

They boy stops at the entrance to the Hôtel and I understand from the number of cars in front that Gabriel's visitors have arrived.

I wipe the perspiration from my forehead. I've never felt such anxiety, never thought I'd be responsible for the fate of two Jewish sisters, nor imagined I'd have to do so in a restaurant full of Nazi scum.

"The play begins." I take a few deep breaths and link arms with the young girl. A forced smile spreads over my face. "Good luck to us." Opening the door to the Hôtel, I march inside.

At the entrance to the restaurant, my legs tremble and I link arms with the girl I'd decided to call Nita. It might have been a mistake because the memory of my old friend only makes me quiver with disquiet.

Soldiers in black uniforms. Soldiers in gray uniforms. Men in luxury suits and women in elegant gowns. Just like an ordinary ball. I try and calm myself, but fail.

"I'm here. We can start the celebration," I call out. And the broad figure in the elegant suit turns around. The small smile on his face doesn't hide the tremor in his upper lip, and I realize that I will have to cope on two fronts this evening.

He comes over to me and, dropping the arms of the sisters, I throw myself at him with a strong embrace. "I'm sorry for being late, *Mon amour*" I kiss his lips. "I went to the train station to pick up my cousins. I got a telegram from them, a complete surprise, I'm so happy they got here on time."

"Then I suppose that your delay is justified." He swings me into the air. "And now that my beautiful wife has arrived, food can be served," he calls out, and the guests stand up and clap.

Waitresses with trays dart among the tables. Champagne is poured into glasses and I stand beside Gabriel, holding his hand, not knowing how to breathe, anxiety taking over my limbs. I shake hands with Germans in gray uniforms, black uniforms and Germans in brown coats. Gabriel exchanges few polite words with them, laughing at their comforting words on the difficulties of married life. Even the commander of the police station is here, and kisses my cheek as if we're old friends.

"Who is that beautiful young woman?" An SS officer looks at the figure behind me and only now, do I understand with terror that the sisters have been standing there all the time.

"Where are my manners?" I turn around and see two white faces staring at me. "These are my beloved aunt's daughters. Nita and…ah…Michelle." I burst out laughing. "All this excitement is confusing." The officer kisses Nita's hand and amiably pats Michelle's head. Her eyes roll upwards and she seems about to faint.

"Ah, *Mon Dieu*." I grab her and sit her down on an empty chair. "I am completely irresponsible, they're after a very long journey and I haven't even offered them food or drink."

"I'll take care of it." Gabriel beckons to a waiter. "And welcome you properly." He kisses Nita's cheek and bends to kiss Michelle. "I'm very glad you managed to come, I know how important it is to my wife."

They both nod wordlessly.

"I hope you'll save me a dance." The officer again takes Nita's hand, lingeringly kissing it. "Where have you come from?"

She opens and closes her mouth. Opens it again and looks questioningly at me. I scratch my head and rock on my heels.

"I asked where you come from." The German speaks more loudly.

"From Cordes-sur-Ciel," Gabriel answers laughingly. "My friend, forgive her nervousness. It isn't every day that a country girl meets such a high-ranking German officer."

"Does my rank make you nervous?" He smiles at her and brushes his hair aside.

"Very much so, monsieur." Nita bows her head. "Only soldiers in gray uniforms have reached our village."

"Wehrmacht soldiers. I understand. I'd be glad to hear more about your village." He takes out a cigarillo and the tension is threatening to undermine my ability to think clearly. I link my fingers with Gabriel's and press his hand.

"Herr Stengel, let's give them time to relax after their long journey." Gabriel says, holding me close to him. "And now it is time for a first dance with my wife." He signals to the band and the singer nods, holding the microphone.

The German clicks his heels and returns to the officers' table. Gabriel leads me into the center of the dance floor and the singer's deep voice fills the space. He holds my hand and places his other hand on my lower back. My feet move to the rhythm he dictates, and when the singer pauses to congratulate the happy couple, a storm of clapping is heard on all sides.

I'm unable to enjoy the dance, my eyes dart between the officers sitting at the tables and the two sisters sitting next to each other and looking at their plates. They look wretched and exhausted. What was I thinking to bring two fragile creatures into the lion's den? My anxiety grows with every passing second, I feel the weight of responsibility on my shoulders. If I fail it will be the end of them. And of me and Gabriel.

I look up at him. His upper lip is trembling as he looks down and I close my eyes and lay my head on his chest.

"Gabriel," I whisper.

He doesn't respond. "Please don't be angry with me now."

He doesn't respond.

I stand on the tips of my toes, put my arms around his neck and put my lips to his ear. "They…they aren't…." I whisper and fall silent.

"If you have something to say, say it loud and clear," he whispers sternly.

"They aren't really my cousins," I find the courage to confess out loud.

"What are you saying…" His angry tone contradicts the gentle caress of his fingers on my head.

I think about apologizing again, but a glance at the sisters prevents me from doing so. Not even my fear can make me feel that I owe an apology for trying to save them.

Other couples join us on the floor and when Gabriel spins me I don't know where Nita has gone. I look right and left and choke when I find her standing close to the SS officer on the dance floor. Her smile is crooked and terrified and she is nodding and responding briefly.

"If you've decided to play the game, you have to think several moves ahead." Gabriel kisses my cheek.

"Then I should change places with her." My voice trembles.

He leads me across the floor until we stop beside them. "Do it properly," he whispers in my ear and kisses me again.

I nod and straighten up.

"Nita," I call and she looks at me in confusion. "You've only just arrived and here you are, commandeering the handsomest officer here?"

She doesn't respond, but the officer's smile broadens.

"With your permission, let's change partners." I giggle and Gabriel pulls her towards him.

The officer doesn't appear to be disappointed by the change and chats ceaselessly. I have no idea what he's saying and can't stop looking at Gabriel who is now dancing with Nita. He holds her gently and seems to be asking her questions. She answers in a whisper and no longer looks fearful.

"I asked if it's possible," the officer says loudly, and I shake my head, not understanding. "I asked if I could come to dinner tomorrow evening. I'd like to get to know your cousin."

If I refuse, it would appear suspicious. If I agree, how will they be able to join the man from the underground who is supposed to get them out tomorrow evening?

"Uh…of course we'd be happy to have you." I pat his arm kindly. "But tomorrow we're having a small family dinner. My husband wishes to get to know them, and I really want them to know the love of my life." I see his expression harden and immediately add, "but the following evening I will arrange a special dinner and you shall be guest of honor!"

I realize that my lie might be costly but right now the only thing that interests me is to get them out of here, and make sure that tomorrow they'll leave the city.

"I accept your invitation." He smiles again and I sigh with relief.

I see that Nita is sitting beside her sister and look for Gabriel on the dance floor. It's hard to miss that tall, impressive man, but harder to miss Marion, close to him in her shiny red dress. Her hands stroke his arms and she giggles every time he opens his mouth.

Hatred can be so strange. I can explain my hatred for Germans in a few words but I can't even explain to myself why I feel so for a woman whose only sin is that I stole her man. A man who doesn't even belong to me.

Their appearance together fascinates me, but nonetheless I pray for the song to finish so I can distance her from him and delude myself that he's mine.

The singer invites the guests to return to their tables and, when the officer kisses my cheek, his lips seem to burn it. I hurry to the table where the sisters are seated and sit down, Gabriel takes the only remaining empty chair. The sisters steal fearful glances at me. Gabriel seems comfortable and full of confidence.

A slim handsome man in a gray suit stands up and taps on his glass. Elegant curls cover his forehead. When he whistles, the guests quiet down and I look uncomprehendingly at Gabriel. He pulls my chair closer and puts his arm along the back of the chair behind my back.

"Good evening, honored guests." The man says in an accent identical to Gabriel's. "Unfortunately, I missed the wedding ceremony of my best friend, but this only happened because of our French friends' dreadful train service. I thought they'd learn from you to be on time." He turns towards the table of the officers in black who laugh with enjoyment. "In any case, now that I'm here, I'll use the opportunity to tell the story of the happy couple's secret romance." My eyes widen in surprise. "The content of the letters I received from Gabriel could easily become a moving novel, of which I will share only a few pearls. The juicy details I will keep to myself." The guests laugh again and I scratch my head in confusion. "He met the beautiful young lady, Josephine, for the first time at a ball several months ago. I'm certain you will all agree that it is impossible to remain indifferent to this lovely girl." The male guests tap their glasses on the tables and call out agreement. "Neither did Gabriel remain indifferent, managing to persuade her to respond to his courtship. He wrote me that this young woman is clever, sensitive and particularly bold." The guests laugh at his inference while I continue to stare at him. "And he constantly praised her dazzling smile." Everyone now looks at me and I smile broadly. "In his last letter, he told me that he'd realized he couldn't imagine his life without her, and that he intended to ask her to spend the rest of her life with him. Thus one more hero has fallen victim to the wiliness of French women."

The guests laugh and Gabriel smiles. "I wish you a happy life together and many heirs with Josephine's beauty and Gabriel's excellent commercial capability." He raises his glass and everyone follows suit. Gabriel hands me a glass of wine and after clinking it with his, he kisses my lips and the guests cheer.

"You've thought of everything," I whisper and sip my wine.

"Always think two steps ahead." He winks at me and goes to thank his friend.

"Soon the evening will be over and we'll leave," I murmur to the sisters who smile tremulously at me. I examine them and cannot understand how in God's name anyone could think they were dangerous. So gentle and noble. So sad.

Gabriel returns to sit beside me. Moving the wine glass away from me, he replaces it with a glass of water.

"Stay focused," he says.

Marion sways her way across the floor and pulls up a chair from a neighboring table. She places it next to the younger sister and sits down.

"Nita, Michelle, this is our neighbor, Marion," I introduce her without enthusiasm and glance at my watch. "They're my dear cousins who have come to celebrate with us."

"So exciting that you managed to come." Marion taps on her glass and signals to Gabriel to pour her wine. He leans forward and fills her glass. She blows him a kiss and I roll my eyes. "You look so familiar to me," she says to the younger sister, who looks down and hides her hands in her lap. "I'm sure I've seen you before, you look just like…"

"That's impossible," I interrupt, "this is their first time in Paris. They live in Cordes-sur-Ciel. It's a village in the south."

"In the south…" Marion murmurs and again fixes her eyes on Michelle. "Tell me about this village of yours."

"It's a village located on a high cliff." Gabriel answers for her. "You must have heard of it."

"You always know everything." Marion giggles irritably. "But I'd prefer to hear a description from this sweet child."

Clenching my fists under the table, I pray for this evening to end.

"She's just a little girl, what description do you expect to hear from her?" I ask without hiding my anger.

"I'd be glad to tell you." The girl surprises me, straightening up and smiling dreamily. "It's an ancient, beautiful village..." she closes her eyes and continues. " It's located on a high mountain, and if you stand on the highest building and raise your head, the sky will caress your hair. If you spread out your arms, you can feel yourself fly like a bird." She waves her arms. "You can smell the sweet, clear, fragrant air and hear the clouds sing. If you look down among the buildings, you'll discover those you love, wandering the alleyways, confident and safe. And if you whistle to them, they will look up at you and signal to you to go on flying. They'll whisper, but you will hear that they love you and miss you, promising that you will always find your way back." She opens her eyes and they're bright. Her older sister looks down and carefully wipes away her tears, and I feel as if my heart is about to burst with pain.

"Oh, the strange imagination of children." Marion bursts out laughing. "They always have to invent all kinds of nonsense."

I nod heavily and Gabriel places his hand on my thigh.

"You certainly don't daydream." Marion turns to Miriam this time. "So tell me what Josephine wrote you about her romance with Gabriel."

"That's our private business," Miriam answers, smiling in embarrassment.

"I'm sure they won't care, but if you refuse then maybe Michelle will tell me and include all the juicy details."

"She doesn't know the juicy details. She's too young," Miriam responds angrily. "I kept those to myself."

"Tell me something anyway. I love hearing romantic stories." Marion sips her wine and leans her elbow on the table.

"I can tell you that she wrote and told me she'd met the handsomest man in the world at a ball. Just like a Hollywood film star." She glances at Gabriel and blushes. "And she told me that he's a gentleman who is courting her in a very special way. That he heaps gifts on her and spoils her, but more important than all, he makes her feel safe." Miriam stopped to take a sip of wine and then goes on. "She told me that he looks at her in a way that no other man ever has. And now that I see them together, it's hard to miss it." She smiles at me and then at Gabriel. "He looks at her as if she were the only person in the room, even when they're surrounded by scores of people."

Cautiously, I look over at him and see how the long lashes half cover his eyes when he gives me that small smile of his. The same smile that effaces the fear and my enormous responsibility.

"Interesting." Marion rises and puts her glass on the table. "I'm willing to swear that I've seen you before."

She pats Sarah's shoulder and goes back to her table.

The waiters clear the tables and set out dessert plates with marvelous desserts. I rub my forehead and sigh.

"It's eight-thirty," I murmur exhaustedly.

Gabriel stands up and taps on his wine glass. Again silence falls.

"Dear guests, I want to thank you with all my heart for honoring us with your presence on this special evening." He motions to me to stand beside him. "Both of us wish to thank you."

I nod.

"I suggest you stay to enjoy the drinks and excellent desserts. With your permission we will leave now for our apartment because my wife has decided that my curfew starts in exactly ten minutes time."

The guests laugh and I hear myself laughing in relief mixed with exhaustion.

The sisters rise, and I stand between them and the guests coming to part from us. After what feels like an eternity, the four of us go out into the street and Gabriel opens the doors of the car for us. The sisters sit at the back and I in the front. He starts the engine and looks at me. I realize he expects me to tell him where to drop the guests but I shrug and bite hard on my lips.

"I understand." The tremor on his upper lip returns, and he gets out of the car and goes back into the restaurant without turning off the engine.

"He's angry with you because of us," Miriam says penitently. "I'm so sorry. I wish we could simply disappear."

"Don't talk nonsense." I tap nervously on the windowpane. "I don't care if he's angry," I lie. "I just want to help you hide until tomorrow and make sure you are safe."

Gabriel returns and the car moves forward. The silence is troubling, I have no idea what to say to him. When the car stops at the entrance to the building, he nods to himself as if I've asked a question and am now receiving an answer.

We follow him upstairs. When he opens the door I urge them inside and turn all the locks. Marie comes into the corridor and looks at us in astonishment.

"You're still here?" Gabriel asks in surprise. "The curfew starts in fifteen minutes, you must go now."

"My knee is hurting." She rubs it without taking her eyes off the sisters. "I thought I'd sleep in the guest room."

"Of course." He responds and lights a cigarette. "Take care of supper for our guests please."

"Are they sleeping over?"

"No."

His harsh response makes me shudder and I look at the sisters with terror. "But…but…" I stammer.

"Be quiet and don't interfere!" He orders irritably. "Leave the drawing room, I need to make a private call."

The sisters hold hands and Miriam looks crushed. She pulls her sister into the corridor. I stay there and look at Gabriel.

"Join them!"

"But…"

"Now!"

Defeated, I walk into the dining room and see Marie entering with a tray of food.

"Where is he sending us? What will happen to us?" Miriam asks tensely.

"I don't know, in a while I'll try and find out," my voice breaks and I struggle with tears.

"Eat, please." Marie points at the tray. "You must take care of yourselves."

Miriam and I look at the tray without moving and only Sarah takes a fork and eats hurriedly.

"Marie." I turn to her, taking her hands. "He'll listen to you, please talk to him. Persuade him not to turn them in. Ask him to let them stay just until tomorrow evening."

"Everything will be all right. He asked for privacy and he'll get it." She presses my hands and leaves the room.

I look at the clock on the wall and every passing minute makes me feel more tired and exhausted. I can't absorb the implications of what has happened.

"I'm sorry. I'm so sorry," I murmur over and over.

Miriam sniffs and embraces her sister. I can't take my eyes off them. They're fragile, quiet, polite and so sad. How will I be able to live with the failure?

"I won't let him do this. I'll hide you myself." Standing up determinedly I stride to the door and then my head meets a broad chest. Defiantly, I raise my head.

Moving me aside with ease, he sits opposite the sisters. "Leave us alone," he asks without turning his head to me.

I open my mouth to protest but he gets up, moves me out of the room and closes the door in my face. I have no idea what is happening. I can't hear what he is saying to them, and my body trembles with nerves.

"Come into the drawing room with me." Marie leads me along the corridor. She asks me to sit down on the sofa, but I insist on standing and staring into the corridor.

Two knocks on the door and I choke. He's informed on them and now they've come to take them. What can I do? What the hell can I do?

Marie opens the door and I see the slim man who made the speech at the restaurant. He bows his head to me and confidently follows Marie into the corridor. The dining room door closes after them.

I can't breathe.

The door opens and can I hear light steps.

"There's no time, we must hurry." The slim man urges the sisters in the direction of the door.

"What is going on here?" My knees are trembling so much I have to lean on the armchair so as not to collapse.

"Thank you very much." Miriam runs to me and embraces me. Her sister puts her thin arms around me and I breathe heavily. "I hope there'll come a day when we can return the favor."

The man clears his throat nervously, and they disengage from me and join him.

"Bon voyage," Gabriel says, opening the door for them, and they disappear with the man down the dark corridor leading to the staircase.

The door closes and the realization that he has arranged a possible escape for them hits me. The relief I feel makes my eyes fill with tears and I cover my mouth with my hands and look at him with adoration. My heart is about to burst with such a strong emotion for this man.

"You're behaving like reckless little girl," he roars at me. "You're putting us all in danger without considering the implications! What the hell were you thinking when…"

I fall upon him and put my lips to his. My fingers slide through his hair and I hold his head and kiss him from the depths of my soul. I don't care that he doesn't embrace me, don't care that his mouth remains closed or that my tears are salting his face. I devour his lips as if they give me oxygen. Finally, I disengage from him, blushing and panting and take a step back. He rubs his thumb along his lower lip and looks stormily at me.

"I want to say so much to you now." I wipe away the tears with the back of my hand. "But nothing I say could reflect what I truly feel for you." Turning, I march into the bedroom.

Taking off my dress, I burrow under the blanket. I don't have the strength to wash my face or the energy to deal with anyone. I want to sink into a deep sleep and let myself escape as far as possible from the terrible reality marking the sisters, two pure souls, as enemies. "Miriam and Sarah," I murmur to myself and close my eyes. "Bon voyage, dear ones."

CHAPTER ELEVEN

Loud knocks at the door make me open my eyes and sit up in alarm, rubbing my eyes. Am I dreaming?

No. The knocking is heard again and again at the apartment door. Heart pounding I jump out of bed, and run into the drawing room, stop at the entrance and look with frightened eyes at Marie and Gabriel who are standing in front of Marion and an SS soldier. He appears younger than Gabriel's friends.

"Where are the women who are staying with you?" Roars the soldier, fixing his eyes on me. He eyes me pointedly and Gabriel turns round.

"Josephine, put on your robe," he orders with clenched teeth and I hug myself in embarrassment and run into the bedroom. Why is the soldier here? And why is he looking for the sisters, could someone have informed on them? I quickly put on my robe over my nightgown. Confused, I don't know whether or not to join Gabriel. A glance in the mirror confirms that I look as terrible as I feel. Remainders of make-up are smeared on my face and my hair is wild. I gather it up carelessly at my neck, sticking in several pins, clean my eyelids with trembling fingers, and press my chest in a vain attempt to calm my heart.

Returning to the drawing room, I watch what is happening from a safe distance.

"Gabriel, I'm telling you she's a danger to you," Marion begs him. "She's lied to you. They aren't her cousins. I recognized the young girl and I'm almost certain I saw her once in Solomon's chemist. He told me she's his daughter. And Solomon is a Jew!"

"What are you talking about?" Gabriel grins and straightens his tie. "You think you saw her in the chemist? A girl who lives in a village in southern France who has never been to Paris…"

I hold my breath.

"I don't have time for this now," barks the German. "Hand them over to me and I'll take them in for questioning."

"I'm sorry," Gabriel responds indifferently. "This morning we received a worrying telephone call that their mother has been hospitalized, and they asked me to take them to the railway station to return home."

"Take her for questioning." Marion stares at me venomously. I back away against the fireplace. "I know this man and he would never countenance such treachery, but she…"

"Be quiet!" Gabriel raises his voice and my eyes roll with an attack of dizziness. "You forget that you are referring to my wife."

"Unless you cooperate, I will have to search the apartment." The German takes a step forward.

"Please do." Gabriel waves his hand and steps aside.

The German brushes Marie aside and walks into the corridor. I hear doors opening and closing, furniture moving and creaking and then hard steps again.

Marion looks at me defiantly, and Marie is frowning angrily but says nothing. Gabriel leans against the wall, folds his arms and smiles his small calming smile.

The German returns to the drawing room, his face flushed and his eyes blazing. "I'll return here with reinforcements."

"*Sharführer*," Gabriel mockingly notes the soldier's rank. "I suggest that before you do so, use my telephone to update your commander that you have burst in here without a warrant." The smile vanishes from Gabriel's face. "Josephine, bring me the photograph, please." He points at our framed wedding photograph on the mantelpiece.

I nod and give it to him.

"If I'm not mistaken, my good friend, Herr Zemel," Gabriel points to the image of the officer in the picture, "is your immediate commander."

"That's right." The German stares at the picture for a moment and steps back in confusion. "But it's a severe offense to hide Jews and must…"

"You dare to repeat your ridiculous accusations?" Gabriel bangs his fist against the wall and the German falls silent.

"To claim that I, Gabriel Augustine, who serves the Fuhrer, is hiding enemies of the Reich in my home? To accuse my wife of treachery? To burst into my home on the basis of a reckless woman's faint memory?"

He momentarily pauses and then smiles again. "I believe that Herr Zemel will be glad to hear personally from me how his soldiers waste their valuable time."

"There is no need for that." The German steps back and opens the door. "I'm obliged to investigate all information that I receive, and if this is indeed false information on the part of your neighbor, I'll be glad to take her for questioning."

"No, I didn't…" Marion stammers and turns pale.

"I think we can forgive her lapse," Gabriel says, blocking the opening to the apartment. "French women are known for their fanciful imaginations. Particularly after an evening of heavy drinking."

"If so, then we count this subject closed." The German clicks his heels and his steps fade away.

Gabriel closes the door and Marion exhales in relief.

"You called an SS soldier to my home?" Gabriel asks quietly.

"You must understand that I'm sure the girl is Jewish. I recognized her. I'm never wrong."

"You called an SS soldier to my home?" He raises his voice.

"Gabriel," she advances and lays her hand on his chest. "I'm concerned for you. I'm telling you that this woman is putting you at risk, she's behaving in a very suspicious manner, and I'm willing to swear that her cousins are in fact Jews that she's hiding in your apartment."

"In her apartment!" He rudely pushes her hand away and moves to stand beside me. "Marion, you are speaking of my wife." He puts his arm around my shoulders. "You must come to terms with the fact that I have chosen her, and you must treat her with respect. If you ever do something like this again, I will not remain silent."

"I'm concerned for you." Her eyes fill with tears, and I can't differentiate between my hatred for the Germans and the hatred I feel for this woman.

"My wife is concerned for me, and you need to get on with your life." He opens the door and gestures to her to leave.

"She's dangerous," Marion sobs. "I'm telling you she's dangerous."

Taking her arm, he forces her out of the apartment. She continues to whine and sob and the door is closed in her face.

My head is spinning, my arms and legs are trembling uncontrollably. Hanging onto Gabriel's arm, I shake my head, trying to dispel the heaviness that is enveloping me.

"Wicked woman." Marie is the first to open her mouth. "I never liked her."

"Not now," Gabriel reproves her. "Please make some coffee for Josephine and we'll sit down to breakfast."

Smoothing her hands over her apron, she nods, but instead of going to the kitchen, she approaches me and strokes my head. "There are several kinds of people in this world," she says, while stroking my head. "Those who survive in order to survive, no matter whom they trample on in the process, and those who survive in order to leave their mark. You've left your mark on the hearts of those sweet sisters. The moment you decided to do this noble deed, you left your mark on my heart too. "

My eyes fill with tears and I nod my head in thanks. Dropping Gabriel's arm I follow her along the corridor and go into the bathroom. Washing my face, I look at myself in the mirror. My eyes are dull and sad. Waking in such a terrible way leaves its signs. I seem to have gained my first worry line. I stroke the tiny line next to my eye and sigh in acceptance, it's a small price to pay for such an emotional reward. Now I must gather up my strength for the difficult conversation awaiting me. I tie the cord of my robe tightly, straighten up and walk into the dining room, sit down and glance at Gabriel.

He puts the newspaper aside and the tremor in his upper lip makes me hide my hands between my knees and bow my head.

"I hope you realize that I'm furious." He clears his throat in an attempt to control the fury in his voice.

"What you did was reckless, irresponsible, and incomprehensible in terms of its risk."

I nod without raising my head.

"I don't understand how in God's name you could do something like that without consulting me, when you know how I'd react."

"I refuse to apologize for it," I whisper.

"When you have something to say, say it clearly and aloud!" He bangs on the table and I straighten up.

"I refuse to apologize," I shout, striding towards the door.

"Come back here at once!" His voice is quiet and threatening.

I try and control my emotional storm and sit down again. I look fixedly at him and refuse to be intimidated by his eyes fixed on mine.

"I'm sorry." The tremor in my voice betrays my distress. "I apologize for being late and for bringing them to the event. I apologize for putting you at risk, but I refuse to apologize for trying to save them." The damned tears return.

Looking at me, he runs his thumb along his upper lip and closes his eyes. "You didn't just put me at risk." His tone softens and he opens his eyes. "And you didn't just put yourself at risk. You put those sisters at risk in the worst way. You chose to bring them into a den of wolves, and you didn't even prepare them sufficiently." He falls silent for a moment, shaking his head in disappointment. "What would have happened if I hadn't been beside them when the officer wanted to know the name of their village?"

I bow my head in embarrassment.

"What would have happened if Marion had remembered last night where she had seen the girl?"

I bite my lips.

"What would have happened if someone there had decided to ask for their papers?"

I sigh.

"Josephine, look at me."

"It's hard to look at you when you're so angry with me." I raise my head cautiously and look into his gentle eyes, which no longer convey anger but sincere concern.

"Yes, I'm angry. Taking on yourself such an important mission, saving the two of them, each one a world in herself, without thinking it through. Do you understand that if I hadn't found a way to get them out last night, all four of us would be in the interrogation room by now?"

"I understand." I shift uncomfortably in my chair, trying to escape his eyes. "But I didn't have any choice. I was their last hope. No-one else could take them, and I just couldn't abandon them."

"I can understand that." He turns my chair so that my knees touch his. "But you have to understand that wanting to succeed isn't good enough. Certainly not when lives are at stake. You should have used that lovely head of yours to make sure you could do it." He cups my chin in his hand, forcing me to look at him. "Close all open ends and plan your actions. Getting into the game is the easy part, knowing how to come out a victor, that's the hard part."

"I can't think about anything right now." I put my hand over his, making sure he left it there on my cheek. "I'm bursting with pride at taking part in saving them, and dazed with anxiety because of the German soldier's terrifying visit this morning."

The realization that I need his comfort and support overcomes my embarrassment. I press his hand and caress my cheek with it.

"I need your assurance that you understand you've done your bit and finished with these adventures." He kisses my forehead. I know he's expecting to hear my response but I can't say a word. "Josephine, I need your assurance that I can stop worrying about you."

I open my mouth and immediately close it, running my fingers over his, enjoying this rare sense of sanctuary.

Two knocks on the door and my sense of protection shatters. Anxiety takes over and I close my eyes, praying for the knocking to stop. For a moment it seems as if my prayers are answered, but again there are two knocks.

"Have they returned?"

"No," he responds confidently, stroking my cheek one more time. "I'm waiting for a special delivery."

I raise my eyes with suspicion, and the small calm smile catches at my heart.

"Come with me." He holds out his hand and I walk with him to the door. Marie has already opened the door and we both gaze in surprise at two boys dragging a tall fir tree inside.

"I thought we should celebrate Christmas as a family." Gabriel laughs and signals to the boys to put the tree in the corner near the fireplace. "But if neither of you feels like it, they can take it back."

The boys look at him in bewilderment. I shake my head and hurry over to the tree. I caress its branches and murmur to myself.

"If you have something to say, say it loud and clear." Gabriel sounds amused, and I turn to him and wipe my tears.

Gabriel takes several notes from his pocket and when he assures the boys that the money is theirs, they bow enthusiastically and leave.

"It looks like a little dream in the midst of this ongoing nightmare." My shoulders droop and I sigh. "It reminds me of better times, but how can we celebrate in these circumstances, I don't understand. I'm not sure it's appropriate."

Gabriel frowns.

"We have to celebrate," Marie scolds me in a motherly tone. "If we sink into despair and mourning, there will be no place for hope. And if they take our hope from us as well, then the heavy price we have paid will be in vain."

"But…it's as if I'm forgetting them." I turn back to the tree to hide my tears. "As if it's all right to go on as usual when they aren't with me." I rub my earlobe and groan soundlessly.

"What do you think they'd expect you to do?" Gabriel is standing beside me, his arm around my shoulders.

"Claude would expect me to go on living. To take care of myself, maybe fight in my own way."

"Well, that's exactly what we're doing." He hugs me and walks away. "Tonight we will allow ourselves to celebrate a little, and I expect that tree to fill with gifts." Taking out a bundle of notes, he places it on the mantelpiece.

"Are you intending to invite your friends?" I ask heavily.

"No, just the three of us this time."

It was the answer I wanted to hear.

Putting on a coat, pausing to enjoy the tree and then nodding to himself in confirmation, he leaves the apartment. I smile at Marie and the door opens again.

"I forgot to ask if I can bring back something that would make you happy." His amused tone lifts my sense of sadness and I laugh briefly, shaking my head. He smiles at me and closes the door behind him.

"If he wants a celebration, he'll get one." Marie pats her apron. "I'll make a meal fit for a king, while you take care of the gifts." Going over to the tree, she examines its branches and her face is sad. "I, too, miss the ones I love." She sighs. "But I am fortunate to be celebrating the holiday with people I care about, and I choose to be happy." The smile returns to her face. "It's a choice we can make. And nobody who loves you could expect you to choose differently."

She disappears down the corridor with her light steps and I know she's right. I'm supposed to choose to be happy, but how does one do that? This is the first holiday that I am not celebrating with my parents or my adoptive family. How does one manage to suppress sadness and anxiety? I miss the sense of warmth and unconditional love, and now all that is left to me, are two strangers who are making an effort to make me happy.

Maybe the time has come for me to make an effort for them. This realization fills me with energy. Half an hour later I leave the apartment.

I reach the first avenue on my bicycle and I seem to have gone back in time; Paris seems to have gone back several years in time. Store windows are lit up and decorated. The sound of Christmas Carols is coming from several stores and the sidewalks are full of pedestrians. Even German soldiers walking in groups seem to be smiling and relaxed, almost as if they were ordinary people.

Going in and out of stores, the basket on my bicycle is almost collapsing with the weight of parcels. I bought dresses, nightgowns and undergarments for myself. The spirit of the holiday had entered me.

In an antique store, I find the perfect gift for Marie, and when I enter a watch store to buy one for Gabriel, I can't choose from the enormous selection. Something doesn't feel right to me. The salesman urges me to take the gold watch, promising to give me a large discount. I have enough money to buy Gabriel three watches with the money he gave me. His money, not mine.

I apologize to the salesman and precipitously leave the store. Sitting down on a bench, I touch the notes in my handbag.

It seems so trivial to use this man's money to buy a gift for him, when he's become my entire world. So inappropriate, but my diamond earrings, the only items I had to barter, are no longer mine.

A female figure sits down beside me. Looking up in surprise, I see Natalie.

"I waited until I could catch you alone." She looks anxiously around her. "You're supposed to hand over the two Fleurs-de-Lis this evening."

"They're already in a safe place." I tap nervously on my handbag.

"How did you manage that?" She asks in astonishment. She takes a pack of cigarettes out of her bag, and offers me one.

"I didn't do it alone. I had help." I wait for her to light my cigarette and then cough in shock.

"You get used to those stinking leaves." She slowly inhales and exhales. "Not everyone can afford real tobacco." She winks at me. "Who helped you?" She whispered without looking at me.

"It doesn't matter. The important thing is that they have left the city and are on their way to a safe place."

"You've managed to surprise me." She strokes my knee. "We weren't sure you'd succeed, and I'm happy to find out that we were wrong."

"I thought I didn't have the option of failing." I try and inhale again, but throw the cigarette away when the coughing starts again.

"We never have that option, but it happens." She rubs her eyes and seems tired. "We have to focus on victory and put aside failure, even when it takes over our dreams."

I sense that this time, she's expecting me to give her strength. I cover her hand with mine but quickly snatch it away when two German soldiers stand in front of us.

"Papers!" One of them orders with a stern look, and we both nervously fumble in our bags.

The soldier bursts out laughing and his friend murmurs an apology in broken French and tries to persuade us to join them in an evening's entertainment.

Natalie falters and seems lost, while I remove my glove and show them my wedding ring. The large diamond seems to impress them. After staring at it for a long moment, they exchange several sentences in German, and then one of them points at a girl on the other side of the street. They laugh and cross the street at a run.

"If they'd been SS dogs, you'd be left without the ring," Natalie says irritably. "Those ordinary soldiers are at least capable of respecting the fact that you're married."

"Both kinds are equally bad." I put on my glove.

"You're probably right." She clings to me and again looks anxiously around her. "You're invited to join us tonight to raise a glass. Maurice will want to hear all the details from you."

"Not this evening," I immediately answer. "I have plans."

"Of course you do." She laughs, momentarily my old free-spirited friend. "What do you want with us when you have the man of your dreams at home?"

I lower my eyes when I realize how her statement hurts me.

"Maybe you'll tell me one day how you managed to trap that perfection. And I'd be glad to hear some juicy details, sometimes I forget how it feels to be courted."

"One day," I respond impatiently.

"We'll wait to raise a glass with you at the next meeting." She plays with her lighter and leans closer to me.

"We've changed the meeting place. Come to the Second District, near the Place des Victoires." She whispers the exact address and stands up, closes the top button on her coat and hurries off.

I smile to myself when I realize that because of me they will celebrate victory this evening and, in the very same breath, regret not being able to tell them that it isn't me who should be praised. My face warms when I remember the embarrassing way in which I thanked Gabriel. I have no idea what was going through my mind when I jumped on him and kissed him. He has always treated me with polite respect and I responded with reckless, childish behavior. I mustn't forget to apologize to him.

CHAPTER TWELVE

I draw the curtain in the drawing room and look out to the dark street. I'm dressed and made up; the tree is decorated and the fragrance of cooking spreads throughout the house. For spend hours on Gabriel's gift and now I'm not sure I want to give it to him. It seems too simple, I should have put more thought into it. I should have used his money to buy something of real value.

His car stops at the sidewalk, and my heart beats faster in anticipation. I go towards the door, smoothing the chiffon on my gown and step back. I wait for him to come in, but don't even know how I intend to greet him.

His loud steps approach the door and unable to resist, I open it. His smile is the only thing I see, and the only thing I want to go on seeing.

"You look beautiful," he says naturally and enters, holding a large box of gifts and several other bags. He looks with satisfaction at the tree and places his gifts next to mine. "I'm sorry I'm late, but now I am all yours. Both of you," he corrects himself when he sees Marie and goes over to kiss her cheek.

She is wearing a short dress that reaches her knees and her gray hair is loose. When Gabriel tells her she looks wonderful, I nod in approval and embrace her.

He asks for a few moments to change and Marie and I set the table. When he joins us, he is shaved, perfumed and dressed in a new suit. I examine him for several seconds too long, blushing when I realize he smiles at me. I lower my eyes and refuse to accept the fact that my heart is telling me it wants more. More than an affectionate smile. More than a comforting caress. More than innocent affection. My heart wants this man to be truly mine. But he isn't. I manage to put a crooked smile on my face, and remind myself to be grateful for what there is.

Marie passes trays of food to us and tells us about life in Paris during the Great War, and about the victory celebrations at the end of it. Gabriel interrupts to ask questions and she scolds him for his impatience. Wine is freely poured into our glasses, and when my eyes catch sight of the clock I'm surprised to discover that two hours have passed.

"Me and my silly stories," Marie says apologetically. "I haven't notice that I was getting carried away."

"Your stories are lovely." I smile at her. "Moving and optimistic. I hope that one day I'll be able to tell my grandchildren my own story, and that it will end with a victory celebration."

"To do that, you'll have to work on the next generation." She giggles and Gabriel grins, I go pale. "I'd be glad to have this home filled with the sound of children's laughter. You two have begun to bore me." She giggles again.

I raise my glass of wine. "I want to take this opportunity to say thank you." I force myself to overcome my embarrassment and look at Gabriel, choosing my words carefully. "I don't take it for granted that you chose me, and I hope I can repay you in the future."

He looks quietly at me and nods.

"And Marie, thank you for receiving me with open arms and making me feel wanted and loved."

"We're family." She dismisses me with a wave of her hand, but her eyes fill with tears.

"Yes, family." I put my hand over Gabriel's. "A family is supposed to give security, and I have undoubtedly gained this." I remove my hand but he takes it back and brings it to his lips, and I feel his kiss penetrate my skin, straight to my heart.

"You've chosen a charming wife." Marie stands up and clears the plates. "I'm at peace now, because even if I'm not here to take care of you, I have a worthy replacement."

I squirm and look at Gabriel with frustration. I'm uncomfortable with this talk of the future and the knowledge that we're lying to her is even harder.

"Marie, leave the dishes and join us in the drawing room." Gabriel stands up and takes the plates from her. "Tonight you rest."

She rubs her back and grimaces. She opens her mouth to protest, but when I stand up and start clearing the dishes, she sighs in relief.

We move into the drawing room and Gabriel opens another bottle of wine. Marie yawns and accepts Gabriel's invitation to stay the night in the guest room. He gives her a velvet box and she takes out an impressive string of pearls.

"Every year he gives me valuable jewelry." She pats his cheek lovingly. "He knows I have no suitable events to wear them to, but it makes me feel young and loved and for that I'm grateful to him." She yawns again and turns in the direction of the corridor.

"Wait." I call her and she stops. "I also have a small gift for you. It isn't valuable," I apologize as she unwraps it. "But I thought you could hang it above the bed, and it'll be the first thing you see when you wake in the morning. The couple sitting on the bench reminded me of you and your stories about Marcel, and I thought you'd like to go back to the bench in your mind and look at the Arc de Triomphe with our flag flying on it. So you can enjoy your Paris with your beloved."

She examines the picture and turns it round to Gabriel.

"Maybe…it was a silly idea," I stammer when her eyes fill with tears.

"It's a wonderful gift." She presses me to her in a strong embrace. "Thanks to you I'll wake every morning with a smile on my face." She kisses my cheek and sniffs. "Thank you." Hugging the picture, she goes into the bedroom. I pick up my glass of wine and meet Gabriel's eyes. He isn't smiling and doesn't say a word, just looks at me in a way that makes my heart contract with frustration.

Quiet knocks on the door and I roll my eyes, guessing who is standing on the other side. Gabriel opens the door and Marion enters without waiting for an invitation.

"Gabriel, Cheri, I've come to apologize to you," She openly ignores my presence. "You know how important you are to me, I didn't do anything malicious." She puts her hand on his arm and turns her head to the side. "I won't let anyone harm you. I hope you understand that and accept my apology."

"It's Josephine you should apologize to," he responds coolly.

"Of course." She turns her back to him and looks at me with an expressionless face. "To you as well." She doesn't wait for my response and takes a white packet out of her bag. "I don't want this to be our first Christmas together without exchanging gifts." She takes out a gold watch identical to the one I'd considered buying for him. Her insolence amazes me, she wants to create the impression that as far as she's concerned they're still together, despite our perfect pretense as a couple.

"It's very handsome." Gabriel smiles at her and I'm glad he is unaware of the nausea overwhelming me. "We also wish to give you something small." He hands her a velvet box identical to the one Marie had received, inside of which was a gold bracelet inset with diamonds. Enthusiastically, she holds out her arm for him to put it on. "You can wear it tomorrow night at the celebratory dinner we are having here."

My mouth opens in surprise, and she uses the opportunity to thank him for the invitation with a quick kiss on his lips. She undoubtedly heads the list of people I most hate, which is very long.

She walks arrogantly into the drawing room, picks up my glass of wine, chattering about the special, festive atmosphere and their exciting pleasures in years gone by. Although Gabriel doesn't appear to reciprocate her enthusiasm, I am starting to feel as if I'm the one pushing in on a private evening and not the opposite.

I walk away from them to the window and open the curtain, reminding myself that it's just a pretense and she was and, perhaps, still is the real thing for him.

"Marion, we'll continue the conversation tomorrow." Gabriel moves behind me. "I promised my wife that this evening will be entirely hers."

He sounds so sincere that instead of being happy, there's a lump in my throat.

"Of course, Mon Cheri." Her voice is cold again. "I look forward to it." I hear her high heels on the tiles and the door closing behind her, but cannot turn around to him.

"Don't let her upset you." He puts his hands on my shoulders.

"You invited her to dinner with us after she brought an SS soldier here to arrest me for interrogation." I try and control the fury growing in my belly.

"I invited her to dinner with us after my wife forgot to tell me that she invited an SS officer to dinner here to meet her cousins."

Alarmed, I turn round and collide with his chest.

"You're right! I completely forgot! What can we do now?"

"Calm down, it's been taken care of." He shakes his head in reproof but doesn't appear to be angry at all. "Fortunately for us, he came to my office today about something else and after I realized that he was expecting to appear here tomorrow, I promised that although your cousins have left, I will make sure he has company that is no less exciting."

"You're pimping your girlfriend?" I ask in surprise, finding it hard to hide the amusement in my voice.

"She isn't my girlfriend." He pours wine into his glass and gives it to me. "And she made a bad mistake deciding to bring that German to our home this morning." Now he does look angry and I weigh my words carefully.

"As a woman, I think I understand her. Especially if she believes that I'm putting you at risk."

"She can't accept the fact that you're my wife." He sits down in the armchair and lights a cigarette. "And don't be too quick to believe her apology. She's making sure to stay close so that at the first opportunity she can push you out of her path."

"Why did you choose to be with a woman like her?" I ask sincerely, thanking him for passing his cigarette to me.

"I think she chose to be with me, and I couldn't find a good enough reason to stay away." He grins and lights another cigarette for himself. "It was comfortable having a non-committed relationship whenever I came to Paris."

"I don't think she believed it was a non-committed relationship." I turn to the fireplace so he shouldn't see my smile.

"I never deceived her," he concluded indifferently. "And you seem to be the only one who hasn't received a gift this evening."

I look down at the large box on the floor and then look at him questioningly.

"It's yours." He nods, and I kneel down and rip off the paper, Opening the rectangular box, I smile broadly.

"A record player." I pass my finger over the delicate design on the lower rectangle.

"You asked and you received." He lifts the record player, places it carefully on the dresser and takes several records out of a packet. He presents them to me and after I point at the picture of Maurice Chevalier, he puts the record on the turntable and turns the handle.

"Mimi?" I ask when I hear the first sounds of the song in English. "I love that song." Gabriel winks at me, lets the song play a while. Then moves the needle and I giggle and move my head with pleasure to the rhythmic sounds of "Valentine."

"The World has Gone Completely Crazy." I choose a record by a singer I don't know, and let the slow chanson warm my heart. "Who would believe that we'd reach such a low point that they'd even limit our music?"

"That's why they'll lose, the Germans." He sits on the sofa and pats the seat beside him. I sit down and he puts his hand in his pocket and takes out a small box. "They'll lose because at some point their psychological war will have no impact, creating the opposite effect." He taps his little finger on the box. "It will make women like you leave their comfort zone and return war, even when they know they might lose everything."

"I have nothing left to lose." I shrug.

"And it's because you believe it that they will lose." He opens the box and I stare at tiny, heart-shaped, diamond earrings. "This is also for you." He takes one earring out and puts it in the palm of my hand. I can't understand why he thinks that buying me identical earrings to those I had, is a good idea. Sadness envelopes me. He opens my fingers and lays a second earring in my palm too. Its clasp is different than the first one's. I put my hand on my mouth in amazement.

"These are my earrings! How did you manage to get hold of them?"

"There isn't a single diamond sold in this city that doesn't ultimately come to me." He cups my chin in his hand and kisses my forehead. "I thought you'd like them back."

"You were right." I cough in an attempt to stop the tears and put them on. "I'm so grateful to you." Leaning forward I gently kiss him on the lips. I know I should keep my distance but I cannot, again I put my lips to his and linger in a kiss. This time, too, it's a one-sided kiss.

"Forgive me." I shake my head and move away. "That's the second time I've imposed a kiss on you." I laugh nervously.

"It's all right." He opens the top button of his shirt and avoids my glance. "Your feelings of gratitude confuse you, and I don't want you to think that I expect you to thank me physically."

"I didn't think so for a minute, and I wouldn't do such a thing." I respond without understanding where I found the courage. "I don't think I've ever met a man like you. You make me feel as if I'm really important to you, that I'm really part of your family and that this is really my home. That not all of this is pretense." I stand up as my courage fades.

"You really are important to me." He looks directly at me. "And you really have become part of the family, but we must remember that neither one of us has chosen this. You must not forget boundaries. You have to think two…"

"Steps ahead," I complete his sentence and nod in understanding. "I'm really sorry for dragging you into this embarrassing conversation, you don't deserve it. And I promise I won't allow myself to get confused again."

"I'm glad we understand each other." He smiles comfortably and I clench my fist to prevent it from caressing my heart that longs for comfort. "And now I expect my own gift," he changes the subject quite naturally.

"Ah, the gift." Picking up the package from the floor, I take my seat at a safe distance from him. "I'm not quite sure whether to give it to you because you may think it's ridiculous." I hug the package and bite my lower lip. "The truth is, I almost bought you exactly the same watch that you received from Marion, but it seemed strange to buy you a gift with your money."

He blinks and looks at the package with curiosity.

"I thought it might be better to make you something that would enable you to know me better, and enable me to have a better idea of whom I'm married to." I place the package on the table and nervously sip my wine. "But now it seems idiotic to me, and I'd be glad if you would forget it even exists. Tomorrow morning I will go and buy you something more ordinary."

"You aren't capable of doing anything ordinary." He takes the package from the table and rips off the paper. I cover my eyes with my hands and refuse to see his reaction.

"You have to explain it to me." He strokes my knee and when I open my eyes he is examining the lace frames I made for the two albums.

"It's my rotten gift." I grimace and move closer to him. On the covers of each album I glued our wedding photograph. On one of them wrote my name and on the other, his name. I take the album with my photograph and open it at the first page.

"On each page I've written something I thought a man should know about his wife." I point out the heading. "Here there's information about my parents, the foods I like, my favorite color." I laugh when I point out the page I painted yellow. "Here, there is all the information a real couple knows about each other." I take the album with his name on it and open it on the first page. "Look, the only thing I know about you is your profession. And that you miss a patisserie and bicycle repair store in the city where you live. Maybe, if you feel like it, you will fill in other details and I can carry out my role in this pretense more successfully."

Mustering the courage to look up, I see that he is gazing strangely at me.

"I told you it was a rotten gift, I just thought…I don't know what I thought." Putting the album down on the table, I hold my head in my hands. Before I have time to blink, I feel his lips on mine in a hard kiss. My heart beats strongly in my breast.

He sits back and his eyes are agitated. "Josephine, this is the finest gift I've ever received."

"Your feelings of gratitude are confusing you." I take a sip of wine and lick my lips, which still feel his intoxicating touch. "I'm just thinking one step ahead."

His spontaneous laughter only confuses me even more and, picking up the glasses, I go into the kitchen. I wash the pile of dishes while he stands leaning against the counter, drying them. His tailored appearance is so contradictory to what he's doing that I laugh.

"What's so funny?" He pokes a finger into my hip and my laughter increases.

"I'm not used to seeing men in the kitchen. I'm not even used to seeing myself in the kitchen, and certainly not when we both look as if we're dressed for the opera."

"I really have to take you." He dries another plate and puts it on the counter. "Maybe if I take care of your social life, you won't have time for those problematic friends of yours."

"They aren't problematic," I say, offended. "And please don't drag me into a conversation I don't want to have."

"You need to learn your place in this game," he says gravely. "You get yourself into situations that are too big for you."

"What do you know about situations like that?" I clench my teeth.

"A lot more than you think." He puts down the towel and straightens up. "I can't prevent you from doing nonsense. I can only suggest you learn how to reduce risks."

I turn off the tap and look him in the eye.

"Rule number one – don't let anything undermine you. Always stay in control. Rule number two – think fast." He puts his finger on my temple. "Sometimes we can get out of impossible situations if we answer a question quickly and confidently."

I frown and make a face as if I were thinking.

'No." He laughs and smooths my frown with his finger. "Don't show them you're thinking. Maintain a blank expression."

I nod.

"And you have to start changing your behavior when we're in company." He takes a bottle of wine and pours the liquid into a clean glass. "Think about it, you're a French girl who has just married the man of her dreams." He winks at me and takes a sip of wine. "Instead of behaving naturally and staying close to me, you make sure to maintain your distance and look hesitant and threatened."

"Let them think I'm strange." I shrug. "I don't think anyone invests too much thought in me."

"You're wrong." He lights a cigarette and swallows the wine. "If you'd gone to Switzerland when I suggested it, you'd be safe now. But you decided to stay and you're still in danger."

"Why?"

"Claude didn't talk in his interrogation and Odette and Brigitte did, but they failed to uncover information that satisfied the Germans. This affair is dangerous and because of its sensitivity, everything passed up the ranks. They're looking for his associates and you were close enough to him to have this information."

"But you said you'd fixed it, that you'd explained to them I had nothing to do with it."

"I explained and I fixed it." He offers me a cigarette and I shake my head. "But the moment your name came up, you were marked. You're no longer anonymous. I hope that the fact that I'm your guarantor is sufficient, but someone could certainly decide differently at some point."

"So what do you advise me to do?"

"I'd like you to leave with me for Switzerland in two days' time."

"Suggest something else," I answer angrily.

"Keep a low profile. Avoid meetings that put you at risk."

I lower my head in silence.

"You drive me mad." Holding my chin he makes me look at him. "If you insist on remaining here, at least start behaving like an innocent person and not like a terrified cat waiting to be caught."

"That is something I can do." I shake off his hand. "Tomorrow you will see that I, too, know how to pretend."

Flouncing out of the kitchen, I close myself in the bathroom, wash my face and exhale in frustration. Every time I think I finally understand what to do, he manages to make me uneasy. I have to be part of the Resistance. If I don't participate, what is the point of my freedom? But now that another player has become important to me, my fear of endangering him makes me doubt my decision.

I get into bed feeling depressed and when he lies down beside me I can't ignore his presence.

"How long are you going for?' I whisper, moving closer to him.

"I don't know." He turns off the light and arranges the pillow under his head. "It's a business trip. I don't have a time limit. I'll return when I finish what I have to do."

"How long does it usually take?"

"Now you're behaving like a married woman." He laughs, pulling me to him. The closeness of his warm body comforts me a little, I put my head on his chest and bend my knees. "I'll return with gifts." He strokes my hair.

"I don't need anything." I'm disappointed by how lightly he relates to leaving me.

"All women like gifts. I'm sure you'll find something you want."

"I've already found it." I smile to myself. "But it's a very large gift, I don't believe you'll manage to bring it back by yourself."

"Try me."

"A company or two of British soldiers." I laugh. "But I won't complain if you bring me Americans instead."

"Your wish is my command." He grins. "I might not be able to bring them to you this visit, but I promise you it will happen."

I close my eyes and smile. This man makes me believe anything.

CHAPTER THIRTEEN

Yawning, I help Marie to set the table with elegant plates.

"A lady should rest in the afternoon if she has guests in the evening." Marie scolds me. "Didn't your mother teach you that?"

"No." I laugh. "But the family I stayed with certainly made sure of it."

"So why did you let him keep you up so late?"

"I didn't. He decided to treat me like a tourist and walked me through the town for hours. I thought he was taking me out for breakfast and to visit the museum but I couldn't stop him." I yawn again and smile to myself. "We visited the Louvre and from there we went to Notre Dame and then he decided I needed to go shopping and made me go into every boutique we saw on the way." I straighten up and turn around so she can see my black, sequined gown. "I thought my purchases would calm him down but he insisted we sit down to coffee on the Champs-Elysees and now all I want is to collapse into bed."

I want to tell her the truth. How every minute with him had been worth more than gold. How I'd never enjoyed myself as much with a man and every time he'd introduced me as his wife, I'd winced in frustration. But I don't dare say aloud what is in my heart.

"It sounds like an enjoyable day." She smiles to herself in satisfaction and arranges the dishes on the table. "I'll manage here. You can rest in the drawing room until the guests arrive."

"No," I shriek. "He'll make me play chess with him again, and I've already lost two games to him."

She shakes her head crossly and scowls. "Come with me!" She walks briskly into the corridor and I follow.

Gabriel is sitting in his elegant suit at the chess table, absorbed in the pieces. When he notices us, he beckons me to join him.

"That's not happening." Marie crossly folds her arms. "You expect her to host guests this evening and don't allow her even a moment's rest."

"Have you informed on me?' He smiles at me and laughs.

"You gave me no choice." I raise my chin defiantly.

"Well. I shall play against myself." Moving the pawn, he again focuses on the board.

I nod thanks to Marie and lie down on the sofa, putting my heels up on a thick cushion, sighing with relief. The last thing I feel like doing is hosting our crazy neighbor and a rude SS officer. Closing my eyes, I yawn. Quiet prevails in the drawing room and I feel sleep drawing me in.

A knocking on the door makes me sit up in alarm and hold my head. I look at Gabriel in panic and he smiles at me and tightens his tie.

"The show begins." He holds out his hand to me and I stand beside him and yawn aloud. "Ready?" He strokes my head and ignores the knocking.

"No." I laugh. "But I don't have much choice."

Together we go to the door and open it and Marion falls upon him with an embrace. I take a step back and she starts chatting about the cursed electricity cuts and how she isn't sure she's properly dressed for a celebratory dinner. She swirls and sways her backside, her pink dress flying and rustling and she blinks and looks questioningly at him.

"You look very pretty," Gabriel says, returning to my side.

"I've brought a bottle of wine." She hands it to me as if I'm just the maid and Gabriel snatches it and places it on the table.

Her colorful presence confuses me and when further knocks are heard at the door, this time even louder, I exhale loudly and scold myself. I have to focus.

A man in a black uniform and a plump, well-dressed woman are standing on the threshold. I try and remember where I know him from…the wedding photograph…it's the officer who was a guest at our wedding and, thanks to our photograph together, the German soldier left us in peace.

Gabriel kisses the woman's hand and shakes the officer's. "Herr Zemel, you remember my wife." He makes way for them and the officer approaches and kisses my hand.

"How could anyone forget such a beautiful fraulein?" He scans me from head to toe. "A beautiful young woman," he translates into perfect French.

Wiping my hand furtively on my gown, I realize I have to pull myself together. "It's an honor to meet you again." I smile at him, swallowing a yawn. "And I'm glad we have the pleasure of being with your lovely wife." The woman smiles at me and Marie hurries to take her coat.

"Frau Anika," the officer introduces her and walks over to examine Marion. She is standing close to Gabriel and I roll my eyes when she introduces herself, placing her hand naturally on Gabriel's arm.

Again there are knocks at the door and the officer I met at the ball enters with his arrogant swagger.

"Herr Stengel." The German officers shake hands and by their ease together I realize they share the same rank.

For several minutes, German is mingled with French until Gabriel leads everyone into the dining room. He sits down at the head of the table and Marion takes the seat nearest to him. He pulls out a chair for me on his other side and, when I sit down, he pulls it nearer to him.

"I so love Paris," Anika declares. "All these beautiful gardens, the museums, and the nightlife. I hope we stay for a long time."

I grimace and feel Gabriel's hand pressing my thigh.

"You can be tranquil on that score. We have no plans to go anywhere else." Her husband smiles arrogantly at her.

"I'm actually glad you're here." Marion giggles. "There's a greater demand for my performances at the Moulin Rouge."

"I think I'll have to come to your performance." The other officer looks at her with frank enjoyment.

"Certainly, you'll be the guest of honor." She sips her wine, and doesn't even thank Marie when she serves her food. "Gabriel came to several of my performances. Tell them how amazing I am." Again she places her hand on his arm and strokes his cheek. When I see Anika's shocked expression, I realize I must pull myself together.

"We should all go." I tap on my wine glass and Gabriel hurries to pour me wine. "Gabriel told me it's a highly amusing performance."

"Amusing?" Marion shrieks.

"Sorry, I meant a special performance." I hide a smile. "But, actually, since he has already seen your performance, maybe we should attend another. There are so many now, thanks to you Germans. Only yesterday, we were saying the time has come to go to the opera. Isn't that so, *Mon Amour*?" I tilt my head to one side and the smile on his face indicates that he understands I have finally joined in the game.

"That's a wonderful idea." Anika claps her hands.

"My wife understands quality." Gabriel kisses my lips and Marion sits erectly in her chair. The expression on her face is not auspicious and I sense this show is growing more complicated.

"Personally, I prefer cabaret." Zemel grins. "Why waste time on singers' howling when one can enjoy the quality of French dancers."

Gabriel nods in thanks to Marie and I smile at her. She looks tired and walks heavily. We're probably the only ones who notice her, she seems to be transparent.

The conversation moves onto general matters and Marion listens attentively. She occasionally interposes a comment or question and, to my surprise, the two officers don't lose patience. As if hypnotized, I look at her, realizing why Gabriel invited her. She has an ability to make everyone feel special and to turn even the heaviest discussion into something lighter and more bearable.

"Don't feel bad if you don't understand anything." Anika looks at me with a bored expression. "When they start talking politics I pray the ground will swallow me."

"We can't ignore what is happening around us." Marion chides her gently.

"Those vulgar Americans are so close now it makes me nervous."

"Don't worry, Fraulein." Stengel puts his arm on the back of her chair. "We're here and we have no intention of going anywhere."

Gabriel offers me a cigarette and when he leans over to light it, he caresses my fingers. I'm aware that these little gestures of his are part of the pretense but I manage to find comfort in them.

"If your agitators don't stop making trouble, the situation here will only get worse," says Zemel in an irritable tone.

"A pitiful underground of limited men playing at war."

I cough when I realize who he's talking about, and immediately smile again. This time I listen attentively.

"They're cutting telephone lines…" He continues venomously. "Putting explosives in factories, damaging train lines. Communist louts. We have to catch them one by one, and throw them into labor camps in Poland."

"The problem is that they're like mosquitoes." Stengel scowls. "They need to be eliminated in each place."

"They also reproduce like mosquitoes?" Zemel bangs on the table. "You catch one and ten more pop up in his place. I have no idea how they manage to recruit women and boys to help them. What on earth are they giving them in return?"

"Hope," I blurt out unintentionally, immediately paling as everyone looks at me in amazement. "That's what they think they're giving them." I laugh and shrug. "It's so foolish. To think that a few miserable criminals could overcome the glorious German army."

"They really are criminals." Unexpected help comes from Marion and Gabriel fills my glass and smiles to himself. "They don't realize that every stupid thing they do jeopardizes innocent French people."

"We have no alternative, Fraulein." Stengel caresses her bare shoulder, which doesn't seem to bother her. "We have to teach them a lesson."

I clench my fists to control the anger swirling inside me.

"My friends, why spoil the atmosphere." Gabriel rises, allowing Marie to clear his plate. "It's a holiday, no need to frighten the women with talk of criminals and punishment."

"A man after my own heart." Anika puts a cigarette between her lips and her husband lights it for her. "I prefer listening to music and talking about culture and art."

"You can move into the drawing room," Marie says to Gabriel. "I've arranged a tray of desserts in there."

"Many thanks, *Cherie*." He observes her stooping posture with concern. "You can go home. We'll manage here."

She turns to me and I realize she is waiting for my permission. I jump up from my place and accompany her into the corridor.

"You don't look very well." I feel her forehead.

"I'm just tired, *Cherie*." Dragging her feet, she walks to the door and puts on her coat. "You have to remember that you are mistress of this house." She becomes grave. "I'm sure you understand what I mean."

"Yes." I button the top buttons of her coat and watch her disappear down the stairs. When I hear the sound of voices and steps approaching, I close the door and stand up straight.

"Gabriel, *Mon Amour*," I say, "let's have some music and we can all enjoy the new record player you bought me." Nodding, he puts a record on the record player. The slow chanson changes the atmosphere at once. Gabriel sits down on the sofa and the guests seat themselves comfortably in the armchairs.

I bring a bottle of wine from the cupboard and see that Marion is sitting so close to Gabriel that there is no room left for me beside him. I make my way directly to him and sit on his knee.

Did I really just do that?

I glance at him and notice the small smile on his face. He seems to be enjoying the situation, which only annoys me further.

"He bought you a record player? Personally, I prefer diamonds." Giggling, Marion proudly shows off her bracelet. "Gabriel always knows how to spoil me."

Anika looks at her then takes sip of wine." "I understand that he buys his wife an object and his lover…ah, forgive me." She reddens. "And his good friend, diamonds."

Now I redden, but not in embarrassment.

"Lover?" I burst out laughing. "Anika, my husband sees Marion as a sister. He relates to her like an older sister." I emphasize the word 'older' and have to fight the laughter threatening to burst out in the face of Marion's shocked expression. "She's lived downstairs for years and they've developed a very special, platonic relationship. And now I'm proud to say that I, too, regard her as part of the family."

"I apologize, that was very rude of me," Anika murmurs, pushing a piece of chocolate cake into her mouth.

Gabriel slides his hand along my back and I move forward slightly to make him understand that I don't like it. I'm furious with him for abandoning me in the battle for my self-respect.

"Frau Anika," he addresses her. "My wife is right. I enjoy spoiling our friends with gifts, but I never neglect her. Josephine, perhaps you will show them the diamonds you received from me?"

I touch my small diamond earrings and he strokes my back again and laughs. "Don't be shy, go and fetch the two boxes I gave you today from the top drawer of the cabinet in our bedroom."

Uncomprehendingly, I turn round and look at him.

"Off you go." He gently pats my behind.

Standing up, I arrange my gown and walk hesitantly into the bedroom.

To my surprise, I find two black velvet boxes in the drawer and return with them to the drawing room. The two women look at me, one with curiosity and the other with fury.

I open the first box and my eyes widen in surprise.

"*Guter Himmel.*" Anika jumps up and bends over to inspect the chain in the box. It is huge and studded with tens of shining diamonds. Gabriel stands up and brushes my hair aside. He puts the chain around my neck and when he lets go, my head falls forward with the weight of it.

"It's magnificent!" Anika gazes at the box then glances at the second one. I open it carefully and discover a matching bracelet. Gabriel turns me around, kisses my wrist and puts on the bracelet. He sits down with a smug smile and draws me onto his lap.

Marion touches her bracelet; she looks as if she's been punched in the belly. Turning away she clings to the German officer.

"Richard," Anika addresses her husband with severity, "you know I like jewelry. I'd like diamonds too."

He yawns without covering his mouth and gives Gabriel an angry look.

"You know I'll always give my friends a good discount." Gabriel laughs.

"Maybe if I were your neighbor, I'd also receive beautiful gifts like these." Anika gazes with interest at the drawing room. "It's such a lovely building, how many neighbors do you have?"

"I'm the only neighbor." Marion puts a cigarette between her lips, blinking as Stengel lights it for her. "Before the war, all the apartments were taken, but the neighbors chose to move."

"Chose!" I imitate her mockingly, shrinking when Zemel looks suspiciously at me.

"Chose to move south," Marion says innocently. "And it's much pleasanter now without all the children jumping noisily in the passages." She sips her wine, while I remind myself to remain calm. "I was living in another apartment, but after they all left, I allowed myself to move into a larger one.

"I'd like to see your apartment." Stengel caresses her thigh and pours her wine.

"It's a charming apartment." Her face lights up. "The residents who lived here left in a hurry, leaving all their furniture, even the paintings. Gabriel says they're very valuable."

"Now I really have to see the apartment." His eyes darted to her décolleté. "If only to make sure you aren't hiding someone there."

"Really, Herr Stengel," she laughs, smacking him flirtatiously. "The only thing I'm hiding there is my jewelry. It's greatly needed these days."

"The hiding places of those mice manage to amaze me again and again," Zemel mutters angrily.

"Just a few days ago, we discovered the escape door the French spy has built in his kitchen."

Gabriel wraps his arm around my shoulders and I swallow.

"To think that for years he tricked us." Zemel scowls. "He hosted us in his home, and humiliated us. I won't rest until I find his associates." He stares fixedly at me and I don't blink. "You lived in that spy's home. You must tell me if you heard something, saw something suspicious, if he met with anyone."

"I've already told you that she was suspicious," Gabriel answered for me. "She shared her suspicions with me, but I wasn't wise enough to believe her."

"That's very serious!" Zemel barked and sat up.

"You're right." Gabriel maintains his calm tone. "I promise that the next time I discover that she's living with a spy, you'll be the first to know."

"But she's living with you," Anika says musingly and then bursts out laughing.

"That isn't funny." Zemel sprawls on the sofa again. "It's reached the highest ranks, and I have to give them answers."

I gather courage and open my mouth. "I didn't see anything. I was suspicious because he talked about you in a way that was inappropriate."

"What did that bastard say?" Stengel asks.

"He said you're dangerous, dishonorable and that you're deluding yourselves that you can control Europe." I notice the angry expression of both officers, and find myself enjoying it. "He also said that you only think you're clever, that in fact, you're stupid…"

Gabriel's hold over my shoulders tightens, but I can't stop. "That you're arrogant, and this arrogance will lead to your humiliating downfall."

I fall silent when his hold makes it difficult to breathe and understand that I've gone too far when four astounded faces stare at me.

"But it always happened only after he drank large quantities of alcohol." I look down. "He had a tendency to overdo things when drinking wine," I lie. "And sometimes, he would say the same things about the British and the Americans and even against the French. So I wasn't sure he really meant it."

"Well." Zemel smiles spitefully. "He can no longer enjoy his wine. If you remember anything else, I insist you come and tell me at once."

"Of course." I nod and take a deep breath when Gabriel finally releases his hold.

"These cakes are wonderful," Anika declares, as if she wasn't present during the difficult conversation, and pushes her fork into the apple pie again. "Josephine, I must borrow your maid next time I have an event."

"Ah…I don't think that…"

"Marie is an elderly woman," Gabriel says firmly. "She won't be able to help you."

"But I must have her," Anika complains. "Richard, tell him he must ask her."

"I'm telling you," Zemel smiles.

"I'm sorry but I can't help you in this matter," Gabriel responds, and I feel his body tense.

"If we lend her to you, how will we be able to persuade you to come again?" I stand up and arrange all the cakes and biscuits on a tray. "I've so enjoyed hosting you, and now I know you'll agree to come again if only for the cakes." Smiling broadly, I offer her the tray.

"You're right." Her expression softens. "It's been a lovely evening. I'm sure we'll be back soon."

The men stand up, followed by the women. We accompany them to the door, Anika holding the tray of cakes like a little girl who has received a bag of candies.

Stengel beckons to Marion to join him. "I'd love to see the artwork in your apartment now."

She glances at Gabriel and when he doesn't react, she links arms with the German officer and straightens up.

She could refuse because of the late hour; she could apologize and fake a yawn, and it would all be accepted with understanding. But no, she smiles sweetly at him and nods. If she wasn't already at the top of my most hated list, I'd put her there now.

The door closes after them, and I lean against it, exhausted.

"Madame Augustine, I have to say that you survived the evening with aplomb." Gabriel winks at me and, rolling my eyes, I totter into the bathroom.

When I enter the bedroom I can no longer stand on my high heels. Sitting down on the bed, I remove them with a yawn.

Gabriel enters the room and unbuttons his shirt. I stare at his broad shoulders and then the light flickers and goes out.

"Perfect timing for an electricity cut." Yawning again, I stand up. He lights the candle on the dresser, stands behind me and removes the heavy chain from my neck. "Thank you for making them think you really did give me this jewelry." I remove the bracelet and put on the dresser beside the chain.

"It really is yours." He opens the zipper on my dress and kisses my hand. A pleasant tingling passes down my back, and I bite my lips and throw the dress on the chair.

"I can't accept such an expensive gift from you." I turn to him.

The light comes on again and his eyes are fixed on my sheer underwear. He is so close to me that I can feel his body heat. He moves forwards slightly, and the thin fabric covering me rubs against his smooth skin. In a second, tiredness fades and my body is alive, excited and longing to feel him closer.

He puts his hand on my shoulder and a quiet sigh escapes me.

"The jewelry is yours. No argument." He kisses my head and moves away.

The heat cools. I hurry to get into bed and cover myself with the blanket.

He turns out the light and lies down on the other side of the bed. "It's important to stay focused," he murmurs, as if trying to convince himself. "If we allow our feelings to confuse us, the game will become too dangerous."

"You're right," I whisper, lying on my belly. "Reason tells me all the time that this is just pretense, but I think I've become fond of you."

His hand closes on my arm and he pulls me to him. His arm lies under my neck and I try to pull away a little so he won't feel the effect of his touch over my heartbeats.

"I won't exploit your sensitive situation." His fingers travel over my arm. "I must admit that thanks to you, I am learning an important lesson in restraint."

Opening my eyes in surprise, I place my hand on his chest. I'm quite sure his heartbeats match my own.

"Josephine." Raising my hand, he kisses it. "I beg you to join me tomorrow morning and allow me to take care of you and arrange a safe place for you to stay."

"I can't leave." I slip my leg between his and rest my head on his chest.

"You aren't making this easy for me." He groans and moves his hips. "I won't be comfortable with you staying here on your own."

"So you regret your impulsive decision to save me?"

"Very much so." He laughs, and I lean on my elbow and hit him on the chest.

He stops laughing. Holding my neck, he brushes his fingers through my hair. He pulls my head back slightly and my lips part in painful expectation of his touch. His glance passes over my face and neck in the direction of my breasts. The transparent fabric allows him to see my nakedness, and he clenches his jaws and gazes at my lips again.

"You really aren't making this easy for me." His face draws close and he emits a faint growl as his lips flutter over mine. His warm breath penetrates my mouth and he pushes me away from him.

I pant with frustration and move to the edge of the bed. "You're confusing worry with passion." I murmur. "I confuse myself too. That's why my body is burning now and in my mind, I imagine your lips and your hands touching me."

"Stop," he commands firmly, and I feel him turn on his belly. "It's only a matter of time before we nullify this marriage. It will happen the moment I know you're safe, and then we can both go back to our lives."

"Yes. Precisely." I grimace as my heart transmits signals of distress. What life is he talking about? What do I have to go back to? Doesn't he realize that right now he's all I have?

His hand finds its way along the mattress until it finds mine and he presses it, continuing to hold it. This time I lie quietly, not allowing myself any illusions about him.

We're merely two strangers living in the same house like house-mates.

And if I continue to repeat this, maybe I'll manage to persuade myself that what I feel for him is just affection.

CHAPTER FOURTEEN

Walking into the dining room, I see the French newspaper placed beside one plate.

Marie comes in and pours my coffee. "Good morning, *Cherie*," she says.

"Marie, why haven't you set a place for Gabriel?" I glance at the door, expecting to hear his steps. "He always sits down to eat with me."

"*Cherie*, he left early this morning. He didn't want to wake you but he left you a note." She points at the dresser behind me and I jump up and eagerly take the note.

> *Have a wonderful day,*
> *Please look after yourself.*
> *We'll see each other soon.*
> *Gabriel*

"That's all?" I turn the note over in disappointment.

"Sit down and eat," Marie orders firmly. "He asked me to look after you and I intend to do so."

"But…are you sure he didn't leave anything else? Maybe another note?" The room suddenly appears cold and alien.

"*Cherie*, men don't excel at words." She smiles naughtily. "What matters is how they make you feel with actions."

I nod heavily and sip my coffee.

I recall how my body has longed for him the previous night, and try to remember if I'd ever felt such passion before. I'd known men in the past, known pleasurable touch and thought I'd known passion, but I'm certain I'd never felt passion that emanated from such a deep, true place.

What matters is how they make you feel with actions. Marie's sentence echoes in my mind. And Gabriel had undoubtedly decided to act for me. My thoughts wander back to the evening when my bubble burst and he went down on one knee and asked me to marry him. His agreeing to have me in his home, the homely warmth he gave me from the moment I came here, the ease with which he cooperated with my risky adventure at our wedding party and his choice to go himself to the Gestapo offices and prevent them from taking me for interrogation.

Putting down my coffee cup, I touch my earrings. I no longer feel confused, I feel agitated. He'd captured my heart without intending to, and I have a terrible feeling that without intending to, he will also be the one to break it.

"Sit down with me," I ask Marie and she sits down in the chair opposite me, as if a deliberate hand had left his chair empty in case he'd surprise me and come in.

"Don't look so miserable." She cuts a slice of bread for me. "His travels are a routine thing. You have to get used to it."

"Did he tell you how long he'd be gone?"

"He never says." She points at my fork and I raise it listlessly.

"But do you have an approximate idea of when he'll be back?"

"It might be a week or two, and it could be a month or several months."

"Several months?" I shriek.

"Now that he has a wife at home, I'm sure he'll try and return as quickly as possible." She gives me a comforting smile. "You'll learn to keep busy when he isn't here. I also learned."

"Do you think you could sleep here while he's away?" I ask hesitantly. "This apartment is a little large for just one person."

"Don't you worry." She stands up and straightens her apron. "He's already asked me not to leave you alone."

"I don't want to ask, only if it suits you."

"I'm happy to do it." She smiles again. "And it's a relief to have someone to take care of when he's away."

"Thank you, Marie." I place my hand over my heart.

She nods and goes into the corridor.

I suddenly realize the depth of my feelings for him. How in God's name will I manage to stay sane until his return? And what would change when this happens? I drum my fingers on the table. It isn't real, it's only pretense. He's emphasized this several times. And perhaps he's right and I really am confusing feelings of gratitude with something stronger and more powerful.

I look at the empty chair and my heart burns. I'm not confused. My feelings are real and my heart knows it.

***

My bicycle creaks with the extra weight I've loaded onto it, and I push it carefully along the sidewalk. The sun is already setting and the edges of the fabrics peep out of the bags I've hung on the handlebars.

I lean it against the wall in the lobby, and go upstairs. Reaching the first floor I hug the bags to me so they won't rustle and make Marion open her door.

I pass her door and breathe a sigh of relief.

"What do you have in all those bags?" Her wheedling voice comes from behind me and I stop in my tracks.

"Just fabrics." I turn around and have difficulty understanding how she dares open the door wearing such a revealing nightgown.

"Show me." She tugs at one of the bags and, to my horror, takes it into her apartment, leaving the door open. "Well, come on," she shouts and I roll my eyes in despair.

I walk into the hall and my eyes open in astonishment. If I were visiting a Parisian brothel, this is exactly what it would look like. I had no idea that so many shades of red existed. The carpets, curtains and even the armchairs, everything is red. I can imagine Brigitte standing beside me and clicking her tongue. This is not the apartment of a lady, she'd say in a shocked tone, leave at once.

"Well." Marion puts her hands on her hips. "Isn't my apartment breathtaking?"

"Breathtaking, indeed." I hide a smile and stop myself adding that it's from shock.

"Can I offer you something to drink?"

I shake my head.

"I think the time has come for us to deepen our acquaintance." She stands in front of the mirror on the dresser and applies red lipstick to her lips. "Now that Gabriel has gone away, we are the only ones in the building, and it's important to look after each other."

"How do you know he's gone away?"

"What do you mean, how do I know?" She waves her hand dismissively. "He tells me everything, and I also had time to say goodbye this morning."

The pinch of jealousy almost makes me lose focus.

"I know that our relationship might cause you discomfort." The tone of her voice changes. "But you must understand that Gabriel was always mine. The relationship with you is only temporary. The quicker you grasp that, the better it will be for everyone."

I look at her in wonder, for a moment I fear he's told her that our relationship is just a pretense.

"He only thinks he's in love with you." She giggles and I sigh with relief. "It's temporary. I know he's never been *exclusively* mine, but this farce of a wedding is something he's never done to me before."

She sits down on the sofa and I glance at my bag she's taken hostage and set down at her feet. "I think he suspects I have another lover for the duration of his time out of town." She sighs and arranges her hair on her shoulders. "I think a broken heart is what made him bring you here. Everything he does is calculated, he is simply trying to make me jealous."

This woman is sickeningly infatuated with herself. Instead of undermining me with her words, the tickle at the center of my belly climbs up into my throat and I burst out laughing.

She looks at me in shock and, continuing to laugh, I bend down to pick up the bag.

"You should find a professional to take care of your emotional problems." I walk out of the door, my body shaking with waves of laughter. "They should replace the blue pills with the red ones, they're stronger."

"You laugh now," she shouts, "but I know you! You're cunning and treacherous and he just cannot see it. But I see everything." She runs to the open door and holds the handle. "I'll go on keeping an eye on your schemes and when I expose you he will realize who you truly are."

"You really are funny. I'm starting to understand why Gabriel is always amused by you." I wink at her and leave the apartment. Ignoring the curses she fires at my back, I go up to the second floor, open my apartment door and laugh.

"What a refreshing sound." Marie stands in front of me, examining me with curiosity. "What amused you so much?"

"Our crazy neighbor." I put down the bags and roll my eyes.

"Ah." Marie grows serious. "Try and avoid her, please."

"I'm trying but she's like a leech. Every time I enter the stairwell, she jumps at me. I can't understand how Gabriel had a relationship with her."

"It's a complicated story. Didn't he tell you?"

"Not all of it. He told me they had a relationship but didn't expand." I fall silent so she can continue to speak.

"You've arrived just in time for dinner," she sharply changes the subject, and I glance at the telephone.

"Has he called?"

"No, *Cherie*. He's probably still on the road." She turns into the corridor and I frown in disappointment and go into the dining room.

"Sit with me," I ask when she sets a plate in front of me.

"It's better we remember my role here." She places a knife and fork on a serviette. "You're the lady of the house and I'm the house-keeper."

"Oh, Marie," I grumble, "it's clear to everyone that you're part of the family. And who cares about those definitions. There are new lords and ladies in our country, we are just pretending."

She laughs and leaves the room; when she returns, she sets another plate on the table and sits down opposite me. "It's so quiet here without him." She looks at his empty chair and sighs.

"At least we're not completely alone." I smile at her and hold out my wine glass.

Knocks at the door make both of us stand up in alarm. Marie is the first to collect herself. She goes to the door and I follow her.

"*Bon Soir.*" This time Marion is wrapped in a silk gown with a broad, false smile on her face.

"*Bon Soir,*" Marie responds coldly.

"I have an important guest so I've come to take some provisions." She pushes Marie aside on her way in and goes directly to the wine cabinet. "Marie, *Cherie*, prepare a tray of desserts please and bring it to my apartment."

Marie doesn't answer and I bite my lower lip.

Marion takes a bottle out of the cabinet and goes into the corridor.

"There is one lady of the house and it isn't her!" Marie whispers angrily.

I look down and clench my fists.

Marion returns to the drawing room with fruit cut on a plate and stands in front of Marie. "Come on, come on, we're waiting for dessert."

Marie turns into the corridor and I block her way.

"Put the plate on the table," I order Marion quietly, and she looks at me in shock. "I told you to put the plate on the table!" Approaching her, I snatch the plate from her. Taking a step back, she hugs the bottle of wine.

"I permit you to take the bottle of wine but not the fruit." Thrusting out my chin, I maintain a blank expression. "And don't expect Marie to come to your apartment. Any request you have of her must go through me." I smile. "I have no idea why you think you can come in here and take whatever you feel like, this house is not your grocery store. Next time you require contributions, make sure to speak to me about it in advance."

I open the door and motion to her to leave.

"Gabriel will hear of this," she says with crazed eyes.

"Please feel free to go to the post office and send him a telegram." I push her out into the passage and slam the door in her face.

"*C'est tout*." I rub my hands together and smile at Marie. "We can return to our meal."

"Congratulations, lady of the house." Marie nods to herself with satisfaction, and returns with me to the dining room. We eat quietly until I put down my fork and gaze at her.

"Please, tell me about their relationship. I just cannot understand how a man like Gabriel could connect with someone like her."

"I don't think it's appropriate." She avoids my glance. "There are things a man should tell his wife."

"But he won't tell me. You know him better than I and you know he isn't forthcoming."

"Men…" she nods her head and chuckles.

"It's important to me to know what I'm facing," I beg her. "I feel as if I must protect our relationship and I don't have the basic knowledge how to cope with her."

I know that I'm lying to this good woman and that my false relationship requires no protection, but inside myself I want to believe that this lie won't hurt anyone except myself.

"You have nothing to worry about on that count." She pours herself a glass of water and seems thoughtful. "But you do need to know that he is sensitive to her and her needs."

"Why?"

"Maybe you should know who you're dealing with so you can be careful." She goes over to the dresser and takes out a packet of cigarettes. It's the first time I've seen her smoke and don't refuse the cigarette she offers me.

"Tell me," I beg her.

"She moved into the building before the occupation," Marie starts speaking and I dare not say a word.

"At first she'd come here every few days with some weak excuse or another. She was smiling and pleasant and very polite."

I try and fail to imagine a younger Marion as a pleasant, cultured young woman.

"She set out to capture Gabriel's heart and in time he responded to her invitations to spend time with her. The visits became more and more frequent and each time he came to town they'd spend time together. She managed to deceive him and, to be honest, myself as well." Marie sighs and inhales. "About two years ago, I started noticing a change in her behavior. She demanded he spend all his spare time with her and began to pressure him to legalize their relationship."

"And why didn't he ask her to marry him?"

"He's married to his work." She laughs. "Until you came, I didn't believe he'd ever settle down. With anyone. It seems he was simply waiting for the right woman."

I nod and touch my earring in discomfort.

"He explained to her that he couldn't give her what she wanted and suggested they end the relationship." She shivers. "Marion became obsessive. She came here at all hours of the day and night, brought other men to her apartment in order to make him jealous, and used every possible stratagem."

"And did this make him return to her?"

"Absolutely not," Marie shrieks. "On the contrary. He simply stayed away longer and made sure to spend as little time in the apartment as possible to avoid her. But when he returned from one of his travels, she surprised him with unexpected news." Her tone became dramatic and I put out my cigarette and lean forward. "She told him she was pregnant."

"Ah, *Mon Dieu*," I murmur.

"Yes…" Marie groans. "She knew he couldn't remain indifferent to her situation. She knew he was a man who would never run away from responsibility, and he behaved exactly as she'd expected. He agreed to marry her and calmed her by taking care of all her needs. At her side, he behaved as if it was the best thing that could have happened to him, but when I saw him at the rare moments he was alone in the apartment, I knew he was broken."

"So why did he agree to marry her?" I ask sadly.

"Because that's my Gabriel. Family values are sacred to him. He wouldn't agree to have a child who didn't bear his family name with pride."

"So did they marry?" I press on my earring until it hurt.

"No." Marie closes her eyes for a moment and when she opens them, they're moist. "Marion refused his pleas to stop performing in the evenings and, during one performance, she began to bleed heavily and lost the fetus."

"Poor woman. That's terrible." I cover my mouth with my hand.

"A tragic event." Marie nods. "Despite the circumstances, Gabriel was crushed. He didn't leave her for a moment. Made sure of the best doctors, tried to comfort and encourage her but she blamed him for it, saying it happened because he didn't really want the child, and she fell into a deep depression.

One evening, Marion dressed up very elegantly and told him she was going back to perform. She refused to discuss the loss and at first behaved like a frolicking spinster. Parties, restaurants, balls, random men…and each time she went crazy, she'd return screaming and crying to him."

"And what did he do?"

"Tried to calm and comfort her."

"Did they get back together?"

"No. He promised her he'd continue to take care of her as long as she needed him, but begged her to get on with her life without him."

"And she can't really do that." I sigh.

"To her credit, she doesn't stop looking for another man." Marie rolls her eyes. "But she knows she'll never find a man like him."

"Damn, I feel sorry for her now," I say, frustrated.

"I'm also sorry for her," Marie says stiffly. "But he is no longer her man and she has to accept it."

"There's something else I don't understand." I frown. "On my first evening here, she said she'd have noticed our relationship because they were together all the time."

"Not in the way you think." Marie chuckles. "This past month she decided to attach herself to him again, and invited herself to the apartment whenever he got home. That woman knows the art of temptation." She shrugs. "She could teach it, but it's a pity she's wasting it on Gabriel. As far as I know, he will never repeat that mistake again with her."

"A problematic situation."

"The situation would be problematic if he didn't look at you in the way a man is supposed to look at his wife."

She smiles calmly at me. "I've never seen him look like that at anyone else, certainly not at her."

I look down, my heart stopping.

"Your performance is perfect."

I raise my head in astonishment and she laughs.

"*Cherie*, it wouldn't be perfect if your performance wasn't real"

"It…isn't…umm…"

"I knew the minute I saw your frightened expression." Getting up, she picked up the plates.

"But I knew it would very quickly turn into the real thing."

"I don't think he sees it as you do." I swallow the lump in my throat.

"You're too young to see what I do. Your special connection will push aside any weight in its way and become a love story that hasn't yet been written. Do you know why?"

I shake my head.

"Because your brief relationship is based on concern, respect and friendship. In time you will both realize that you didn't meet by chance. Your love is written in the stars."

She leaves the room and I continue to gaze at the empty chair she left behind. The compassion I feel for Marion blends with my sensations of frustration and confusion. I can't understand how I found myself in this situation. How can a stranger, who chose to save me, become the center of my world?

I have to get out of here.

I have to remind myself that I have a purpose and that as long as Paris is occupied by those loathsome Germans, it is more important than anything else.

Peddling hard, I chastise myself for the nonsense I put in my head. The quiet, dark streets and the flags with their swastikas return me to the bleak reality, and I refuse to think any further about Marie's words.

The new address Natalie had given me brought me to an old building surrounded by wild foliage. I leave my bicycle at the entrance floor and run up to the third floor, knock twice on the door and the sounds of conversation inside stop. I hear steps coming to the door and I whisper "Fleur-de-Lis." The locks rattle and the door opens. I'm pulled inside and the door closes behind me.

"I thought you'd decided to abandon us." Natalie runs to me with open arms.

"Have we won the war?" I ask gravely.

"Not yet." She laughs.

"Then it seems I will continue to be one of you." I smile at her.

Maurice comes up to me, pats my shoulder and introduces me to those present. The little drawing room is filled with cigarette smoke and rickety old furniture, but the energy in the air is electrifying. This time there is no main speech but a scattering of small groups. Some of those present are sitting in armchairs and some are standing and talking quietly. Each group seems to consist of people who otherwise would never have met. Natalie takes me to a group sitting round the dinner table. There are two men, a woman and three youngsters. She introduces me to the woman who motions to me to sit next to her.

Within a few seconds, I realize that the woman's name is Veronique and she's the leader of the group. Coolly and impassively, she allocates tasks to everyone. Each one receives a small parcel and when I look questioningly at her, she nods and hands me a paper bag of documents.

"Josephine," she says with a meaningful glance. "Our team's tasks may not include physical fighting, but each link in the chain relies on us."

Examining the bag, my eyes narrow uncomprehendingly.

"We're the courier team," she says proudly, gesturing to the members of the group. "Every document in your bag impacts a life."

"Are these false documents?" I ask, taking one out of the bag.

"Don't look at them!" Angrily, she tugs the paper away from me. "You don't need to know the names, you don't need to see the pictures and don't try to understand whom they're for. The less you know, the less of a risk you are in."

"Understood." I hand her the bag so she can return the documents in her hand.

"We all want to know whose life we're saving." She softens her tone. "It could be a Jewish child, an elderly communist or a young girl who has gotten involved in a dangerous affair with a German. Ultimately, it doesn't matter. These documents must pass from your hands to a contact and with that your involvement ends."

I nod.

"You have exactly one hour to deliver the parcel to this address." She points to a map, making sure that only I see it. None of the group tries to peep. I memorize the address and she gets up and accompanies me to the door.

"Do you have a bicycle?"

"Yes."

"Hide the bag in the basket and put this packet of fruit on top of it."

She hands me one of the packets on the dresser near the door. "Ride slowly, don't lose your composure if you're stopped at a check point and when you reach your destination, go round the building and enter from the back door. Ask for Madame Distel, only she may receive the parcel from you. Is that clear?"

"Yes."

"Come back tomorrow at noon for another mission."

Nodding, I leave the apartment. Putting the documents on the bottom of the basket, I settle the fruit on top of them, as ordered. I ride my bicycle slowly, shivering with cold but continuing to peddle steadily. I pass two pedestrians and turn at the next street. Pass a patrol of three soldiers, and when the tension makes itself felt, I start soundlessly humming Maurice Chevalier's "Valentina."

Arriving at the street of my destination, I stay close to the first building. Dear God, if I'd realized what address she was sending me to, I might not have been so enthusiastic about going out on a mission. A lot of cars are parked at the sidewalk and German soldiers are standing in groups, drinking, laughing and smoking.

"To the back entrance…" I mutter to myself and push my bicycle along the narrow path between the buildings. Reaching the common yard, I drag my bicycle up to the building with lighted windows and blaring music.

Putting the documents into an inner pocket of my coat, I pick up the packet of fruit, climb three steps and knock on the door. No answer. I knock again and the door remains closed.

I consider running away but reason commands I complete my mission successfully. Turning the handle, the door opens easily. The lighting is dim but I see that I am standing at the entrance to the kitchen. I take a hesitant step forward and the door slams behind me.

"Are you the new courier?" I hear a shrill voice and, turning my head, I see a young girl in a lace robe that shows far more than I wish to see. I look to the side and stare at another young woman wearing a long skirt and corset. She is sitting on a high stool, eating a red apple.

"What have you brought us?" The first girl snatches the packet from me and inspects the fruit with disappointment. "Why don't you ever bring chocolate?" She grumbles. "Or jewelry." Her eyes brighten as she approaches me, looking at my diamond earrings. She holds my ear lobe in two fingers and pulls at it to closely examine the earring.

"Leave her alone."

The order comes from an older female. I step back. The red curtain separating the kitchen from the rest of the house is parted and in the opening, stands a tall, buxom woman. She is wearing a corset that makes her breasts burst out generously, and a skirt with many layers of fabric. Her graying hair is gathered up in a gold clip and her heels tap on the wooden floor as she approaches me.

"Stop your laziness," she scolds the young women. "New clients have arrived, go and serve them."

"Gladly, Madame Distel." The young woman sitting on the chair throws the apple into the sink and arranges her breasts in her corset. Pulling her friend with her, they disappear behind the curtain.

"You're the new one." Madame states, peeping into the packet of fruit. "Where is it?" She gives me a hard look. I open the buttons of my coat and hand her the bag of documents.

"Good girl." She counts the documents and then lifts her skirt and slips the bag under a red garter at the top of her thigh. "Make sure your friends get this tomorrow." She takes a folded note out of the depths of her décolleté and, when I hide it in the pocket of my coat, she shakes her head crossly and pulls me to her. Removing the note from my pocket, she pushes her hand into my décolleté.

"What are you doing?" I shudder.

"Making sure of a better hiding place." She removes her hand and I feel the note close to my breast. She smiles mockingly and then steps back and examines me with interest. "If you're hungry you can eat something." She gestures to the refrigerator.

"No thank you."

"You don't really look hungry." She tilts her head to one side and narrows her eyes. "That body of yours could earn you a lot of money here. A beautiful young woman like you would be much in demand among the officers."

"With your permission, I'll go now." I glance at the exit door.

"You could go on with your missions and earn money in these hard times." She's insistent.

"I'm not interested," I answer firmly.

"Pity." She approaches me. "If you reconsider, you know where to find me." Her eyes are fixed on my earrings. "And if you decide to sell those diamonds, I know a dealer who pays a fair price."

"They aren't for sale." I touch the earring and run outside, lean against the door panting. I'd managed to keep him out of my thoughts for several hours and now, in one sentence, this woman had shaken me.

I push my bicycle through the yards of the buildings and come out at the end of the road. Peddling hard, I bite my lips. The knowledge that he won't be waiting for me in the apartment saddens me, and the force of my longing surprises me.

Only at the entrance to the building do I grasp that I was so focused on my thoughts of him that I was spared the anxiety that had accompanied me on my way to my first mission for the Resistance.

Going up the stairs I pause at the entrance to Marion's apartment. I'm so used to the door opening every time I pass by, that when it doesn't happen I stop in surprise. I hear music and her rolling laugh and then the amused sound of a German accent. I shudder when I realize with whom she is enjoying herself. I thought that the fact that it is a German officer would shock me, but it's the fact that she is hosting a married officer shocks me even more.

The sounds of laughter change to murmurs and groans and holding to the banister, I run up to the second floor. Quietly opening the door to the apartment, I go inside.

"You shouldn't be wandering around outside at this hour," Marie scolds me, getting up from her chair.

"I was visiting a friend," I lie, locking the door.

"Josephine, the curfew begins in a few minutes. And apart from that, a married woman doesn't return alone at such a late hour." She rubs her eyes and goes into the corridor. "You must remember that you are married to a man whose reputation is very important to him. He won't like it and please don't ask me to lie to him."

"Did he call?" I ask excitedly.

"No." She sighs. "And I'm too old to worry and wait up for you in the drawing room."

"I apologize."

She nods heavily and goes into her bedroom.

I drag the armchair over to the telephone and sit down, crossing my legs. It's hard to go into the bedroom when I know he isn't there, and it's harder to cope with the fact that this man has become the center of my world.

I look longingly at the telephone and pray he will call just so that I can tell him that if he wants to make me happy, he must come back.

CHAPTER FIFTEEN

The raindrops make it hard for me to maneuver my bicycle between the puddles, and by the time I reach the building that serves as a meeting place, I am wet to the bone. My muscles hurt from a disturbed night in the armchair and the disappointment that he didn't call gives me no peace.

My teeth are chattering when I whisper the password and the moment the door opens I leap inside, looking for a source of warmth. To my disappointment, the fire is out, and I wrap myself in a faded blanket one of the men hands me.

No-one present seems concerned by my plight. Veronique nods to me and goes on briefing the boy sitting opposite her. He asks her a question and she responds with a smile, affectionately pressing his hand. Only now do I see the similarity between them. Cursed reality that forces a mother to risk her son's life. After he leaves, she continues to gaze at the closed door and then pulls herself together and beckons me to sit in the chair opposite her.

"You probably worry about him every time he goes out on a mission." I smile sadly at her.

Her expression hardens and she blazes furiously. "Do you know his surname?"

I shake my head.

"Do you know the mission he's gone out on?"

"No." I shrug in embarrassment.

"Have I ever told you of our relationship?"

"No."

"Then how dare you make assumptions?" She raises her voice and everyone in the room falls silent and looks at us.

"My name is Veronique," she speaks quietly again. "And your name is Josephine. This is the only thing we know about each other. Is that clear?"

"Yes." I nod and take the note out of my brassiere, wordlessly putting it down in front of her.

She reads it, gets up and gives it to a man with a mustache who is sitting with two others in the kitchen. They whisper and she returns to her seat in front of me.

"You must deliver a package to an address in another neighborhood," she says without mentioning the note. "It's a heavier package." She picks up a package wrapped in newspaper. I see the barrel of a revolver, and my heart pounds wildly. "Don't think about it," Veronique scolds me. "It's just another package you have to deliver."

My intuition screams to me to refuse, but I find myself nodding.

I put the package at the bottom of the basket and the packet of fruit on the top. The only thing that calms my anxiety is the heavy rain that leaves the streets empty.

I ride carefully and German soldiers protecting their heads with black umbrellas look at me indifferently. I pass another street, no longer knowing if my body is trembling with cold or tension.

I stop at the entrance to the building at the address given me, and lean my bicycle against the wall in the lobby. Old newspapers and cigarette butts are scattered on the floor. I take the package and look around to make sure no-one is following me.

The desire to get rid of the package overcomes the anxiety gnawing at me, and I quickly go up the stairs. Two knocks, whisper the password and the door opens. I wave my hand to disperse the smoke burning my eyes, and someone takes my elbow and pulls me inside.

"*S'il vous plaît.*" I hand over the package to a filthy man with black shaggy hair.

Taking the package from me, he tears off the newspaper and examines the revolver with satisfaction.

"The new courier doesn't look too bad." Another man who is sitting on a mattress smiles at me, inhaling a cigarette.

"Much better than the boy who came here yesterday." The man standing in front of me laughs.

"I must go now." I turn to the door and my arm is pulled again.

"What's the hurry?" The man pulls me to him and I cough from the stink emanating from him. "You can't leave us here alone. A man who is fighting for your freedom needs a little appreciation."

"I'm just the courier." I try to get away from him.

"You should contribute a little more to our war effort." The man sitting on the mattress stands up. "The Germans are fucking our women and we don't even get left-overs." He comes towards me and I realize in terror that unless I do something drastic, I won't get out of here so quickly.

Clinging to the man who is holding me, I grab the revolver from him.

"What are you doing?" He sneers.

I stretch my hand forwards and aim the revolver at him.

"I said I am only the courier." The tremor in my voice reveals the tension blurring my senses. "Let me leave in peace now, or I'll press the trigger."

"You don't have the guts to do that." The second man grins but remains standing at a safe distance.

Turning my arm, I feel for the door handle. My eyes are fixed on the man standing in front of me. The moment the door is open, I throw the revolver on the floor and run quickly downstairs. I don't stop to see if they're after me, and the moment my feet reach the entrance, I get on my bicycle and peddle away with all my strength.

A loud whistle is heard and a German in a gray uniform signals to me to stop.

"Papers," he orders quietly.

I take my papers out of my pocket and wipe the perspiration from my eyes.

"What's that?" he points at the packet of fruit.

"Just some fruit I managed to get." I try and smile at him.

He fumbles in the packet and then to my consternation picks it up. My heart beats in my chest and I have to remind myself that I've already gotten rid of the package.

"You may continue." He waves his hand and I thank him soundlessly and ride on. This time more slowly. I'm supposed to return to the apartment we convene in but instead I go on to my apartment. I am incapable of thinking about anything except those terrible men waiting for my delivery. I realized the hard way that the fact that someone is on my side doesn't necessarily mean he's a good man. This realization shocks me.

Leaving my bicycle in the entrance, I go upstairs, exhausted. Marion's door remains closed and this time I don't pause to work out whom she's hosting.

Entering the apartment, I put down the packet of fruit at the entrance.

"This is no weather to be out in," Marie scolds, taking my coat from me. "You'll get pneumonia."

"I know." My teeth are chattering.

"There's hot water." She rubs my back. "Get in the bath and I'll make some hot soup."

I follow her into the bathroom, strip off my clothes and lie down in the hot water. I burst into tears. Reality is supposed to be clearer. There are good and bad people. How can good people forget it? How can my devotion to my purpose make me pay such a heavy price?

Not even the hot water comfort me. I get out of the bath, envelope myself in a robe and stumble into the dining room.

I sniff as I sip my soup.

"Do you want to tell me anything?" Marie sits down in front of me and looks at me with concern.

"No. Just a strange day…" I avoid her gaze.

"Maybe you should stop visiting that friend of yours."

"She isn't feeling well," I murmur. "She really needs my help."

"I think she's a lot sicker than you can deal with."

Looking up, I see pain, much like mine, in her eyes. I realize she knows what I'm doing.

"You want to help her, but there are others who are helping. More skilled and mentally stronger."

"If everyone gives in to the difficulty, who will help her?" The tears return.

"You're right. But at least wait until Gabriel comes back. He will look after you while you look after her."

"I can't." I wipe my tears with my serviette, "I can't sit by and watch others helping her while I do nothing."

"You're a good friend." She sighs heavily. "I hope I live to celebrate the day she recovers, with you."

"I also hope I live to see it."

Marie leaves the room and I decide to allow myself to hide away in the apartment for the rest of the day. Anxiety, tension, exhaustion and longing, all gather together in one hurting, distressed heart.

CHAPTER SIXTEEN

The rain has stopped and I ride my bicycle through the gray streets.

A week has passed. Seven days and seven nights and I refuse to enter his bedroom. I sleep on the sofa and wait for the telephone to ring, but it remains silent.

I go our meeting place and sit opposite Veronique. I chose not to tell her what happened to that damned delivery I made, and she didn't ask why I hadn't returned for other packages that day.

"This time I want you to return here to make other deliveries." She says coldly.

"That's what I've done over the past days." I refuse to be put off by her tone.

"Today it's particularly important, and it's hard to know with you."

"If you have something to say, say it loud and clear." I clench my teeth.

"All right." She smiles but it doesn't reach her eyes. "Everyone here knows you aren't completely committed to your role. You come and go as you please. It's merely a game to you."

"A game?" I ask quietly and feel waves of anger pierce my belly. "I come here day after day, in all weather, and carry out every one of your deliveries without asking questions."

"That's exactly what you're supposed to do." She grins.

"You should have warned me last week before sending me off to that den of scoundrels." I raise my voice and all the others fall silent.

Natalie crosses the room to stand beside me. "Is there a problem?" She asks, fixing her eyes on Veronique.

"You know I appreciate and respect all the volunteers here." Veronique moderates her tone. "But I can't suppress my suspicions about her." She points at me. "Look at her, coming here in her beautiful clothes, clean and perfumed, always refusing to eat with us and yet to part from her pretty diamond earrings. What is she really doing here? How can you be sure that she isn't a spy?"

I open my mouth to reply, but Natalie bangs on the table and curses. "Apologize to her!"

Veronique lowers her eyes and shakes her head.

"I told you to apologize." Natalie pulls her hair, forcing her to look at me.

"Leave her alone." I address Natalie firmly. "It's between me and her. We'll work this out between us."

"Demand an apology," Natalie says angrily. She lets go of Veronique's chair and returns to her place beside Maurice.

"You know nothing about me." I say in a whisper. "And in your situation, I would probably be suspicious too. If I wanted to implicate anyone here I've had enough opportunities."

Veronique drums her fingers on the table, and doesn't say a word.

"What is your dream?" I ask, putting my hand on hers.

"I'm a practical woman. I leave dreams to the young."

"You wouldn't be here now if you didn't have a dream." I press her hand. "Please, answer my question."

"To be free," she says in an annoyed tone. "To be free in my own country, and to be proud of it. A simple dream, isn't it?"

"We don't know anything about each other. Two strangers who work together without even knowing each other's surnames." I pat her hand and straighten up. "Two women who are complete strangers, but who apparently share the same dream."

She gives me a long considering look and her eyes tear up.

"I'm sorry for attacking you," she finally says. "You have to understand that I have a lot to lose, my two sons, all that is dear to me in this life."

"Well, my risk is not equal to yours." I stand up and take the packet of documents. "I've already lost those who were important to me. And now it looks as if I'm fighting for those who are important to you."

I leave the apartment with a feeling of heaviness, mount my bicycle and hurry off towards my destination.

When I return for another delivery, Veronique checks my packages carefully and re-sorts them. She doesn't ask me to clarify my last sentence, but the way in which she addresses me shows I've managed to gain her trust.

I leave to deliver another package and only return to my apartment late that night. I'm hungry and exhausted by the long hours of tension throughout the day, but find comfort in the fact that Marion's door remains closed. My personal spy is busy amusing herself with her married German, and for several evenings, I have passed her apartment without cross-examination.

"Dinner is ready." Marie welcomes me with her habitual smile.

"Has he called?" I ask my usual, monotonous question and when she nods, my eyes open in surprise.

"He asked about you." She helps me take off my coat. "I explained that you're busy taking care of a sick friend."

"But…did he say he'd call again?" I ask, disappointment dulling my senses.

"He said he'll call again tomorrow evening at eight." She strokes my back. I'm not comforted. I have waited impatiently for that call and missed it. Missed the opportunity to tell him I want him to come back so much.

I eat dinner apathetically, and every sound makes me jump, hoping it's the ring of the telephone. But the telephone refuses to ring. I lie down to sleep on the sofa, repeating to myself the only thing that is important to me to tell him. Please come back.

***

Morning breaks and I make myself go out to another routine day of collecting and distributing packages.

I take a package of medication to a young girl in a square, return to our meeting apartment and from there to a luxury apartment in the sixth District. Time passes slowly and I keep looking at my watch. I'm grateful for the workload and even agree to share a meager lunch with my friends at our meeting place.

I continue to deliver package after package, and the constant anxiety that accompanies me becomes bearable. My thoughts focus on the telephone call I'm expecting this evening. Everything else is secondary.

Seven o'clock comes. I refuse to take another package and quickly leave for home. I pedal fast through street after street and almost fall off my bicycle when I encounter the end of a human line.

"What's happened?" I ask the girl standing in front of me.

"Check point." She says nervously.

"Why so thorough?" I shudder at the careful body search two soldiers carry out on an old woman.

"I heard that members of the underground damaged electricity cables at the main headquarters," she whispers, biting her lip.

"When we harass them, they harass us in return."

I fumble in the fruit packet in the basket, making sure nothing suspicious is still underneath it.

Everything is all right. I sigh with relief and glance at my watch again. It is seven-thirty.

The soldiers check the documents of two boys, asking all of us to step back when they take a small penknife from one of them. He explains that he uses the penknife for work in his uncle's carpentry shop, but his explanation doesn't appear to satisfy them.

Shouts and commands in Germans. A black car glides forward and the two boys disappear inside it.

"They'll find out." The girl turns round to me and seems on the verge of fainting. "I...I must get away." Turning her head from side to side, she rocks on her heels.

"Calm down," I whisper firmly and move closer to her. "Show me your papers."

She takes her papers out of her coat pocket, grasping them.

"Show me," I ask again and she hands them to me with trembling fingers.

I look at the picture and then at the girl, quickly read what is written and return the papers to her.

"Mademoiselle Eve Clouseau, it's perfect." I smile at her.

"And what if they find out?" She continues to tremble and look around her fearfully. "What will I do? Where will they take me?"

"You must calm down." I hold her hand. "Smile and say nothing, just answer what they ask you."

Again I glance at my watch. A quarter to eight. I no longer have any chance of getting back in time for the call. I sigh with disappointment. Another glance at the terrified girl reminds me of what really matters and I scold myself for my lack of proportion.

"Papers," the German orders us, and I smile at him and hand him mine. "Papers!" He barks at the girl and she nods and hands them to him.

He examines mine and then hers, glances at her photograph and narrows his eyes to see the stamp. He hands the papers to the second soldier and signals to me to turn around. His hands fumble in my pockets and then touch my body. He feels my hips, my buttocks and then, with complete indifference, my breasts.

"This one has a special permit," he says to the soldier beside him, nodding at me, and waving me aside. He carries out the same search on the girl, and when he reaches her breasts, she chokes and he grins mockingly.

"Papers!" He yells at the man standing behind us, and the second soldier returns our papers. Holding my bicycle, I pull the girl along with my other hand.

She appears amazed and doesn't stop looking back.

"Come on. Look in front of you," I scold her, and she shakes her head and walks along the sidewalk with me.

"Thank you," she murmurs.

"You're welcome. I didn't do anything." I caress her head.

"I don't leave the house a lot," she whispers. "I don't know what I was thinking when I decided to take a walk in the fresh air today of all days."

"Do you want me to walk you home?"

"I live in the next street." She stopped at the entrance to an alleyway and hugged me. "I was paralyzed with fear," she says with a sob. "It doesn't matter how often they explain to me how to deal with the checks, when I see those gray or black uniforms, I just get paralyzed."

"You aren't alone." I blurt out with a bitter laugh. "We're all afraid of them."

"Maybe one day I'll understand why they're so afraid of me." She kisses my cheek and disappears into the alleyway.

I sigh and look at my watch. It is one minute past eight. Mounting my bicycle I ride slowly along the sidewalk. Even though I missed my call, I gained a rare moment of peace. I witnessed the sweet, tiny victory of a young girl. Instead of being drawn into a painful sense of disappointment, I prefer to be reinforced by a sense of satisfaction that was overwhelming me.

I open the door to the apartment at ten past eight and look sorrowfully at Marie.

"He hasn't called yet." She sits down in the chair next to the telephone table and I put my hand over my heart and hurry to sit down on the sofa. "It isn't like him to be late, he is always so punctual." She looks at the telephone and I do the same.

"Maybe something's happened." I bite my nails, and jump to my feet when the desired sound is heard.

She points to the receiver and I step back, shaking my head. All the anticipation drains away the second the phone rings, and I don't remember what I wanted to say to him.

Marie picks up the receiver and greets him enthusiastically. She tells him about her back pain and the weather and even about her impressive shopping on the black market.

I stare at her without being able to move.

"Yes, she's here." She hands me the receiver, and I step forward and grasp it fearfully.

"Josephine?" I hear his strong voice.

"Gabriel."

"I missed you yesterday."

He sounds so far away, and my heart beats faster. "I was taking care of a sick friend," I say, and fall silent.

"How do you feel?"

"All right, and you?"

"Fine."

"Good. I hope business is good." I hit myself on my head when I understand that I'm wasting precious time on casual conversation.

"Always." He laughs. "And I hope you're taking care of yourself."

"Always."

"Is there anything I can do to make my wife happy?"

Come back. Come back. Come back. The words echo in my mind again and again.

"Everything is fine, I don't need a thing."

"So take care of yourself," he says quietly.

Come back. Come back. Come back.

"You too."

I continue to hold the receiver even after he hangs up, and then collapse on the sofa. Why didn't I tell him I miss him? Why didn't I ask him to come back to me? Why didn't I tell him I miss him so much my heart weeps with longing for him.

Curling into a fetal position, I close my eyes. I wasted a precious conversation on senseless words, and now he is far away again. So far away, physically and mentally. I sense Marie covering me with a blanket, and can't even open my mouth to thank her.

I wake and my body is trembling and I'm breathing heavily. The room is filled with light and I have difficulty opening my eyes, refusing Marie's pleas that I move into the bedroom. She wanders around me all day and when my fever refuses to drop, she begs me to allow her to call a doctor. I hear myself murmuring it's just a cold and sink into dreams again.

I occasionally open my eyes and seem to sense his presence, smell his scent and even take pleasure in his comforting caress, but then the room grows clear and I find it deserted. I drink a little tea and fall asleep again. Drink some soup and stumble to the bathroom. Sleep and wake and again sink into dreams.

All those dear to me come to visit. My father scolds me for being irresponsible, and I try and justify myself. He explains that I got myself into a strategic game that is too big for me. That I'm just a pawn on a board who always sacrifice themselves. I try and hide my hurt and am determined to stand up for myself, but his image fades and Claude takes his place in the armchair.

"I'm so glad you're here," I murmur with feeling. "I didn't have time to tell you how proud I am of you."

"Smile," he orders quietly, and I look at him uncomprehendingly. "I sacrificed myself for a great purpose, and you can't even carry out a few dispatches without collapsing."

"But…but…"

His hair tumbles in ordered ringlets to his shoulders, and I blink, trying to understand how Odette came to sit in his place.

"You can't afford to look like a beggar." She giggles and arranges a clip on her head." Fix your dress and powder your nose. Didn't I teach you anything?"

"I have a cold."

"A girl of your class in a brothel?"

"Brigitte?" I ask excitedly and she shakes her head in disappointment.

"What do you think your man will say when he hears about it?"

"He isn't really my man," I whisper, trying to hold her hand. "It was just a trick to save me."

The space around me whirls and the drawing room is painted in shining white. The sofa is in the center of a field of white lilies, and I lean down to pick one and bring it to my nose.

"How can anyone be afraid of something so delicate and noble?" The girl

I encountered at the check point asks me with a broad smile.

The lilies darken, likewise the walls of the room.

I take a deep breath and sit up heavily.

"The fever is breaking." Marie strokes my forehead, and I squint in an effort to understand if she is real.

"That was a hard night," I pant.

"Night?" She laughs and pours hot water into a cup on the table. "You've been holding entire conversations with yourself for five days."

"That's impossible." I sip the tea and look suspiciously at her.

She walks into the corridor and returns with a newspaper in her hands. When I look at the date my eyes open in surprise.

"Yesterday, I was at the door, about to call a doctor." She feels my forehead again. "I stopped myself when you started talking again. It was too dangerous."

"What did I say?"

"What didn't you say?" She laughs. "If the doctor heard you he'd have thought you were carrying the burden of the entire war on your shoulders."

I frown with embarrassment.

"Get up and wash." She helps me to get up. "Your husband will call in an hour, and we don't want him to worry."

"Has he called since the last time?" My heart signals a beat of existence.

"Yesterday. And he was a bit disappointed not to find you at home to take his call."

"So you didn't tell him I have a cold?"

"I didn't think it right to worry him when he is so far away." She accompanies me to the door of the bathroom and urges me inside. "If you permit me to interfere, maybe in this conversation, you should tell him something he expects to hear." She leaves me and goes into the kitchen.

I wash quickly, put on my robe and sit down on the sofa next to the telephone table. Again and again, I imagine the conversation I wish to have with him, praying for the courage to tell him just one thing.

The hands of the clock refuse to move. I stand up, go to the window, peep out and return to the chair. I go to the dresser, light a cigarette and immediately put it out. Walk to the door of the bedroom, knock on the door and drag myself back to the chair.

The ringing of the telephone sounds as if it's coming from a dream. Only on the third ring do I manage to lift the receiver'

"Gabriel?"

"Josephine?" His voice plays on my heart strings.

"Yes?"

"How are you feeling?"

"Everything is fine."

"I understand that you are still visiting your sick friend every day."

"Yes." I laugh quietly.

"Are you taking care of yourself?"

"Trying."

"Are you doing something I wouldn't do?"

"Probably."

He laughs, and I close my eyes and absorb the sound that warms my heart.

"If so, can I do something to make my wife happy?"

Come back. Come back. Come back.

"Ah…everything is fine. Marie is taking care of me." I can hear the cracks in my heart and bite my lips.

"Good. So take care of yourself."

"You too…" I wipe away the perspiration from my forehead and beat my breast in disappointment. "Gabriel?" I raise my voice.

"Yes?"

"I…I think there is something else you could do." I can't breathe.

"Yes?"

"Come home."

"Your wish is my command."

My sigh of relief seems to merge with his, and I put down the receiver and hug myself. My heart is dancing and my lips widen in a smile.

CHAPTER SEVENTEEN

I glance at the date on today's newspaper and then at the one Marie brought me on the day I last spoke to Gabriel on the telephone.

It's hard to believe that three weeks have gone by. In the first week, expectation controlled everything I did. Waking excitedly alternating with hours of disappointment, and then those damned evenings when the apartment door refused to open and the man my heart longed to see, remained so far away.

From the second week, expectation dulled and disappointment became an integral part of my existence. Sometimes it seems to me that if the anxiety of carrying out my missions wasn't so strong, I might even have enjoyed them.

I leave the brothel as speedily as I entered, buttoning up my coat. My short stay there shocks me again every time the *Madame* observes me, making me feel too exposed. I still don't understand how the girls working there can degrade themselves by serving men in general, and the soldiers of the occupying army in particular. Those Germans also claim ownership of French women, which revolts me. The girls whose giggles and flattering words I heard this evening, disgust me even more than the soldiers who exploit them.

Feeling the note in my breast, I wheel my bicycle through the yards. An hour later, I'm at the meeting-apartment door, holding the handle, two knocks, the whispered code and I'm inside. Maurice stands there, erect and tense, his arms folded, the members of the organization seated in front of him. "You shouldn't have brought him here," he said, looking at a small shrinking figure seated between two men.

"We did you a favor by agreeing to put ourselves at risk." The man on the right of the figure stands up, and I retreat when I see he's the filthy man who received the revolver I brought.

"You should have waited until tomorrow and taken him directly to the contact," Maurice raises his voice.

"I don't work for you." The man tosses a cigarette butt on the floor. "Our place is in the forests, shooting Nazis in the head, not babysitting some stinking child."

"It's no less important." Natalie stands next to Maurice. "These rescue missions are no less important." Walking forward quietly, I sit on the armrest of Veronique's chair.

"You're the ones who decided it's important," the man says spitefully. "Putting us at risk to save the life of a parasite."

"Don't say that!" Natali clenches her hands. "Does this little boy look like a parasite to you?"

I turn and look at the small figure, trembling at the sight of a frail child holding his knees and looking down. His hair is coal-black, his skin pale and he looks exhausted and starving.

"Anyone who interferes with our fighting is a parasite." The man smiles provocatively at her.

"Let's get down to business," Veronique intervenes. "He has to be hidden until tomorrow and, unfortunately, I can't take him home with me."

"Maybe we can take him?" Natalie looks beseechingly at Maurice.

"We ourselves are in hiding." He caresses her head. "I have no idea where we'll be tonight, how can we take a child with us?"

"So we'll let him loose in the street," the man said indifferently, lighting a cigarette. "Someone will find him. And if he's lucky, it won't be a German soldier." He grins and I can't stop looking at the child.

"Really, Phillipe?" Natalie cried out. "Would you really do something like that?"

"Easily." He drops ash on the floor. "You've forgotten we're fighters. We have a great and crucial purpose, we can't involve ourselves with trivialities. We have to liberate France, no matter what the price is."

The boy looks up and his doe-like eyes gaze at me.

"I'll take him," I hear myself murmur, paling when all heads turn to me, and I realize what I've taken on myself.

"If I'm not mistaken…" The man steps forward and examines me. "I suggested you serve the fighters in a more effective way."

"Shut up!" I stand up and push him aside, go over to the boy and kneel down in front of him. "What are we fighting for?" I ask quietly, stroking his knee.

"*Vive la France,*" Philippe shouts, smiling. "Liberate our country from the bastards who've invaded it."

"Is that really our purpose?" I blurt out with a bitter laugh. "Liberate France from those German bastards so bastards like you can be free?"

The smile is wiped off his face.

"We're supposed to be the good ones and they, the bad." I shake my head in disappointment. "We're supposed to liberate France from the evil that rules her, not adopt evil. They also justify their evil in a thousand different ways. You've just done the very same thing." I hold out my hand to the child and he grasps it, getting down from the chair. "Unlike you, along with liberating France, I'm fighting to restore my pride." Straightening up, I hand Veronique the note I'd received from Madame Distel.

Philippe waves his hand dismissively, the others remain quiet. All heads are bowed, while Maurice and Natalie smile painfully at me. Veronique follows us to the door and hugs me.

"Tomorrow at six in the evening, be at Place de la Bastille without him," she whispers in my ear. "Wait on the bench and you'll be contacted with instructions."

I nod.

"Josephine, thank you for making me proud now." She presses my arm and returns to her seat.

Philippe starts making a speech about the need for recruiting more fighters and nobody is looking at us. This mission is mine, and its failure or success is solely up to me.

I take the child downstairs and start to realize the implications of my decision. How can I even think about failure when the price is so high? A cold sweat envelops me, and the small hand almost slips from mine.

"My name is Josephine," I whisper. "What's your name?"

He neither responds nor raises his head to look at me.

"How old are you?'

He doesn't respond.

I put him on the bicycle seat, glance into the street and wipe the perspiration from my forehead and neck. I don't feel the cold, only increasing, terrible anxiety. I wheel the bicycle out of the building area. and we are now completely exposed.

"Better you don't talk," I tell him, but am actually speaking to myself, "You're the son of a sick friend and I'm taking you to stay with me tonight."

I wheel the bicycle along the sidewalk and he stretches out his arms to grasp the handlebars and closes his eyes.

"You must be afraid. I'm also afraid," I murmur. "The truth is I'm really, really afraid. If we're caught it won't be pleasant."

We pass an old man. He stands close to the wall and smiles at me.

Dear God, I've never been so afraid. I shudder when I notice a group of soldiers marching towards us on the sidewalk, and turn the bicycle into an alley. It takes us double the usual amount of time, each time I think I spot danger, I turn into one of the narrow alleyways. Just as my body seems to be petrified with anxiety, we reach the corner of my street.

"We're here." I look round, exhausted, and help the boy off the bicycle. He holds out his hand and we go upstairs. When we reach Marion's apartment, I remove my shoes and put my finger to my mouth, signaling him to be quiet.

The groans and murmurs from the apartment are in French and German and I can't breathe. I pick up the child and tiptoe, praying the cursed door won't open.

When we reach my apartment, I stumble inside, setting the child on his feet and bolt the locks. Only then can I take a deep breath.

"I'm glad you're in time for dinner…" Marie falls silent, staring at the child.

"This is…my sick friend's son," I stammer, wiping away the perspiration from my forehead.

"He looks so dirty and hungry." Marie grimaces sadly.

"Yes. She asked me to look after him tonight."

"So, what are you waiting for?" She shakes her head and looks reproachfully at me. "Come on, we'll fill him a warm bath and make him some dinner."

"Thank you, Marie." Hiding my eyes with my hand, I fight off tears.

She leads the child gently into the bathroom and fills the tub with warm water. I strip him and try to hide my distress at the sight of his thin body. He doesn't speak a word, just occasionally glances at the bath.

Marie lifts him easily into the water. Asking me to soap him, she bends over the sink, scrubbing his clothes.

The sense of anxiety doesn't leave me and my movements are clumsy. I almost drop him when taking him out of the bath, and murmur words of apology.

Marie leaves the room, returning with one of Gabriel's long, flannel vests. When she dresses him, it reaches down to his feet and he gives her a small, shy smile.

"So you know how to smile." She gives him a motherly smile, and I can't understand her lack of the fear that is blurring my senses.

Marie takes him into the dining room and seats him at the head of the table in Gabriel's chair. She strokes his head and goes into the kitchen. I sit down beside him and bite my nails. With each glance at him, my fear increases. I have never felt such terror. Not even when I brought the sisters to my wedding party, then it didn't leave me dizzy and unable to breathe like now.

Marie returns with two plates. The child looks wonderingly at the meat and looks at me.

"Eat." I nod.

He doesn't pick up his fork.

"Eat. It's for you." I pick up the fork and hand it to him.

He points at my plate and I shake my head uncomprehendingly.

"He's waiting for you to start eating," Marie says in a choked voice.

I look at the boy and he nods.

"You have good manners." I cough to hide the tremor in my voice and put some meat on my fork.

He holds the knife and fork, cutting small pieces for himself and eating slowly and quietly, every now and then taking a sip of water from the glass. I'm incapable of eating, drinking or breathing. I can only gaze at the child, my heart ripped to pieces.

He eats several pieces and then puts his hand on his belly, contracting with pain.

"That's enough. You've eaten very nicely," Marie declares with false cheerfulness. "Now we'll put you to bed." She lifts him from the chair and he puts his arms around her neck. The sight of them together, an old woman and a frail boy clinging to her as if to a savior, makes me choke.

She walks confidently into Gabriel's bedroom and I follow her. She puts him in the middle of the bed and he closes his eyes and yawns.

"It would be best if you slept with him tonight," she whispers. "If he wakes in the middle of the night, you must make sure he doesn't make a sound."

"Sleep?" I look from him to her. "Marie, I am so afraid, there is no chance of my sleeping tonight. And if I do fall asleep, there's every chance I'll wake up shrieking with fear."

She smiles understandingly at me and lights a candle on the dresser.

"I'll sleep with him." She strokes the boy's head and turns off the light.

Going into the drawing room, I light a candle on the mantelpiece and switch off all the lights in the house. I sit down in the armchair next to the window and peep into the street. Tears roll down my cheeks and I sob quietly. The lullaby Marie is humming in the bedroom penetrates my veins and my mental pain is so strong I understand how it feels when the heart weeps.

I light a cigarette and sniff, not even trying to stem the tears burning my skin. The minutes pass and I light cigarette after cigarette, my throat burns, my eyes burn and fear closes in on me.

"May I join you?" Marie whispers, sitting down on the sofa.

"I'm so afraid."

"You have to calm down. If by some chance someone comes here, I will say I brought him," she says sternly.

"Do you think I'm afraid for myself?" The snort of laughter becomes a wail. "I'm willing to go out into the street at this very minute and shout that I'm to blame for this war. Marie I'm terrified by the thought that someone will come here and decide that this tiny chick lying in that bed constitutes some threat and must be punished." I walk from the fireplace to the passage and back. "I can't breathe." My hand closes on my throat and I cough. "I'm so frightened by the thought that something might happen, and the fear is suffocating me."

Standing up, she pulls me onto the sofa, sits beside me and rubs my back. "Take a deep breath." Her whisper caresses my ear and I try to breathe in and cough. "Again." I open my mouth and feel the salty taste of my tears.

"I'm afraid, too, for the very same reason." She pats my back and sighs. "But we must be strong and make sure this chick reaches a safe haven."

Hugging myself, I burst into tears.

"Shhh…" Glancing at the door, she shakes me. "Josephine, you have to pull yourself together! We have an important task now, you will feel terrible if we fail because you can't control your emotions."

"Forgive me, you're right." I put my hand over my mouth and forcefully stop the sobbing. "It's just that I feel I've taken on a role that's far too big for me."

"No, it is exactly the right size for you." Spreading a blanket over the two of us, she leans back.

Neither of us says a word when Marion's door closes and loud steps are heard on the stairs, but my breath seems to stop. The sound of a car engine cuts through the silence, and both of us sigh with relief when quiet is restored.

My head jerks and my eyes close, but I make myself open them and stay focused. Again my eyes close and I sit up in alarm, refusing to fall asleep.

Marie gets up and goes into the bedroom, returning after a few minutes. Her head rests on my shoulder, and every time I wake, both of us turn and look fearfully at the door.

"I'll make coffee." She yawns, drawing the curtain slightly.

Tiredly, I look out at the illuminated street, realizing that we'd got safely through the night. Getting up, I go into the bedroom and lean against the door. I gaze at the child who has taken over Gabriel's side of the bed. His small hands grasp the blanket, holding it to his neck. The brief moment of relief fades and again helplessness overwhelms me.

As if sensing my gaze, the tiny body stretches and he sits up and stares at me.

"Good morning." I smile at him. "I hope you slept well."

He nods and gets down from the bed, goes by himself into the bathroom, stands on the tips of his toes, opens the tap and washes his face and hands. When he's dried himself, he turns his head and his big black eyes look questioningly at me.

"We'll have breakfast now." I smile at him, waving in the direction of the dining room.

He follows me into the dining room, standing until I am seated. Only then does he very naturally sit in Gabriel's place.

Marie comes in, puts a jug of coffee on the table and a plate of fruit, leaning over to kiss his head. He gives her his gentle smile, and I rub my chest to calm the burning of my heart. She goes out again, returning with a tray of food. She sits down opposite me and only after we begin eating, does he pick up his fork.

"What's your name?" Marie asks, stroking his hair.

He continues to eat quietly.

"How old are you?" She tries again.

He doesn't even raise his eyes from the plate.

Marie looks at me and I shrug.

"This afternoon, I will receive information about his address," I say, and we both glance at the clock on the wall.

She nods, continuing to gaze at the boy. He appears to be in a world of his own, completely unexcited by what I've said.

After the meal, I take him into the drawing room and ask him to be quiet. It's such a stupid request to make of a child who hasn't made a sound since I met him, but fear of an unexpected visit from our neighbor drives me crazy.

He sits down on the carpet in front of the fireplace and Marie brings him paper and pencils. Her behavior is natural and calming and I feel even more clumsy and confused. He draws for a few minutes and then, putting the picture down on the table, he goes over to the chess board and sits down. We both examine the drawing with curiosity, and I wonder how a drawing in only one color, gray, can look so colorful. A sun with burning rays, a rainbow penetrating a cloud and two large figures holding the hands of two small ones, a boy and a girl. They're all smiling.

I put my hand over my heart and find it hard to stop the tears.

"A beautiful picture," Marie declares in a trembling voice and escapes into the passage so he won't see her tears.

I blow my nose and hear the faint sound of tapping coming from the chess board. The boy is holding a pawn and tapping with it.

"Would you like me to teach you to play?" Getting up, I sit down opposite him. "I'm not really very good at the game but I can teach you the rules."

Frowning, he focuses on the board.

"The bishop moves in straight lines." I point to it and continue. "The rook moves diagonally, the pawns are the minor soldiers and the queen…"

Before I have time to finish, he moves his pawn.

"So you know the game?"

Without responding he stares at my piece.

I make my move and a light seems to gleam in his eyes. He doesn't pause to think before making his next move, and I continue to move my pieces whenever it's my turn.

"Ah, I think you've won." I scratch my head in confusion and a little smile spreads over his handsome face. He arranges the pieces on the board once again and for several hours I suffer one defeat after another. I plead for a break and, fortunately, Marie calls us for lunch, but immediately afterwards, he returns enthusiastically to the chess table.

This time I try a more serious challenge, but no matter what strategy I choose, he seems to anticipate all my moves. I smile when he shakes his head in disappointment after knocking over my queen, and I look at the watch on my wrist.

I stand up in alarm. "I didn't notice the time."

He arranges the pieces again as if he hadn't heard me.

"I have to go and meet someone," I tell him. "Marie will stay here with you and I'll try and get back as soon as possible."

Putting on my coat, I open the door and peep out into the stairwell. The building is quiet, but again anxiety grips me and I can hardly breathe.

I pass Marion's apartment and the silence there only makes me more anxious. She might decide to pop in at any minute, and I have no idea of whether Marie would be able to cope with her interrogations. Briefly I regret not taking the boy with me. I'm not sure what puts him more at risk, staying at home or wandering outside.

The way to the square passes safely and when I arrive I lean my bicycle against the bench and sit down. I'm certain the tension is obvious in my face but nonetheless smile at passersby. None of them sit down beside me.

The minutes pass. The square darkens and the cold penetrates my bones.

"Bon soir, madame." An eastern looking man sits down beside me.

"Good evening to you, too." I hold my bag tightly.

"I understand you have a fleur-de-lis in your apartment."

I nod.

"I have new papers for him. I need you to return to the apartment and bring him here." He puts a folded newspaper down beside me and, putting it in my lap, I hide the paper inside it in my bag.

"Where will you take him?"

"To a safe place."

"I need to know where."

"Better not."

"I won't bring him to you unless I know where you're taking him."

"The papers show his name is Khalil," the man whispers, opening the newspaper to hide his face. "I'll take him to the Great Mosque where the Imam will take care of him."

"But he isn't a Muslim." I fold my arms tightly, eaten up by tension.

"From now on he's a Muslim child called Khalil. And you agreed to take care of him today until I finished work."

"Is there no other place? Maybe somewhere he'll be with others like him. Maybe…"

"Do you really want him to go to a place where others like him are being held?"

"No, I meant that…"

"Don't worry." He puts his hand over mine. "Our aim is the same. With Allah's help we will do everything to keep him safe until war ends."

"I wish I could stop worrying." I smile at two passing German soldiers.

"The fleur-de-lis will be safe with us." He looks through the newspaper. "But I need you to bring him to me as soon as possible so that I won't attract attention by waiting here."

"All right." With a sigh, I hold my bicycle. "I have no other choice but to trust you."

I mount my bicycle and ride back home, stop for a routine check of my papers and continue to peddle hard. I reach the corner of the street and blink several times to make sure I'm not hallucinating and that Gabriel's car really is parked in front of the building.

My heart starts to beat wildly. I throw down my bicycle in the entrance and rush upstairs. Excitement overcomes anxiety and only when I reach the door do I stop. If I'm disappointed this time, I'll be crushed.

Quickly opening the door, I enter quietly and catch my breath.

The man who has captured my heart and my dreams is sitting in his elegant suit in front of a chess board and, on the other side, in clean, ironed clothes, sits the small boy. Both are concentrating on the board, and then Gabriel looks up and sees me.

"Josephine." He rises. Putting my hand over my heart, I bite my lips.

He strides towards me, his eyes fixed on mine, and when I feel he is close enough I drop my bag on the floor. I cling to him and put my head on his chest. His hand touches my head and for several precious seconds nothing else exists in the world save for this man. I close my eyes and breathe in his scent, his confidence and his comfort, and then open them again. Bitter reality is like a blow to my belly.

"I apologize." I force myself to move away from him. "I'd like to stay with you but…" I turn my head to the child, he is still gazing at the board.

"I have to take him to his father. He is waiting at the *Place de la Bastille*." Gripping Gabriel's hand, I long to sense his confidence for one moment longer, and then I rub my forehead and pull myself together. "His name is Khalil, he's the son of my sick friend and his father is waiting for him."

"I'll come with you."

My heart sinks and my eyes open in surprise.

"I don't want to put you at risk. I prefer…"

"No arguments." He presses my hand and takes his coat from the hook.

I nod, unable even to open my mouth to thank him. I merely stare at him, feeling as if I can now release the huge stone pressing down on my shoulders.

Marie comes out of the passage, a knapsack in her hand, she seems worried and confused. She explains in half sentences that she's put food in the knapsack and can't stop looking at the boy. She opens the knapsack, rubs her forehead and closes it again.

"Maybe I should add a few things," she murmurs.

"I'll take it." I take the knapsack from her and her anxiety fuels my own. I'm about to hand over my frail chick to a man I don't know and pressure blurs my senses. "I can't send him off with just a bit of food." I bite my nails and hug the knapsack. "Give me some money," I plead, turning to Gabriel, who takes a number of notes out of his pocket and hands them to me. I hide them in the depths of the knapsack and start breathing heavily. "It's not enough," I mutter, running into the bedroom and returning to the drawing room, holding the black velvet box with the diamond necklace in my hand. "I know you gave me this as a gift, but I prefer him to have it. Maybe it will help him."

Gabriel looks quietly at me and nods consent.

Removing the packet of food, I put in the notes and the box. On top, I replace the food and turn back to the boy.

"We have to go now," I say in a choked voice. He moves one piece on the board and gets up, buttons up his coat and stands beside Gabriel. Putting his small hand in Gabriel's large one, he smiles at him.

My heart is beating wildly.

"Leon, we're taking you to a safe place now." Gabriel bends down and strokes the boy's head. Marie covers her mouth and sobs quietly.

"How do you know his name?" I bite my lip.

"He told me." Gabriel lifts the child in his arms and goes to the door.

"From now on, your name is Khalil," I tell the child and, when he doesn't respond, I look at Gabriel.

"He'll be all right," he hugs my shoulders.

"*Bon chance.*" Marie smiles a sad smile. "I'll pray to God to keep you safe." Standing on the tips of her toes, she kisses the boy's forehead.

Gently stroking her cheek, he smiles.

Coughing again, I sniff, and Gabriel opens the door. We go quietly downstairs and as we pass Marion's apartment, I blush. The groaning and murmuring in German and French are clearly heard in the corridor, and when I glance at Gabriel, I see him rolling his eyes.

Opening the back door of the car, he seats the boy and I sit down next to him. The moment the car starts moving, I take the child's hand and stroke it.

Rain drops dirty the windscreen. Gabriel drives slowly, occasionally glancing at us in the mirror.

I see two German soldiers inspecting a passerby's papers and shrink in my place. The anxiety is so strong I suspect that if we're stopped I won't be able to hide it.

"We're here," Gabriel says quietly and parks at the curb.

"I'll take him to his father," I say, choking when I see the child's excited expression. "It's just a man who has agreed to help us pretend in order to help you," I explain apologetically, and the boy's face falls. "He's a good man, he'll make sure to take you to a safe place where you'll stay until your parents return." The child looks down and nods. "You must remember that your name is Khalil and that this man is your father, otherwise we'll all be in great trouble."

"Josephine, he understands." Gabriel sighs and gets out of the car. He opens the door, waits for me to get out and lifts the child into his arms.

"Lead on," he says, stroking my arm.

Walking slowly, I notice the man sitting on the bench. Raindrops fall on his hat and clothing and the newspaper he's holding, is wet and crumpled. The few people passing in the square walk quickly, and those without umbrellas try to cover their heads and escape the rain.

I sit down beside him and he looks suspiciously up at Gabriel.

"This is my husband," I calm him.

Gabriel whispers something in the boy's ear, kisses his forehead and sets him on my knees. He walks away from us and lights a cigarette.

"It looks suspicious for me to be sitting in this rain." The man puts the newspaper on the bench and smiles at the boy.

"Better you give him to me now."

With shaking fingers I take out the boy's papers and give them to the man.

Three German soldiers march towards us and the man continues to smile but his eyes are darting about uneasily.

Gabriel stands in front of the soldiers and they stop. I can't hear what he says to them, but they point at the monument in the center of the square. A few seconds later he offers one a cigarette and laughs.

"We don't have time," the man whispers tensely.

"Very well." I stand the boy on his feet and hug him. "You must go with him now." The boy nods.

"I will try to come and visit you." I quickly wipe the tears from my eyes.

"Be a good boy and take care of yourself."

The man stands up and take's the boy's hand.

I put the knapsack on the boy's shoulders and when I step back, the boy takes my hand and puts his lips to it. He kisses it delicately and a wail rises in my throat.

"Au revoir, Josephine." He smiles the most beautiful smile I've ever seen.

"Au revoir, Leon," I stress his real name and walk away from them.

Raindrops fall on my face and I know the heavens are weeping with me. A large arm is placed around my waist, I put my head on Gabriel's shoulder and allow him to lead me to the car. I sit down in the front seat and when he is seated beside me, I sniff and press my head to the window. The man who has taken my fleur-de-lis has vanished and the sadness is unbearable.

Gabriel puts his hand on my thigh and strokes it. I put my palms together and hide them between my knees. Even his touch, which I have craved for so long, cannot comfort me now. Taking my hand he puts it to his lips and kisses it while maneuvering the car through the cold, gray streets. He says nothing, but I know he feels my pain.

He doesn't let go of my hand, not even when we reach our building, pressing me against him as we go upstairs. My tears have dried but my heart continues to weep.

Sounds of laughter come from Marion's apartment, and I feel that the universe is laughing at me. I shudder and frown with nausea.

"You're amazing," Gabriel says the minute the door closes behind us, and his small smile tugs at my heart strings.

"I don't feel amazing right now." My body clings to his and I put my head on his chest.

"You must learn to accept this pain and allow yourself to celebrate your victories." He caresses my head.

"There isn't any victory here." The tears return. "Only losses. They're still here and now it seems as if they'll stay forever."

"No. They won't." He disengages from me and takes off his coat.

"Do you know something I don't?" Tiredly, I wipe my tears.

"Many things." He winks at me.

Marie enters the drawing room and looks questioningly at us.

"He's in good hands." Gabriel smiles at her and when she sighs, it seems to me that she's aged ten years at least.

"I've made dinner for you and now, with your permission, I'll return to my apartment." She looks grief-stricken.

Gabriel helps her put her coat on and when she hugs me the current that passes between us makes my heart contract with pain. A fateful collaboration between two women who, until recently, were strangers, and who now share a terrible sadness.

"The bath water is hot," she says to Gabriel. "You should freshen up after your long journey. And try and let Josephine rest, she didn't sleep all night."

He nods and opens the door for her.

I find it hard to absorb that this man really is here. With me.

"I'll be quick." He loosens his tie and turns into the passage. "I know you're tired, but I'll be glad if you'll join me for dinner tonight."

"Of course." I yawn and stare at his huge back.

"I hope you're done with your adventures for today." He stops and looks round at me. "In about half an hour, the SS will raid some Resistance buildings."

"What?!" I step back in alarm.

"There's nothing to be done now," he says firmly. "You're lucky to be here and not wandering the streets."

"But…I must warn my friends." I look at the telephone and then at him.

"Josephine, it's out of the question." He opens his eyes warningly and walks on down the passage.

Thoughts whirl through my mind and I start walking about the drawing room in confusion. I look at the clock and then at the door and again at the clock. I hear the water in the bathroom and shake my head.

Natalie, Maurice, Veronique…they may be in the apartment and here I am, safe and protected. I can't call and warn them, I don't even know the apartment telephone number. And I can't put Gabriel at risk. What can I do?

I look at the clock and my shoulders droop. Half an hour. I might get there in time.

Quickly opening the door, I run downstairs. Marion's apartment is quiet and immediately after I pass it, I hear her door open.

"Where are you running off to?" Her voice makes me jump but I refuse to allow her to delay me and I continue to run.

The rain is stronger and I peddle hard. One street, then another and another and, apart from the scraping of my bicycle on the sidewalk, there isn't a sound to be heard. I don't stop to look at my watch or to apologize when the wheels of my bicycle splash two passing women.

Adrenalin overwhelms me. One more street and I'm there. Only one more street.

The wheels sail forward and I crash into a puddle on the street. My stockings tear and my knee is bleeding. I feel pain in my cheek, but pick up the bicycle and walk alongside it. The walk becomes a run and I trip in fear when I hear the sound of firing.

I hold my breath.

Shouts in German, pleading in French and again the sound of firing.

I've come too late.

Limping to the next building, I stand on tiptoes to look through the window overlooking the yard.

"Dear God," I hear myself mutter, and cannot tear my eyes away from the terrible sight in front of me.

People in civilian dress on their knees, their hands on their heads, and a score of Germans in black and gray uniforms shouting and continuing to drag more and more people out of the building.

I can't see their faces. I can't comprehend the shouts. I can't absorb the images.

Falling to my knees, I put my head in my hands. More shots.

The door of the apartment in front of me opens and I raise my head in alarm.

"Please, let me in," I beg the woman looking at me in shock.

She steps back when more shots are fired, and then she half closes her eyes and examines me. "Give me the earrings," she whispers, glancing fearfully at the door to the building.

Pulling them from my ears, I crawl forwards.

"In exchange, I won't tell them you're here." She takes the earrings from me and slams the door in my face.

Sobbing, I stare at the closed door. The shouts, weeping, pleading, shots, everything seems so close, and my body has turned to stone.

After a few moments, I manage to crawl to the staircase and tuck my body into the alcove underneath it. I pull my knees up to my chest and put my head on my arms. My body is tired, in pain, and my soul is crushed.

Every time I hear loud steps outside the building, I hold my breath and close my eyes, expecting to hear a shout directed at me. Expecting to feel a hand grasp my hair, dragging me outside, imagining the barrel of a gun held to my temple.

The icy cold penetrates my coat, freezing my bones and the sounds outside grow muffled. Anxiety turns my breathing into groans and as time passes, I can't understand how they don't hear me. Another shout. Another shot. More pleading. My limbs contract more and more until my body seems to become a steel ball.

And suddenly, quiet. Silence.

I squint in an attempt to see the hands on my watch. A few minutes after nine.

The curfew has begun and I'm still imprisoned here under the staircase. They missed me but I can find no comfort in that.

I hug myself and close my eyes. Every time I think I hear shooting, my eyes open in terror. Every time I think I hear steps approaching, a wail bursts from my throat.

I seem to sink into sleep and then wake in darkness. From time to time, I manage to straighten my arm to look at my watch and, at some point, I think that if the Germans don't put an end to me, the cold will do the work for them.

"Somebody left a bicycle here." I hear an excited voice speaking in French and I choke. My eyes open slowly and the lobby is filled with light. Two boys are examining the bicycle with interest and then start arguing over who saw it first. The tall boy pushes his friend and grabs the handlebars. Both of them leave the building laughing.

I try to straighten my legs and moan, managing to drag myself out of the alcove to rest on my knees. My jaws are locked and my teeth chatter. Any movement causes unbearable pain. Leaning against the wall, I get up.

Step by step I leave the building. My eyes are burning and I try and regulate my breathing.

My eyes fall on the place where the slaughter had taken place the night before, and I try to figure out where the people have disappeared to. The muddy ground is empty and apart from some bloodstained clothing, nothing is left of that cursed night.

I tighten my coat around me and walk to the end of the road. People pass by, all immersed in their own affairs. Nobody notices my distress. Slowly, I walk on, one street after another.

There is only one place in the world I want to be now and my mind commands my feet to keep moving forward.

I reach the entrance to the building and lean exhaustedly against the wall. Walking upstairs seems an impossible task. I've never felt so tired, so heavy and with every step, I seem to hear my bones cracking.

Dreamily I look at the tall figure leaning against the doorpost in a red silk robe.

"Where have you been all night?" Marion blows cigarette smoke towards me. "You look terrible."

"Thank you…" I manage to mutter and continue up. Another step and another and my teeth chatter even harder. The physical cold fuses with the cold in my heart. Hanging onto the door handle I throw myself inside the apartment.

"Good God!" Gabriel roars. "I thought they'd managed to catch you. Because of that damned curfew, I've been wandering about the apartment like a caged lion imagining the worst."

Staring at his ironed suit, I blink exhaustedly.

"Do you have any idea how irresponsible you are?" He sounds furious. My eyes fall on the bunch of keys in his hand. "I was about to start hunting the streets for you, and if I didn't find you, I'd have gone to the Gestapo offices. Because of you, I've spent the whole night thinking you were imprisoned in their cellar under interrogation."

"They didn't take anyone for interrogation." My voice trembles and I collapse on my knees.

"What happened?" He hurries towards me and kneels down. "What did they do to you? Did they harm you?" I feel his gentle caress on my head and groan in pain.

Cupping my chin in his hand, he carefully raises it. His eyes dart about my face uneasily.

"Gabriel, I think this game is too much for me." I collapse forward and feel his arms around me. Tears scald my skin and I shrink into his large, protective body.

"It's too much for all of us." He kisses my head and gets up. His arms are still holding me and I feel him walking me to the passage. I hear the door to the bathroom open and, unwillingly, I leave his embrace. The mirror above the sink reveals my broken image. My hair is disheveled, my cheek bruised and bleeding and there are dark smudges on my eyelids.

I look at the steam rising from the water filling the bath and close my eyes. "I am so sorry for making you worry." My voice cracks and a groan escapes my throat.

"Let's make sure it doesn't happen again." He doesn't sound angry, and I have to straighten my arms when he removes my coat.

"I'll manage from here." I hug myself and wait for him to leave the room.

I take off my clothes and get into the water. The heat shocks my body and I rub my arms in a despairing attempt to let the heat in. The sounds of firing echo in my mind and I groan in pain. A terrible sense of loneliness spreads through me.

Standing up I cover myself with the robe. The longing I'd felt for Gabriel during the time he was gone drains to a single point in my belly and presses there. I hurry to the door and open it. He leans against the passage wall in front of me and his strong, beautiful face looks quietly at me.

"I'm so glad you're back." Putting out my hand I place it on his chest, making sure I'm not hallucinating and that he really is here.

"I shouldn't have left you here alone for such a long time." He puts his hand over mine, and this touch makes my heart tremble. I cling to him and rub my cheek against his shirt. A rare moment of warmth and safety in the chaos of my mind. "Do you want something to eat?" He asks quietly. "Or should I make you a cup of tea?"

"No." I breathe in his intoxicating smell and sigh. "I'm tired. So tired…"

He puts his arm around my waist, my legs leave the floor and I feel him walking forward with me. My body lifts and is set down on the mattress. I can't open my eyes.

"Don't leave me alone."

"I have no intention of doing so." I feel the warmth of the blanket covering me and then his body sinking close beside me.

"Gabriel, I'm sorry. I shouldn't have asked you to return." I yawn into the pillow and feel for his arm. "Sometimes I forget it's just an act." I put his arm on my body and sigh with relief.

"I don't think either of us are very good actors." He slides his other arm under my neck and the upper part of his body is close to mine.

"I lied. I'm not really sorry…" My voice sounds to me as if it's coming from a dream and my thoughts evaporate into the mists of sleep.

CHAPTER EIGHTEEN

The sound of firing deafens my ears. Another shot. And another…

The lit candle on the dresser illuminates the large figure seated in the armchair opposite me. Gabriel smiles his small smile at me, and for a moment my heart seems to be slowly healing. I could stay lying here, looking at him for hours. A stranger who had taken me in and became my safe haven.

"I waited to have dinner with you." Gabriel scratches his chin without taking his eyes off me.

"Is it evening already?" I stretch my arms.

"I considered waking you a few hours ago, but Marie insisted I allow you to go on sleeping." His hypnotic smile returned to adorn his face.

"I think she was right." I yawn and sit up. "If the firing hadn't woken me, I could have gone on sleeping."

"What firing?" He turns his glance to the closed curtains then back at me.

"In my mind." I point to my head. "I heard it again and again."

"You should have listened to me," he murmurs, then stands up. "Will you join me in the drawing room and I'll bring you a glass of tea before dinner?"

I tie the belt of my robe and follow him. He goes to the kitchen and I go into the drawing room. Sitting on the sofa I gaze at the chess board. My foot jerks restlessly and I realize that the physical distance between us, even if it's only a passageway, troubles me.

He returns with a jug and a cup and I can't stop looking at him. He notices my gaze and responds with a small smile. He hands me the cup which I put it to my lips, having difficulty looking away from him.

"Would you like something stronger?"

I shake my head.

Gabriel pours himself a small glass of cognac and, as he brushes his fingers through his hair, loud knocks are heard at the door.

"They've come for me." I get up in confusion and Gabriel frowns irritably, gesturing to me to sit down again. "I must get dressed…I think it's better if…" Hysteria overwhelms me.

"Josephine, let me handle this." His tone is quiet but firm. "Don't say a word."

"Open the door."

The shout makes me shrink back in the chair. I recognize the voice and my heart starts beating frantically.

Gabriel opens the door, continuing to hold the handle. "Good evening, Herr Zemel." He greets the German with ease.

"Monsieur Augustine." The German clicks his heel and doesn't hold out his hand to shake. "I've come to take your wife for questioning." He pushes open the door and now I see Marion standing beside him.

"Gabriel." She walks hesitantly inside. "I warned you about her. I told you she's dangerous." Gabriel ignores her and continues to look at Zemel. "Why do you have to take my wife for questioning?"

"She left the apartment yesterday evening and only returned this morning." Zemel responds vindictively. "She spent the night outside while the SS was arresting members of the Underground. It is important that we investigate her connection with these criminals."

"I saw her," Marion interrupted. "Last night and this morning as well when she returned wet and filthy. What the hell was she doing outside?"

The sounds of firing return to echo in my mind, but instead of increasing the anxiety, they dull it as hatred burns in my belly. Suddenly, I feel clearer than ever.

"I think there's been some misunderstanding." Gabriel folds his arms. "Josephine spent…"

"Don't lie to them on my behalf, mon amour." Standing up, I tighten the belt of my robe. Marion and Zemel look at me in surprise whereas Gabriel's eyes are warning.

"I'm willing to come in for questioning." My voice is level. "I'll be glad to come in for questioning." Walking around the sofa, I stand in front of them. "I'll tell all the interrogators there that my beloved husband is betraying me." I glance harshly at Gabriel and see his eyes contract uncomprehendingly. "After weeks away and leaving me here alone, he finally came back yesterday and tells me he has to go to the office. To the office!" I say with fake anger. "I sensed he was lying." I swiftly glance at Marion. "I went out into the corridor and heard noises coming from her apartment." I point accusingly. "I went downstairs and the sounds coming out of her apartment left no room for interpretation. She had a man with her and they were engaged in sexual activity."

Marion's cheeks redden.

"I have no doubt she was with my husband." I gaze fixedly into Zemel's frozen eyes. "Do you understand? He's broken my heart!"

Zemel frowns and I cover my face with my hands and sob. "I left the apartment distraught and went to sleep at a friend's apartment. I don't want to be here. I prefer to be anywhere else, even the offices of the Gestapo, just not with this traitor."

"She's lying…" I hear confusion in Marion's voice.

"Be quiet," Zemel reprimands her.

"I'll be happy to discover that I'm lying," a shriek bursts from my throat. "In fact, I insist you take me for questioning, but take both of them as well!" I don't dare look at Gabriel. "Maybe your interrogators will succeed in making my husband confess to his affair, because I can't."

"We don't investigate such silly things." Zemel barks irritably.

"Why not?" I bark back at him. "Doesn't it matter to you that someone in the service of the Fuhrer is an unfaithful man who can't be trusted?"

"Your husband wasn't with her last evening." Zemel lights himself a cigarette and the expression on his face changes.

"How can you be so sure?"

"He was with me." His lie shot into the space of the room with ease. "I was with him at his office and then he joined us for dinner."

"Gabriel?" I turn questioningly to him.

Expressionlessly, he nodded.

"It's hard for me to believe. I'm sick and tired of her flirtatiousness. Sick and tired of her refusing to accept that you chose me. She simply won't understand that you are **my** husband. And if you weren't with her, then who was?" I look at Marion again.

"No-one was with me." She looks fearfully at Zemel. "You were probably imagining it."

I scratch my head and sniff. "Then…you aren't having an affair with my husband?"

Clenching her teeth, she shakes her head.

"Oh, I am so sorry." I approach Gabriel and wind my arms around him. "My jealousy is driving me mad."

"It's all right." He kisses my head. "I should have stayed with you yesterday and put off the work that had accumulated."

"Yes." I rub my cheek against his shirt, wondering if my act is succeeding or failing.

"I think you've received an explanation from my wife with regard to her absence last night." Gabriel sounds amused. "A rather embarrassing one, I'd say…"

"Yes." Zemel grins. "You must explain to her that this is no time to be talking of betrayals."

"Perhaps you'll join us for a drink?" Gabriel addresses them without pushing me away.

"Not tonight," Zemel responds, exhaling smoke. "I have other plans." He pulls Marion back, clicks his heels and shuts the door behind him.

I open my mouth, take a deep breath and step away from Gabriel.

His eyes are distressed. He turns his head and gives me a stunned look.

"I thought two steps ahead." I point at the chess board. "I knew he was with her," I whisper, going over to the fireplace, emptying a glass of cognac and smiling bitterly. "I knew he was spending the evening with her. We both heard them yesterday when we took Leon to the square."

I pour myself another glass of tea and feel him around me.

"I hope I didn't embarrass you." I murmur reflectively. "Do you think I overdid it?" I turn to look at him.

"Utterly and completely." His arm encircles me and before I can blink, my body is pinned to the wall, his hips close to mine.

"What...what are you doing?" I pant in alarm.

"Something I should have done the first evening you arrived." His hoarse voice is full of passion. The ardor that spreads through my body makes it difficult to think logically.

"I think you're confusing your concern for me with passion. I think that..."

His hand cups my chin, forcing me to raise my head and look into his eyes with their long, thick lashes. His blazing, deep green eyes makes me forget the rest of the sentence. His thumb flutters delicately over my cheek and his lips caress my forehead.

"You're confused. You...worry about me like a brother worries about his little sister." I close my eyes as his lips touch the end of my nose, settling above my lips.

"It would be really bad if a brother wanted to do to his sister what I want to do to you right now." He gently bites my lower lip and my thighs tremble with the heat pulsing through them. "Why did you want me to come back?"

"Because...because I..."

"If you have something to say, say it loud and clear." His tone hardens.

"Because I was going mad here without you! Because I missed you so much. Because my heart shattered when you left."

"You've taken over my mind." His whisper makes my lips tremble in anticipation.

"Gabriel, it will change everything." I make myself move my head back.

"Everything is already different." His hand holds my neck and he kisses me hard. The voices in my mind stop and all I feel is my burning body, craving for his touch. I slightly part my lips, enabling his tongue to penetrate my mouth and explore it at leisure. The faint groan bursting from my throat enflames him further. His hand slides up my thigh, parts the fabric of the robe and I feel him hardening. A groan erupts from his throat and I realize that I've never longed for anyone as much as I long for him now. I clasp my fingers behind his neck, holding his hair and pulling him closer to me. Kissing him harder, I groan into his mouth.

"I want you so badly." Panting, he kisses me again. "I have to feel you." His lips move to my neck and he scatters small kisses there. "But I have to know that you realize the implications of what we are about to do."

"I only realize one thing." I wind my legs around his hips. "My heart wept from the moment you left and now I hear it singing."

He bends to kiss the fabric above my heart and then his arms lift me up. He strides resolutely towards the bedroom, unties the belt of my robe and flings it on the floor. He lays me down and when I try to cover my naked body with the blanket, he pulls it away and shakes his head.

His eyes devour my body and he quickly strips off his shirt. I openly examine his chest muscles, moving uncomfortably, only too aware of my nakedness. I bite my lip again and again, trying to work out if my passion has overcome my reason.

"What's bothering you?" Gabriel smiles his small smile as he stretches over me. His hands embrace my head.

"That maybe we're making a mistake." I can't resist stroking his shoulder.

"Do you feel it's a mistake?" Bending his head, he buries it in my neck. His lips cling to my skin and I moan.

"I feel it's the best thing in the whole world to do." My nails slide down his arm. "But…"

"Josephine, this is not the time to think two steps ahead," his tone is firm, and my back arches as his tongue tastes my skin. "Now only one move is right, and this time I'm making it." His lips cling to my breast. Breathlessly, I sink into his touch, groaning with pleasure when he kisses the other breast.

It's incredible how such a large body can simultaneously create such a gentle yet firm touch. He pulls back and his lips kiss my belly. I close my eyes and relax my limbs. Each kiss and caress allow me to disconnect from reality. There is nothing in the world except my need to feel him mine. Only mine.

"You're so beautiful..." He whispers hoarsely, parting my legs. "So beautiful and so my own..."

His head settles between my legs and I let out a loud groan and my nails dig into his broad shoulders. All the frustration, the sadness and confusion merge in one sensation. Pleasure. Supreme pleasure approaching the threshold of explosion.

"Gabriel," I murmur his name and he raises his head and kisses my belly. I want to protest his denying me the explosion, but he leans on his elbows and the sensation of his hardness between my legs makes me pant in anticipation. I move my pelvis to receive him and he retreats slightly.

I frown with frustration and his small smile confuses me. Raising my hand, he kisses it and removes the wedding ring from my finger.

I look at him uncomprehendingly.

"Josephine Portiere" he whispers and kisses my lips. "I swear I will do all I can to make you feel safe." He kisses my neck. "I will do all I can to protect you." He kisses my chin. "I will do all I can to make you feel loved." He gently bites my shoulder. I can't breathe. "I will do all I can to prove myself worthy of you." He straightens up and his eager eyes meet my own. I put my hand over my heart. "My Josephine, will you be my wife?" He kisses my little finger and my heart beats in my chest.

Tears fill my eyes and I choke and nod.

"I didn't hear your answer." His eyelashes cover his eyes and I feel his hardness between my legs.

"There is nothing I would like more than to be your wife." My thighs cling to his pelvis and my head drops back.

"Then the time has come to consummate this marriage." The ring slides onto my finger and, grasping my shoulders, he takes me wildly. Sucking at my lips, my skin and caressing my soul. Opening my eyes, I gaze into his chiseled face, feel his gaze penetrate my heart, enveloping it in layers of protection.

My blood is rushing and my body trembling as he slows, bringing me to my peak. With each penetration I feel my heart expanding to contain the intensity of emotion, and when the explosion happens between my legs, I murmur his name and let my arms fall.

He stops and gazes at me for a long time. "My beautiful wife."

I caress his face and he kisses the palm of my hand. My body becomes his, and he penetrates me one more time, groaning aloud as his body trembles and he collapses onto the mattress beside me.

I'm drawn into his arms and, holding my chin, he kisses me for a long time. Locked in his body, I listen to his heartbeats, knowing I have found my place. I will never wish to be anywhere else.

"I should have fed you before." His fingers caress my back.

"Of all the things in the world, you're thinking of food now?" I ask, confused.

He laughs, an open spontaneous laugh that makes my heart tremble, and lies on top of me again. His chest presses on mine, and when I realize his body is aroused again, I open my eyes in surprise.

"Do you understand why you should have eaten before we came to bed?"

"Yes," I murmur as my body grows hot again, but the only hunger I feel is for the body of the man who'd made his vows to me a few moments ago.

I gaze up at him. His body takes up half the bed and his skin is shining with sweat. For the first time, I allow myself to look at him with a woman's eyes, and my hunger becomes unbearable. I sit on him, my legs apart. That small smile of his, which makes his eyes close, and my heart flutter.

His face is strong and peaceful, not one worry line disturbs its wholeness. I pass my hands over my forehead and around my eyes, knowing that at this special moment, my face, too, is free of worry.

"I have a small debt to pay." I slide my body forwards until my fingers intertwine with his.

"Tonight we won't be paying any debts." His upper lip trembles. "I really hope you don't think I'm expecting you…"

"Gabriel," I interrupt him and remove the wedding ring from his finger. "I have a small debt to pay, and I think I should say what I have to say before I lose my courage."

I sit up again and he places a pillow under his head and looks expectantly at me.

"Gabriel Augustine." My eyes are fixed on his and my heart beats even faster. "The first time we met I was certain you would be the end of me."

His eyes narrow and he caresses my thigh.

"That night, you said you'd never force me to smile, and what I didn't know was that you're the only person who can make me really." I put my hand over my heart. "I swear that I will never lie to you." I bend down to kiss his lips. "That I will do everything I can to make you feel loved." I lightly bite his chin. "And that I'll do everything I can to prove myself worthy of you." I lick his neck and straighten up. "My Gabriel, in such a short time you have become my entire world. You've become my home. Will you marry me?"

Holding me, he throws me onto the mattress. His body shields me and his pelvis latches onto mine.

"I didn't hear your answer." I laugh through a veil of tears.

"Nothing would give me greater pleasure and pride than to be your husband." He kisses me hard and allows me to return his ring to his finger.

He caresses my face, then my neck and, feeling his love filter into me, I yield to him body and soul.

CHAPTER NINETEEN

My body shakes with a sudden attack of cold. I pull the blanket around me and snuggle in. My thighs and arms are tingling, and I smile as the memory of last night returns.

The caresses, kisses, words of love…

Turning my head I discover that Gabriel isn't there beside me.

In a flash, the sense of sublime pleasure is replaced by confusion. I didn't dream it. My body and heart had experienced a night of intoxicating sensuality. Putting on my robe, I open the curtain a little. Paris is still gray.

I long to sense again the safety I feel only in this man's presence. "My husband," I murmur and a slight apprehension lingers. For me, perhaps, it was the highlight of my life, but for him was it just another conquest? Maybe he chose to love and comfort me only because of the experiences I have undergone while he was away.

I find it hard to come to terms with the sublime joy that had burst into my life in my darkest hour. I have to know if it's as real for him as it is for me.

I enter the drawing room and continue along the corridor to the bathroom. The sound of a newspaper is coming from the dining room which causes my heart to beat wildly. He is so close to me. The answer is two steps away and I still can't deal with it.

I wash my face and look at the image reflected to me from the mirror. My cheeks are flushed, my lips swollen and my eyes are shining. For a moment, I can see the Josephine of another time. A time when Paris was illuminated. I brush my hair and try to calm my heart. I owe this man so much. I owe him my life and nothing that happens could change that. But my heart refuses to calm down. The time has come to receive an answer.

When I enter the dining room Gabriel raises his eyes from the newspaper and smiles his small, perfect smile at me.

I can't breathe.

Sitting down beside him, I look at him quietly.

"How do you feel this morning?" The way in which he is looking at me makes me blush.

"Umm…I feel good." Lowering my eyes I try and understand what the hell is happening to me.

"Then why is my wife sitting so far away from me?" He smacks his thigh and I jump up from my chair and snuggle in his body. "Why are you trembling?" He asks with concern and rubs my back. "Are you cold? Shall I bring you a blanket?"

"No." I put my arms around his waist. "Those cursed thoughts don't let up. I woke and you weren't beside me, and I wasn't sure you were glad of the decision we made."

Two seconds of silence threaten to shatter my heart and when he distances me from him, anxiety bites into my belly. His hands close on my waist, he sits me on the table and stands between my legs. His upper lip trembles and I'm puzzled as to why he's angry.

"Do you think I'd do such a thing if I weren't sure I wanted you to be mine?"

"I don't know." Staring at his buttoned shirt, I long to feel the warmth of his body again. "Brigitte always told us that men are motivated by passion whereas we, women, are motivated by reason."

"I won't lie to you." Untying the belt of my robe he continues to gaze at me. "I have never felt so attracted to a woman." His hand slides along my inner thigh and I close my eyes as my body flames. "I have never longed to feel I belong to someone, and I've never wanted anyone to feel she belongs to me." He spreads my legs and I open my eyes and see he is undoing the buckle of his belt.

"But with you, it's different." He takes off his trousers and underwear, "you were mine from the moment you chirped your nonsense about loyalty to the Reich." His small smile adorns his face. "Even then I realized that no matter what happens, I would never sacrifice you to save someone else. Not even myself."

I groan as he takes me. All my fears dissipate when I feel his heart sending love to my heart. I choke when steps are heard in the corridor. The blood drains from my face and I try and sit up.

"Gabriel…" I murmur and bite my lips as my climax approaches.

"This is your home." He leans forward and brushes his lips against mine. "We can consummate our marriage anywhere we please."

The footsteps stop briefly and then fade away down the corridor.

"Dear God." I groan as my body bursts in a wave of pleasure.

He kisses my lips as if he were drawing my pleasure into himself and then straightens up again and fills me with his love until we're both panting in satisfaction.

"Do you think we've consummated our marriage sufficiently for you not to consider running away?" He caresses my thigh and stands back.

I burst out laughing and wrap myself in my robe. "I think we even have a witness." I glance uneasily at the door and hurry into the bathroom.

A few moments later, I return to the dining room and see Gabriel reading the newspaper and sticking his fork into his food. His plate is exactly where I was sitting before. He notices my gaze and grins.

"Just the thought of you sitting here…" he drums his fork on the table, "makes me hungry."

"Where are your European manners?" I blush and sit down next to him.

"I keep my manners for my colleagues." He takes my arm and kisses my hand. "With my wife, I prefer vulgarities. So would you please get yourself back here?"

Pulling my hand away, I burst out laughing.

"A melody!" Marie enters the dining room with a broad smile and I pale. "To hear laughter in this house is like hearing a wonderful melody." She sets a plate in front of me and I try and work out if I'm still eating the food I got myself.

"Don't even think about it," Gabriel says without taking his eyes off the newspaper.

"How do you know what I'm thinking?"

"My food is your food, and you will no longer stand like a beggar in line for food rations."

"Don't suddenly turn into a man like that," I complain, but can't control the hunger and stick my fork into the pie.

"A man like what?" He asks while turning a page. "Who takes care of his wife? Or a man who is unwilling for her to take any unnecessary risks?"

Marie pours my coffee, looking amused by our conversation.

"No." I exhale irritably. "A man who tells me what to do and expects me to obey him."

"Welcome to the institution of marriage." Marie chuckles and avoids my glare.

"Gabriel, you do know that I have no intention of stopping…" I fall silent for a moment, thinking about how to continue my sentence. "Stop doing everything I can to justify my existence."

Without responding, he hands me the French newspaper. I sigh when I see he has censored entire articles.

"You don't have to do this either." I look at him through the torn newspaper.

"You do not want to see the photographs of the night you spent outside," he stated decisively.

I really don't want to see them. Just the thought of what I might have seen shocks me, and the illusion of safety I feel in his presence shatters, making my eyes fill with tears. My friends, all the brave people who made me feel part of such an important organization are gone. And now who is left to fight?

Gabriel puts the newspaper aside and taps his finger on the table. Marie is quick to leave us alone, as if they have a secret code.

"Josephine." He leans forward and takes my hand. "Your friend survived."

"Natalie?" I ask eagerly.

He nods. "Her friend also survived. They weren't in the apartment when it was raided."

"Maurice." I murmur, holding tightly to his hand. "Veronique? Her sons?"

"I don't know."

"Can you find out?"

He nods once, pulling the newspaper towards him.

The relief I feel is only partial. Natalie and Maurice survived, which moves me to tears, but these are not just tears of happiness, I grieve for those who didn't survive. In my little piece of Eden, reality hits me in the face.

"I expect you to understand that nothing has changed even after consummating our marriage." I try to sound firm.

"Everything has already changed," he responds indifferently.

"I don't understand. If fighting my own small war bothers you so much, if you can't accept the fact that what I do is an inseparable part of me, how can you think I am truly yours?"

"You're completely mine." His upper lip trembles but I refuse to back down.

"If what I do, defines me, and you cannot accept me as I am, you can't possibly want to be with me. You can't possibly choose me."

He folds the newspaper and straightens his tie. His eyes bore into mine and my heart misses a beat.

"I chose you precisely because of who you are." He holds my face firmly. "I fell insanely in love with you, precisely because what you do defines you." He runs his thumb along my lower lip, and I battle not to leap on him. "I know you can't obey my request to stop your involvement in the Resistance, and I didn't expect anything else."

I open my mouth for an explanation, but he silences me with a kiss.

"You will move into the big players' game." He sighs, and I frown in incomprehension. "You will accompany me, this way I can guarantee your safety."

"I'll start dealing in diamonds?" I look at him in wonder.

Gabriel laughs and stands up. "You will obey me in a different way." He puts on his jacket and sips his coffee. "I will teach you how to attain valuable information, and you'll contribute even more to the Resistance."

"How exactly? What am I supposed to do? When…"

"I'm sure you didn't ask so many questions before going out on a mission that your gang assigned you to."

"No, but…"

"No buts. You will do as I say without asking questions."

For a moment, I don't recognize the hard expression of the man who makes my heart tremble, but then the small smile returns to his face.

"You will contribute more, that I can promise you. But in exchange, you must promise not to ask unnecessary questions."

I bite my lips hard. So many questions rise up in my mind and I know I won't get any answers. But more than anything, I know with all my heart that he is speaking the truth. I nod.

"Tonight you will accompany me to a ball. If you accept your first assignment."

Again, I nod.

"I believe I could learn to love this obedient side of you." He grins and I open my eyes in irritation.

"I ask you not to contact your friends." He bends to kiss me and leaves the room.

I hide my hands between my knees and my mind is feverish with thoughts. I didn't nod so I'm not lying.

CHAPTER TWENTY

Sitting beside him in the car, I hug my handbag. Gabriel holds my hand, stroking it. Since he picked me up from the apartment, his expression has changed. If I didn't know him, I'd suspect he was worried.

"I received notice today that the location of the ball has been changed." He glances at me.

I shrug my shoulders. "What does it matter where we meet with those bastards?"

"The new location might cause you discomfort."

"I always feel uncomfortable in their company."

Gabriel is quiet and then brings my hand to his lips. "The ball is at Claude's house."

"What?" I try and pull my hand away but he holds it firmly. The infinite serenity I feel in his presence is dispelled, and a cold sweat covers my forehead.

"Herr Zemel and his wife are the new residents there. I should have told you before."

"Yes, you certainly should have." I turn my head to the window, surprised I didn't recognize the route. I was so engrossed in the sense of false safety he gives me, that nothing else captured my attention.

"If you want me to turn round and take you home, I will do so now." He stops the car at the entrance to the street, and I feel his steady gaze.

"What is my assignment tonight?" I ask without turning my head.

"Josephine…"

"Gabriel, what is my assignment tonight?"

"In the main bedroom, under the bed, there is a key taped to the lower right-hand bedpost. I need that key."

"Claude and Brigitte's bedroom?" I ask in a suffocated voice.

"Yes."

"I will try and get it."

He kisses my hand once again and continues driving. The car passes the house and he finds a parking spot next to the sidewalk.

Gabriel opens the door for me and helps me put on the black fur coat he'd given me, covering the tight satin dress that reaches my ankles. Sliding his hand across my back, he leads me up the path to the house. The large, familiar entrance door now looks so threatening to me, and I stop and lean against the wall. I cover my mouth, overcome by a terrible wave of nausea.

"This was a stupid idea," he says contritely, hugging me. "I'll take you home now."

"No." I shake him off and grit my teeth. "I will do whatever it takes to help the Resistance. This is not the time to think of myself and my childish emotions."

He doesn't seem convinced but he nods, gesturing to the staircase.

With each step, my breath becomes more labored and the blood drains from my face. When the door opens and Gabriel leads me inside, I'm quite certain I'm about to faint. My legs are trembling and my heart is beating fast.

"Madame Josephine, what a pleasant surprise. Wonderful to meet you again."

I give Lucille, the housekeeper, a hostile look.

"I heard you'd married this charming man." She holds out her hand for my coat and a strange sound emerges from my mouth as I imagine how I'd grasp her throat and throttle her. Revolting, treacherous creature.

"Indeed she has," Gabriel answers for me, taking my coat. He gives her his coat too and then puts his arm around my waist and leads me from the foyer into the ballroom.

Everything looks exactly the same. As if I'd returned in time to the house of my adoptive family. I gaze around me, searching in vain for those I love. The sob that escapes my throat surprises even me.

Gabriel stands in front of me. "Darling, you look wonderful tonight." He carefully caresses my elegantly styled hair and bends to kiss my cheek. "If you've decided to play the game tonight," he whispers in my ear, "then pull yourself together. Now!" His assertive tone shocks me and I nod, swallowing.

He puts his arm around my waist again and we cross the hall to stand before Zemel who appears smug with pleasure.

"Good evening." Gabriel addresses him with a smile.

"Good evening, Monsieur Augustine." Zemel clicks his heels together and shakes his hand. "I'm glad you're able to attend the first ball in my new mansion."

Again the wave of nausea.

"And I see your beautiful wife has accompanied you." He winks conspiratorially and I cough to fight the bitter wave rising in my throat. "Anika will be happy to see you've arrived. Go and say hello to her."

"As soon as we've had something to drink." Gabriel turns and we hurry to the bar. Gray and black uniforms are intertwined and elegant dresses fill the hall with bright colors. I pull myself together.

"Two cognacs, please," Gabriel addresses the bartender while he strokes my back. He hands me the glass and after clinking it with his, I take a long sip. "Come and dance with me." He smiles his small smile at me.

"What about the assignment," I whisper faintly.

"First, dance with your husband." He finishes his drink in one gulp and waits for me to put my glass down on the counter.

We walk towards the dance floor and Gabriel is constantly greeted on all sides. I find myself smiling and nodding, praying to be left alone.

He stands in the center of the dance floor and leads me into a slow waltz. I look around uneasily and he cups my chin and kisses me gently on the lips.

"Learn to disconnect from emotion on your assignments."

"That's probably what the Germans tell themselves." I smile bitterly at him.

"Learn to disconnect from emotion, not bury it."

"It's emotions that motivate me." I quickly wipe away the tears in my eyes and smile again. "I'd never believed that I would reach a time when my heart is filled with such strong hatred."

"Leave a little room for love." His fingers pass over my back.

"I feel it." I cling to him and inhale the scent of his eau de cologne. "But now I'm embarrassed. I have no right to love, to dance and smile in the home of those who have been taken from me."

"So let's win for them too." He rubs his cheek against mine and miraculously his quick breath on my skin strengthens me. The confidence is no longer faked, when he's beside me, his strength seems to pass onto me, filling me with determination. "I'll get the key instead of you." He kisses my cheek when the song ends.

"No.' I can do it," I answer confidently. "Let's go and greet our hostess." He bows to me and, arm in arm, we walk towards Anika. She is wearing a blue dress, which doesn't flatter her figure. She is talking to an elegant woman who is standing in front of her.

"Josephine." She kisses my cheek and holds out her hand to Gabriel. He kisses it and smiles easily. "I've asked Richard several times to invite you to dinner." She is sullen. "But he works so hard. He hasn't had a single free evening."

I know exactly where he spends his evenings, but I don't feel even an iota of compassion for this betrayed woman.

"I hope you don't feel uncomfortable spending time in this house." Her expression becomes grave. "I know you used to stay here and it must..."

"Not at all." I cut her off with a wave. "I'm so glad you have the opportunity to live in this beautiful house."

"Isn't it simply incredible?" She spins around. "I barely had to make any changes."

I nod, biting my lips when I notice the pictures of the Fuhrer hanging on the walls and the large swastika hanging in the center of the staircase.

"But I had to change the curtains and the carpets on the top floor. I don't understand who could have chosen the color white. So boring." She grimaces and I seem to be grimacing with her. "Yesterday, they changed it all to blue. As you've probably noticed, that's my favorite color."

"I have to see it." Disengaging from Gabriel, I linked my arm in hers. "I always thought that white so boring," I lie without batting an eyelash. "Blue is such a calming, special color. Have I told you that I studied fashion design?"

"I'd be happy to show you." Her face is alight with eagerness. "But I think I should stay here to greet the guests."

"It will only take a few minutes," I beg her. "Gabriel, will you excuse us."

"Of course." He smiles and winks at Anika. "I'll keep Herr Zemel occupied with stories of the war so he won't notice you've disappeared."

"So boring." Anika laughs and goes upstairs with me.

Climbing the stairs makes me dizzy and I find myself holding on to the banister and breathing heavily. Don't think about them, I command myself. Don't think about them, don't think about them...

Fortunately, Anika was busy chatting about the treasures she'd found in the house, and didn't notice my distress. She proudly, points at the horrible blue carpet and I nod, pretending enthusiasm. I glance towards my bedroom and groan soundlessly. We pass Odette's bedroom and I touch the door and ask forgiveness in my heart.

"I must see the curtains." I point to the door of the main bedroom.

"Fortunately the housekeeper has tidied the room." Anika giggles. "I'm so disorganized." She opens the door and, when I see that a picture of the Fuhrer hangs above the bed in place of the picture of the lilies, my legs buckled. The contents of my bag scatter and Anika bends down in alarm.

"These heels," I murmur in confusion and look at the bed post, realizing that my fall was to my advantage. "They make me clumsy."

"I won't tell anyone." Anika laughs and collects my make-up products that have dropped on the carpet.

Approaching the bed, my fingers quickly feel for the key. When I feel it, my heart jumps in my chest.

Anika straightens up a moment after I manage to tug it off and hide it in my fist.

"The curtains are simply wonderful!" I cry aloud, and when she turns to look at the window I hide the key deep in my décolleté.

"Yes." She goes over to stroke them while I try and regulate my breathing.

Loud steps are heard outside the door, making both of us turn our heads.

"What in hell's name are you doing in the bedroom during a ball?" Zemel barks at her.

"Herr Zemel, it's my fault." I bat my eyelids. "I just had to see the changes your wife has made here!"

He looks at me with his icy eyes and doesn't say a word.

"She has a rare gift for interior design, everything is in such good taste." Passing by him, I walk to the door.

"Curtains and carpets." He says angrily. "The nonsense with which women are preoccupied."

"Precisely. While you men talk of war, we women deal with the really important things."

"Exactly." Anika laughs with enjoyment and walks towards us. She hands me my bag and the three of us go downstairs.

Mission accomplished but air refused to fill my lungs. Looking round, I notice Gabriel's burning expression. He is leaning against the bar, glancing at Zemel and his upper lip is trembling. I'm unable to smile at him. The hall is spread between us and it seems an impossible mission to reach him without oxygen. The walls swirl around me. I look to the right and approach a door leading to the garden. I part from Anika with murmured thanks, hurrying to the door and collide with a man in a gray uniform. I hang on the handle as if it were a lifesaver, the door opens and I thrust myself outside.

Air.

I stumble along the tiles and lean against the wall. The cold penetrates my bones and I fill my lungs with air.

"When you are absent from the hall, it loses its beauty." The deep voice from behind makes me close my eyes and relax my limbs. His jacket is placed around my shoulders and his arms encircle me.

"I want you to take me home."

I sniff as tears fill my eyes.

Turning me around, he takes my bag. He opens it and I know he is looking for the key. To my surprise he says nothing when he doesn't find it, just smiles his captivating smile that makes his eyes close and then he kisses my lips.

"I don't want you to feel that you've failed." His lips flutter over my forehead. "I'll find another way to get it. It was a mistake to bring you here. You're not ready yet."

I don't know if my heart is expanding because of the way in which he's trying to comfort me or because I know I'm about to make him proud of me.

He leads me back into the hall, holding me close as we pass the tables. He stops to say goodnight to Herr Zemel and walks determinedly to the foyer. He orders Lucille to bring us our coats and within a few minutes I find myself seated in the car. His hand covers mine and he strokes my thigh.

We don't exchange a word as he drives; I lean back against the seat and allow the tears to flow down my cheeks.

"Curtains and carpets," I say angrily as the car stops at the entrance to the building. "They're occupiers, threatening, murderers and she's replaced the curtains with blue ones."

Gabriel gets out of the car and comes to open my door.

"How could such a ridiculous nation manage to conquer us?" I ask as we go up the stairs. "What does it say about us? What does it say we are?" I look at him questioningly but he doesn't respond.

Marion's door is closed and he urges me to quicken my steps.

"Actually it isn't 'us.'" I continue talking to myself as we enter the apartment. "Because 'we' refers to the French nation, and you aren't one of us. Why should a citizen of a neutral country put himself at risk for us?"

"Not everyone in my country is neutral." He takes off his coat and hangs it on the hook in the entrance. "There are those who understand that this is not a war between countries but between good and evil. I prefer to be on the side of good." He takes my coat and hangs it up with my bag and goes to pour us drinks.

The easy, comfortable way in which he presents things makes me look at him in confusion. The external chaos cannot penetrate this apartment and again the illusion of safety envelopes me.

Can one person envelope me with so many layers of protection?

"You handled yourself very well this evening." He hands me the glass and returns to lean against the fireplace. "I'm sure that if Zemel hadn't surprised you upstairs, you'd have managed to get the key."

"Why is the key so important?" I sip my drink and look at him with curiosity.

"War costs money." He answers, lighting a cigarette. "And that key opens a safe containing a great deal of money."

"So why not break into it?"

"It's in a place with a lot of people around."

"Where?"

"Didn't I ask you not to ask questions?" He sounds amused.

"If I know where the safe is, maybe I could surprise you with its contents." I approach him and take the cigarette from his fingers.

"It's difficult for me to believe you'd succeed without the key." He laughs. "But I'd be glad if you'd surprise me in the bedroom."

One sentence and my body shifts from ice to unreasonable heat.

"Who says I'll have to do it without the key?" I return the cigarette and sit down opposite the chess board.

He gives me a look of surprise and hurries to the hooks in the entrance. He checks my bag and frowns.

"Want to play?" I gesture to the chair opposite me and smile slyly.

"I'd be glad to play." He takes off his tie and throws his jacket on the armchair.

"Begin." I point at the white pieces in front of him, and he moves a pawn forward. His eyes are fixed on mine and I move my piece. He moves another piece and his expression confuses me. I bite my lower lip and move another piece. My eyes disengage from his and I try to focus on my moves, but every time his fingers move I imagine them pleasuring me.

"I had to sacrifice my queen to save my king." He grins arrogantly. "You've lost again."

"Not so." I stand up and knock over my king. "Tonight I won." I start going in the direction of the bedroom but am suddenly pulled backwards to collide against the muscle mass of his chest.

"Give it to me," Gabriel asks quietly.

"Give what to you?" I raise my eyes innocently to his.

"Where have you hidden it?" He steps back to scan my body.

"Your friend at the brothel taught me there are better hiding places than a handbag." Turning, I walk quickly into the bedroom. I sit down on the edge of the bed and when he enters the room his top lip is quivering.

"Brothel? Did you say brothel?"

"Yes." I refuse to be cooled by his furious look.

"And what in hell's name were you looking for in such an unsavory place?"

"I was carrying a message." I realize that this conversation is not going as I expected and rub my orphaned earlobe.

"What did you think would happen if one of my acquaintances would have seen you there?" He grits his teeth.

"I went in the back door. Handed over a parcel and left. Nobody saw me."

"You're reckless and irresponsible!" He raises his voice and I get angry and stand facing him.

"It isn't a war between countries or between more ethical or less ethical people. It's a war between people who have lost their way and those who still believe there is a right way." I remind him of his words. "I don't care if I'm required to carry out a mission in a mosque or a brothel, I will carry it out with the same determination."

"There are so many women in this world," he sighs, running his fingers through his hair. "And I have to fall in love with someone who drives me crazy."

"But the one who drives you crazy," I point to myself, "succeeded in getting you the key."

The small smile appears on his face and, holding my hips, he throws me onto the mattress. My body flames and I long to feel him on top of me.

"Turn over," he orders passionately and I lie on my belly.

His fingers open the zipper on my dress and his lips travel over my back, covered in the thin fabric of my underwear. When he kisses my lower back I sigh in anticipation. He removes my dress and turns me over. His eyes burn into me.

"Where is it?" Gabriel kisses my lips gently and when his tongue penetrates I yield to the flame between my legs.

"It is…"

"Shhh…" He silences me with another kiss. "I actually like this game." His lips pass over my neck and I arch my back to bring my chest closer to his. He pulls down the strap of my petticoat and kisses my shoulder. From there he continues to my collarbone and then to my chest. "We wasted so much time in boring games when we could have played here." He pulls down the other strap and then my petticoat, settling between my legs and kissing my belly.

"You're over dressed," I complain, stroking his back.

He removes his jacket and opens the buttons of his shirt. "I still haven't found the key." He gazes at my chest, "and I really like this game." Lying on his back, he pulls me up until I'm sitting on him.

"Maybe it's here." He pulls me down and kisses me hard.

"Getting warmer." I groan and writhe on top of him.

"Maybe here," He kisses my neck, gently biting me.

"Getting warmer."

He brushes his lips over my collarbone.

"Really getting warm…"

He opens my brassiere and the key falls onto his belly and, ignoring it, he turns me over on my back.

He pulls my arms up so my hands grip the bars of the bed.

"Don't move until the heat burns," he orders, and for long moments there is no trace of the gentlemanly man who has shaken my world. Instead I am taken, intoxicated by a man motivated only by animal urges.

"This is the first time you're playing with me and I don't feel defeated," I whisper exhaustedly, tensing and relaxing my fingers.

"You always defeat me." He laughs, holding me close.

"I only hope you haven't lost the key." My back is against his chest and I snuggle into him and yawn.

"I have no problem looking for it again." He strokes my thigh and when I move away from him, he pulls me back.

His arms embrace me and I rub my eyes and yawn repeatedly. My body is exhausted and I can't understand how he isn't collapsing with exhaustion.

"We have to go to sleep. You have to get up for work." I try and move away from his hold, but it's too strong.

"I'm my own master. There is no reason we shouldn't continue our search tonight." He bites my shoulder and I fake a sob.

I feel around for the key and when my fingers grasp the cold metal, I dig my elbow into him and show him the key.

"I've found it. Now let me sleep!"

"I don't think so." He grins and throws the key on the carpet.

"Where is Gabriel?" I shriek as he climbs on top of me. "Return the gentleman I married. He will certainly respect my request to go to sleep."

"I've already told you." He bites my lip and smiles smugly. "Manners have no place in the bedroom."

"Tomorrow I'll return to the brothel for some advice from your friend…" I groan as his lips cling to my neck.

"You are never going back there." His face grows grave. "And I suggest you don't test my boundaries."

I lick the lip he bit a few moments ago and regret not remaining silent. To my surprise, he bends and licks it gently, and I enjoy his caressing, gentle taking me until I climax in a way I've never known before.

CHAPTER TWENTY-ONE

The light penetrating the curtains makes me open my eyes for a second, but I close them immediately, covering my head with the blanket. I long to stay in bed and enjoy the intoxicating safety I feel here.

The loud voice coming from the drawing room belongs to the man who has chosen me, and all I want is to be near him. Wrapping myself in my satin robe, I go into the drawing room.

Two men stand up when I enter. One, curls covering his forehead, has an embarrassed smile, and the other looks at me in horror, his upper lip quivering.

"Forgive me." I blush and tie the belt of my robe, noticing a tall woman sitting on the sofa. "I didn't know we had guests." I hurry into the passage, closing the bathroom door behind me. When I finish washing, I open the door a little.

"Marie," I whisper, and she appears from the kitchen, smiling at me. "Bring me some clothes, please."

She nods her head and goes into the bedroom, she returns with the clothes and enters the bathroom, closing the door behind her.

"A wild night?" She examines me, chuckling.

"You are so nosy." I laugh in embarrassment.

"I'm just happy for you both." She shrugs.

"The man in the drawing room, he's Gabriel's friend. He's from Switzerland," I murmur while buttoning up my dress.

"He's a good man."

"And the woman?"

"Probably his partner."

"I should join them." Looking at my watch, my eyes open in surprise. "Have I slept that long?"

"It will be dark again soon." Marie gestures to me to bend down and puts a few slides in my hair.

When I enter the drawing room Gabriel falls silent and the two men stand up again.

"Vincent, you know my wife." Gabriel draws me to him.

The young man holds out his hand with a warm smile and I shake it.

"Josephine, this is Jeanne, Vincent's fiancée." The young woman holds out her hand, and examines me at length. Her light hair reaches her ears in a fashionable *carré*, and a short fringe adorns her forehead. Her eyes are blue and her features straight and delicate. She's beautiful.

"I have never believed I'd meet a woman who could domesticate Gabriel," she says without smiling.

"I was also surprised when it happened." I turn to look at him and that small smile of his makes my heart skip a beat.

"I suggest you put on something more elegant." He slides his hand over my lower back. "We're going out for a formal dinner and cocktails."

"We'll meet you there." Vincent beckons to Jeanne to join him.

"But I still haven't received a decision about…"

Both men give her a hard look and she falls silent.

"I shouldn't have spoken in front of her." She smiles for the first time and I feel as if I've interrupted their private conversation.

"I'll leave you alone." I have difficulty hiding my hurt and go into the bedroom.

I hear the whispers from the drawing room and am unable to understand why Gabriel invited me to join them. I grumble as I put on a long, cream dress, tighten my garters and continue to grumble as I sit down to put on my make-up.

The closeness I feel for the man waiting for me in the drawing room is replaced by a troubling coolness. How can I feel close to someone I don't know?

I hear the apartment door slam and return to the drawing room.

Gabriel is leaning against the fireplace, smoking a cigarette. "You're beautiful," he says, approaching me and I step back.

"If I disturb you all, there is no reason for me to join you this evening."

"Disturb us?" He tries to approach me again.

"Yes, disturb." Raising my hand, I signal him to stop. "If there are things I shouldn't hear, why do you want me to join you? I'll only feel as if I'm butting in. I have no problem with your going out without me."

"Josephine, there are things I don't want you to hear because I want to protect you." He ignores my hand and draws me to him.

"If you are at risk, I want to be at risk with you."

"I know, and nonetheless…" Holding my chin, he gently kisses my lips. "I have the right to try and protect you, even if you prefer otherwise."

"I thought you wanted me to learn to play with the big boys."

"I want you to play with me in one place alone." His lips flutter over my cheek. "But since you have chosen to play in a way that puts you at risk, I prefer to have the possibility of taking care of you."

"I thought I proved my ability yesterday."

"On so many fronts." He squeezes my behind and blows into my ear.

"All right. I'll come." I quickly step away from him, already longing for the evening to end, so that I can come back here for private time with him.

I sit next to him in the car, and the moment he takes my hand I feel my mood shift. He seems alert. He is quiet the whole time, and only he turns to me when the car stops at the curb.

"Your task tonight is to listen." He kisses my hand.

"Listen? To whom?"

"At events like these, people tend to talk too much." He looks at me, but it seems as if he's looking through me. "Talk less and listen more. At the end of the evening all you need to do is tell me what you heard." He gets out of the car without further explanation.

When we enter the restaurant, I regret I didn't insist on staying home. Black uniforms, gray uniforms, French police officers and, of course, well-dressed women displaying fake smiles. Only when I'm close to the man now holding my hand do I remember how it feels to smile from the heart.

Gabriel introduces me, exchanges polite words with several men, and leads me to a corner table. Vincent stands and waits for me to sit while Jeanne sips her glass of wine nonchalantly. I listen to Gabriel and Vincent discussing the prices of gold and diamonds and the deals each had closed. The waiter offers me more wine and I happily agree, losing interest in the conversation.

"Mon Cheri," the enthusiastic voice makes me shiver.

Marion pushes her chair in between mine and Gabriel's. "Are you still angry with me? You know I only want to protect you." She puts her hand on Gabriel's and he pulls back his shoulder. His upper lip quivers but his expression remains blank.

"Everything's all right, Marion, I wish you a good evening."

"Won't you dance with me?" She persists, and Jeanne chuckles and sips her wine.

"Something amuses you?" Marion asks spitefully.

"You." Jeanne raises her glass and nods her head. "You were and remain pathetic."

I believe I'm starting to like Jeanne.

"I'm not the only pathetic woman at this table." Marion stands up. "I always thought I was a threat to you, and now I'm certain you were no less surprised than I when you discovered that he'd adopted a child who has turned his head."

What is going on here?

"You have never been a threat to me." Jeanne chuckles again, glancing at me. "If you haven't heard, I'm engaged to Vincent." She waves the diamond ring on her finger.

"We all compromise at some point." Marion flounces away.

"Just that I don't compromise with a German cock…" Jeanne is suddenly silent, grimacing in annoyance.

"All right, we should go to the bar for something stronger to drink." Vincent motions with his head to Gabriel.

Gabriel stands and caresses my shoulder. "Josephine, do you want something?"

"Brandy," I say, continuing to gaze at Jeanne.

The men are swallowed up in the crowd, and Jeanne moves to sit beside me.

"What month are you in?" She asks tapping on her glass.

"What?"

"You shouldn't be drinking in your condition."

"I'm not pregnant."

"He's married you, so why should you hide it?"

"I said I'm not pregnant!"

Pushing back her chair, she examines me at length.

"So why the hell did he marry you?"

"Why shouldn't he marry me?" I start to lose my temper.

"Gabriel is not the marrying kind," she declares confidently. "The only woman who almost trapped him is that cunning whore."

She is the second woman to refer in such a way to Marion, whereas Gabriel didn't find it necessary to tell me himself.

"Tell me how you managed to persuade him to marry you."

"The truth is I didn't persuade him at all." This conversation is starting to exhaust me. "He proposed and I accepted. That's the whole story."

Standing up, I try to work out in which direction to escape. In the crowd, I notice the commander of the police station with SS officer Herr Stengel. I hadn't seen him since the dinner at our apartment, and now it seems a lot more tempting to listen to him barking than to the intrusive questions of my husband's caustic friend. Putting a fake smile on my face, I approach them. Beside them are two soldiers in gray uniforms.

"Herr Stengel." I hold out my hand. "How nice to see you again."

He falls silent and kisses my hand. The police station commander bows his head, and both uniformed men look at me with curiosity.

"Madame Josephine, it's really a great pleasure to see your beautiful face among all these ugly ones."

He has certainly been blessed with elegant manners.

"Maybe you can settle our argument." He beckons to a waiter, taking a glass of champagne from the tray. Handing me the glass, he impatiently waves away the waiter.

"I'd be glad to try." I blink and remind myself that my task is to listen.

"If the dogs always escape southward isn't it foolish to set up blocks to the north of the city?"

"But we've received reports they attempt to escape to the *Saint*-Denis District," the police station commander interrupts.

"The reports you receive always turn out to be false," Stengel barks at him. "In the end, we'll suspect you of collaboration."

The police commander pales and Stengel turns and smiles at me.

"And what does the young lady think?"

Gazing at the pink liquid in my glass, I consider my answer. I'm supposed to listen, not take an active part in the conversation. Stengel's gaze makes it clear that I have no option but to reply.

"I think that the honored policeman has always proved his loyalty and if he says north then it's north."

I shrug my shoulders and giggle.

"In that case, we'll increase forces in the north of the city." Stengel clinks his glass with mine.

"I very much hope you haven't involved me in a political or military discussion. You know that the only things on which I can offer an opinion are the impressive dresses of the women here this evening."

The soldier in the gray uniform standing beside Stengel approaches me, putting his hand on my back.

"I'd actually like to hear your opinion of several other subjects." His cheeks are flushed and I can smell alcohol on his breath as he whispers in my ear. "Would you care to dance with me?" His hand slides down to my backside, and when he squeezes it, I choke.

"I think this soldier has forgotten how to behave like a gentleman." The loud voice behind me sounds angry. Gabriel draws me to him, putting his arm around my shoulders.

"And who are you to teach me manners?" The soldier is furious.

"Her husband," Gabriel responded coolly, "and I expect you to apologize to her for forgetting what a gentleman should do with his hands when he meets a married lady."

Everyone around us falls silent, and Stengel looks amused.

"Apologize?" Spit flies out of the soldier's mouth. "I expect you to apologize for forgetting that your country has new masters, and everything here belongs to us. Including your wife."

"I think you've had a glass too many to drink." Gabriel smiles his small smile, but his upper lip is quivering. "And we're not leaving until I hear your apology."

"I'll put a bullet in your head." Screams the soldier and the crowd around us grows.

"Gabriel," I whisper.

"Don't interfere!"

"Come outside and I'll show you how the Germans apologize," the soldier continues to roar.

"If so," Gabriel turns to Stengel, "would you please explain to the Fuhrer why the flow of money to main headquarters has stopped."

Stengel frowns, no longer amused. Tossing his glass at the wall behind him, he approaches the soldier with a chilling look.

"Apologize at once to Monsieur Augustine and his wife," the command is fired directly at the astonished soldier.

"A German doesn't apologize to…"

"I told you to apologize!" Stengel roars, shacking his body.

The soldier's friend steps back and the crowd around us quickly disperses.

"Apologize or I'll make sure you're stripped of your ranks this very night." The soldier gazes at him incredulously. The flush that had covered his face disappears and he is now as pale as a sheet.

"Yes sir, Herr Stengel." He clicks his heels and turns, looking directly at me, his face burning with hatred.

"Madame, please accept my apology, and you, too, Monsieur."

I nod energetically and the soldier crosses the hall and disappears out the entrance door.

"With your permission, I'll take my wife back to our table." Bowing his head to Stengel and the police station commander, Gabriel leads me slowly and erectly back to our table.

Jeanne narrows her eyes, gazing suspiciously at me, whereas Vincent looks concerned.

"Come and dance." Vincent pulls her up, leaving me alone with Gabriel.

"Has something impaired your memory?" Gabriel asks quietly without looking at me. His upper lip refusing to stop quivering.

"No."

"So you haven't forgotten that you're a married woman?"

"No." I draw the glass of brandy closer and hold it tightly.

"I thought you'd forgotten, otherwise how could you allow another man to touch you?"

"What the hell did you expect me to do?" Putting the glass to my lips, I take a long sip.

"What I did," he slightly raises his voice, and I thump the glass down on the table.

"You expected me to demand an apology from him?"

"Yes."

"And when he refuses, humiliating me, what would I have done then? Maybe threaten to tell his commanding officer? Or the press? Or maybe stop economic support for the Fuhrer?" I laugh scornfully. "Ah, forgive me, only you can do that."

"I expected you to demand an apology and maintain your self-respect!" He holds my wrist tightly.

"He conquered our country and everything here belongs to him." I quote the German soldier, tears veiling my eyes. "He believes that and I have no way of protesting against it." Sniffing, I look down.

"You have me." His hold on my wrist slackens and Gabriel cups my chin in his hand. "You have pride, you have honor and you have **me**."

"I don't feel proud now." Cautiously raising my eyes to his, I feel the tears on my cheek.

Gabriel sighs and gently kisses my lips. "What can I do to make you happy now?"

"Get me out of this snake pit."

"Your wish is my command." He stands up but gestures to me to stay seated. "Let me say goodbye to some people and then I'll take you home."

I nod, watching his back moving away from me, swallowed up in the crowd. I want to stand on a chair and shout that I'm in love with this man. So much in love that I'd be willing to be a buffer between him and all the forces of evil surrounding him at this moment.

"You've put a spell on him." Jeanne declares, sitting down next to me. "It's not like Gabriel to attract so much attention because of some wretched, drunk soldier's despicable behavior." She pours herself wine, and looks straight into my eyes. "In Switzerland, we speak about the impressive ability of French women, but my Gabriel is too smart, so the only logical explanation is a spell."

"He isn't your Gabriel." My eyes are unwavering. "He is my Gabriel. And if anyone has put a spell on someone, it must be him, because I am so much in love with him that if the soldier had pulled out a gun, I'd have thrown myself in front of Gabriel."

Jeanne looks up and I realize someone is standing behind me.

"Josephine, we can go now." I feel pressure on my shoulder and pale. Gabriel had heard my embarrassing confession and didn't say a word. I murmur goodbye to Jeanne and leave with him in silence.

The silence in the car increases my embarrassment. I wonder why he is traveling away from our destination.

When the car stops, I look out uncomprehendingly.

"Arc de Triomphe?"

"I thought I should remind you of what you are fighting for." He kisses the palm of my hand. "And take the opportunity to explain to you that I will never allow you to sacrifice yourself."

Looking into his eyes, my heart spins in my breast. "I really think I'd have done it. I don't know anything about you, and I still feel you are all I have."

Holding my neck, he kisses me fiercely. The saltiness of my tears merges with his taste, and my fingers tangle in his hair as I hold him closer to me, imbibing his air, his confidence, and the comfort only he can give me.

"Josephine, when this cursed war is over, you will know all there is to know about me." His fiery eyes look at me lovingly. "We'll build a home and have a child and he will know what a heroine his mother is."

"A child?" I contract on the spot.

"Even two." He laughs. "I'm sure they'll be as impulsive and irresponsible as their mother, but they'll learn to act from their father." He puts his hand on my thigh and strokes it as we drive along the street.

It's the first time he talks to me of our future, and I have difficulty imagining a reality different from the gray one surrounding me on all sides now.

"Do you really want children with me?"

"I dream of having children with you." I see the small smile appear on his face. "Why are we putting ourselves at risk if not for the right to continuity?"

For a moment, I can imagine small children running about our apartment, laughing and fooling around, Marie scolding them affectionately and Gabriel sitting in front of the fireplace with me tucked in his arms. A spark of light and hope warms my heart until loud knocks are heard in my imagination and I tremble.

"Cursed reality."

"It won't last forever," he states confidently and stops the car at the entrance to our building.

When we enter the apartment, I remove my shoes and lie on the sofa while Gabriel lights the fire.

He pours us a drink, leans back against the wall and looks at me.

"You asked me to find out about your friend."

"Veronique." Alert, I sit up and look at him.

"Unfortunately, I don't have good news."

Moaning in pain, I rub my forehead.

"But her sons managed to escape." He sits next to me, caressing my head.

"It should comfort me but all I feel is guilt." Closing his arms around me, he pulls me onto his knees. "I disappeared and I have to go back. I belong there, to the national Resistance. I shouldn't be going to balls and smiling at those bastards. I want to go back to them but I can't hide it from you."

I feel his distressed breath on my head and his embrace almost cracks my bones.

"I should remind you that you are my wife and have a duty to obey me." He pulls my hair back, stretching my neck, and I look at him through a veil of tears. "I won't do it. I'll merely ask you to be careful because if anything should happen to you…"

I heap kisses on him and my heart spins with love.

Yawning, I lie in bed, held in Gabriel's protective arms. "Gabriel, I think I might have heard something important this evening."

"You mean apart from my groans?"

"Yes." I laugh, stroking his cheek.

"Tell me." He takes my hand and kisses it.

"The dogs always escape to the south, but the forces are spread out in the north of the city."

"Are you sure?" He sits up.

"I suspect I had something to do with the decision. Why?"

"I have to go." He jumps out of bed. I sit up and look at him in alarm. "Don't worry." He winks at me. "I'll be back soon."

I don't have time to ask him the meaning of what I said or how he understood it so quickly, when he enters the dressing room and comes out dressed in a new suit.

"Wait up for me." He bends, kisses my lips and leaves.

The apartment door slams, and my body shivers. One moment I'm in my private, safe harbor, and a second later I'm thrown into gloomy reality.

Lying, I wait for the sound of the door re-opening. My eyelids are heavy and I try and fight my tiredness. My eyes close and I try to keep them open but they droop again and I promise myself that I'll rest only for a few moments.

CHAPTER TWENTY-TWO

I'm hot. Snuggling into the body enveloping me I refuse to open my eyes. If it's just a dream, I don't ever want to wake up from it.

I feel his breathing above my head and sigh with relief. He's back. But I didn't wait up for him. I turn carefully. Gabriel is lying on his back, his eyes closed and his breathing is heavy. He's asleep and I long to wake him. Leaning on one elbow, I gaze at his strong, male face. Every feature is perfectly carved, everything put together as a work of art.

I find it hard to believe that I have gained the interest of this man. There's no lack of women who are more beautiful than I am, more elegant, and mistresses of the secrets of temptation. Quite simply, I was there, and he was forced to save me. I'm saddened by this thought. Am I supposed to feel gratitude for the fact that this cursed war, which has taken so many lives, linked me with this man?

My hand slides over his chest muscles and his eyes remain closed. I bend down to kiss the small plume of hair on the slope of his belly. Thoughts fade and the only sound playing in my ears is that of his groans.

"Compensation for my falling asleep yesterday." Smiling at him, I sit up.

His arms close around my hips, pulling me back and tossing me down. His body shields me and his fingers caress my lips. "I don't know what destiny has in store for us, but I do know that I can't see a future that doesn't include you."

"If you didn't have to save me, you wouldn't have married me." I meet his eyes. "Jeanne told me that you married me either because I'm pregnant or because I put a spell on you."

"She's right." He responds unsmilingly and removes my nightgown. "You've put a spell on me."

"Yesterday I watched a cat fight over you and I took no part in it at all."

"Why should you take part in a fight you've already won?" His lips close on my neck.

"Gabriel, I want to know more about you." I groan.

"You already know I'm crazy about you." He kisses me. "You know there is nothing I wouldn't do for you." He spreads my legs. "And you know that I fully intend to take you." I raise my arms to hold the bars of the bed. "Is there anything else you absolutely have to know now?" He kisses me hard, breathing into my mouth.

I don't answer, merely close my eyes and yield to him completely.

While eating breakfast, I leaf through the censored newspaper. Gabriel reads the German newspaper, glancing periodically at me.

"You didn't tell me that you sold your earrings again." He says quietly from behind the newspaper,

"I didn't sell them." Regretfully, I touch my earlobes. "On that terrible evening, I had to give them to a woman who threatened to turn me in."

"Well, I hope that this time they'll stay with you." He puts a velvet box in front of me. I open my eyes in surprise. "I paid more money for these diamonds than any others." He grins.

I open the box, see my earrings and fall upon him with kisses.

"It was worth buying them again." He gently pats my backside and I sit down and put them on.

"Thank you, I promise I will make it up to you." I turn them and feel the pinch of longing in my heart.

"Josephine." Gabriel folds the newspaper and puts it down on the table. "I have to go away again."

The news is an unexpected blow. I sip my coffee and try to calm my heart beats.

"For how long?"

"I'm afraid that this time it will be a long trip." He strokes my fingers. I put down my cup and allow him to take my hand and kiss it. Fear and frustration choke me.

"How many weeks?" My voice trembles.

"I won't be back in the coming months."

"Months?" I feel tears burn my eyes and look down.

"You know that if it weren't important, I wouldn't leave you." Turning over my hand, he gently kisses my wrist.

"I know." My response comes without thought and I want to shout that he cannot leave me for a few months, or for a few weeks or even for a day. But I'm silent.

"Vincent and Jeanne are staying in the city. They will take care of anything you need."

"I don't need them to take care of me." I can't raise my eyes to look at him. "I need my husband to take care of me."

"I am taking care of you." He pulls me onto his lap and embraces me. "The day will come when you realize that this trip too is for your protection."

"When are you going?" I wipe my eyes and wonder what he means.

"Now."

"At this very moment?" I shriek.

He nods, and my shock prevents me from thinking clearly.

"I'm sad." I rub my cheek against his shoulder.

"I'd be a little disappointed if you weren't." He tries to speak lightly, but I can feel his worry.

"I've bought you a new bicycle. It's at the entrance to the building."

"Thank you." Again I wipe my eyes and try to pull myself together.

"Come, walk me to the door." He kisses my head and I stand, holding hard to his hand. Parting from him grieves me and I try to remind myself that it is only a temporary parting.

Marie runs into the passage and hugs him. She murmurs parting words and he smiles calmly at her. He takes his bag and then pulls me with him to the fireplace and picks up the album I made for him.

"Reading material." He winks at me and smiles. "I've added some details to my album, so you can stop complaining that you know nothing about me."

I nod but cannot smile. I accompany him to the door, and Marie leans against the door post and sniffs.

"What can I do to make you happy?" He draws me to him and kisses my lips.

Don't go. Don't go. Don't go.

"Make me feel that even though you're far away, you're thinking about me."

"Your wish is my command." He kisses me gently, bows his head and my hand lets go of his.

The door slams behind him and I put my hand on my mouth and burst into tears. His steps fade and my sadness is unbearable. The suddenness, the transition from peak to abyss, will he really be away for a few months now?

Marie hugs me but I feel no comfort. I want to run into the bedroom and hide from the world until my man returns to me. In an instant I feel as if the apartment is cold and alien and I have no idea of how to shake off the weight bearing on me. Sitting down on the sofa, I stare at the burning coals in the fireplace and cover myself with a blanket. How many months will pass before we meet again? How many days will pass until I see the smile that rocks my being? How many hours until I am pleasured by the touch that makes me feel unconquerable?

Only a few moments have passed and I already feel grief-stricken.

Marie sets a jug of tea on the table and I notice the album on the mantelpiece. Getting up, I hug it to me, trying to persuade myself that I'll look at one page every day. In this way, I'll feel him even when he's far away from me.

Sitting down on the sofa again, I cover myself with the blanket and stroke our wedding picture. I look at it intently for the first time. The young woman in the white wedding dress looks stunned. She looks straight at the camera and her eyes convey pain and confusion. I don't recognize myself in this young woman. Beside her stands a tall man in an elegant, three-piece suit. One hand is hidden in the pocket of his trousers and the other is on the woman's shoulder. He isn't looking at the camera but at the woman. A small smile is on his face and he appears calm and strong. As if his body shields her from the unwanted guests and his arm is her support. Mine.

Placing one hand over my heart, I kiss the man's image. If only I could turn the clock back, I'd look back at him. I'd smile at him, convey the love threatening to crush my heart.

Sipping my glass of tea, I open at the first page. The heading I'd written is: **A place you miss.** What I wrote underneath, **the bicycle repair store and the patisserie,** was erased and in Gabriel's distinctive handwriting, **mine and my wife's bedroom.**

My heart expands painfully. I glance towards the bedroom and rub my thighs. My man, who is a model of European manners for any other man, has taught me what animal passion is.

I look at the page again, stroking the precise, round handwriting.

Don't turn the page. Don't turn the page…

Breathing aloud, I turn it.

Heading: **My favorite color.** Answer: **Yellow. The color of the first rose you dropped, which made me realize that my heart belongs to you.**

I close the album and sob with pain while remembering his sharp rebuke and my sense of frustration.

He'd felt me from the very first moment, yet it took me so long to feel him.

I look at our picture again and, without noticing, turn the pages.

Heading: **My favorite smell.** Answer: **My wife's sweet smell when her body trembles underneath me as I sink into her.**

I cross my legs when I feel that pleasant tingling and my cheeks are suffused with color. I smile to myself with embarrassment and turn the page.

Heading: **My favorite taste.** Answer: **The taste of my wife's body when I take her.**

"Good God…" I murmur as the tingling between my legs increases. I lean back and breathe aloud. How the hell can I survive until he comes back to me? I turn the page.

Heading: **My favorite flower.** Answer: **Fleur-de-lis.**

Fleur-de-lis? How does he…I shake my head and continue reading.

The knight's shield that signified the way of nobles. The lily consists of three petals and, for me, you signify the middle petal, walking the middle path and resisting temptations to left and right, determined to maintain your own path while the right petal has forgotten the way and the left attempts to make you bow your head, accepting defeat.

Frowning, I read his answer again. So much hidden meaning in three brief words. So much history, so much power. Now I feel that my petal is withering. There is no-one to water and protect it from the storms outside. I hurriedly turn the page.

Heading: **Your dream.** Answer: **To wake every morning with my wife's black hair spread on the pillow beside me. Her beautiful eyes look at me through the veils of sleep, and the smile on her face makes my heart miss a beat. I dream our home is a protective oasis for her, and that the sounds of children's laughter will erase the worry line from her forehead.**

I feel the tiny line in the center of my forehead and sigh. Such a simple, dream, and it still seems like an unattainable fantasy to me.

I know I didn't write any more but I turn the page nevertheless. He added a heading in his own handwriting: **Who are you thinking about now?** Answer: **You.**

I smile. Closing the album, I kiss his image in the picture.

"I'm thinking of you too and the time has come for my petal to stand up with pride."

CHAPTER TWENTY-THREE

I put on my long brown coat, my black wool hat and carelessly gather up my hair, returning to the grayish appearance that allows me to blend in without attracting attention.

A new bicycle is waiting for me in the lobby. This time it is completely white, as is the basket in front. In it is a single, yellow rose. I pick up the flower, smell it and replace it next to my handbag.

I reach Natalie's parents' home. I know there is only a slim chance of finding her there but I have no other way to find her, and I'm determined to return to my friends in the Resistance. I wheel the bicycle up three stairs leading to the building entrance, lean it against the wall and quickly go up to the second floor.

I knock twice and hear her father's angry voice. The lock rattles and an angry face looks at me.

"Good evening, Monsieur, do you remember me? I'm looking for Natalie."

"I have no idea where that wretched girl is." He says crossly. "Instead of taking care of her elderly parents she's out in the streets. I haven't seen her for two weeks."

My shoulders droop dejectedly and I nod.

"In any case, if you hear from her, would you tell her that Josephine is looking for her. I'm going to Leon's bar and I'll wait for her…"

The door slams in my face.

I return to the street. The same gloomy scenes. Gray buildings, wet streets, Reich flags proudly fluttering, and people trying to disappear into the background.

I ride slowly. No-one is waiting for me at Leon's, no-one is waiting for me at the apartment. I reach the quiet street and leave my bicycle at the entrance to the bar. The same young man is standing behind the bar. I sit down in front of him, drumming my fingers on the faded wooden counter and sigh.

"What strange cocktail would the young lady like tonight?" The young man asks, grinning. "You haven't been here in a long time."

"It seems to me that I'm not the only one." I jerk my head in the direction of the empty tables.

"It's still early." He takes a jug of red liquid from the shelf behind him, and pours into a wine glass. "The drinkers will start coming in about an hour. And this is on the house." He puts the glass in front of me and I sip and make a face.

"This is dreadful," I shriek.

"No need to be insulting." He pretends to be hurt. "After two glasses of that you'll forget it isn't the Cabernet Sauvignon you prefer."

"Nonetheless, I think I'll have a glass of water." I smile at him and he shrugs and pours me a glass of water.

"Look, you see? The drinkers are coming." He nods in the direction of the door and I look in astonishment as Vincent enters.

"Good evening," He says with a broad smile and sits down at a corner table. Getting up, I sit down opposite him.

"What are you doing here? Has something happened to Gabriel?"

"Everything is fine. Just looking after you." He winks at me and beckons to the barman. "I'll have what she's having."

"Water?" The barman asks, disappointed.

"No." Vincent laughs. "What you hide in the right hand cupboard." He takes a few notes from his pocket and the barman snatches them and goes back to the bar.

"I don't need a bodyguard," I whisper. "Don't follow me, it's dangerous."

"Why? Are you planning something?" A small smile appears on his lips and immediately disappears.

"No." I shake my head. "But it doesn't look good…"

The barman puts two glasses of cognac in front of us and I give him a cross look.

"I didn't think you could afford it," he apologizes and returns to the bar.

"So, do you want to go on sitting here or do you want me to give you the address of your friends' meeting place?"

"Are you serious?" I ask eagerly.

"Always." Leaning forward, he whispers the address.

"I should go there now." I get up.

"Sit down!"

I sit down and look questioningly at him.

"Don't be reckless. Drink your cognac, smoke a cigarette with me and then go to your meeting."

His rebuke reminds me of my man. Embarrassed, I nod and smile at him.

"He wasn't lying when he said your smile made him fall in love with you." Vincent lights a cigarette and hands it to me.

"Gabriel talked to you about me?" I bite my lip with annoyance.

"I'm his best friend, ever since we were a year old. I had to interrogate him to discover who had enticed the eternal bachelor into matrimony."

"Tell me something about him that I don't know." I inhale and then exhale the heavy smoke.

"What do you know?" He plays with the curls on his forehead and lights another cigarette for himself.

"That he's Swiss, thirty-four years old. A diamond dealer and… that's it actually."

"Then you know everything you need to know." Vincent laughs.

"You can't blame me for trying." I sip the strong drink and laugh.

"You know he worries about you?" His expression is grave.

I nod.

"You know he wouldn't leave you if it weren't necessary?"

I nod.

"You know he's crazy about you?"

Putting my hand over my heart, I nod.

"Then you know what no other woman knows about him."

"You're a good friend." I stub out the cigarette in the ashtray and stand up. "I really do know all I need to know about him."

I push my bicycle outside and peddle away. I no longer feel alone. Even when he's away from me, he fights my loneliness. This time I have a clear aim and am full of hope.

The shabby building is only a few streets away from my apartment. I have to hide in an alleyway until three Wehrmacht soldiers finish their patrol and vanish at the end of the street. I'm afraid to leave my bicycle at the entrance, so I take it with me up to the fifth floor. Standing in front of the door, panting with the effort, I knock once.

On the second knock, I whisper "Fleur-de-lis."

The locks rattle and I'm pulled inside. The door closes behind me.

"Josephine." Natalie calls gladly and runs to hug me. In the dim light, I recognize several figures I've seen before, and there are some new faces. "I thought you'd given up on us." She leads me to the sofa and Maurice gets up and bows in greeting. "I thought that after that terrible raid and our bad losses, you decided to leave us."

"I didn't have to hear about the raid." I scan those sitting quietly in chairs and looking at me. Some smiling and some indifferent. "I was there that evening."

"So you saw what happened?" Maurice asked, surprised. "So how did you manage to escape?"

Two boys whom I recognize as Veronique's sons, stiffen and look at me tensely.

"I didn't see anything." I lie so I won't have to detail the horrifying scenes. "The moment I heard firing, I hid in the next building."

"You didn't see anything?" One of the boys addresses me painfully. "Do you know if they begged for their lives or accepted their fate honorably?"

Looking down, I decide to lie.

"I heard a shot and then another, and then I heard our anthem. They sang loudly, all together, until a volley of shots cut off the singing."

I hear sobbing around me and don't dare look up.

"They went like heroes. None begged for their lives. They left us proudly and determinedly."

"Thank you for sharing with us," Maurice says, and I cautiously meet his eyes. I see from his gaze that he knows I've lied, but his sad smile tells me that I acted correctly.

"And we're glad you've returned to us." Natalie strokes my back. "We've lost many good people and now we're crying out for help."

"I'm here to stay."

"If so, then we should start assigning deliveries." Maurice rubs his eyes, appearing exhausted from sleepless nights. Members around me are equally lacking in vitality, Natalie's eyes are sunken and framed in gray. Surprisingly, she seems even lovelier to me.

"I was at your home," I whisper to her as people disperse to different rooms. "Maybe I shouldn't have."

"Did you get an angry welcome from my father?" She smiles.

"Yes."

"Good. He's behaving just as I told him to."

I look at her in surprise. "He looks older than I remembered," I murmur.

"That's what war does to people." She sighs. "We've lost the magic of youth." She yawns and half closes her eyes that glint mischievously. "You haven't yet lost the magic, but I suspect that has something to do with your charming man. Does he know you're here?"

"Yes," I answer without knowing if I'm telling the truth. "He had to go away, and I'm afraid that by the time he returns I'll have lost the magic you're talking about."

She looks yearningly at Maurice. He's bending over a map, explaining something to a bearded man. "When we're together, he manages to make me forget the horror outside and I feel like a woman." She strokes her belly and closes her eyes for a moment. "He is so excited about my pregnancy but I'm unable to be happy."

"Oh," I whisper, staring at her flat belly. "That's wonderful news. Congratulations."

"We only found out a few days ago. I'm still trying to absorb it." She hugs herself. "What reality is waiting for this child?" She asks, continuing without waiting for a response. "Every night we have to stay with friends who are willing to put themselves at risk for us. But who will be willing to risk it when we arrive with a crying baby?"

I stroke her back, trying to think of a comforting answer.

"I suggested to Maurice that we get rid of it." She shuddered and I choke. "He won't hear of it, but I am so afraid."

"You aren't alone." I hold her and see that Maurice has raised his head from the map and is looking at us in distress.

"I'll help in any way I can."

"Thank you." Embarrassed, she wipes the tears from her cheeks and shakes her head. "No more whining, it's time to work. Are you ready?"

"Of course." I kiss her forehead and join two boys who are being briefed by an older woman. Her hair is completely white but when she looks up at me and smiles, I find it hard to tell her age.

The boys hurriedly take the parcels she hands them, and I sit down in front of her. Within a few minutes, I'm peddling through the streets, anxiously glancing at the basket full of fruit. The yellow rose lies on top, the packet of documents carefully hidden and the constant fear returns, becoming an inseparable part of me.

CHAPTER TWENTY-FOUR

I wake only at noon. My thighs burn from the effort of yesterday's ride. Marie is humming a new Edith Piaf song in the drawing room and, listlessly, I get out of bed.

I grumble on my way to the bathroom, giving Marie a bitter half-smile.

"Good afternoon," she calls, wiping a window.

"What's so good about it?" I respond, closing myself in the bathroom.

There's a knock at the door and I freeze. It isn't the arrogant knocking of the Germans, but it's too hesitant a knock to be someone I know.

And who would come to visit me?

I quickly wash my face, return to the drawing room and see Marie standing and smiling at me with a yellow rose in her hand.

"I didn't even have time to thank him for you…" She hands me the flower and I smell it and put my hand over my heart.

"Good afternoon." Marie chuckles.

"It is now." I say joyfully, spinning around.

She yields to my pleas to join me for lunch and afterwards I set out for my friends' meeting place.

I carry out mission after mission, discovering that the hours pass quickly. Only when I return to the apartment, a few minutes before curfew, my heart torments me again. Without my asking, Marie spends the night in the guest room, and I sink into a night of loneliness accompanied by somber dreams.

A knock at the door makes me jump in alarm. I get out of bed, managing to get to the door before Marie, and open it to see the back of a boy skipping quickly down the stairs.

"Wait a moment," I call. "I'd like to tip you."

Not even turning his head, the boy vanishes.

I pick up the yellow rose and smile at Marie. If only I could show him that I'm thinking of him, that not a moment goes by when he isn't in my thoughts, but I have no idea where he is or how I could make contact.

I look longingly at the telephone and sigh. Another day begins and I'm already waiting for it to end.

Gobbling down my lunch I go out into the corridor leading to the stairs. Noise coming from the top floor is so unusual that I stop to work out what I'm hearing.

The sound of children talking and laughing.

I pause a moment longer then go downstairs. Marion's door opens and she comes out into the corridor and makes a face.

"New neighbors have arrived." She inhales, dropping ash from her cigarette onto the floor. "They've got small children!"

"Yes, I heard," I say, passing her.

"But don't worry," she calls after me, "I have contacts, I'll try and get rid of them."

I roll my eyes, in a hurry to leave the building. Next to my bicycle is another gray one I've never seen before. I ride my bicycle to the meeting place and have to wait a long time in the alleyway until the street is empty of pedestrians.

Temperatures have gone down in the last few days and by the time I enter the apartment, my face is frozen and my teeth are chattering. Inside isn't much better. The small stove in the middle of the room is out, and everyone is standing and rubbing their arms.

"What's wrong with the stove?" I ask a girl I don't recognize from previous meetings.

"The wood supply hasn't arrive," the bearded man Maurice had been briefing the day before answered. "Some idiot decided it was more important to transfer it to a hiding place for Jews."

I grimace and search for Natalie or Maurice, but apart from the older woman who had assigned me my deliveries the previous day, I don't' recognize anyone. They're all new members.

"I gather you're also in favor of those leeches." He says, an expression of revulsion on his face, continuing to sort bullets.

"I'm in favor of people in general." Turning my back on him, I sit down opposite the older woman. "And I don't really care about their religion or beliefs."

He chuckles to himself and I realize that none of those present intend to condemn his terrible words.

"He's right," the woman whispers to me. "We're here to beat the Germans, not to fight a war that isn't ours."

Rubbing my forehead, I stare at her. She looks so old and ugly now.

"Our people risk their lives, suffer cold and hunger. We have to remember our priorities." There is a hint of rebuke in her voice.

I'm unable to respond. The noble figures of the two sisters appear in front of my eyes, replaced by the frail little prince I hosted. Again the good becomes evil. A terrible frustration overwhelms me. I no longer understand the purpose I am risking my life for.

"Pity you weren't here earlier." She continues to whisper. "There was a stormy discussion about this very subject when Maurice asked us to help find a hiding place for a Fleur-de-Lis." She grimaces as she uses the *nom de plume*.

"Everyone, apart from three, voted against."

Without her telling me, I guessed that these were Natalie and Veronique's two sons.

"So he got irritated, took the wood supply and left us here, cold and hungry."

"Good for Maurice," I murmur and get a vindictive look from her. "I, ah...I'm not feeling very well." Putting my hand on my belly I fake a wretched expression. "Forgive me, but I can't do any deliveries today. I'll return tomorrow."

I make for the door and run down the steps. When I reach my bicycle I wheel it into the street, lean against the wall of a building and vomit. I no longer need to fake physical pain. My belly tingles and my throat burns. Gabriel was wrong. One side had indeed lost their way, but the side I thought was mine, has moved over to the other side. It wasn't trying to make me come to terms with defeat, it was making me lose the will to win.

A German soldier stops, politely asking if I am all right. Instead of replying, I bend over and vomit again and he quickly retreats. I'm supposed to return to my apartment but refuse to wallow in my distress alone. I wipe my mouth on my wool glove and turn my bicycle. An hour later, I lean it against the wall at the entrance to Louis's bar and go inside.

"Madame, you look terrible," the barman calls out with a smile, while narrowing his eyes in concern.

"I feel terrible." I sit down in front of him and put my head down on the counter.

"I'll get you some water on the house." He laughs and then falls silent as the door opens. "Or maybe your friend would like to spoil you with something better."

Straightening up, I turn quickly and, surprised, see Vincent entering with his calm step. His external appearance is so different from Gabriel's. He is tall like him, but thin with untidy, curly hair. Yet both have a quiet power. And maybe it's his closeness to my man that instantly makes me feel safe.

"Will you join me?" He points to the corner table and I nod, going over to sit down opposite him. "If you don't feel well, why didn't you go home?" There is no rebuke in his tone, only concern.

"I don't like being there alone."

"Isn't Marie with you?"

"She is, but he isn't." I bite my lip.

"You're very pale. And I saw you leave the building and vomit so maybe you're preg…" He chokes and looks suddenly embarrassed.

"Pregnant?" Amused, I raise one eyebrow. "You can relax. Before leaving the house I found out that the aunt had come to visit."

"What aunt?"

"The aunt." I burst out laughing. "The one who visits women every month."

"Ah…" He avoids my glance and beckons to the barman. "Bring us what we drank yesterday." He gives him several notes and the barman puts them in his pocket.

"But I'm not ill." I change the subject when I realize he is still embarrassed by our conversation. "I had to leave the members there when I realized that I'm no longer sure I want to be a part of them. I vomited because they disgusted me."

"Did someone try to hurt you?" He asks and, for a moment, I imagine that my man is sitting in front of me, his upper lip quivering. I blink, and the image I so long to see, vanishes,

"No." I sigh, nodding thanks when the barman puts the glasses in front of us. "Nobody tried to hurt me but I am so confused."

"Tell me." He lights a cigarette and offers it to me and I smile and take it.

"I don't know what I can tell you." I inhale, moving uncomfortably in my chair. "I don't know what you know and what I may share with you."

"I think that if your husband put me in charge of your safety you can rely on me," he says gravely and I know in my heart that he's right.

"The evening I lost those dear to me, I realized it was a wake-up call to join the Resistance," I whisper. "So I joined and felt I'd found a reason to live. Suddenly I have a reason to get up in the morning, suddenly my pride is restored, and suddenly I'm part of something important that fills me with hope."

He nods without saying a word.

"But, today, I discovered that I no longer want to be part of these people. I discovered that their opinions are dark, they believe all means are legitimate as long as they serve the cause. But not all of them are like that." I explain with frustration. "There are some who haven't disconnected from their feelings, who haven't forgotten their humanity. And they're the ones who make me envious of their sense of calling and devotion."

Vincent shrugs indifferently. "So leave."

"But if I leave, and my friends leave, who will remain?" I ask, tapping ash into the ashtray.

"The bad on both sides will remain." He sips his drink and I sigh.

"It's impossible to leave only the bad in the system. Maybe they don't know they're like that, maybe they need to be reminded to be good. To follow their conscience."

"You don't sound very confused." He clinks his glass with mine and winks at me.

"I'll go back tomorrow." I nod to myself. "I will just have to fight on two fronts sometimes."

"Nobody said this war is a child's game." Vincent stands up and waits for me to join him.

We leave together and I mount my bicycle and start peddling. When I turn my head a few moments later, he has disappeared.

CHAPTER TWENTY-FIVE

Picking up the rose from my doorstep, I smile sadly at the back of the boy skipping swiftly down the stairs. For several days I'd left a note on the spot he leaves the rose, but the note remained there. I realized he didn't want my money but I wished to find a way to thank him. One morning, Marie baked an apple pie. I cut a large slice and put it on a plate next to the door.

When I heard the knock on the door, I opened it and found an empty plate. It's impossible to explain the joy that comes from giving, but I feel it now too, when I find that the packet of cake disappears with the delivery boy.

I look at the vase and count fifteen roses. I'd already dried twenty-six of them and placed them in an album. Forty-one days have passed since Gabriel went away, and my longing for him increases by the day. Not feeling his touch at night, not seeing his small smile in the mornings and not even hearing his soothing voice. I glance at the album on the mantelpiece and long to page through it again. I have done this so many times I can recite his answers by heart. But I don't have time to sink into depression, I have work to do and deliveries increase from one day to the next.

"Have a good day," Marie smiles at me and takes the vase away to change the water, as she does every day.

"You, too, my dear." I put my hand on the door handle and stiffen when the ring of the telephone disturbs the quiet. Dropping the handle I cross the drawing room.

"Gabriel?" I gasp.

"Josephine." His deep voice sounds so far away.

"I'm so glad you called. Is everything all right? When are you coming back?"

"Everything is fine, my love. I…" The line is noisy and I hear him in snatches.

"Gabriel?"

"Can you…hear…"

"Gabriel, I can't hear you." There is frustration in my voice.

"Jos…" Loud noises are heard and then quiet. The line is silent.

"Gabriel? Gabriel?" I raise my voice but receive no answer. Only the cursed silence.

I wait a few seconds and then put down the receiver and look sorrowfully at Marie.

"Maybe he'll be able to call again." Approaching me, she looks expectantly at the telephone.

"Yes…" I murmur, sitting down in the armchair. My eyes are fixed on the telephone and I rock impatiently.

One minute is followed by another and the cursed telephone refuses to ring. I drum my fingers on my thighs and finally stand up. Half an hour has passed and the call I long for doesn't come.

"I must go out," I say to Marie. "Maybe he'll call again tomorrow."

Hugging my handbag, I leave the apartment. My disappointment is so great, I'm incapable of thinking about anything else apart from his deep voice that continues to echo in my mind.

I bump into a woman and nod in confusion to the new neighbor. She came to my apartment a month before to introduce herself, but I can't remember her name.

"Is everything all right, dear?" She asks, passing a bag of groceries from one hand to another.

"Yes. Wonderful." I continue on my way downstairs and get on my bicycle.

I didn't think the city could look any grayer, but now it seems as if it is painted in dark shades of black. I ride my bicycle and the people I pass look as if they're in a tragic film about my life. They're all gray and tired, hurrying to another meaningless destination, lacking any hope that something inspiring would happen to take them away from their wretched reality.

I leave my bicycle in the lobby of the building, and go upstairs. When I reach the apartment, I sit down opposite the older woman and nod impassively as she explains the new delivery. I make myself repeat the address of the destination and take the bags from her. In one are dozens of bullets and in the other rotten fruit.

"Be careful." I hear her shout after me and I shrug indifferently.

I put the bag of bullets on the bottom of the basket with the fruit on top. As I wheel my bicycle, the bullets tap against each other. Taking my papers out of my coat, I put them between the bag of bullets and the fruit and reluctantly start peddling.

I didn't have time to tell him I miss him. I didn't have time to tell him I love him… I didn't have time to enjoy his soothing voice. I didn't have time to get answers to my questions. I didn't have time …

I stop my bicycle, climb down and look incredulously at the crowd opposite me. Loud orders in German. Frightened screams in French and a quickening movement of people. Some disappear like rats into alleyways and I blink, trying to work out what I'm facing.

"Five! I want five French vermin!" The shout in a heavy German accent shocks me and I lose my grip on the handlebars. The bicycle falls on its side and I look fearfully into the basket. Some fruit had fallen on the ground but the bag of bullets is still hidden.

"Bring her to me!" Another shout and I'm dragged by my coat into the middle of the street, standing next to two shocked men and a hysterical woman, who doesn't stop screaming. "Another one!" The German in the black uniform screams, and another man is dragged from the sidewalk to stand next to me. "Nobody leave the area." The German gestures and a troop of soldiers stand in lines on either side of the street.

"Papers." A young soldier approaches the last man in the line, who hands over his papers with a trembling hand. The soldier nods to the officer standing behind him who takes out his gun and shoots just one shot. The man collapses on the ground and screams are heard from all sides. My throat burns from the scream that bursts from my throat.

"This is punishment for killing one of ours." The man in the black uniform screams. "Five of your miserable lives for one of ours."

I remember Gabriel's instructions with regard to my papers. I have a special stamp from the Reich thanks to my marriage to a collaborator, and I can show it. But if the soldier discovers the bullets I will save myself now in exchange for torture in the cellars of the Gestapo and a certain death sentence later on.

I'm so stupid. Tears well up in my eyes. Reckless and irresponsible. I hear Gabriel's loud voice scolding me, and pray to hear it just once more.

Another shot is heard and my body trembles. I don't dare look at the dead bodies lying next to me. An immediate death sentence as opposed to torture and an agonizing wait for execution. And I'm not only risking myself. Gabriel's fate is linked to mine. Once they're done with me, what will happen to the man who has become my entire world?

The dilemma is no longer a difficult one. A cold sweat breaks out on my forehead and I bow my head and hear the begging of the woman beside me.

"I'm a collaborator," she shrieks and weeps. "Last week I informed on my communist neighbor who was hiding two wanted people."

"Do you have more information for us?"

"Uh…no…but please…"

"Then we thank you for your contribution to the Reich." The officer grins and the woman's pleading is cut off by another shot.

"Papers." The young soldier addresses me. I don't dare raise my head. I close my eyes tightly, refusing to accept that he will be the last thing I see in my short life. "Papers!" He roars, and I shake my head. A strange peace envelops me. I smile to myself when the image of my father approaches and holds me in a strong embrace, and then the arms become more muscular. Gabriel, my love, I say in my heart. Don't be angry, Gabriel. I've had the privilege of loving you enough for a lifetime.

My hair is wrenched back and I refuse to open my eyes.

Gabriel. *Je t'aime, mon amour.*

"Leave her alone!"

Have I heard Vincent's distressed voice interrupting my intimate parting?

"Leave her alone. She's married to a man who works for the Fuhrer." The voice is louder and stronger. "She has special protection. Her papers will prove it."

Is Vincent really here? I'm not hallucinating?

Cautiously, I open my eyes, raise my head and find Vincent's anguished eyes in front of me. He is really here.

I nod my head in confusion.

"Where are your papers?" He raises his voice and thrusts his hands into my coat pockets.

"Ah, what?" I have difficulty answering him and stare at the officer's revolver.

"I asked where are your papers!" Vincent slaps my face hard and I shake my head. I point at the bicycle and put my hand on my burning cheek.

The German turns towards the sidewalk, but Vincent is before him and runs to the bicycle. Bending over, he rummages in the basket, takes out the papers and pushes the fruit back into the basket.

"Here they are." He waves the papers and runs back. He adds his papers to mine and I hear them rustling in the soldier's hand.

"Why did this foolish woman refuse to present them?" The officer barks, and my body turns to stone.

"She's in shock. Look at her." Vincent holds my shoulders and shakes me.

"All right, get her out of here." The officer hands him back my papers. I'm unable to move.

Vincent takes my hand and drags me towards the sidewalk.

"Get me someone else," the officer screams and when I hear the hysterical weeping of the woman pushed into the road, I open my mouth and shriek.

Vincent's hand covers my mouth and I can neither scream nor breathe. A shot is heard and I'm not sure I ever want to take another breath. He commands me to be quiet and takes his hand from my mouth. I open it to take a breath and can't stop trembling.

He lifts my bicycle carefully and puts his arm around my waist. He leads me towards the line of soldiers blocking the way and two of them move to allow us to pass. Their eyes are hollow. Unfeeling. The war has turned them into soulless, engineered creatures. If I remained near them for even just a few seconds longer, they would have infected me and I would have never returned to myself.

I mutter to myself, unable to contain what I'd been through.

"Everything is all right now." Vincent slows his pace a little. "I'll take you home." He adds, realizing that I don't intend to answer.

My life was saved at the cost of another woman's life. This fact is a blow and I fold.

"You're in shock, it will pass." He rubs my back and I am unable to utter a word.

I recognize my street through my tears and manage to blink only when I'm seated on the sofa in front of the fire.

Vincent talks on the telephone and Marie scurries around me. She covers me with a blanket, pours me a glass of tea and murmurs soothing words.

He finishes his conversation and stands in front of me. "The delivery?"

I open and close my eyes in a desperate attempt to focus on Vincent.

"I'll take care of it," he says.

"But…" I try to protest.

"Address?" He responds firmly.

I murmur the address in confusion and hear him order Marie not to leave me alone even for a moment.

The door slams and Marie sits down beside me. She holds my hand as if she's afraid I'll suddenly get up and run away. I rest my head on her shoulder and weep.

CHAPTER TWENTY-SIX

The sound of liquid poured into a glass causes me to open my eyes, and I look exhaustedly at Jeanne who is sitting in the armchair opposite me.

"Marie, she's waking up. Please bring her a glass of tea."

I rub my eyes and sit up, examining the elegant figure in front of me. She is sipping wine and smoking a long cigarette.

"Want one?" Jeanne asks, noticing my eyes on the cigarette.

I shake my head. The memory of the events overwhelms me and putting my hand over my mouth, I burst into tears.

"Josephine, it's all right to feel terrible." She sighs. "Facing the angel of death and Satan is a jarring experience."

"That's not why I'm crying." I sniff, thanking Marie with a crooked smile when she joins us with a jug of tea. "At that moment, I'd come to terms with my end. I think I even managed to smile when I realized that despite everything I'd lost, I'd gained the right to love."

"And be loved," Marie adds, handing me a glass of tea. "But nobody wants their life arbitrarily cut off in the middle of the street."

"True." Trembling, I sip the hot liquid. "And I won my life back, but I don't feel victorious because someone else paid with theirs…"

"That has nothing to do with you!" Jeanne says firmly. "We have the right and the obligation to fight for survival in these painful times. You didn't choose to invade another country. You didn't choose to humiliate its inhabitants. You didn't choose to execute the innocent. All you did was choose to live."

"And that choice cost someone else her life," I insist, my heart refusing to be soothed.

"Deal with it. If you have papers that entitle you to live. Anyone would choose life."

"In terms of official protocol, that sounds logical." I put the glass on the table and lean back. "But my heart will always remember what happened."

"Don't distress yourself, *Cherie*." Marie hugs me. "This reality isn't logical. It tosses us into situations no human being should have to experience. We aren't the bad ones in this story. They are. I hope they burn in hell."

"Amen." Jeanne raises her glass to Marie.

"I was standing next to a woman who begged to be saved because she'd informed on her neighbor." I grimace.

"Fool." Marie snorts in irritation. "Some pitiful French people exploit the situation to settle a score."

The ring of the telephone makes my heart jump and I look breathlessly at it.

Marie goes to the dresser but Jeanne is quicker and answers.

"Jeanne speaking."

She is silent, smiling to herself.

"Good evening to you, too, Cheri."

She listens quietly and I hug myself so I won't leap forward and snatch the receiver from her.

"As usual. Work, restaurants, going out." She laughs like a girl being courted. "Yes, yes. She's fine. I'm keeping an eye on her."

Silence again. My fear that the conversation will cut off before I have time to talk to him drives me crazy.

"Tell me how you are," she says, and I roll my eyes in frustration. "Yes. Of course. I'll let you speak to her."

Ignoring her disappointed expression, I jump up from the sofa. Holding the receiver, I gesture to her to vacate the armchair.

"Gabriel?"

"Josephine, my love." His sigh of relief makes me dizzy.

"I didn't have time to tell you some important things in our last conversation," I speak fast, terrified the conversation will be cut off.

"I'm listening." His deep voice is so calm and comforting.

"I miss you."

"And I you, my beauty."

"I love you."

"Not as much as I love you."

I let out a groan of longing and close my eyes. "I beg you, look after yourself."

"Don't worry yourself about me. Focus on taking care of yourself."

"Yes…I'm trying."

"You're not doing a very good job of it." Here is the rebuke I was waiting to hear, and a smile spreads over my face.

"Be focused. Don't be reckless or irresponsible. And always think…"

"Two steps ahead," I interrupt him, bursting into tears.

"Don't cry." His tone is distressed. "I shouldn't have scolded you when I'm not there to take care of you. It's only because I'm eaten up with guilt."

"No, no, I'm not crying because of that." I take a deep breath and forcefully pull myself together. "I'm crying because you're right. I lost focus. And I miss you so much."

"What can I do to make you happy?"

My heart shrieks to tell him to come back, but I know that my request will only bring unbearable expectation.

"Every time you look at your watch and see it is ten o'clock at night," I say quietly, "remember that I'm in our bed alone, imagining the gentleman who married me undressing and taking me in any way he chooses."

The line is quiet and I'm not sure if he'd heard me. "Gabri…"

I hear a quiet growl and fall silent.

"Your wish is my command."

"Talk soon?" I'm smiling from ear to ear.

"Whenever I can."

The call is disconnected and I kiss the mouthpiece and close my eyes.

When I open them, two figures are staring at me. Marie is smiling mischievously and Jeanne is biting her lip with embarrassment.

Vincent enters the apartment without knocking and looks questioningly at the three of us.

"Cheri, Gabriel called," Jeanne explains, sitting down on the sofa.

I tilt my head and when he nods, I understand the delivery reached its destination.

"How are you feeling?" Vincent asks, smiling at me.

"Much better now." I glance at the telephone and sigh.

"I apologize for…" He slaps himself and grimaces in embarrassment.

"It was necessary." I dismiss him with a short laugh.

"If you want us to stay the night with you, you only have to ask."

"No need." I pull the blanket over me and snuggle into it.

"All right." He doesn't sound convinced. "We'll leave you to Marie's devoted care. But if you need us, you can call The Ritz and leave me a message in Reception."

"And what should I say? The message could easily reach one of the Germans staying there, maybe even Herman Goering himself."

"The Commander of the Luftwaffe isn't interested in a girl asking to meet with a close acquaintance." He winks at me. "He's too busy looting art works."

"I wish that was all he's busy with." Jeanne links her arm in Vincent's and smiles at him. He looks lovingly at her and my heart contracts for a moment. Does he really not see that his fiancée longs for another man?

"Vincent." I go over to him as he opens the door. "I haven't thanked you." I hug him and he laughs in embarrassment.

"I didn't do anything your husband wouldn't do for me."

"You saved my life." Moving away from him, I put my hands together. "I want you to know that I'm grateful."

"You can thank me by being careful."

Again he reminds me of my man. They leave and I drop into the armchair and pray that soon I won't have to imagine him anymore.

CHAPTER TWENTY-SEVEN

I walk back and forth in the drawing room like a caged animal. A week has passed since my terrifying ordeal, and I can't find the courage to go out into the street.

Marie doesn't try and urge me to go back to my routine. On the contrary, she goes out early in the morning and returns with treasures. Fabrics, buttons, thread and a variety of other accessories which keep me busy for hours, designing and sewing dresses I have no reason to wear.

Two knocks at the door and Marie runs along the passage to the drawing room.

"It's me, Marion. Open the door."

"Marion," she whispers, the lines in her face deepening as she grimaces.

"Come on, I'm freezing out here in the corridor."

I roll my eyes and open the door.

"What took the two of you so long?" She enters and goes straight to the fireplace. She is wearing a red robe and heeled shoes in the same color and her face is made up. "It's so cold in this building."

"If you didn't wander about naked, you'd be warmer," Marie responds with a grin, disappearing into the passage.

"Josephine, I have good news." She sinks into the armchair and takes a cigarette from the packet on the coffee table. "But first, perhaps, tell me why you're looking as if you've been run over by a truck?" She narrows her eyes and examines me at length.

"I don't feel well." I lean back against the sofa and drum my fingers impatiently on it. "And we aren't friends. There is no reason for you to take an interest in how I am, or share your good news with me."

"Josephine, really." She waves a hand dismissively. "Are you still angry with me about the visit with Richard?"

"Your visit with Herr Zemel wasn't a social call!"

"You can't blame me, I was concerned for Gabriel." She refuses to get upset. "I was really afraid you were putting him at risk with traitorous behavior."

"You call a Gestapo officer here to take me in for questioning at the Gestapo offices, and then come here as if we are friends? I don't understand your insolence."

"I have to admit it was hard to accept your romance…"

"Marriage," I correct her.

"Yes, That. But I'm over my jealousy. I'm able to be generous to you." She inhales smoke and licks her lips. "I'm in love."

"That really is good news." I don't try and hide my cynicism. "I'm very happy for you and invite you to return to your apartment."

"That isn't the news." She stubs out her cigarette, stands up and puts her hand on her belly. "I'm pregnant!"

"Oh no…" I murmur.

"That's not the right response from a friend," she says, insulted.

"We aren't friends."

"Of course we are," she insists. "We're two women alone in Paris. Close neighbors who share an affection for the same man."

"Marion, we aren't…"

"O well, we don't share the same affection." She swiftly corrects herself. "But I don't have any friends, and I really need a friend now."

I look at her in despair. Does she really expect me to be her friend now?

"I know you're shut up in here all day on your own with that cross old woman," she continues. "I'm sure you also need a friend."

"I'm really tired." I fake a yawn and go to the door. "Good luck, and I hope Herr Zemel is as excited as you are."

"He doesn't know yet." She giggles. "He's coming tomorrow night and I'll tell him."

Closing the door, I look fearfully at her. I have no idea why I feel responsible for this dreadful woman, but I think that if I'd lost Gabriel maybe I'd also be temporarily insane.

"Marion," I whisper. "He is a German officer and a married man. Are you sure he'll be glad to hear your news?"

"Don't talk nonsense." She frowns. "He's head over heels in love with me. The moment I tell him, he'll leave his wife. If I have to move with him to Berlin, I'll do it. You know that true love beats any difficulties."

"Maybe you should think about it for a while."

"I thought I'd invite you tomorrow to raise a glass with us. But after your behavior this evening, I think I'll give up the idea." Pushing me aside, she leaves the apartment.

Marie peeps out from the passage, her hand over her mouth. I assume we're both thinking exactly the same thing.

***

A new rose lies on the threshold and I smile to myself when I see the empty cookie plate.

Putting the rose in the vase, I return to the dining room. A score of fabrics are spread out on the table, and I hum quietly as I sew. The escape from the outside world turns out to have been the right decision. Here I'm protected. I don't need to think even one step ahead. Just focus on the rising, falling sewing machine needle and create more and more impressive dresses that will impress no-one but Marie. I know that in the evening hours I will again feel imprisoned and the walls will close in on me, but at this moment, the quiet is good and pleasant.

Hesitant knocks on the door and, reluctantly, I disconnect from the sewing machine and walk into the passage.

Marie is standing in front of Natalie, who looks pale and exhausted.

"Let her in," I call out and pull her towards the sofa.

"I'm sorry for coming to your home." She rubs her eyes. "I was just so worried about you, I had to make sure you were healthy and in one piece."

"You were worried about me?" I cover her legs with a blanket.

"We heard about the miracle that happened to you. Saved like that at the last minute." She smiles at me. "We thought you'd come back and we'd raise a glass with you, but you simply disappeared."

"Even if I'd returned, I wouldn't have wanted to raise a glass." I sit down beside her. "Who could celebrate the murder of five innocent people?"

"You're right. I shouldn't have said that." She takes my hand and strokes it. "I was just so happy you'd been saved that I felt the need to celebrate. Our reality is completely distorted."

"Natalie, I think I'm still in shock." I bite my lip nervously. "I can't leave the house. I don't ever want to encounter any of those Germans again."

"I don't think I'd want to leave this comfortable apartment either." She leans her head back and yawns. "And don't feel guilty. You've been through a terrible ordeal and you need time to recover."

"I don't know if I'll come back at all."

"I understand." She smiles at me again and puts my hand on her belly. "You can't see that I'm pregnant yet but that doesn't mean I don't feel all the side-effects."

Marie hands her a glass of tea and puts a plate of fresh pastries on the table.

"Josephine, you are in Eden here." She puts out a hand to the plate and closes her eyes as she takes a bite of the pastry. "If I stay here a few more minutes, I'll forget there's a war outside."

"So stay," I plead. "You can rest here and get your strength back as much as you want. We'll spoil you and take care of you…"

"It won't happen." She licks her fingers and massages her neck. "Maurice will never agree to abandon the struggle and hide here with me. And even if he did agree, I don't think I could do it." She settles a cushion in the corner of the sofa and lays her head on it. "I've become used to living like an escaped convict. Being on the move all the time so they won't catch me." She yawns. "The Gestapo know about us. Our names came up in interrogation. They're looking for us everywhere, but we always manage to get away." I hear the pride in her voice and shrink in embarrassment. "I've stopped counting the number of people we've helped to escape. I no longer remember the faces of each Fleur-de-Lis we've taken to a safe hiding place, and I'm quite certain that the weapons we've passed over are helping the fighters in the forests." She yawns again and pulls the blanket up to her shoulders. "I'll just rest a while and then I'll go back to my missions."

Her breathing becomes heavy and I continue to sit beside her, looking at her beautiful, anguished face. As if all the burden of France lies on those slender shoulders.

I get up to lock the door and return to the dining room. I undo the seams of the blue wool dress, adding material to the top part. Three hours later I call Marie to see my new creation. A long, pretty dress with silver buttons on the breast and a thin belt for the hips. The belt expands and contracts as needed, making it the perfect pregnancy dress.

"Sorry I fell asleep." Natalie appears in the doorway. "Thank you for your hospitality."

"We aren't done with you yet." Marie obstinately folds her arms. "I've warmed you water for a bath and made you dinner. When you finish, you can leave."

"But ... they're waiting for me, and…"

"Natalie, the war will manage without you for one evening!" Holding the new dress, I lead her into the bathroom and when she sees the bath in the center, her eyes sparkle with excitement. "Take your time." I close the door behind her and return to the dining room to clear the table. I help Marie set the table and when we finish, Natalie joins us. She is wearing the dress and doesn't stop touching it. "I don't know what to say." Her eyes well up with tears. "It's perfect, and you didn't even take my measurements."

"It will expand with you." I wink, showing her how to release the tucks in the belt.

"You were always a level above the other students." She sits down and looks in astonishment at the food. "The day will come when I go into a boutique that sells your creations and I'll proudly tell that I studied with you." Hesitantly, she takes a roll, and Marie leans forward and heaps food on her plate.

"That's too much." She smiles shyly.

"You're eating for two," Marie scolds her. I sit down and lower my eyes, having difficulty coming to terms with the abundance given me every day while she is fighting and starving.

"You probably think I'm judging you." She puts down her fork and looks gravely at me. "I'm not judging you at all. I'm glad for you. And I respect you even more for choosing to join us when you don't have to fight for your survival."

"Our struggle is identical." I straighten up. "I'd give it all up without turning a hair. But I realized that it's better I do it when I'm physically strong."

"You're right." Natalie pours herself a glass of milk and sips it pleasurably. "Better you enjoy it than those stinking Germans." She glances fearfully at Marie.

"Don't worry." Marie winks at her. "I use far worse words to describe their stink."

The conversation around the table grows nostalgic. We recount our memories of when we were studying and laugh when Natalie imitates some of our strict lecturers.

"I'll never forget how Nita burst into tears when the new lecturer maintained that her skirt was more suitable for milking cows than a fashion show." Natalie laughs and then pales. She bows her head and rubs her belly. "She could have saved herself." Her voice trembled. "On the cursed night of the *Vel d'Hiv* hunt, I hid her in my apartment. Her parents refused to believe that the deportation would take place, and they insisted that they were merely damn rumors. When they started picking up Jews at around four in the morning, we were sitting weeping in my drawing room." Natalie sniffs and her expression grows somber. "At eight o'clock she hugged me and said that her parents needed her."

I feel my cheeks grow wet with tears and hear Marie sniffing.

"My pleading was of no use. She was determined to join them no matter what. When they took them to Drancy I was still cautiously optimistic, but then I heard they'd been sent to those camps…" She coughs and sips her milk. "Since then I have a blacklist. Not of Germans, but of the French. Rene Bousquet and Louis *Darquier head the list, and several others have been added since then.*" She smiles bitterly. "The day will come and they'll pay the price and I hope I'll be there to see their faces a moment before they're hanged from the Arc de Triomphe." She falls silent and I gaze at her with grief stricken eyes.

"This Fleur-de-Lis is in memory of Nita." Natalie stands up and takes a yellow Fleur-de-Lis badge out of her pocket. "She always said that this symbol would decorate the sign of the boutique she'd open on the Champs Elysees."

Natalie opens the top buttons of her dress and pins the badge to the lining of the dress. "She won't be able to do it, but maybe one day one of us will do it for her."

She closes the buttons and pats the fabric over her heart. "It will happen on the day I manage to stop hating and open a place in my heart for the love I felt for her."

Natalie puts on her coat and hugs Marie. Her words have moved me so deeply that I am unable to stop the flow of tears.

"We'll prepare packets of food." I say in confusion, "we have so many things here and I'll gladly share it with you. Actually, I'll give it all to you." I go past her to the kitchen but she holds my arm and stops me.

"It will look suspicious if I leave this apartment with bags of food." She smiles sweetly and rubs her neck. "I have to be very careful."

"I didn't think of that." I murmur and see her to the door.

"If you decide to come back to us, I'd be glad if you spoil me with one of those pastries." She points to the tray in the drawing room, and I hurry to bring her two pastries. She thanks me with a nod and puts them in the pocket of her coat. "Maurice will spoil me tonight in exchange for these." She winks at me and leaves the apartment.

I turn to look at Marie and shrug. "I won't be able to hide here forever. You heard her…there's a special boutique waiting to open on the Champs Elysees."

CHAPTER TWENTY-EIGHT

I'm received in the hideout-apartment with utter indifference. I didn't expect anything else. They all seem to be forcing themselves to walk back and forth about the room to avoid freezing. Natalie and Maurice aren't here and I listen with half an ear to the whispering of several men about the need for a more powerful armed resistance. The only information I have about the war between the Allies and the Germans is based on the awkward details I hear from Marie. She listens to BBC broadcasts at night and tells me her exciting news in the morning. The wretched state of the Germans in Russia, the Allies' stubborn war on Italian ground, and the power of the American army. But at this moment, in the filthy, freezing apartment, it seems to me that the war will go on forever. Or at least until the moment when the last of the Resistance freezes to death.

I receive my delivery and set out. This time I am alert and cautious. Dodging into alleyways time after time, avoiding all uniforms. Fear filters into me and flows through my veins. Maybe because for the first time, I realize I have something to lose. I dream about the future and am not sure whether this is a blessing or a curse.

I arrive at the street of the brothels and cautiously cross the back yards. When I reach the steps leading up to the kitchen, I leave my bicycle and go up. This time I don't knock but immediately enter. The kitchen is empty.

Putting the documents inside my coat, I sit down on a chair. The noises on the other side of the curtain indicate a great deal of activity. Not even the loud music hides the sounds of laugher and pleasure. I grimace in distaste when lewd words in a heavy German accent evoke a flirtatious, Parisian feminine response.

Minutes pass and it doesn't look as if the curtain will open any time soon. I walk forward, reach the curtain and retreat. Approach again and this time peep inside the room. The floor of the foyer is covered with a red carpet and on the walls hang pornographic pictures.

"Where are you running off to?" A German soldier chases a young girl with bare breasts and she giggles and skips up the stairs to the top floor.

Retreating, I lean against the wall. In this cursed place the German doesn't seem to be a soulless creature. He seems alive and enthusiastic. My revulsion increases.

I sit down and wait. The ceiling shakes with the creaking of beds and the sounds of women and men groaning reaches me from beyond the walls. I'm undoubtedly in the most despicable place in the world. No pride probably existed here even before the war, but now it is irretrievably buried under the tiles.

"Have you been waiting long?" Madame Distel closes the curtain behind her and holds out her hand.

"Long enough to know I really don't want to be here." I hand over the parcel of documents.

"I can understand that." She sighs. "You'd probably prefer to take deliveries to noble, elegant women, but they prefer to sit in front of the fire eating croissants, while I am willing to put myself at risk."

"Aren't you afraid that after the war you'll be punished for this?" I whisper, pointing at the curtain. "For hosting and indulging those animals?"

"Do you think I deserve to be punished?"

"Yes…no…I don't know."

"Well let's agree that I won't judge you for how you get your food at this time, and you won't judge me." She raises her arm to a shelf, takes a bottle of perfume and liberally sprays her neck. "Are you waiting for a tip?" She slips her fingers into her décolleté and I shake my head and run outside.

I wheel my bicycle between the bushes and look in horror at a swaying soldier urinating in the yard. He smiles when he notices me.

"Come here." He laughs, shaking his exposed penis.

Without replying, I escape on my bicycle.

"Madame, where are you running off to?" He shouts and when I turn my head I see he is trying to run after me, but his pants are down and he trips.

I peddle fast, slowing down only at the third street. What would have happened if he hadn't been drunk? Fear gnaws at my belly, and I force myself to peddle slowly, hiding in alleyways whenever I think I see a uniform.

I leave my bicycle at the entrance to the building with a sigh of relief. The door to Marion's apartment is closed and I pause in front of it and listen to the music and sounds of laughter. Could she have told him and is he really excited for her? For them? But I have no intention of joining in their celebration, all I want is to wash off the filth of the last delivery.

Marie welcomes me in the drawing room and I realize from her expression that she shares my relief that the day has ended. I bathe, put on the record player and join her in the dining room.

Loud knocks on the door make us both jump in alarm.

"I'll open it." Marie shakes her head and walks swiftly to the door. I follow, standing behind her. My heart is beating wildly.

"Madame Josephine." The new neighbor looks distraught. "I'm sorry to disturb you, but I think there's a problem on the first floor."

"What problem?" I move to stand beside Marie.

"I don't want to interfere…" She looks fearfully behind her. "I've been out shopping and just returned." She waves a bag. "And I heard shouting and blows and ran upstairs, but when I looked down, I saw a German officer leaving the apartment."

I put my hand over my mouth and go out to the corridor.

"Has he gone?" I whisper.

"Yes. But he might come back." She shifts uncomfortably.

"I don't think he'll be back." I nod to Marie to accompany me and the neighbor follows us on tiptoes.

"My husband will kill me," she murmurs irritably. "He's forbidden me to meet the neighbors."

"Then go back to your apartment," I order quietly.

"I have to make sure she's all right."

I knock once on Marion's door and hear a faint moan.

Marie opens the door and the three of us stare in horror at the figure in the red nightgown lying on the carpet. Her face is swollen, her lips bleeding and she is holding her belly and sobbing.

"What has he done to you?" I run to her and brush the hair from her forehead.

"Josephine, get me out of here." She wails.

"We'll take you to the hospital."

"No!" She raises her voice and bursts into sobs. "I don't want anyone to touch or question me, I just want you to get me out of this apartment."

"We'll take you to our apartment." Marie bends down and takes her arm. Marion groans in pain and I help her to sit up. The neighbor gazes at her in utter shock.

"Close the door behind us," I ask her, dragging Marion to our apartment with Marie's help.

We sit her on the sofa and Marie hurries to the bathroom. She is back in a minute with a wet cloth, and carefully wipes the blood of Marion's lips.

"I have to go," says the neighbor with embarrassment. "If my husband were to return and start asking questions…" I nod, continuing to gaze at Marion with concern.

The apartment door closes.

"You were right." Marion looks down. "Maybe I shouldn't have told him." She sniffs. "You probably think I'm a fool for believing that he was in love with me."

"No." I stroke her hair. "I think you're a fool for believing there could be a relationship with that scum of a human being."

She laughs briefly and groans again. "He always treated me with respect, spoiling me, bringing me gifts, promising to take me to visit Berlin and suddenly…" She chokes. "He became a different man. I thought I was imagining it when he slapped me the first time." She rubs her swollen cheek. "We danced, drank, laughed, made love." Marion shrinks and trembles. "And then, when we returned to the drawing room, I poured him a glass of wine and told him I'm pregnant." She hugs herself and closes her eyes. "If you could have seen how his eyes darkened." She shivered. "As if the devil had got into him, He began to scream and break things in the apartment. And then he turned his rage on me. At first I tried to persuade him to stop. That I love him and he loves me. That he could leave his wife and I'd take care of him. But then he broke the wine glass on me." She bows her head and fingers the stains on her nightgown.

"Human scum," Marie bursts out.

"He demanded that I get rid of the pest tomorrow." Her gaze is fixed on the wall in front of her. "He called it a pest."

"And what do you intend to do?" I try to keep my voice steady.

"Keep it, of course." Her jaws tighten with determination. "I've already lost one baby and I won't lose another."

Marie and I exchange glances. Marion stares at a mysterious spot on the wall again.

"I don't think you should tell him that you're keeping the baby," Marie says, when she returns with a jug of tea.

"Men like him are very dangerous, you know very well how he'll react."

"I'll think about it." Marion yawns, looking like a lost little girl. "Could I stay here tonight? I promise not to bother you, it's hard for me to go back to my apartment now."

"Of course," I respond at once. "I'll go to your apartment to fetch you a change of clothing, and in the meantime you can use the bathroom."

Marie helps her to get up and I leave the apartment and go downstairs.

The new neighbor passes and, apart from a nod, ignores me. I wait for his door to close, then go into Marion's apartment.

The apartment looks like a war zone. The carpet is covered with glass fragments and blood stains. The dresser is overturned. A vase is smashed.

I hurry into the untidy bedroom and open the closet, take out some things and escape upstairs.

When I enter the bathroom, I'm horrified by the number of bruises on Marion's body. She doesn't try to hide them but dresses slowly, allowing me to help her. It's the first time I've seen her in a modest flannel nightgown, and am sorry she doesn't understand how much prettier she is.

She brushes her hair and looks at herself in the mirror. Her eyes well up. "Everyone gets what's coming to them," her voice trembles.

"Nobody deserves a beating like this." I sit down and look at her with pain.

"I deserve it. I fell pregnant through trickery because I was head over heels in love and knew my man, your man now, wouldn't leave me in that situation. But I wasn't smart enough to keep the baby. After I lost it, I got very depressed and started doing stupid things."

I no longer feel hatred for this woman, only pity.

"And then, when I saw you and the way he looked at you, I was mad with jealousy. I wanted to feel loved and it seems I was willing to compromise with anyone."

"You don't have to compromise. You're a good, beautiful woman who has lost her way a little."

"I've completely lost my way." She puts the comb down on the shelf and turns to me. "I was determined to get rid of you, only because I couldn't bear the fact that he's in love with you."

"You can find your way again," I plead with her. "I'll help you hide. I know some people who will help you escape and…"

"I knew I didn't suspect you for nothing." She narrows her eyes and I go pale. "I'm incorrigible, talking nonsense again." She smiles crookedly. "I should thank you but I have to refuse. The baby in my belly and this apartment are the only things I have right now." She briefly strokes her belly and straightens up. "I don't think running away is the solution. Tomorrow evening he's supposed to come and see if I've carried out his order, and I'll deal with what's coming."

I want to shake her and explain the consequences of her decision, but she resolutely leaves the room and I find myself praying for my man to return and explain to me what my next steps should be.

CHAPTER TWENTY-NINE

I stay in the apartment for the entire day. Marion doesn't talk much. She joins me for breakfast and then goes back to the guest room. She joins me for lunch and returns to bed.

I hug the yellow rose that came for me today, and refuse to put it in the vase, longing to inhale its strength and wisdom. Not even my escape to the sewing machine can calm me. For the first time, I watch the hands of the clock as I sew, praying that they will stop moving so fast.

"What will we do?" Marie whispers, sitting down beside me.

"I have no idea." Pulling the fabric from the machine, I irritably undo the crooked seam. We both look up at Marion who is leaning against the door frame.

"I'm going back to my apartment now." She drums her fingers on the wall. "And you two have to stop looking so worried."

"He will hurt you." Standing up I walk over to her. "Please consider my suggestion, it isn't too late."

"I'm going back to the apartment." She retreats into the passage. "He'll be angry, he'll shout, hit me and that will be the end of it. I'll tell him I don't expect anything from him, that as far as I'm concerned the relationship has ended." She doesn't wait for my response and leaves the apartment.

"That woman has no sense." Marie stands up and lights a cigarette.

"Maybe he'll just shout this time." I sit down again in front of the sewing machine, but unable to thread the needle. The fear is nerve-wracking.

"I thought she has sense." Marie walks back and forth. "You should know it will end with far worse than a few slaps."

"What can I do?" I raise my voice. "I gave her another option and she refused."

"She's a wretched, foolish woman." Marie sighs and goes to the kitchen. When she puts dinner on the table neither of us can touch our plates. Finally, I get up and walk to the door. Putting my hand on the wood, I put my ear to it. The corridor is quiet and apart from children's voices on the floor above, I can't hear a thing.

"Well…" Marie puts her ear to the door. "Did you hear anything?"

"Nothing." I turn to the fireplace, light a cigarette and go to the door. I return to the fireplace to get rid of the ash and walk back and forth until the cigarette is finished. "Maybe he won't come this evening."

"Shhh…" Marie puts her finger on her lips, and I hurry to put my ear to the door.

Steps thunder up the stairs and both of us step back in alarm. A door opens, slams shut, and then silence.

"Maybe we should go there." I put my hand on the handle and Marie pulls it back.

"Are you mad? Do you want him to hurt you too?"

"So what the hell are we supposed to do?"

She looks just as helpless as I do, and we both lean against the door again and listen tensely.

Silence.

I press Marie's arm when I think I hear a cry.

Sounds of breaking. Shouts. Wails. I drop my hand from Marie's arm and open the door.

"Stay here!" I order her, but she shakes her head and sticks closely to me. We go quietly down the stairs and the roars increase. Now there is clearly a battle going on in the apartment, Marion's cries are horrifying.

Putting my hand on my chest, I try to calm my pounding heart glancing in alarm at Marie. She tries to take my hand and pull me back up the stairs, but I shake her off and stand in front of Marion's door.

"Wretched French whore," the roar of the familiar voice shocks my ear drums. "I told you to get rid of that garbage in your belly." The sound of breaking, blows and wails. "I gave you a chance to end this story and now you've left me no choice."

"Please, please, don't!" Marion's terrified scream makes me dizzy. "No-one will know. I will never tell our secret."

"We have no shared secret," Zemel scoffs. "But now I will have a private secret."

I can't hear Marion's answer, just a horrifying choking sound. My hand presses the handle and the door opens. Zemel is sitting on Marion's belly and choking her. Her eyes are staring out of her head and her mouth is open in a despairing attempt to breathe.

"Leave her alone!" I shriek, and his hold slackens as he turns his head and looks at me, his eyes wide open. I have never seen such a satanic expression. I retreat horrified.

"Get out of here now or you will come to the same end." His tone freezes my blood. I can't move. Marie holds my hand and says nothing.

I see Marion waving her hand and removing his revolver from his belt. Zemel looks back at her, laughing, as he easily takes the gun out of her hand.

"That really will be quicker." He aims the barrel at her forehead. She screams and manages to knock the gun out of his hand to the carpet. He leaps towards it but Marion screams again and pulls his leg. He kicks her and my eyes are fixed on the gun. She doesn't give up. Biting, scratching, shouting; I take a step forward.

"Stinking whore." Zemel straightens up to kick her, and I throw myself forward to lie on the gun. I hold it with trembling fingers and see his fist fly up, but this time towards me.

"Shoot him!" Marie shouts, and I close my eyes and press the trigger. I'm thrown onto my back and the gun falls to the carpet.

Silence.

I cautiously open my eyes and see Marie bending over the large body in the black uniform. Her face is as white as a sheet.

"You shot him…" Marion murmurs, holding her throat. "He'd have killed me but you shot him."

Marie turns to close the door.

I look at my fingers and then at the huge hole in Zemel's throat. Blood is bursting from his body and I put my hand over my mouth and choke.

"You had no choice." Marie kneels down and strokes my head.

"I killed him." I feel panic stricken and have difficulty thinking logically. "Marie, I've killed a human being. I've killed a human being."

"Not a human being." She continues to stroke my head. "A devil. A particularly vicious devil."

"You saved me." Marion bursts into tears and drags herself over to me. "Now we only have to tell the truth, it was self-defense."

"You can't be serious." I continue to look at the lifeless figure lying on the carpet. "I killed an SS officer, do you really think someone will care about the reason? They'll put me in front of a firing squad and shoot me without blinking an eye."

"Then we'll go to the French police." Marion insists. "They'll believe us. They'll help us."

"Nobody will help us." I clench my fist to stop the trembling of my fingers. "They'll hand us over to the Gestapo and after torturing us, they'll kill us."

"I won't be able to cope with their torture." Marion retreats from me, wailing hysterically.

"Josephine, first of all, let's go back to our apartment." Marie holds my arm and helps me up. "None of us can think clearly with his body looking at us."

I nod in confusion, my eyes fixed on the expressionless blue eyes. They look even more threatening.

We help Marion get up and peep out into the corridor. The coast is clear. The three of us go quickly upstairs to my apartment. Marie locks the door behind us.

"We don't have much time." Marie lights a cigarette and walks nervously up and down the drawing room. "When do you think they'll notice he's disappeared?" She asks Marion, who pours herself a glass of brandy.

"He usually stays with me until the early hours of the morning." She sips her drink, her eyes darting back and forth.

"Does anyone know about your romance?" I go over to pour myself a drink.

"I don't think so." Marion scratches her head. "We've never been seen in public, his driver doesn't bring him here and I don't believe he told anyone. His wife comes from a family very close to the Fuhrer, and he stressed several times that our connection must not be discovered." She sips her drink again and taps the glass several times.

"And you chose to tell him you're pregnant?" I raise my voice.

"Calm down. Only you and Marie know about us."

Hesitant knocks at the door and the three of us look fearfully at each other.

"Keep calm!" Marie orders and goes to open the door.

"I heard a shot." The neighbor bursts inside looking distraught.

"A shot?" Marie asks musingly, putting a cigarette between her lips.

"Yes. Yes. A shot. I was putting the children to bed and I heard it."

"Ah…" I nod. "The shot…yes, we also heard it, from the street."

"It sounded really close." She peeps out into the corridor. "I was afraid the German I saw yesterday came back to hurt her."

She points at Marion.

"There was no German!" I raise my voice and she steps back. "You're confused. Marion fell downstairs yesterday and we ran to help her."

"I'm quite sure I saw…"

"her trip on the stairs," Marie interrupted irritably. "You didn't see anyone, and I'm sure your husband won't want to spend time with you in the cellars of the Gestapo."

"You're right. I didn't see anything." She pales. "I didn't hear anything either. Sometimes the children so confuse me I imagine things."

"I need to be more careful." Marion mutters, pouring herself another glass. "Those stairs are very slippery."

"Yes." The neighbor peeps into the corridor again and then looks up at the top floor. "I should go back to my children." She goes out and closes the door.

"She'll inform on us," Marion says.

"She won't." I try and calm her as well as myself. "But maybe we should pack a bag and get out of here. If anyone else knows and comes here…" Fear prevents me from completing the sentence.

"We need to find a better solution." Marie paces back and forth again and I bite my nails. Running away indicates guilt. And we'll probably be caught. And what will happen to Gabriel? My Gabriel… I go to the dresser, lift the telephone receiver and ask the switchboard to transfer my call to The Ritz Hotel.

"Bon Soir," a pleasant male voice answers in French.

"Bon Soir." I take a deep breath. "I wish to leave a message for a guest in room 152."

"Monsieur Vincent Godard?"

"Yes. Would you tell him that Josephine wants to see him?"

"Certainly, Madame."

"Wait!" I hold the receiver so tightly my fingers turn white. "Actually, tell him that Josephine longs to see him. Longs very, very, very much to see him."

"I will gladly do so."

"Did you write down 'very'?"

"Three times Madame." He sounds amused.

"Thank you." I put down the receiver and start pacing the drawing room.

None of us utter a word. Each one is sunk in thought. As time passes, I feel despair invading me and my fear increases.

"He'll come." Marie nods to herself and walks over to stand in front of the wall clock. "It's only seven o'clock. Still two hours to curfew."

Steps outside in the corridor make all three of us stare at the door, but they continue up to the top floor.

"He'll come. He has to come," I murmur, looking at the clock.

"We are in so much trouble." Marion sobs, touching her injured, swollen face.

Two knocks are heard. Embracing Marie, I go to open the door.

"If you so long to see me, it must be important." The winning smile on Vincent's face makes me fall upon him in an embrace.

Marie closes the door, and when I disengage from him, the smile is wiped off his face and he looks worriedly at Marion.

"We have a little problem," I whisper.

Taking my arm, he leads me into the dining room, closes the door and lights a cigarette.

"Vincent, I had no choice." I hug myself and shake my head. "He'd have killed her, and I wasn't thinking about the implications when I shot him."

"French or German?" He asks quietly.

"German." I lower my eyes. "High ranking. Extremely high."

I hear the curse bursting from his throat.

"I had no choice, I swear."

"I believe you." He sighs. "Where is he?"

"In her apartment, on the first floor."

"Understood." He puts out the cigarette, opens the door, and I follow him into the drawing room.

He goes to the telephone and makes a quick call in German, then turns to us.

"Before I take care of our little problem," he clears his throat and takes a sip of the drink I left on the coffee table. "I need to know if anyone else witnessed the incident."

"Just the three of us," Marie is the first to respond. "The neighbor upstairs thought she heard a shot but we made her believe she was mistaken."

"Will she be a problem?" He asks me.

"I don't think so."

"Marie, I'd be glad of your help until further help arrives." He smiles at her and she nods in confirmation.

"Josephine, wait for a telephone call." Vincent bows his head to me and leaves the apartment with Marie.

Marion collapses on the sofa. She licks her hurt lips and rocks her body. I stand by the telephone dresser, unable to calm myself. I walk to the window, draw the curtains and go to the fireplace, pour a drink, and return to the dresser.

The ring of the telephone breaks the silence. Holding the receive I put it to my ear.

"Josephine?" Gabriel's deep voice is suddenly heard, and I put my hand over my mouth to stop the sob wanting to come out.

"Gabriel." My voice trembles and I cough.

"I've missed you." He sounds so calm. The tears flow down my cheeks.

"I wish you were here with me now." Biting my lips I remind myself not to say anything that could incriminate me.

"There is nothing I'd like more than to be with you now. I think you should go out and enjoy yourself, it will be good for you."

"Enjoy myself?" I repeat uncomprehendingly.

"Yes, *Cherie*, I'm sure that enjoying yourself in a place with lots of people around will be good for you."

"I don't understand why you want me to go out without you."

"People will start to suspect I forbid you to enjoy yourself without me." He laughs. "We don't want that to happen. It's important my wife be seen to be enjoying herself even when I'm not with her. That a lot of people see…"

I frown and nod. He wants me to create an alibi for myself.

"You're right, my love. I'll take Marion and we'll go out and have a good time.'

I see her looking at me in horror and I put my finger to my lips, signaling to her to be quiet.

"Wear a beautiful dress and I'll imagine I'm with you." He is silent for a moment then adds, "Go to the restaurant on the Grand Boulevard, the one where I proposed to you."

I realize the conversation is coming to an end and my heart burns. "Gabriel, I love you."

"I love you more."

The call disconnects and I continue to look at the telephone. Our common dream seems even further away than ever.

"Get up!" I order Marion. "We're going out to enjoy ourselves."

"I have no desire to go out." She shrinks. "I'm terrified. And see what I look like!" She touches her face and sighs.

Going over to her I whisper firmly in her ear. "We are going out to enjoy ourselves and we'll make sure we're seen by as many people as possible. So if they come to question us, there will be enough witnesses to corroborate our story."

Her eyes narrow and she jumps up from the sofa.

"Yes, that's what we'll do. We'll attract attention. And it will be difficult to believe that we'd go out after committing murder."

Going quickly to my closet, she goes through my dresses and chooses an olive green dress. She puts it on and I look at her. This woman undoubtedly has a magnificent body, nobody could remain indifferent to her.

"Your face…" I whisper as I put on a short, sequined dress.

"Don't worry, I'm a make-up artist. And I'm not a bad actress either." She stands in front of the mirror and pats her face with a napkin, spreading a thick layer of base on her face. "If I manage to survive this war, I'll move to America and try my luck there."

I look on in astonishment at how she hides her bruises. Within a few minutes I have to look at her from close up in order to discover any signs of the struggle. "I'll hide this with a hat." She points to the gray mark on her forehead.

She tries on my high heeled shoes but they are too small.

"I'll have to go to my apartment." She slips her arms into lace gloves, frowning with frustration.

I look at the clock. It is already nine-thirty and time isn't on our side.

Going downstairs, we knock at the door to her apartment. Marie opens it a little, peeps out, and examines us in surprise.

"We have to go out, we'll be back before curfew," I explain to her and Marion enters the apartment. When she comes out, she looks stunned and distraught.

"What's happening in there?" I whisper as we go out into the street.

"Nothing I haven't seen in horror movies." She walks fast in her high heels and I hurry after her.

Two women in fur coats and lace-edged hats will certainly attract attention in the quiet, gray, Paris streets. She waves her hand to stop a cyclist with a passenger rickshaw. I give him the name of the restaurant and we sit down in the rickshaw. Marion plays with her cigarette box and I turn the earrings in my ears until they hurt. The sight of the hollow-eyed Zemel haunts me, and my fingers tremble when I recall Marie's command to press the trigger.

The moment the rickshaw stops at the entrance to the restaurant, Marion puts a broad smile on her face and lights a cigarette. I pay the boy and ask him to wait for us.

"I'll make sure no-one forgets we were here." Marion winks at me and goes inside.

She giggles with the hostess and, instead of sitting down opposite me, passes among the tables, chatting cheerfully with all the uniforms she encounters. She had undoubtedly managed to meet a few Germans since they'd occupied our city, and I stare in admiration at her perfect performance. No-one but myself noticed the tiny spasms of pain in her face or the artificial smile she flung in all directions. She returns to our table accompanied by Herr Stengel, begging him to join us. He kisses my hand and seems delighted by the attention he is receiving from her.

"Madame Augustine, has your husband returned to Paris yet?" He asks, lighting a cigarette for Marion.

"No, unfortunately, not yet." Playing with the edge of the tablecloth, I command myself to remain calm.

"It isn't healthy for a man to leave his wife alone for so long." He grins. "Especially when friends at my table ask about her."

"My husband is on business for the Fuhrer," I respond firmly with a forced smile. "I'm sure your friends respect this."

"Of course. Of course." He raises his hands in surrender. "We are all grateful for his important activity. Wars are very costly and every diamond helps us to arm ourselves."

"I love diamonds." Marion displays the diamond bracelet she'd received from Gabriel. "And I also love singing!" She laughs with pleasure. "So go back to your seat and allow me to indulge you with a song dedicated especially to you."

Raising his eyebrows in surprise, he nods enthusiastically.

"Maybe that's drawing a little too much attention," I whisper uncomfortably as he walks away from us.

"There is no such thing as too much attention." She taps her glass against mine and sways her hips as she approaches the stage and whispers to the pianist.

When she opens her mouth and starts to sing, the audience falls silent. Her voice is soft and velvety and when she closes her eyes, I close mine, and feel the words that emerge from her throat plucking at my soul. So much pain. So much suffering. And tonight I took the life of a human being. A cruel monster of a man, but in my worst nightmares I never believed I could ever be in such a situation. Placing my hands on my thighs I try to draw comfort from the gentle sounds of the piano and the sweet voice that makes me shiver. Her song sounds like a prayer and I move my lips and join her in a whisper.

A storm of clapping makes me open my eyes. Marion carefully wipes away a tear form the corner of her eye and bows to the audience. She seems so vulnerable and yet stands erect, looking proudly around her. For a moment, it seems to me that she is the perfect equivalent to my beloved city. Wounded, bruised, sad and still trying to prove her pride.

She attempts to return to the table but is blocked by men and women who congratulate her. When she reaches me she is flushed and excited.

"The manager offered me a permanent job here." She sits down stroking her belly and sighing. "I think we have enough witnesses to our evening of enjoyment." She winks at me and thanks the waitress who serves us two glasses of champagne, courtesy of Herr Stengel.

I nod and fake a yawn. The curfew starts in half an hour, and although I have a special permit, I have no intention of using it tonight. I had enough for one evening.

Marion attracts attention on our way out too, not missing a parting from a single acquaintance.

When we get into the rickshaw, it seems that my forced smile will never be erased. The short journey passes in silence. Each of us deep in thought. I know how I left the building, but I have no idea what I'll find when I return, or who will be waiting for us. I press Marion's hand and she responds with a despondent smile.

The entrance is quiet and the building dark. We go upstairs and stop at the door to her apartment.

"Open it." I tell her and rub my forehead.

Marion cautiously opens the door and peeps inside. "I've never seen my apartment so clean and tidy." She enters and I follow. The sight of the officer lying lifeless, blood welling from his neck, won't leave me alone, and I have to blink several times to shake the terrifying memory.

But now, there is not a sign of the officer. No sign of blood. The apartment is shining and clean.

"Where did they put him?" Marion fearfully opens the doors of her closets.

"They wouldn't have left him here," I declare confidently, following her into the bedroom and peeping into the closets. "We should get our stories straight in case someone comes to ask questions."

She nods and takes off the dress, tossing it on the carpet in the bedroom, and puts on a revealing nightgown. We return to the drawing room and she pours us a drink, sitting on the sofa with crossed legs and examining her apartment with great interest.

"You spent the day with me so I could sew a dress for you." I point towards the bedroom.

"Who would believe that you sewed it?" She scoffs, rolling her eyes. "Isn't that a dress from Coco Chanel's collection?"

"No." I try to control my need to shake her. "That really is a dress I designed and sewed."

"Don't you think we have enough lies to tell?" She scolds me. "Find another excuse. A more reasonable one."

Going into the bedroom, I return with the dress.

"Marion, this is what I do all day. Design and sew dresses." I straighten the folds of the dress and display it to her. "I know each stitch in this dress, and I have sketches that will prove it is the fruit of my creation."

"*Mon Dieu.*" She raises her eyebrows in surprise. "How come I didn't know that until now?"

"You were busy trying to give me up to the Gestapo."

"I've already apologized for that." She smiles at me and blinks.

"Very well. So focus." I lose patience. "You spent the whole day with me trying on the dress and in the evening we went out to celebrate so that everyone could see my creation."

"You have to send a picture of it to Coco Chanel. I know her, I'll help you get to her." She stares at the dress.

"I will never ever work for that traitor!"

"All right." She waves her hand in surrender.

"Do me a favor and focus." I tell her in despair.

"I'm focused. I spent the whole day with you taking measurements and we went out to celebrate and show off your creation."

"Exactly." I sigh with relief. "And try to behave as usual tomorrow. Do exactly what you do every day."

"That's easy. I'll simply stay home."

"If you're afraid to stay here, you're welcome to sleep in our apartment," I offer, not sure if I really mean it.

"The man I was afraid of can no longer hurt me." She becomes grave and stands up. "Thanks to you I can keep my baby, and you should know that I will never forget it." She embraces me.

"As long as you leave me alone and don't send me any more German officers, as far as I'm concerned the story is closed." I pat her back and she giggles.

Leaving her apartment, I go home. Marie, exhausted and troubled, is waiting for me. I relate the cover story I coordinated with Marion and collapse on the sofa. My body is drained. My heart anguished and fear gives me no rest.

Covering myself with a blanket, I think only of my man. He is so far away from me and the closest to me in all the world.

CHAPTER THIRTY

The sewing machine works unceasingly from early morning and I already have difficulty holding the fabric taut without yawning. Trying to thread the needle, I prick my finger.

Have three days passed? Or maybe four or five?

I count the roses in the vase Marie placed in the dining room.

Eight roses.

I count them again, finding it hard to believe that eight days have passed since the terrible evening I shot the German officer. So many hours of sewing, and I haven't completed one dress.

Any unusual sound from the street makes me jump. Any step in the corridor makes my heart miss a beat, and every time the delivery boy knocks on the door at his usual time I can't breathe.

The newspapers reported that the body of Herr Zemel had been found in an alleyway in the fifth district. A note in French had been pinned to his uniform saying the Resistance had taken revenge for the occupation and demanded the immediate release of France.

It seemed an ingenious move but, in the newspaper the following day, I was forced to see pictures of retaliatory actions. The lives of more innocent people had been taken and this time it was entirely my fault. My guilt is unbearable, and I'm unable to leave the apartment and cope with life outside. I try to remind myself that it was self-defense, a life for a life, but feel that I have blood on my hands and I will never be able to cleanse them.

Headlines in the newspaper today announced a considerable cash prize for anyone helping to find the members of the underground who were responsible for the murder of the German hero. I can't eat or sleep and even the fabrics I so love refuse to cooperate with me.

"Stop distressing yourself." Marie moves the fabrics aside and sets a plate of food in front of me. "You aren't responsible for all the horrors taking place in this world."

"But I'm responsible for some of them." I put my head down on the table.

"Would you blame me if I had pressed the trigger?"

"Of course not." I yawn.

"Then why are you blaming yourself?" She holds my shoulders and makes me straighten up. "This is the situation and this is life. And even if it is terrible right now, we need to deal with it."

"You're right, but…"

"No buts." She puts the fork in my hand. "Stop whining. Eat, shower and try to sleep. Tomorrow you will leave this apartment and go back to all your nonsense."

"It isn't nonsense," I answer grimly, sticking the fork into the potato. "But you're right, I've mourned enough. It's time to go back to routine."

She sits down opposite me and doesn't move until I finish my meal. "Now, into the shower." She stands up and leans against the wall when loud knocks are heard at the door.

"It's them." I swallow the suffocation in my throat and stand up. "Someone has informed on us, they've come for us."

"We don't know…" She murmurs, trembling when the knocking threatens to break down the door. "I'll open the door and you will insist on your cover story!"

I nod and she goes into the passage. I dip my fingers in the glass of water and wet my face. The barking in German from the drawing room makes me tremble at the knees and when I hear Marie's stammering answers, I realize I have to pull myself together.

Straightening my dress and standing erect, I go into the drawing room.

An SS officer in a black uniform and five Wehrmacht soldiers surround Marie and the officer is yelling at her.

"Good evening." I put an artificial smile on my face and approach them. "How can I help you honorable gentlemen this evening?"

"Bring her in!" The officer barks and Marion is pushed into the hallway. She looks terrified but when she looks at me her eyes become clear and she shakes her head and tightens the belt of her robe.

"Where are the other residents?" The officer barks again, and our new neighbors are dragged inside. The woman is pale and trembling and the man is grinding his teeth. "Sit down on the sofa!"

We're all pushed onto the sofa, one next to the other. The officer places the armchair before us and sits down with a combative expression.

"Which of you hosted Herr Zemel?" He shoots out the question.

"I did of course." My answer is the truth and I manage to calm my breathing. "Herr Zemel is a close friend of my husband." I look down. "I was shocked to hear of that terrible murder. He was an honored guest at our wedding and later came here with his charming wife, Anika."

"I also met him at that dinner." Marion played with the ends of her hair.

"So did I." Marie shrugs.

"And what about you?" He barks at the couple, and they both shake their heads.

The officer grimaces in anger, and then looks at me with icy eyes.

"His driver says he dropped him off here twice."

"Twice?" I wrinkle my forehead. "He came here for dinner once with his wife, and the second time he…"

"He came looking for Monsieur Augustine," Marie completed my words. "He didn't know that Gabriel had already left on his mission."

"Yes. That's right." I smile at her and nod.

"And you?" He turns to Marion. "How well did you know Herr Zemel?"

"I knew him very well." She smiled flirtatiously and I look at her in shock. "And his wife, of course," she adds, and I give a sigh of relief. "We met at several social events and he gave the impression of being a real gentleman."

"So how do you explain the fact that we have evidence of his car being here on the night of the murder?" He looks at me again, and his small mean eyes seem able to penetrate my mind.

"I have no idea," I murmur, and pray that Marie will have a logical explanation. "I went out that evening and didn't see any car when I left or when I returned."

"Who went out?" His lip curls in a menacing smile.

"We did." I point at Marion and she nodded.

"We went out to that delightful restaurant on Grande Boulevard, and I'm sure there were several people there who will remember us." She blinks again. "If I'm not mistaken, Herr Stengel even joined us at our table."

"That's right." This time I corroborated her words. "Marion went up onstage and sang a charming song. It was an enchanting evening. If we'd only known what horror was taking place that evening, I imagine we'd have chosen to stay home."

"So none of you can explain why his car was parked on the sidewalk opposite your building on the night of the murder?"

The officer's scream makes all of us shrink in fear. "Maybe you'll remember more details when the Gestapo interrogates you!"

"I might be able to explain it." The loud voice from the entrance to the apartment made my mouth drop open in surprise.

"Gabriel!" I run to him, pushing between the row of Germans and fall into his arms. "I can't believe you're here." I press my nose into his chest, knowing that even if fear is making me hallucinate, I will cherish these seconds forever.

"I'd have preferred to return without discovering that my wife is being questioned about having a good time." He presses my head to his chest, strokes it once and then gently disengages from me. I hold his hand, refusing to let go.

"Monsieur Augustine." The officer stands and clicks his heels. "She isn't being questioned about having a good time, but about her involvement in the murder of Herr Zemel."

"Herr Borman," Gabriel addresses him by name, approaching him with his erect gait. "I believe it would be a little difficult to commit murder while seated in a restaurant surrounded by our dear friends." He stops next to the armchair and beckons me to sit down.

Reluctantly I release his hand and continue to look at him while sitting down.

"His car was here!" Borman raises his voice irritably. "Someone has to provide answers to that."

"I said I could explain it." Gabriel pours two glasses of cognac, giving one to the officer. "I made a telephone call to headquarters a few days before this terrible murder took place. I informed them that I'd be returning earlier, so Herr Zemel probably came here looking for me."

"He could have called!"

"But he never does." Gabriel lights a cigarette. "It seems he came up to the apartment and found nobody here."

"And where the hell were you?" He looks threateningly at Marie.

"I went home to my own apartment before curfew." She shrugs. "I don't live here."

"It's a very sad event." Gabriel sighs. "On my way here, I paid a condolence visit to Frau Anika. I offered to help her with anything she might need, but she is returning to her parents in Berlin."

Borman sips his drink and looks tensely at Gabriel. It seems to me that he is waiting for him to break under his interrogatory eyes, but Gabriel keeps an expressionless countenance.

"I'm not done with you." Borman glares at us, surveying each of us from head to toe.

"We will undertake a thorough investigation of the murder of a German hero, and the bastard who committed it will pay for it with his life."

None of my fellows under investigation dared say a word.

"We'll be glad to cooperate with your investigation." Gabriel accompanies him to the door, and the soldiers are thrust out into the corridor. "Richard was a dear friend of mine, it will be a privilege to help investigate his murder."

Borman clicks his heels and arranges his hat on his head. "We'll get them. It's only a matter of time."

Gabriel continues to stand at the door until the clicking of heels fades, and then he turns to us.

"Who are you?" He coolly addresses the couple.

"Your new neighbors," the woman answers, wiping the perspiration from her forehead.

"Forgive my impoliteness," says her husband, pulling her to the door. "We would like to live here quietly, we have no need to befriend our neighbors."

Gabriel moves aside so they can leave then goes to the bar. Folding his arms on his chest, he looks at us quietly.

"I am so happy you're back." Marie is the first to approach him and he pats her back affectionately. "I think I've experienced enough drama for an entire lifetime."

"I'm also glad you're back." Marion smiles sweetly at him. "I'd stay to raise a glass with you but respect your need to be alone."

He looks at her suspiciously and she stands up and laughs. "I've stopped fighting a losing battle. I have something more important to fight for." She strokes her belly, kisses his cheeks and departs, Marie goes out of the room, leaving us alone.

I continue to sit in the armchair, gazing dreamily at him. The moment I'd been waiting for has come and I don't know how to cope with my stormy emotions.

"I didn't get a rose today." I bow my head in exhaustion. "Only now do I realize that I didn't get a rose today."

I feel his hand on my head. All the emotional upheavals of the last months come together like a fist to my belly and I burst into tears.

He walks away from me and I look up in fright. He stops at the door, bends over his suitcase and then straightens up. When he turns around to me, his small smile envelops my heart with layers of protectiveness. His arm is behind his back and he goes down on his knees in front of me.

"My Josephine, I thought you'd like to receive the rose from your husband."

He presents me with the flower and I cover my mouth with my hand, not managing to stop the tears. "I hope those are tears of joy." He wipes my cheeks with his thumb and I sigh, snatching the rose from him.

"I so love my roses." I sniff. "And I also hate them." I grimace angrily. "I know they symbolize the fact that you are thinking of me."

"Not a day goes by when I don't think of you," he corrects me.

"Yes, but each one reminds me that another day has gone by and I have no idea when you'll return to me. They commemorate our love and I don't want to commemorate it, I want to live it."

"Then there'll be no more roses." He puts the rose on the table and cups my face with his hands. "And now that we're here alone, do you want to welcome me like a wife is supposed to welcome her husband?"

He doesn't have to ask twice. I embrace him and kiss his lips, pushing my tongue into his mouth and driving all thoughts from my mind.

"I've missed you," he whispers, biting my lips. A groan bursts from his throat as I grab his hair and pull his head to me. He takes control, kissing me fiercely, his hands exploring my body. I feel them on my neck, my back, my hips, and then they're pressing my thighs. I open my eyes to his roused expression.

"The bath is ready for you," Marie calls from the passage. "And supper is heating in the oven."

He tries to straighten up but I press his arm and shake my head, aware that my eyes convey distress. There is no way I will let him move away from me now.

"With your permission I'll go home now." She rubs her back and yawns. "Too many dramas for an old woman." She winks at me and I smile at her.

"Thank you for everything." I blow her a kiss.

Gabriel stands up, drawing me to him. "Marie, I'll drive you home." He puts his hand into his pocket and takes out his keys.

"Certainly not." She quickly puts on her coat and picks up her bag. "Now that you're here, I can stop worrying about her. So make sure she takes a bath and goes to sleep. Too many troubles on her little shoulders." She leaves the apartment before he can protest, and the moment the door slams, he turns to gaze at me.

"I've been ordered to make sure you take a bath." He raises an eyebrow and loosens his tie. "I think I can carry it out successfully only if I get into the bath with you."

"I suspect there is no other way to obey this order." I smile, still finding it hard to believe that he really is here with me. Taking my hand he pulls me along behind him. We go into the bathroom and while I undress, he sits on the chair watching me.

"I thought you were getting in with me." I say, disappointed, and remove my underwear.

Gabriel tilts his head and his eyes survey my body. He lingers over my breasts and then my belly, my thighs and the meeting place between them. He scratches his whiskers and smiles the small smile that makes my belly turn over.

"I've imagined your body so many times." He stands up and undoes his shirt. "I've imagined it lying underneath me, leaning over me…" He removes his trousers and gestures to me to get in the water.

"I've imagined it on the chess table, the sofa, the dining room table. This is the only place I didn't imagine it." He bites his lip as I lie down in the bath with the fragrant bubbles enveloping my body. "Now I don't have to imagine it."

Sitting down opposite me he tries to stretch out his legs. I laugh when he has to raise his knees and the water splashes onto the floor.

"Your body is too big for a bath together." I lean my head back and put my feet on his chest.

"I think we'll manage." He holds my foot, gently massaging it.

I close my eyes and sigh. I'd also imagined his body in every possible position, and this is now my favorite.

"I understand you've decided to join a more active Resistance," he says quietly, and I open my eyes and look up.

"I had no choice." I rub my face. "I tried to think how to extricate Marion from that very difficult situation, and couldn't find an acceptable solution."

"After everything she's done to you, you still chose to help her." He continues to massage my foot, and though it wasn't a question, I feel I need to explain.

"She came here very excited, declaring she was in love."

He rolls his eyes.

"Gabriel, she told me she was pregnant," I bite my lips and wait tensely for his response.

He nods and sighs.

"I know she lost your baby," I say sadly, and he narrows his eyes as if trying to understand how this affects me. "You should have told me yourself."

"True. I should have." He kisses my toe.

"When she told me she was pregnant by a married German officer, I had a feeling it wouldn't end well. But she was so sure of their love…I didn't try hard enough to persuade her not to tell him."

He doesn't say anything but nods, telling me to go on.

"The next evening, the new neighbor knocked on the door in hysterics, asking me to go with her to see what had happened to Marion." I exhale aloud. "She also said she saw a German officer leaving her apartment."

Gabriel combs his hair with his fingers, his eyes begging me to continue.

"We found her bruised and bleeding on the carpet."

"Bastard."

"We brought her here, took care of her and when she told us that he demanded she get rid of the baby, I suggested she go into hiding. I explained that I could help her, that I know people…

"Weren't you afraid she'd try and inform on you again?"

"No." I smile sadly at him. "Maybe I'm naïve, but something in her has changed. As if she's realized that she now has something more important to fight for."

"She isn't a bad woman." He starts massaging my calves. "Just confused, alone, and not very wise."

"She refused to run away. She decided she's going to cope come what may. I knew that she was in way over her head. The next evening Marie and

I heard the struggle taking place in her apartment, and at a certain stage I couldn't stop myself, and we ran there."

I look down.

"I burst into her apartment and saw him bending over her, throttling her. I saw her mouth opening so she could breathe. She was in a dangerous state. She managed to pull out his gun but he grabbed it back and do you know what he did?" I raise my head.

Gabriel shakes his head.

"He laughed and put the gun to her temple, but she continued to fight like a lioness and knocked the gun onto the carpet." I scratch my forehead. "All I remember is seeing him leaping at the gun again and Marion struggling. So I jumped on the gun held it and shot him. I didn't think; I had to stop that terrible monster." I dry my tears and gaze into the perfect face of the man looking lovingly at me. "I really didn't have a choice." I shrug and cover my face with my hands.

He pulls my body forward between his legs. My back leans against his chest and his arms are around me.

"I'm proud of you." He kisses my head, and I choke when I realize that this was exactly what I needed to hear from him.

"There were retaliations. Innocent people were murdered." I put my hands on his arms to make sure he was still embracing me.

"And what does that have to do with you?" He asks sharply.

"Because…I…"

"Millions of innocent people have been killed on the battlefield or in retaliations since the outbreak of the war. You did what you had to do, and that's the end of this discussion."

"A thousand times I tried to think about what you would have done if you'd been here." Leaning my head on his shoulder I flutter my eyelashes on his neck, enjoying the sense of security he gives me. "But every time I reached an impasse."

"You did the right thing." His hand caresses my belly.

"But what would you have done?" I bite his earlobe. "What would you have done in my place?"

"There's no point in asking questions like that." His fingers caress my thigh, and I close my eyes.

"If you'd had a better solution, I'd like to learn from you." I close my hand around his fingers.

"Why? Do you intend to eliminate a few more German officers in the near future?"

"Please," I murmur, sitting up.

"I'd have suggested she receive him lying in bed, bitter over the loss of their baby." He sighs and holds me close to him. "I'd have found a decent French doctor and, fortunately, there are still a few around, who'd be willing to say he'd carried out an abortion."

"But Zemel would have found out that…"

"You insisted on an answer so let me finish." He gently bites my shoulder. "He wouldn't stay around to take care of her while she was depressed about the loss of the baby, and he wouldn't return even after she pretended to recover. Within a week, two weeks at the most, she'd have found another man who'd follow her around and win the right to be the proud father of her baby."

"But lie to him about being pregnant with his child?" I turn to look at him in surprise.

"Not necessarily." Gabriel grins, taking the opportunity of turning me around to face him. My chest is close to his and my legs are on either side of his body.

"I understand," I whisper. "A man who'd lie for her."

"That's what they call thinking two steps ahead." He kisses the tip of my nose.

"Would you be willing to lie for her? Would you be willing to be that man?"

"We'd find someone who wasn't waiting impatiently for his wife to give him the news." He strokes my hip.

"Are you disappointed that I haven't yet fallen pregnant?"

"It just means I have to continue trying." His small smile makes me dizzy.

"And now perhaps you'll stop asking questions and tell me what I can do to make you happy?" I feel his body craving mine, tilt back my head and take a deep breath.

"Exchange the gentleman who is touching me as if I might break for the wild man who taught me the power of passion."

"Your wish is my command," he responds hoarsely and takes me fiercely.

"Gabriel, I love you," my whisper is accompanied by a loud groan.

"I love you more." He drops his head on my shoulder and his thighs tremble under me.

My breathing is heavy, and he rains kisses on my neck until I manage to stand up. The adrenalin that burst out of me has faded, and now a strange peace envelops me. I put on my robe and watch him getting out of the bath and smiling at me. I don't have time to cover my mouth while I yawn.

He laughs when I'm overcome by a wave of yawns. "I was ordered to put you to bed."

"I'll sit with you while you eat your dinner." I blink with frustration. My eyes are burning and tearing, and I have to bite my lips to stop another yawn.

"I've just devoured my meal." He winks and hugs me. "And if you don't go to bed now, I can't promise I won't insist on dessert."

I laugh and yawn aloud into his chest and he leads me into the bedroom and covers me with a blanket.

"I don't want to sleep without you," I say as he moves back.

"I have to make one telephone call and I'll join you." He turns off the light.

"Gabriel," I whisper.

"Yes?"

"I only wanted to hear you answer me and know I'm not dreaming."

His body leans over me and he brushes aside my hair and kisses my lips. "Josephine."

"Mmm…" My eyes close.

"You can relax. I'm here now and will take care of everything."

I feel my lips smile and fall into a sweet, nightmare free sleep.

CHAPTER THIRTY-ONE

I peep through the rough tear in the newspaper and roll my eyes.

"Gabriel, after everything I've been through are you still censoring the newspaper for me?"

"At least while I'm here I will make sure you are exposed to as little of the horror taking place outside as I can," he responds drily, continuing to look through his newspaper.

I gaze at his large figure in the elegant suit and my heart constricts. "How long will it last this time?" I ask fearfully. "Your stay here?"

Putting down his newspaper, he pulls my chair close to him. His long lashes rise, exposing the soothing color of his eyes.

"The Allies are fighting determinedly." He strokes my cheek and looks directly into my eyes. "I know you are a prisoner of the terrible reality here, but things will change soon, and we will see the end of this wretched occupation."

"You haven't answered my question." I place my hand over his.

"The moment they need me I will have to leave. But there is no point in worrying about it now. I'm here and I intend to make sure you stop looking so worried."

"Not even you can make me stop worrying." I sigh. "If the situation is as optimistic as you describe, then this is the moment for me to continue taking part in the Resistance. We'll fight them on all fronts."

"Not in the near future." He straightens his tie and stands up. "You are still under a magnifying glass and I am unwilling for you to put yourself and your friends at risk."

For a moment I consider protesting, but since he mentioned my friends as well, I am silent.

"I'll be back this evening and we'll go out and enjoy ourselves," He says placating me.

"I have a better idea." I stand in front of him touching his tie. "Come back this evening and we'll enjoy ourselves here, just the two of us, without having to fake smiles." Looking up at him, I put a false, exaggerated smile on my face.

"It's a date." He laughs and kisses me. "I will never force you to smile against your will."

This time the smile on my face comes from my heart and I continue to stand looking at him as he leaves the dining room. Before I have time to sit down, he returns.

"I forgot to ask. What can I do today to make my beautiful wife happy?"

There hasn't been a single thing I've asked for that he hasn't managed to bring me. I don't think I took it for granted, but I wasn't surprised. As if it were the most natural thing in the world that he could make any dream of mine come true.

"Make me believe, if only for one evening, that Paris has been liberated and the war is over."

"Your wish is my command." He bows his head to me and leaves.

Funny. He doesn't even blink. As if something like that could be achieved.

Marie arrives late in the morning carrying bags of groceries. She prances all the way to the kitchen. It's been so long since the last time I saw her so full of vitality and racket. When she starts humming and smiling I realize I'm not the only one affected by Gabriel's presence.

He doesn't have to be in the apartment for her to be full of confidence. He only has to be nearby, and for us to know he will return in a few hours' time.

Even the weather seems to welcome my man. The rain stops and the sun comes out, and when I look at the sewing machine the desire to flirt with it returns. I work on the machine for a few hours, sewing a short floral dress. The design is simple and ordinary, something I wouldn't usually design, but I love the result. It looks light, optimistic and joyful.

I smile at Marie when she comes in with a plate of cookies, continuing to smile to myself when she goes out. A momentary, raw and pure happiness. The knocks on the door toss me back into reality and for a second the smile is wiped off my face.

"It's not their knocking," Marie says as she passes the dining room.

She's right. But I already recognize all types of knocking. The Germans,' Marion's, the delivery boy's and even the neighbor's from the top floor. I don't recognize this one, so who the hell could it be?

Leaving the table, I quickly enter the drawing room. Marie is standing in front of the neighbor blocking his way in.

"Madame Augustine," he addresses me, pushing Marie aside. I don't like the rude way in which he shoves her aside, and the expression on his face bodes trouble.

"Monsieur…"

"Mathieu Bouznet." He strides inside with a slight limp. It's the first time I've noticed his limp.

"How can I help you?" I look at him as he sits down in the armchair uninvited.

"I'd prefer to speak with you in private." He jerks his head towards Marie.

"Anything you have to say to me can be said in her presence." I fold my arms. "And it might be better for you to wait until my husband comes home and talk to both of us."

"I believe you'd prefer to hear what I have to say in private." He leans back comfortably and smiles arrogantly.

"Very well." I grit my teeth. "Marie, leave us alone please."

Wiping her hands on her apron and grimacing in anger, but without saying a word, she goes into the kitchen.

"You may start talking."

"Have you heard of the monetary prize offered to anyone who reveals the identity of the German officer's murderer?" He continues to smile.

"No." I shrug, commanding myself to hide my storm of emotions. He has come here because he knows, and now the extortion begins.

"A lot of money. A great deal of money."

"And what has that to do with me or you?" Turning my back on him, I pour myself a drink.

"I'd be glad to taste that superb liquor," he says without answering my question. I close the bottle and turn, holding only one glass, and it is I who sip from it.

The way he is looking at me tells me he's angry. "It has to do with you because you are directly involved with his murder, which has to do with me because I know about it."

"What you are saying is very dangerous." I take a cigarette from the packet and light it.

"It is. I'm glad we both know just how dangerous it is for you."

"For me? It might have been dangerous for me if it weren't the stupidest thing I've ever heard!"

"Madame Augustine," his tone becomes conciliating. "My wife doesn't know how to keep secrets from me. I know about the officer's visit, about the beating and even about the sound of the shot."

"And I still have no idea of what you're talking about." I refuse to show hysteria.

"Your husband is a well-known figure and respected among the Germans. How do you think he'd react if he hears his wife is party to the murder of one of his German friends?" He whispers, stroking his leg. "I've done my homework. I know to whom you're married, and I have a feeling that he himself will hand you over if he knew."

"Knew what?" I persist. "Your wife's invented stories? I'm sorry to tell you, but she apparently suffers from an overly rich imagination."

"*Cherie.*" He stands up. "You live here in great luxury. Drink expensive liquor, smoke expensive cigarettes and eat well, as if the war has passed this home by."

"It hasn't passed by any home."

"While you eat meat, I struggle to bring home leftover potatoes for my wife and children. This injustice stops now."

"What the hell do you want?" I raise my voice. "Food? Alcohol? Cigarettes?" I scoff.

"If you'd asked, I'd be glad to share it all with you. I don't understand why you think extortion will be effective."

"I don't need your charity." He pretends to spit on the floor. "I'm onto you. And starting tomorrow I expect a consistent weekly payment. Your husband doesn't have to know anything about it." The menacing smile returns to his face. "Just tell him you want to buy another new dress."

"Why would my wife need a new dress?" Gabriel is leaning against the door frame looking at him with a stony expression.

"I was just having a neighborly conversation. Nothing that would interest you." Mathieu strokes his thigh and straightens up.

"Sit down!" Gabriel orders and I look at him uncomprehendingly.

"I'd better leave now."

"You'd better sit down." Gabriel trips Mathieu who falls into the armchair. "Anything to do with my wife is of interest to me."

"I came to apologize for our strange behavior as neighbors. It's just that the situation since the beginning of the war…"

"He's lying." I turn to the fireplace and pour an extra glass. When I hand it to Gabriel I see that Mathieu is looking at me in shock. "He didn't come to apologize. He came to blackmail me. He claims that his wife is certain I have something to do with Herr Zemel's murder, and if I give him a weekly allowance he won't tell you."

Gabriel bursts out laughing and Mathieu pales.

"If you are in collaboration with her, I'll go directly to the Gestapo."

Mathieu tries to get up but Gabriel pushes him down, preventing him from moving. "I'll get the money I deserve from them." He manages to say through gritted teeth.

Gabriel presses his shoulder and from Mathieu's expression it's not pleasant.

"These are grave accusations," Gabriel says quietly, sitting down in the armchair opposite him. "Do you have any solid evidence?"

"My wife saw the German officer." Mathieu raises his chin. "And she saw the bruised neighbor and heard a shot. I think this is sufficient evidence to take her for questioning." He tilts his head in my direction without looking at me.

"Yes…" Gabriel murmurs and scratches his chin. "I'm sure the Gestapo will be happy to give you a respectable sum for this information."

Supported by the back of the chair, Mathieu starts to get up.

"But by the same token, I can also go to my friends at the Gestapo and tell them that my wife has remembered a few interesting things." Mathieu sits down again and looks at him.

"Yesterday evening, she recalled seeing a German officer going up to your floor. I believe only you live there, am I right?"

"Yes, but…"

"And she also heard something that sounded like a shot."

"My wife heard a shot…"

"And she recalls seeing your wife distraught in the course of the evening."

"She was distraught because…"

"Because she doesn't know my wife, and she was certain this information would get out."

"That's ridiculous!" Mathieu shouts and stands up. "I tried to give her the opportunity to understand the advantage in cooperating with me, but if you aren't willing to understand then I have no choice but to go to the Germans."

"I'll come with you." Gabriel stands smiling in front of him.

I look from Gabriel to Mathieu and back, biting my lips.

"You're invited." Mathieu grins.

"The question is whom will they believe?" Gabriel raises an eyebrow and continues to smile. "A French fellow who fought them. Or, more accurately, wanted to fight them but was injured in an embarrassing accident and sent home."

"You don't know anything!"

"I know that your brother really did fight while you slipped under the wheels of a French military vehicle. And I know that he was later taken to work in a German factory."

Mathieu looks at him in shock.

"And I know that apart from the need to take care of your wife and two children, you also have to help your brother's wife and three children. No simple matter."

"No simple matter at all, but the sum of money will enable me to live as you do." Mathieu surveys the apartment.

"The big question is whom will the Germans believe." Gabriel shrugs his shoulders. "A former soldier who returned with a wounded leg and has to keep two families, which means he doesn't like them very much, or a Swiss citizen who helps them with the war effort, is invited to their balls and holds special permits from the Reich."

"Your wife isn't Swiss. She's French, and I'm willing to gamble on that."

"Then you're a very brave man." Gabriel steps back and puts his arm around my shoulders. "They would probably question my wife but I have no doubt that after her evidence they will also question you. They might decide you're telling the truth and she's lying, in which case you will receive a considerable sum. But they might not." Gabriel lights a cigarette and hands it to me. I take it with trembling fingers and look at his small, relaxed smile. "And then…after a very harsh interrogation of your wife, that will probably include physical violence…"

I see the color draining out of Mathieu's face.

"They might decide you're both traitors and then your end will be a lot less optimistic than you imagine. So sad that your children will become orphans." Gabriel lights another cigarette and then disengages from me and approaches Mathieu. He hands him the cigarette and Mathieu grasps it and places it between his lips. He seems terrified.

"You could have paid me and all this could have been avoided." His voice is trembling.

"You could have asked for help and we'd have given it gladly." Gabriel returns to stand beside me.

"I'm not asking for charity."

"And we aren't paying extortion fees." Gabriel turns to smile at me.

I'm unable to return his smile. The tension makes me dizzy.

Mathieu limps to the coffee table, stubs out the cigarette in an ashtray and straightens up in front of us.

"I think we can put an end to this story with a handshake." He holds out his hand to Gabriel but the latter shakes his head.

"You'll have to put an end to it with my wife. After your shocking allegations, I think it best if she decides whether or not to approach the Germans."

Mathieu briefly looks down and then looks at me.

"Madame Augustine, I realize that my wife has a very vivid imagination. I hope we can put an end to this story and forget her absurd allegations."

"As far as I'm concerned, the story is over and done with." I hold out my hand and he shakes it with relief.

He bows his head in Gabriel's direction and leaves the apartment.

I give a loud sigh of relief and drop to the armchair. Gabriel stands behind me, bends forwards and kisses my neck.

"How did you know all those things about him?"

"It's important to know your neighbors," he answers playfully.

"But how did you know he'd believe you really would go to the Germans?"

"Do you remember my scolding you when you didn't sacrifice your queen to save your king?"

"Yes."

"Well, sometimes it's possible to make your opponent think you intend to sacrifice the queen." He laughs.

"Oof, I don't understand anything." I stand up and walk around the armchair. "But I'm sure about one thing." Standing on tiptoes, I kiss his chin. "There's no way I'll waste precious time on dinner when I can escape from the horror I've just experienced."

"And how do you intend to do that?" He puts his arm around my waist.

"I have several ideas, but for that you'll have to join me in the bedroom." I wink at him, and burst out laughing when he tosses me in the air and rushes into the bedroom.

CHAPTER THIRTY-TWO

I draw the curtain and look out at the quiet street. If I weren't shut away here due to my need to disappear, I might stay shut away out of choice.

Several weeks of virtual reality with my man have allowed anxieties to fade, and I'm no longer sure I want to go back to routine. But even now, when the sun is shining, it doesn't light up the dark corners of my heart.

The swastika flags flutter on the buildings and I'm not free to live my dream. At any moment there could be knocks on the door, bursting the protective bubble Gabriel has created for me.

Going into the dining room, I don't say a word when I see the ripped French newspaper.

"Have we won yet?" I ask, paging through the newspaper.

"That, my darling, I wouldn't censor." Gabriel smiles at me.

"So why has nobody looked for me?" I sigh. "I thought I was important in this struggle, even if I don't fight physically."

He doesn't respond and returns to his newspaper.

"I thought that at least Natalie would want to know why I've disappeared."

"I believe she does want to know."

"Why do you say that?" I ask in surprise.

He doesn't respond.

"Gabriel?" I pull the newspaper away from him.

"Last week a letter came for you from her that was pushed under the door." He says drily, sipping his coffee. "And another came this morning."

"And you didn't say anything?" I shake my head uncomprehendingly. "Where are they? I want to read them."

"I tore them up."

"But they were addressed to me!"

"Josephine." His upper lip quivers. "It has become too dangerous. You can't continue to be seen with them."

"That's not your decision to make." I stand up. "I have never lied to you, and I don't intend to start doing so now. If you don't tell me what was written in them, I will have to walk the streets and look for her. I will find her in the end, but don't you think it would be a relief to know what she wrote to me?"

"I'm telling you it's too dangerous." He bangs on the table.

"It's more dangerous to go back to all the meeting places to try and find her. But if you leave me no choice, that's exactly what I'll do." I walk to the door.

"You're not walking out in the middle of a conversation." His forceful tone stops me. "Please come back and sit down."

Clenching my fists I sit down.

"I told you that things are about to change soon." He puts his hand over mine and I angrily pull it away. "You have only to wait patiently."

"I asked if we'd won yet and you said no." I grit my teeth. "So nothing has changed. And, anyway, you have no right to keep letters addressed to me!"

"I'm your husband, and I have the right to try and protect you."

"Gabriel, I know you want to protect me." I take his hand and press it to my lips. "You are the best thing that has happened to me and not a day goes by when I'm not grateful, but it was only a matter of time before I realized that I cannot live in isolation." I kiss his hand and stroke my cheek with it. "I must know what she wanted to tell me. Please let me do it."

He pauses a few seconds and finally nods once. "She asked to meet you at seven o'clock this evening at the Jazz Club."

"Did she write anything else?"

"Only the address."

"Thank you." Leaning forwards, I kiss him on the lips.

"You aren't going alone." He pulls me onto his lap. "A married woman shouldn't wander around clubs on her own."

"I don't think it's a good idea for you to join me. I prefer to keep my personal life with you separate from my Resistance activities."

His laughter makes me look up at him.

"My beautiful wife, everything you do is linked to me." He gently kisses my lips.

"I don't want to put you at risk. If you are seen with members of the Resistance then…"

He silences me with another kiss. "I'm with you in any choice you make, even if I don't like it."

He pats my backside and stands me on my feet.

I continue to look at him while we eat, certain that I've never felt such powerful love.

***

The tension and anticipation accompanying me during the past hours has almost faded completely when I hear the sound of Gabriel getting ready in the bedroom. I put on my blue hat and my gloves.

He emerges from the bedroom and I gasp. I've never seen him wear anything except an elegant suit when going out, and here he is, standing in front of me, wearing a tailored pair of black pants and a white sweater.

"I thought it better not to attract attention in a dim club with a suit and tie." He winks at me.

"How do you know it's a dim club?" I run my hands over his chest and step back before I capitulate and stay in the bedroom with him.

"I used the day to find out where I'm taking my beautiful wife." He hands me my bag and opens the door for me.

Looking up at the top floor, I smile when I hear children's voices. I've never thought of myself as someone capable of being a mother, but now that my man is holding my hand it seems there is nothing I want more than to give him and myself this joy.

We pass Marion's apartment and I chuckle.

"Strange to think that I feel so safe in a place where the neighbor from the ground floor and the neighbor from the top floor tried to send me to the cellars of the Gestapo."

"That is the way of war." Gabriel opens the car door for me, waiting until I'm seated. "People mistakenly believe that any means is justified in order to survive." He starts to drive slowly. Apart from several cyclists, the road is completely empty.

We stop near a bus stop and watch people crowding and pushing each other to get onto the bus.

"It doesn't matter if we're dressed simply," I murmur. "Anyone traveling by car attracts attention."

"You're right." Gabriel puts his hand on my thigh and cautiously overtakes the bus. "I thought of suggesting we use the Metro, but it's just as crowded as buses."

He continues to drive in a leisurely pace, finally parking in a street parallel to the club. "We'll go on foot from here." He gets out of the car and opens the door for me.

We walk hand in hand until I notice a few people standing at the entrance to an industrial building. I press his hand and close my eyes.

"There's a feeling of normality." I open my mouth and take a deep breath. "As if we're just another couple going out to have a good time in the most romantic city in the world."

"Not just any couple." He draws me to him. "A man who is in love with his wife with an intensity unmatched by any other love."

Opening my eyes I look at the small smile that makes his eyelashes cover his eyes. My heart beats in my chest and I can't find the words to respond. Embracing him hard, I hope he feels what my touch conveys.

Holding my hand again, he leads me to the doorway of the club. Men standing at the entrance glance at us indifferently, and as we go downstairs the music becomes louder. Standing on the last step I look around in astonishment. A world within a world, but this time it reminds me of my life before this damned occupation.

Men and women fill the tables, drinking, laughing and talking amongst themselves. Several couples are dancing on the small dance floor and on-stage, are three older men playing rhythmic jazz music.

"I'll order us drinks." Gabriel leads me to the bar, but I stop him when I notice Natalie sitting at a side table, talking to a woman. "Go to her." He releases my hand. "I'll wait for you at the bar."

Nodding, I push through the tables. A broad smile spreads over Natalie's face when she sees me, and she gets up to embrace me. I am happy to see she is wearing the dress I'd sewed her, lingering over the small swell of her belly.

"Only now I am starting to show." She chuckles and points to the empty chair. "Did you have any problems getting here?"

"No, Gabriel drove me." I glance in the direction of the bar and roll my eyes when I realize that even when he doesn't wear a suit, he is unable to blend into the crowd. He's a head taller than the men standing beside him and his elegant, relaxed appearance attracts the attention of the young women standing nearby. They push in to order drinks from the barman as if he's handing out gold.

Gabriel turns his head and gazes into my eyes. His small smile enhances his face, and he raises his glass to me. I smile and turn back to Natalie. She lowers her head and bites her lip.

"What's wrong?" I ask with concern. "Is it Maurice? The baby?"

"Leave us alone," Natalie addresses the young woman sitting beside her who gets ups and moves to another table.

"Natalie, what's wrong?"

"I thought you'd come alone." She glances at the bar.

"I came with Gabriel," I say uncomprehendingly. "With my husband."

"And what do you know about your husband?" She whispers.

"What a strange question." I rummage in my bag for a cigarette. "He's my husband, I know all I need to know about him."

Natalie sighs. "Promise me this conversation will remain between the two of us."

Lighting the cigarette, I nod.

"You know that what we are doing is more important than any relationship you or I have."

"Of course." I try to gauge where she's going.

"So I'll repeat my question. What do you know about the man you married?"

"I know he's a Swiss diamond dealer."

"And what else?"

"That he loves and takes care of me."

"That I don't doubt." She takes a sip of water and looks at me. "It's impossible to fake the way he looks at you."

I smile crookedly when I realize the conversation won't end there.

"Several questions have arisen for us, and I thought you should have an opportunity to answer them."

"I have no secrets from you."

"Why did he choose to save you, but failed to save Claude and his family?"

"It's a little complicated…"

"Brigitte and Odette did not survive the camps," she drops the bomb, and I groan in pain, bowing my head. "And on the night of the raid, did you come to warn us? How did you know? Was it he who gave you the information?"

I open my mouth to respond but close it again. Her previous news shocks me and I'm unable to join in the conversation.

"What exactly does he do for the Nazis?" She ignores the emotions I'm going through. "Why does he have a special permit as if he were one of them? Why does he trade in diamonds for them? What is his connection to the Fuhrer? What does he…"

Dear God! Her questions are like a fist in my belly. Why haven't I asked him all these questions? Instead of shocking me, I'm enraged by her daring to suspect him.

"Shut up!" I look up. "He isn't one of them. He never has been nor could he be. I know my husband and I know there's a logical explanation for all your questions."

"So why aren't you able to answer them?" She asks in pain, leaning forwards to lay her hand on mine.

I pull my hand away and put it between my knees.

"Josephine, we believe he has used you to get and convey information about members of the underground…"

"I told you to shut up!" I throw the cigarette on the floor. "I know the answers to questions that are important to me." Standing up I hug my bag. "After everything he's done for me, I am certain beyond any doubt that he is on our side and nobody, not even you, can undermine my confidence in him."

"Done only for you," she says in rebuke.

"You're wrong. You don't understand anything." I refuse to let her see how insulted I am.

"If so, I understand that your decision to disengage from us was the right one." Her expression becomes graver. "We'd be glad if you'd avoid attending any more of our meetings."

"This struggle isn't only yours." I raise my chin.

"You can return the moment you have answers."

I turn my back on her and close my eyes tightly. I won't let her see my tears, I won't let her undermine my confidence.

I push through the tables and my pain becomes physical. Pressing my hand to my chest, I groan.

"Are you done?" The deep voice of my man comes from behind me and I nod, going quickly up the stairs.

Going out into the street, I continue to walk with him beside me. Her questions continue to echo in my mind, and I'm unable to look at him.

"Josephine, is everything all right?" He holds my elbow, turning me to him.

"Why didn't you tell me about Brigitte and Odette?" I drop my eyes, blinking in a desperate attempt to stop the tears.

"I wanted to spare you further pain." He pulls me into his arms.

"So you knew…" I murmur exhaustedly and Natalie's questions make me dizzy. "How did you know?" I push him away.

"I have sources of information."

Again a question left without an answer. I shake my head and walk away from him. He catches up and walks beside me. He doesn't say a word, not even when we get in the car, and when he places his hand on my thigh, I close my eyes and lean my head against the windowpane.

Cautious optimism is replaced by anguish and mourning and, for the first time since I met him, I feel he is a stranger to me. So many questions have been left unanswered, and I lack the strength to fight for answers. My heart clamors to believe him, but Natalie's questions eat away at all the organs in my body.

CHAPTER THIRTY-THREE

I look apathetically at the newspaper, ignoring the male presence in the chair beside me. For three days he has tried to get me to talk to him and share the pain, but I am too immersed in my anguish. How can I explain to him that my safe island has been undermined, that after all he's done for me, I have doubts.

Gabriel folds his newspaper and draws me to him. He caresses my head and says words of comfort, but I don't feel the comfort. Only deep anguish.

"I'll try and get home earlier this evening." He sighs, kisses my head and, still holding me, he stands up. For a moment I place my forehead on his chest and choke.

How did I get into this situation? Why am I pursued by these questions? He has saved me so many times. He has helped me complete such important missions. He loves me, I'm certain of it, but what double game is he playing?

He leaves the room and I sit staring reluctantly at my plate.

"*Cherie*, losing people we love is hard." Marie sits down opposite me.

I nod, avoiding her glance.

"Try and take comfort from the great love you have. I know it isn't easy, but you have a great deal more than others."

Looking up, I stare at her. An elderly, noble and kind-hearted woman. She'd know if he was using me. She'd warn me.

She smiles at me and her wrinkles deepen. I know with all my heart that she is on the side of the good. I know she's on my side, but maybe she's as blind as I am? I nod again and give her a half smile.

"It's all right to grieve." She stands up, smoothing her apron. "It's even important. Just don't get too absorbed in it for too long. I'm talking from experience."

She leaves the room and I clear the table and put out the sewing machine and fabrics. The questions return. How did he know about the raid? I sew the hem of the dress with no defined aim. How does he get his information? What does he do for the Reich? What kind of relationship does he have with the Fuhrer? I bang myself on the forehead and continue sewing diagonally. Did he use me? Did I provide the information about the meeting point?

Not one answer satisfies me regarding the man who has set my world spinning. His expression, smile, touch...but could Natalie be right? Maybe the love is real, but not enough to place him on the right side of the board?

I look up only when Marie enters and puts lunch on the table, then return to the fabrics.

"Get dressed, we're going for a short walk." The deep voice makes me raise my head. And I look at him through a veil of tears.

I shake my head and try and slide the fabric under the needle.

"Josephine, get dressed." He pulls the sewing machine aside. I put my hands between my knees and look down. "Please get dressed and join me. We'll go for a short walk and then I'll leave you to yourself."

Realizing that he did not intend to give in, I go into the bedroom. On the bed is the pale blue dress I sewed when he was far away from me. Even then I felt he was closer than I feel now.

Reluctantly, I put it on and look at myself in the mirror. I don't feel like a peacock spreading its feathers. I feel as if they've all been pulled out, extinguishing the light in me.

I rub my eyelids, gray from lack of sleep. A short walk and then I'll return to my mourning.

Going back into the drawing room, I look at the large figure smiling at me. He holds out my gloves and fixes his tie. I was always told that French women use their beauty to trap men. Now, as I look at his perfect features,

I try and work out if I was trapped by his rare good looks.

He opens the door and offers me his arm. I want to distance myself but he draws me to him like a magnet and, supported, I go downstairs with him. For a moment, it seemed I've gathered the courage to cope with the answers to the questions clamoring in my mind and I look up at him. The strange noises from the street make me stop in my tracks.

"Come on." He puts his hand on my lower back and leads me to the lobby.

My mouth opens in astonishment and I take a step back.

"You asked me to make you feel, at least for a few hours, that the war has ended." He pulls me to the sidewalk. "I hope I've accomplished the task."

I open and close my mouth. Open it again and can't say a word.

A French flag is hanging on the building opposite. Several tables are arranged on the sidewalk in an impromptu café, and around them sit couples who are drinking wine and eating pastries. A woman in high heels is walking her dog and two boys are playing ball.

Gabriel leads me to the table and even after sitting down, all I can do is stare at the colorful figures. They're all smiling and seem so relaxed. I turn my head to the other side, trying to understand where the music is coming from.

"Madame, what would you like to drink?" A waiter in a beret jovially addresses me.

"Ah…" I scratch my head and my eyes are fixed on Gabriel. His beautiful smile is reflected in his eyes and I feel my heart is about to explode.

"Two glasses of Cabernet Sauvignon," Gabriel answers for me, and I stare at the boy holding a basket and suggesting that one of the young men buy a rose for his partner. Even the street lighting seems stronger. I squint my eyes in an effort to understand what is written on the signs on the opposite sidewalk. The launch of a new film and an invitation to a show.

"Ah, Ah, *Mon Dieu*…" I murmur, putting my hand over my heart.

The waiter pours wine into my glass and, clinking on it, I look at the flower seller who is now standing next to us.

"Flowers for the lady?" He asks Gabriel.

"I'll take the yellow rose." Gabriel hands him a note and receives the rose in exchange. He puts it down in front of me and I raise it to my nose. Even the flower is more fragrant.

"Gabriel, how did you manage to organize all this?"

"I told you, every wish of yours is my command." He caresses my hand and I turn my head to the clock the waiter is hanging on the wall. I blink my eyes to read the clock and then look again at my watch. He even made sure they turned the clock back an hour, the time in France before Germany took control even of our time.

"But how did you manage to organize all this when they're everywhere?" I look at him in wonder.

"I know people who know people." His smile broadens, and I feel as if my heart is cracking. Straightening up, I lean back. My breathing becomes labored and my distress increases. "Whose side are you on?" The cursed tears are burning my eyes.

He looks at me in bewilderment. "Isn't that obvious to you?"

I see the pain in his eyes but am unable to let go. "Gabriel, answer one simple question. On whose side are you?"

Instead of answering me he stands up and, in addition to the tears, sobs rip me to shreds.

He gives a short whistle and all the actors look at him. "Take it all away now!" His order is quiet and like the flick of a wand, the tables are collected, along with the signs and the flag, and all the people disappear into the alleyways.

The only thing still in place is the chair I am sitting on.

"Come on, we'll go home." Gabriel holds out his hand.

"And will I receive an answer to my question there?" Sniffing, I look at him.

He nods just once, and I take his hand and go upstairs with him.

"Are you finished already?" Marion emerges from her apartment wearing a long dress and pulling on her gloves.

"Yes." Gabriel continues upstairs.

"But I haven't had time to do my little performance," she complains.

"There will be other opportunities." He says, urging me up the stairs.

I follow him into the apartment and Marie runs down the passage with a tray of cookies in her hands. When she sees my miserable expression she frowns and looks questioningly at Gabriel.

"Everything's all right," he says coolly. "Marie thank you for your help, you can finish for the day."

"Was she disappointed?" Marie asks in confusion, and when his upper lip quivers she puts the tray on the coffee table and hurries out of the apartment.

His hand still tightly holding mine, he leads me into the bathroom. He opens the taps of the bath and looks around.

"Lately, it seems to me that they're listening to us even through the walls." He puts a towel on the floor and motions to me to sit down on it.

Sitting down, I lean my back against the tub. Gabriel takes off his jacket and sits down beside me.

The flowing water behind us slightly muffles my quiet sobbing.

"Josephine." He takes my hand and puts it on his thigh. "From the moment you met me have I done anything to make you doubt that I would do anything to protect you?"

"No." I sniff.

"Have I done anything to make you doubt my integrity?"

"No."

"Have I done anything to make you think I might hurt you?"

"Of course not."

"Are you certain of my love for you?"

"More than anything in the world." I rest my head on his shoulder and the tears return.

"So isn't it clear to you that I'm on your side?" He kisses my hand.

"I'm certain you will do anything to protect me," I whisper. "I'm certain I can put my life in your hands. I'm certain you're the best thing that has happened to me, but…" I fall silent, covering my mouth with my hand as the tears increase. "But she raised questions I couldn't answer."

"Natalie?"

"Yes."

"And how did you react to her questions?"

"I told her to shut up. I was angry. I told her I was more certain of you than any other human being in the world. That you are my husband and I know all I need to know."

He turns and kisses my forehead.

"Gabriel, those questions give me no peace." I cling to him, seeking warmth, comfort and safety. "How did you know to warn me about the raid on the apartment where we met? How do you get your information? What do you do for the Germans? So many questions and I have no answers." Holding his hands I press them hard. "She claimed you're using me to get information about the underground. It sounds so ridiculous and illogical, but when I have no answers, how can I cope with the questions? How can I be certain that your feelings for me make you save me while sacrificing all the others?"

He seats me on him, my legs apart, and I look painfully into his hypnotic eyes.

"I tried to hide information from you to protect you." He caresses my cheek. "My need to protect you is stronger than anything that happens around me."

"I tried to shut her up with a logical explanation." I bite my lip in frustration. "I wanted to shout that she doesn't understand anything, that her questions are crazy. But then she dropped the bomb about Brigitte and Odette and shamelessly stated that you are using me, and I had no answers."

"Better for both of us that you didn't." He leans forward and kisses my lips.

"I need you to restore my confidence." I lean back and look pleadingly at him. "I need my safe island, and I need your comfort and love. Please, please Gabriel, explain which side you're on."

Setting me up on my feet, he strips off his clothes.

"Join me." He nods at the bath and I don't understand. "I'll explain it all to you." He sighs. "But I prefer to do it with you close to me."

"Because I'll want to run away after I hear the explanation?"

"No." He smiles and sits down in the water.

I strip off my clothes and settle down between his legs, leaning my head on his chest, unable to calm the storm inside me. I wait tensely for him to start speaking.

"In the last war my father chose a side." He kisses my neck and leans back. "A Swiss diamond dealer with a flourishing business who chose to put his comfort aside and join the British."

I gasp.

"Since he had good relations with the Germans he was recruited to the British Secret Service, and managed to attain important information."

"*Mon Dieu*, and he managed to..."

"Let me finish."

Falling silent, I bite my lip.

"A few months before the end of the war, he was exposed and executed."

"I'm so sorry." I put my hands on his arms and feel his pain penetrate me.

"He took into account that he could pay a painful price, and he did."

"It must have been terrible for you and your mother and siblings."

"We're only two brothers." He rests his chin on my shoulder. "Vincent and I."

"Vincent's your brother?" I ask in surprise. "But you have different surnames."

"My mother moved to Britain and her mental state didn't allow her to raise us, so they separated us and we were raised by two different adoptive families, though they made sure we stayed in touch."

"It sounds awful."

"It wasn't as awful as it sounds." He flutters his lips across my shoulder. "But living with the need for revenge...that is something else entirely." He falls silent, and I long to turn and hug him but make myself wait quietly for him to continue his story.

"When I came of age, I joined the British Secret Service, and Vincent joined after me. We came up with a cover story as diamond dealers, and it turns out that our talent is in the genes because we succeeded in creating a business empire based in Switzerland."

"But how did you contact the Germans?"

"It was a long process. Years of establishing a social and business status in European countries in general, and in Germany in particular. And then, when the winds of war began to blow, I knew how to offer them what they needed."

"Money?"

"A lot of money."

"But doesn't that conflict with British interests? Money allows the Germans to buy equipment and arms."

"Information in wartime is worth far more than conventional weapons."

"Gabriel, I'm so sorry." I turn and sit on him, my face close to his.

"What are you sorry about?"

"For doubting you." Tears flow down my cheeks and my shame is overwhelming. "My heart knew I'm in the right place. That you are my home. But the questions simply gave me no peace."

He wipes away my tears with his thumb and his small, beautiful smile makes my heart tremble.

"You have to understand that my desire to win is no longer motivated by revenge, but by love. It is far more than I could hope for."

"Why didn't you warn my Resistance friends? You're on the same side. We're on the same side." I insist on an answer to my last question, which still bothers me.

"It is complicated." He sighs. "We frequently warned them in time, and we tried to this time as well. It doesn't always work."

I press my forehead against his and put my arms around his neck. "Why haven't you told me until now? After all, I would never expose your true identity."

"Josephine, I'd be much calmer if you knew nothing. If I could hide you here until this cursed war is over."

I pounce on his lips and kiss him fiercely. My fingers tangle in his hair and

I can't stop wringing from him everything I have missed in the past few days.

"I don't need all the actors you brought so I'd feel as if the war was over." I lightly bite his chin and then kiss him again. "Here, like this, exactly as we are, I feel the safest in the world." I exhale in anticipation when I feel his passion.

"I have one more dream to realize." He caresses my hips. "And when that happens, you will make me the happiest of men."

"Make love to me." I whisper, closing my eyes and feeling his love rock my soul with each penetration, caress and kiss.

CHAPTER THIRTY-FOUR

Wartime routine is deceptive. Particularly when I experience it with Gabriel by my side. I wake every morning wrapped in his arms and fall asleep after hours of intoxicated feelings.

His ability to make me forget the horrors taking place outside, no longer surprises me, but now, standing in the bathroom and trying to remember when I had my last period, I feel an equal sense of excitement and foreboding.

Tying the belt of my robe I enter the dining room. Gabriel and Marie are standing next to the radio, and when I move a plate both motion to me to be quiet.

"What's going on?" I ask, approaching them on tiptoe.

"The Allies have invaded Normandy." Marie lifts her arms and bursts into tears.

"What? What does that mean?" I try to understand if I need to comfort her.

Gabriel turns to me and tosses me up in the air. "Josephine, my love, it means the time has come to destroy those bastards."

I open my eyes in surprise and he laughs and kisses me. The three of us return to the radio and Gabriel translates the transmission from English to French. Finally, he switches it off and we sit down around the table. Marie taps on the plate with her fingers and Gabriel frowns, looking worried. Only I eat with pleasure, smiling to myself when my imagination takes flight to the moment I will see the victory march in Paris.

"I need to go to the office." Gabriel stands up and puts on his jacket.

"Shall we celebrate this evening when you return?" I ask, accompanying him to the door.

"We'll save the celebrations for the right moment." He still looks worried.

"I believe we have something else to celebrate," I murmur hesitantly.

"If you have something to say, say it loud and clear." Taking the key ring from the hook, he turns to me, his eyebrow raised.

Blushing, I cautiously stroke my belly.

His eyelashes lift and I think I've never seen such huge eyes. "Do you think that...?"

"I only think so, I haven't yet been examined by the doctor."

"*Mon Dieu*, Josephine!" He kneels down and kisses my belly. "I think that's the best news I could have received this morning."

"Better than the Allies' invasion?" I laugh.

"Better than anything." Standing up, he hugs me. His arms encircle me so strongly that my head is pressed against his chest and I can't breathe.

"Gabriel, I'm suffocating."

He releases his hold and his eyes scan me from head to toe, then he cups my face and kisses me.

"It's still not certain," I murmur shyly. "I haven't been examined and I don't want you to be disappointed."

"There is nothing about you that could disappoint me." He kisses me again. "Just knowing it could happen for us moves me."

Combing his hair with his fingers, he seems distracted. "I'll find out who is the best doctor in the city and we'll go together to see him tomorrow."

"Very well." Holding the door handle, I gaze after him as he goes downstairs. When he has disappeared from sight, I close the door and lean against it.

"Two pieces of good news in one day." Marie looks at me from the passage, a wide smile on her face. "It's high time we started celebrating good news in this house!" She hugs me and raising my head, I pray that this goodness will continue.

The hours pass swiftly. The apartment is full of light and the sun rays warm it. Even the buildings don't look so gray. An optimistic heart can illuminate whole streets.

The ring of the telephone echoes in the drawing room and I run to the dresser with Marie behind me.

"Josephine."

"Gabriel, why are you calling me?" I laugh.

"I need you to get dressed because I'll be coming soon to take you to a restaurant." His voice sounds too grave for a routine invitation.

"All right." I answer, fear settling in me. "Anything else?"

"No, my love. Just be quick because I'll be there soon."

He rings off and I turn to Marie, scratching my head.

"What's wrong?" She is no longer smiling.

"He asked me to dress quickly because he's coming to take me to a restaurant."

"Then, off you go. Get dressed." She runs to the bedroom and I follow, wondering why she seems so stressed. She takes out a simple brown dress, urging me to take off my robe.

"But we're going to a restaurant, shouldn't I wear something more elegant?"

"It's good enough." She says drily, going to the closet to fetch shoes with low heels.

"Marie you're behaving very strangely." I put on the dress and sit down on the chair.

"Are you done?" She asks impatiently, gesturing to me to get up. She puts a shawl around my shoulders and hands me a pair of gloves. Realizing that I'm not going to get an explanation for her strange behavior, I shrug.

Leaving the room, she returns with my handbag. Opening the drawer, she takes out the diamond bracelet I received from Gabriel for Christmas, puts it into the bag and adds my old papers.

"Marie, *Mon Dieu*, what's going on here?"

The front door opens and we both run into the drawing room. Gabriel puts down a large suitcase at the door and looks at us with distraught eyes.

"You're ready." He states rather than asks, and I nod, looking at the suitcase.

"Aren't we going to a restaurant?" I put on my hat and arrange its lace above my forehead. My heart beats faster and I try to reassure myself that all the terrible scenarios going through my mind will vanish as soon as Gabriel explains what the hell is happening.

"Marie, did you put her old papers into the bag?" He ignores my question and turns to her.

"Yes, everything is in the bag." She lowers her eyes and I find it hard to understand why her voice is trembling.

"Thank you very much." He hugs her, then bends down to look into her eyes. "Thank you very much for everything!"

She nods, stroking his cheek.

I watch both of them quietly, panic creeping into me. It looks like a farewell scene, and I don't understand who is parting from whom and why.

"Josephine," He leaves the door and takes me with him to the fireplace. "I've been ordered to return to Britain. In the suitcase is a great deal of money, and we decided it should reach the right hands."

"So when are we going?" I ask, closing my eyes when a harsh sensation strikes me.

"Look at me!"

Opening my eyes, I make myself look at him.

"We aren't going together, because very soon they'll understand that I haven't reported to Headquarters to hand over the suitcase and they'll come in pursuit."

"I don't want to stay here without you." Tears blur my vision. "Not now, when at long last we are starting to see the end of this war."

"You aren't staying here." He holds me tightly in his arms. "Vincent and Jeanne are waiting for you in a car down below, and they will take you to Belgium to a safe place until I come to fetch you."

"But why aren't you coming with us? Why doesn't he go to Britain instead of you to carry out the mission?"

"It's impossible, my love." He disengages from me, looking at his watch. "Time is against us and we must leave now."

"I can't." Holding tightly to his hand I shake my head. "I'm so afraid this is the last time I'll see you. I have a bad feeling and I can't let you go."

"Josephine, they'll soon come looking for me here. There is not a chance I can allow them to find you here. You must leave the building with me now and get into the car with Vincent."

"I haven't packed a suitcase." I burst into tears.

"We don't want anyone to suspect you're running away." He pulls me towards the door and stops only to let Marie hug me. I don't have time to hug her back or say any parting words. Fear is making me dizzy. I hear him part from her again, and feel him pull me outside. In one hand he holds the suitcase and with the other my arm.

We reach the door of the building and Vincent hurries towards us.

"The moment they arrive here, they'll set up roadblocks," Vincent addresses Gabriel, and I don't think I've ever seen him so stressed.

"I need two hours to cross the check point, and then I'll change identity." Gabriel puts the suitcase in the back of his car and thumps Vincent on the shoulder. "This is the time to start praying." He winks at him and then looks at me.

His eyes are burning with love for me, and standing on tiptoe I caress his cheek, memorizing each feature of his perfect face.

"What can I do to make you happy?" He caresses my belly and holds my chin. His gaze electrifies me.

"Promise me that this isn't the last time I'll see you." I fall upon him and kiss him fiercely. "And make sure you bring me a yellow rose."

"Your wish is my command." He holds me tight and then gets into the car. He smiles his hypnotic smile through the window. "I'll bring two roses. One for you and one for my heir."

Unable to breathe, I watch the wheels of the car travel away, disappearing at the end of the street.

"Josephine, we must go." Vincent pulls me towards the car and I see Jeanne sitting in the front seat, I nod, rubbing my chest. I've never felt such emotional pain. Never.

"Wait." I shake him off and run to the building door. "I've forgotten something important."

"Hurry up," he shouts, and I run up the stairs to the apartment.

"I forgot the album," I tell the alarmed Marie, I grab it from the shelf above the fireplace. "I must have something of his with me." I hug her and run to the door.

Screams in German make me choke and the album drops to the floor.

CHAPTER THIRTY-FIVE

The entire building seems to shake with the loud steps coming upstairs, accompanied by orders in German.

The blood drains from my face. I turn my head to Marie and take a step back.

"They're here," I hear myself say but don't recognize my voice.

Marie looks terrified but stands in front of me, blocking the door like a human wall. I push her aside and grit my teeth. "You will not put yourself at risk. You are only the housekeeper. Go to the kitchen immediately!"

She steps back and leans against the wall in the passage. I see all my own fears, doubts, and anxieties reflected in her face and manage to smile at her.

The door is kicked open and ten Wehrmacht soldiers burst in. I remove my hat, hug my bag and gaze as if in a nightmare at the SS officer who pushes between them to stand in front of me.

"Where is he?" His voice grates and his dark eyes look at me with burning hatred.

"Who?"

My head is knocked sideways from the force of the blow I receive, and I hold my ear and try to calm the burning whistle in it.

"I asked you where he is."

"Do you mean my husband?" I try to straighten up but the blow comes from the other side this time, and in addition to the whistle I also hear the terrible scream coming from Marie.

"Yes. I'm talking about your husband the traitor." The officer grins.

I blink and my eyes are fixed on his watch. I'm shut in here without any possibility of escape. I'm surrounded by loathsome Nazis who won't allow me to leave the apartment, but Gabriel has already left. He needs two hours to get past the roadblocks…he needs two hours…the whistling in my ears has stopped, and my mind is clear. He needs two hours, and instead of praying I can try and buy him that time. Rubbing my cheek, I smile a small smile.

"I don't know why you are calling my husband a traitor. He works for the Reich on a special mission for the Fuhrer, I don't think he'll appreciate you striking his wife."

By the devious, mean smile on the German's face, I realize my tactic isn't the most successful.

"We planned to go out for dinner," I continue to speak fast before receiving another slap. "He came here ten minutes ago but I said I'm not feeling well. I think I have a fever." I frown and wipe the perspiration from my forehead. "He went to fetch a doctor to examine me."

The officer taps his fingers on the revolver in his belt and narrows his eyes. "What's the address of this doctor?" He tilts his head, examining me in a way that makes me feel sick.

I look down and think.

"What's the address?" He roars and I nod vigorously.

"Thirty-three Rosier Street," I give the address of the Jewish doctor who lived near Nita before the war, but not his name.

The officer turns his head to the group of soldiers standing at attention, signaling them to leave the apartment. They leave at a run and I glance at Marie. She is as white as a sheet and still leaning against the wall.

"With your permission, we'll wait here for him." The officer goes over to the fireplace, pours himself a cognac and sits down in the armchair. He beckons me to sit down on the sofa, grasping my bag. He doesn't stop looking at me, and I try with all my strength to maintain a calm expression. My heart is pounding and the perspiration on my forehead seems about to become a flood.

The hands moving on the clock above the mantelpiece sound like a melody. Each movement confirms that another minute has passed, and another, and as the minutes pass I allow myself a cautious optimism.

The officer pours himself another glass and lights a cigarette. He examines the drawing room and stands up to examine the pile of records.

"Garbage." He breaks one record and goes on to the second and the third. "All garbage." He speaks with his foreign accent and breaks the record hanging on the wall.

I don't react, just watch the hands of the clock. Forty minutes have passed and I pray the soldiers will be held up. The loud steps coming from the stairs make me shrink back, and I take a deep breath and get to my feet.

"Sir, he hasn't been there," the soldier states with an icy expression. "We checked with the neighbors as well. There is no doctor at that address, a Jew doctor used to live there."

I collapse back against the sofa when a blow hits my jaw. I try to open my mouth to scream, but manage only to cough and spit out blood.

"Stinking French slut." The officer grabs my hair and pulls me to my feet. "I asked you where your husband the traitor is and you lie to me?"

"No. I didn't lie." I raise my hand to protect my face. "I was confused." I put my hand on my belly. "I suspect I'm pregnant and it's one of the reasons I keep forgetting things. It irritates Gabriel too."

The dark threatening eyes are fixed on my belly, and the blow that falls under my ribs makes me collapse and vomit on his shoes. The officer curses and kicks me, starting to scream in German.

"Wait." I pull myself up. "I've remembered. He said he has a friend, a gynecologist with a private clinic. He asked me to wait until he brings him here."

"Yes, I think I heard him say so," Marie murmurs, wiping her hands on her apron. ""Something about a clinic on Saint Savore St. He's probably late because the doctor is greatly in demand."

"You aren't on my lists." The officer pages through his notebook and looks at her again.

"Because she's only our nosy housekeeper," I shout, wiping my lips.

The officer waves his hand and the two soldiers hurry out of the apartment.

Sitting down on the sofa, I again look at the hands of the clock. I remember Vincent and Jeanne who waited for me in the street and pray they had time to escape.

The officer stands in front of the chess board and arranges the pieces on the board. "Come here," he orders without turning his head.

Groaning with the pain in my ribs, I go over to stand beside him.

"Do you know how to play?"

"A little." I cough.

"Sit down." He pulls back the chair with an ostensibly gentlemanly air, and I sit down and look at the white pieces. "Start." He sits opposite me and lights a cigarette.

I move the pawn and glance at the clock. He moves a piece and blows smoke right into my face.

Unable to concentrate on the moves I make, I move another pawn. The officer grins and knocks it over. I move the knight and the officer rolls his eyes in disappointment and moves another piece.

"It's like playing with a four-year-old," he says crossly, and placing my elbows on the table, I rest my head in my hands. While staring at the pieces, I recall the Fleur-de-lis who sat here and beat me time after time. The memory of the little prince makes me smile, and I move the knight again.

"Worse than a four-year-old," the officer barks, irritably over-turning the board. The pieces scatter across the floor, and I shrug and return to the sofa.

The officer paces back and forth, tapping on his revolver. I turn to look at Marie who is also looking tensely at the clock. Only now do I realize why she chose the address of the clinic. She made sure they'd have a long journey.

I want to smile at her and indicate that I understand, but the risk is too great.

"Search the house." The officer waves his hand and the soldiers who'd been standing at attention scatter through the rooms.

The sound of shattering and breakage indicates the destruction and wrecking of the house, but nothing reaches me. An hour and a half have gone by, time is in my favor.

Doors open and close. Furniture crashes on the floor. Plates in the kitchen shatter and the hands continue to move.

"Josephine?" I hear Marion's frightened voice from the doorway and stand up quickly. I open my eyes threateningly, and she steps back in alarm.

"You do appear in my notes," The officer strides towards her and smiles his devious smile. "The neighbor…" He mutters, looking at her round belly. Blinking, she puts her hand on her belly. "The actress, singer, lover…have I forgotten a particular title?"

"No." Leaning against the door, she giggles, "But I'd remove the title of lover. I've had a partner for a few months now."

"Maybe you know where Monsieur Augustine is while his pregnant wife waits for him."

"You're pregnant?" She opens her eyes in surprise and examines me. By her anxious expression I realize that my swollen face matches the physical pain I'm feeling.

"Perhaps." I shrug and immediately regret it. I should have thought of something else.

"I have no idea where Monsieur Augustine is." Marion arranges the ribbon wound round her head. "I heard a noise and came to see if my neighbor needs help." She glances at me and I see she is distressed. I close my eyes and shake my head, allowing her to escape this cursed place.

"I'm really late for the performance, so if there's nothing I can do to help, you can find me in my apartment in a few hours' time."

The two soldiers burst into the apartment and she uses the distraction to escape to the stairwell.

"Sir, there is a clinic there, but he hasn't been there."

The fist hits me in the center of my belly and I double over, crying out.

Another blow to my forehead and I collapse on the floor. Cold metal is pressed against my temple.

Closing my eyes, I murmur parting words. My body is aching and, suddenly, the possibility that the pain will pass and I'll be able to rest doesn't appear so terrible. I murmur parting words of love to my man, managing to raise my head and look at the clock. Another five minutes and he'll be safe. I can rest now.

"I'd happily finish you off now." The officer returns his revolver to his holster. "But the Gestapo will want to ask you some questions."

He shouts several orders in German and all the soldiers gather in the drawing room.

I'm pulled to my unsteady feet by my hair. He continues to shout orders and the soldiers run to the stairs. The scum of humanity who are hurrying to trap my man. But two hours have passed. My man, the love of my life, is safe. They're too late.

I manage to raise my chin and look directly into the officer's evil eyes. Smiling broadly, I lick my burning lip.

"Even a four year-old child knows that sometimes one has to sacrifice the queen in order to save the king." I burst out laughing, and my eyes roll upward when his fist shakes my belly.

"It's time to wake up." My cheek burns from continued vigorous slaps, and I try to open my eyes but my eyelids are too swollen and heavy. "Get up!" The slap is harder and I manage to recognize sounds through the veil of mist.

Looking around, I try to work out where I am. The room is dark apart from a night lamp on the dresser in the corner. The walls are peeling and the floor is filthy. Two men in civilian dress are standing in front of me. One of them bends down to slap me again.

"Welcome to our warm office." The second man smiles at me. I try to breathe but without success. I bend my head when another slap comes. My face contorts at the sight of blood pouring between my legs.

"Did I get my period?" I ask in confusion, shrinking from a sharp pain that pierces my belly.

"I think your poor hygiene is the least of your problems right now."

The man who is slapping me, his hair and eyes black as coal, laughs and steps away.

The second man approaches, he looks young and so handsome. His appearance fascinates me. For a moment I think that such a handsome man could never be cruel. The blow to my ribs corrects my mistake.

"We will ask you a series of questions, and you will answer them as quickly as possible so we can release you to your home." He rubs his fist and I cough and nod.

"Is the carriage waiting for me outside?" I blurt out a laugh mixed with a cough that burns my throat, and stare at the ceiling when the fist to my forehead knocks my head backwards.

"What is your husband's name?"

"Gabriel Augustine." Coughing I manage to straighten my neck.

"A good beginning." The young man smiles like a model for toothpaste. "What nationality is he?"

"Swiss." I answer unhesitatingly.

"What does he do?" The other man opens a notebook and scribbles something.

"He's a diamond dealer."

"Who does he work for?"

"Herr Fuhrer." I salute and feel my elbow crack as he lands a blow on it.

My eyes roll upward but the slaps wake me up.

"We'll try again." The man pages through his notebook. "Who does he work for?"

"For the Reich, Monsieur."

The fist in my ribs makes me drop into a pleasant darkness and again the cursed slaps make me open my eyes.

"You can no longer save him." The young man grimaces with fake disappointment. "We have roadblocks at every exit from the city. We will catch him and we will hang him. But you can still save yourself."

I nod in exhaustion. Knowing they won't catch him dulls the pain.

"It would be to your advantage to tell us what you know about him, and do it now!"

Nobody emerges unscathed from a Gestapo interrogation. I won't leave here unscathed either, and I might not leave at all. I'm aware of this and, in a strange way, manage to contain it. A small spark of pride fills my heart and I feel complete.

"I know a great deal so you'd better sit down." I use my right hand to settle my left hand on my thighs, and the pain suffocates me. The men smile at each other and pull up two chairs. They sit down opposite me and open their notebooks.

"Gabriel is the love of my life." I close my legs tightly as the blood flows down my thighs. "I know that the place he misses most is our bedroom."

The young man grits his teeth in irritation and starts to rise, but the other man holds his arm, signaling to him to stay put.

"I know that yellow is the color he loves the most, because it is my way of commemorating your atrocities." I smile bitterly and see that the other man is also losing his patience.

"His favorite smell is that of my body trembling underneath him as he sinks into me." I sniff and my face contorts. "He probably doesn't mean the smell of decay coming from me right now."

The dark man stands up and punches my jaw. The taste of blood fills my mouth and I laugh and cough.

"His favorite taste is that of my tongue when he sucks it."

Another punch, and I no longer feel any pain. I blink constantly and the walls swirl around me.

"His favorite flower is the Fleur-de-Lis because I am determined to find my way even though you poor bastards have lost yours."

The kick to my belly knocks me off the chair and I hear a strange laugh emerging from my throat.

"And his dream. We mustn't forget his dream…" I no longer try to protect my head from the blows, and in my mind I see him sharply and clearly. He is leaning against the bar, a head taller than the other men. His white sweater emphasizes his tan, and his small smile makes my heart contract.

"My Gabriel," I murmur. "I beat them for you. Our love is truly written in the stars."

A shriek of pain deafens my ears and then silence.

I can't hear my breathing and or feel the pain. My eyes open a crack as I try to work out if I've parted from this world.

"She's fainted. We'll come back in an hour and wake her."

I don't make a sound.

"She's loyal to the man who abandoned her." His guffaw rips out my heart, and if there was anything in me beyond despair, I'd have risen and screamed that he'd never have abandoned me.

"When we start pulling out her nails she'll remember what we want to hear." Another guffaw. "At that stage, they all remember."

Their steps fade and I stare at the light coming from the corridor. My eyes close, opening slightly when I seem to hear a whisper.

"Are you alive?" The perfect French accent makes me moan, and I seem to see the face of a boy looking fearfully at me. "I have five minutes to try and get you out of here. The patrol will return to the corridor soon."

"I won't tell you anything." My cheek is comforted by the cold touch of the floor tiles.

The boy straightens up and takes a yellow flower out from behind his back. He puts it in front of my eyes and strokes my head.

"That's…from my Gabriel?"

"This time it's from me." He lifts me in his arms, his face grimacing as he tries to maintain his balance. "Thank you for all the pastries and pies you left me in the stairwell."

I hear my cry of pain and hide my head in his bony chest.

"Shhh…" He starts walking and I bite my lips fiercely to stop the cries. He pauses at a door, takes something from a dresser and peeps outside. "Pray hard we manage to get out of here."

I can't find the strength for even one brief prayer. The pain is so strong I focus solely on fighting to breathe.

The light is stronger as he turns into the corridor, and I feel he is striding unsteadily to bear my weight. He turns again, and then I seem to hear a door opening. Now my body is shaking as he descends stairs and I slide in and out of consciousness.

"Help me," he whispers.

"Are you crazy? She's already half dead."

"Shut up and help me."

I feel his arms rising and my body is passed through a narrow window.

Loud steps. I hear loud steps from inside a building. I want to shout out a warning but no longer hear the steps. Now I'm in the arms of another boy, and even through the veil of mist I can see his terror. He turns back and the delivery boy jumps down from the window and gathers me into his arms.

Each movement makes me dizzy. I open my mouth and hear broken sounds coming from my throat. They run next to each other, stopping beside a bicycle attached to a rickshaw.

"Drive slowly," the delivery boy orders his friend. "Don't draw attention."

"All right." He looks at me again and then sits on the bicycle.

The delivery boy puts me into the rickshaw and sits holding me in his arms. The rickshaw starts to move and I cry out again.

"Now all we need is to pray they haven't discovered you aren't in the room, and that we manage to reach the brothel." He falls silent for a moment. "And that she agrees to take you in." He murmurs to himself and strokes my head. "I hope you survive. You deserve to survive."

"What…what…" I hear my voice crack and cough.

"My name is Frederique." He pips and exhales with difficulty. "Vincent called to tell me what happened."

I open my mouth to ask how they know each other, but can only cough.

"I've never heard him so upset. He didn't even speak in code. He screamed that the Germans had taken you and he had to get Jeanne out of the city before they put up roadblocks. He begged me to talk to the underground to try and get you out." He is silent when the rickshaw stops and sighs with relief when it continues. "Nobody agreed to risk a rescue attempt so I thought I'd better try myself."

I stare into his gentle face. So young and good-looking, but his forehead is as lined as an old man's.

"For some years I've been making deliveries for those bastards as well."

He looks down in embarrassment. "The advantage is that nobody suspects a delivery boy who is there all the time."

I try and open my mouth to warn him not to return there but again the coughing starts.

"I'll have to hide now." He smiles at me as if understanding what I'm trying to say. "But if I know you'll make it, I won't have risked my life in vain."

I barely manage to raise my right hand to touch his arm.

"You'll make it. I have no doubt." I don't know if he is trying to persuade me or himself. "You probably don't remember…" He brushes my hair off my forehead and continues to smile. "Once you lived in a huge fancy apartment and I delivered flowers to you from Monsieur Augustine."

I murmur weakly to signal that I remember.

"You suggested I join you for dinner." He laughs shyly. "I was so hungry I almost ate the bouquet of flowers, and you offered me something nobody had ever offered me in any other house. Delivery boys are invisible. They come, deliver and go. But you saw me, and that evening I ate the best stew I'd ever had in my life."

I feel the fire in my eyes as the tears burn down the cuts on my face.

"We never forget the angels we encounter on the way."

The driver stops and my body rocks forwards and backwards. The pain is now unbearable and I lose consciousness.

CHAPTER THIRTY-SEVEN

My body is resting on a soft bed and I seem to hear whispers. I feel as if my head has been replaced by a rock that weighs several tons. My eyes are burning and my belly is on fire.

If the pain is so severe then I haven't yet breathed my last, but where am I?

My eyes try to adjust to the dim light creeping through the narrow slit of my eyelids, and I stare at several female faces examining me with concern.

"I told you she wasn't dead," the chirpy voice whispers.

"You meant she isn't dead yet," another voice joins the echoes in my mind.

"And she won't die on my watch." The firm tone is familiar to me, and I can't understand whose it is. "You! Go and call the old doctor."

"But he's a gynecologist, what can he do for her?" The chirpy voice argues.

"Someone has to stop the bleeding between her legs," the familiar voice rebukes her. "If she continues to bleed she will die tonight."

I feel a moist towel on my forehead and murmur exhaustedly.

"Everything is going to be all right, *Cherie*." The towel is pressed to my cheek. "And all of you, stop standing here doing nothing. We don't want our clients to suspect something. Go and amuse them and make sure you make a lot of noise."

"Yes, Madame Distel."

I hear the tapping of heels and moan as the dizziness intensifies.

I'm forced to wake up when unpleasant hands touch me. I want to protest and cry out to be left alone.

The pain is too strong. My knees give in and I shout soundlessly.

"Why did you call me?" The voice of an older man sounds angry. "It's been years since I practiced medicine. She has had a miscarriage, and I don't have the necessary equipment to perform a D&C."

The weak moan comes directly from my heart. Miscarriage? Was I really pregnant and did I have a miscarriage? The emotional pain veils my physical pain.

"I know those diamond earrings." Again I seem to recognize a familiar female voice. "Papa, I know her. I met her in the line for food, she took me with her to the black market and because of her we ate like kings for a whole month."

"And how does that help this poor woman now?" He asks drily. "Francine, I can't take care of her. Look at her. She won't get through the night."

"Papa, please try," the gentle voice pleads.

"I'll pay you with her diamond earring." Madame Distel offers.

"I won't take payment for work I can't do."

I seem to hear more pleading, and then cold metal is pressed against my thigh. My eyes roll up and I fall into the pleasant darkness.

"I'll inject her with morphine."

Silence.

"Pass me the speculum."

Silence.

"Hold her knees."

Silence,

I blink rapidly and my throat burns with the creaking of my vocal cords.

"Poor child. I've done what I can. Even if she pulls through, she will never be able to bring children into this wretched world."

"Gabriel…" I call him in my mind and my heart cracks, shattering into a thousand pieces. I can see a picture of me in his arms, lying in our bed and opening my eyes to his small hypnotic smile. The sound of children laughing in the drawing room, and he strokes my hair and whispers loving words. Laughter turns to weeping, the picture darkens and fades, with it my desire to live.

"She's been burning with fever for three days now."
Silence.
"We need to call a doctor who can set her arm."
Silence.
"She needs another infusion."
Silence.
"I don't think she wants to recover."
Silence.
"Sit up, *Cherie*, maybe you'll be able to eat something."
Silence.

I'm lying on the bed in our bedroom. My man has his arms around me. The small smile adorns his face and he kisses the tip of my nose. The sound of children laughing…

"I've set her arm. Don't ask me to come again. It's too dangerous."
Silence.
"Go and take care of our clients!"
Silence.
"How long do you intend to keep her here? It's putting us all at risk."
"Shut up and get back to work!"
Silence.

You've made me the happiest of men. His green eyes are shining with emotion. The laughter of children fades and I hear the sound of weeping.

"Don't, *Cherie*, don't cry. You're safe here."

I blink, trying with all my strength to sink back into my sweet dream, but the voice pleads with me again and again to open my eyes.

"You've returned to us." Madame Distel clasps her hands in relief and the tears blur her large frame.

"Don't cry. You're safe now. I'm taking care of you. Nobody will find you here."

I open my eyes to ask her to let me be. Let me sink into my dream. But she puts another pillow under my head and makes me lean forward. Unbearable physical pain, but the pain in my heart is by far worse.

"We've been fighting for you for two weeks now." She sits down beside the bed. "I knew you were a fighter. That you wouldn't give up so easily."

I look at her exhaustedly and nod.

"I'll bring you some soup." She stands up and leaves the room.

I close my eyes and stroke my belly. I will never be able to make my man's dream come true. It's unbearable. I didn't think it was possible to feel such an onslaught of mental anguish. The realization comes very gradually. I've not only lost the ability to fall pregnant but also the right to hope he will continue to want me. I've had the privilege of loving enough for a lifetime, and now I need to be fair and release him to realize his dream with someone else.

My eyes stream with tears and the sobbing makes my body tremble.

This war has taken so much from me, but there was always hope.

Now hope, too, has been taken from me.

CHAPTER THIRTY-EIGHT

I listen to Madame Distel read the newspaper headlines to me. If we were exposed only to news circulated in pro-Nazi newspapers, we wouldn't know that during the weeks I fought for my life, the Allies continued to establish their hold in Normandy, and were slowly moving into French territory.

Madame Distel rolls her eyes every time she comes to an item that praises the heroism of the Wehrmacht soldiers and, finally, folds the newspaper and points threateningly at the tray of food on my lap.

"How long has it been?" I ask, chewing reluctantly on a roll.

"Since the invasion or since you arrived here?"

"It happened on the same day." I smile at her, lowering my eyes to avoid her noticing my tears. A day that started with great emotion and ended in a great crisis.

Looking at the newspaper headlines, she raises an eyebrow in surprise. "You've been with me for almost two months."

"Have I thanked you?" I frown, gazing into her good eyes.

"Too often." She laughs with a dismissive wave of her hand.

"The real thank you I want is to see your smile again."

I contort my face in a crooked smile.

"Not like that," She rebukes me affectionately. "The real smile of someone who got her life back." She goes to the door, making sure it is locked. "Josephine, that sweet boy managed to get you out of the flames of hell. Have you ever heard of anyone who was saved from the cellars of the Gestapo?"

I shake my head.

"I have." She points at me and sits down again. "Soon this war will end and your husband will return to you. Time will heal the suffering and you will build yourselves a happy life together."

Putting my hand on my belly, I burst into tears.

Her eyes are fixed on my hand and she sighs. "You aren't the first woman who won't bring children into the world. If your love is strong enough, it won't matter at all. He will understand that he has won you against all odds, and you will find a way to build a family."

"It matters to me." I wipe away the tears and lean my head against the pillow. "Gabriel will take me back. He will love and protect me, comfort me, but I will always know that I have taken away his dream. He deserves more. He deserves a woman who can give him children of his own." Putting the tray on the dresser, I turn my back on her.

"There are many women who could make him happy, he doesn't need a broken woman. I will make that decision for him."

Standing up, Madame Distel covers me with a blanket. She leaves the room without a word.

***

With every passing day, my body gets stronger. I manage to bathe without help, help with the cleaning and cooking, and even go out once a day to sit for a few minutes on the back stairs and breathe some fresh air.

The moment clients start arriving, I go to my room, forced to listen to the girls pleasuring our enemies for long hours. I manage to go inward and cope with my thoughts.

Memories of all the goodness I have experienced in my short life comfort me, and I no longer burst into tears every time Gabriel's image appears in front of my eyes. My conviction that I'd made the right decision, affects me like well-oiled propaganda. He deserves the very best and I am no longer good enough for him. Now I only have to fight against my dreams. There,

I am still healthy and carrying our child. We are so in love and happy and his small smile never fails to make my heart tremble. I wake again feeling nauseous, the reality of the dream, but this time I don't hear the clients. The quiet in a house that is always noisy, makes me sit on the bed in alarm.

"Josephine, come quickly." An excited cry comes from the other side of the door, and I stand up and cautiously approach. They'd never knocked on my door, never called my name aloud and never invited me to join them, unless I chose to do so.

Opening the door, I peep out. The passage is empty and the doors to the rooms are open.

"Come on, come on." One of the girls waves at me and skips downstairs. I tighten the belt of my robe and tiptoe to the staircase.

The entrance floor is quiet. I go downstairs, peep into the abandoned drawing room and enter the kitchen. All the women are sitting around the table and Madame Distel points to an empty chair beside her.

"Where is everyone?" I ask anxiously.

"Josephine, *Cherie*, this cursed war is coming to an end." She pours tea into my cup and clinks her glass of wine against it.

"I've been hearing that for several months now. What's new?"

"The stinking Germans have taken thousands of political prisoners out of the city to Germany."

"That's dreadful." I look at her uncomprehendingly.

"Yes. Dreadful." She nods. "But they've also decided to take all the weapons away from our police."

"They deserve it." I shrug.

"The police and underground workers have gone on strike!"

"Too little, too late." I sip my tea indifferently.

"Not this time, *Cherie*." Madame Distel pats my shoulder. "The communists have called for a popular uprising, and you'll see that the French will finally raise their heads."

"Anything else?" I stand up and gaze at the excited girls, unable to join in their excitement.

"It's a lot," she responds, and I roll my eyes and go back to my room.

***

The sequence of events over the coming days proves her right. The postal service joined the strike the following day, and two days later a general strike broke out in the city. But I refuse to get excited. The Germans are still here, and they are as cruel as ever. The news that thirty-five members of the Resistance were caught by the Gestapo, interrogated, tortured and executed, was a blow. The only thing that slightly comforts me is that Natalie and Maurice weren't on the considerable list of heroes who sacrificed their lives for their country.

I no longer care who is declared the victor or the loser because, in this war, everyone has lost. Claude, Brigitte, Odette, Nita. Myself included. Anguish has become an inseparable part of me, and no physical pain equals my mental pain.

Rumors of the destruction of the city arouse hysteria at home and the clients don't return. Madame Distel tells me that the advance of the Allies is driving away the Germans and their collaborators, and looting has turned the city to chaos.

"The real struggle for the liberation of Paris has begun!" She declares enthusiastically, drawing back the curtains. Bright light floods the room and I continue to sit on the bed and gaze at her. "Our flag is flying above Police Headquarters and our police has taken over the building. Armed resistance has begun. The Germans are unable to suppress the revolt, and our people are fighting in the streets."

"So, it's really happening?" I rub my elbow. It hasn't completely healed and my arm hangs at a strange angle.

"*Cherie*, it is really happening." She laughs. "While you are lying here in bed, the city looks like a battlefield." She settles her bosom in her corset and looks out the window onto the street. "Now everyone is waiting for Charles de Gaulle."

I feel my body vibrate with excitement and sit up. "Madame Distel, I need to ask a favor."

Turning, she looks inquiringly at me.

"I need to leave."

"Leave the house? It's not safe to leave now. I told you, it's a battlefield."

"No." Absentmindedly, I stroke my belly. "I want to leave Paris. Leave France and go to my parents in New York."

Her rolling laugh disappoints me and I look down.

"*Ciel*! What are you talking about? You can't leave this house, how do you think I can get you out of the country. And to America of all places…"

"You must know people who know people…"

"I'm just an old whore who runs a brothel. Not a magician."

Jumping off the bed, I take her hands. "You're an extraordinary woman who has put herself in danger to save me. I will always owe you a debt of gratitude, and I will never forget what you have done for me."

Her face grows sad and her eyes mist with tears.

"Please don't say no. All I need is for you to try."

Nodding, she leaves the room.

Suddenly I have a purpose. The war will end, Paris will be liberated and I'll be able to spread my wings and fly from here. I'll reach my parents in New York and start a new life, and I'll leave all the mourning, anguish and sorrow behind me.

I'll leave my heart here too, but I consciously surrender it. It will forever remain with the man who will never again be mine.

CHAPTER THIRTY-NINE

Women are festively dressed. Men are cheering and the Avenue des Champs-Élysées is decorated with the flags of France and a multitude of excited faces.

The military march makes the crowd burst into the anthem and I gaze in astonishment at the tall, impressive figure of Charles de Gaulle, proudly leading his soldiers.

Paris is illuminated, but I am unable to enjoy its light. My momentary excitement is replaced by suffocation and I shrink back against one of the buildings. I make myself invisible, unwilling to join in the festivities.

I listen to the victory speech and watch men and women cheer enthusiastically.

"Paris. Battered Paris. Destroyed Paris. Tortured Paris. But also, liberated Paris…"

Enthusiastic cries and applause. While I lean against the wall of the building and stroke my belly.

"The enemy sways but is not yet defeated…in order to feel satisfaction in light of what has happened, we want to invade their territory as we should, as victors…"

Making my way through the crowd, I let out a bitter laugh. What victors does he mean? Those who chose to inform on their neighbors in exchange for favors? Or maybe those who starved to death, or who were kidnapped in the streets and executed? Those who joined the Resistance and didn't get to hear his speech? No. He probably means those who dreamed of a liberated

Paris, like me, but the moment it happened, they realized they'd already lost too much. There are no victors in this war. Only losers. And this Paris is no longer my Paris.

Returning to the brothel, I shut myself in my room. For three days I refuse to join in the victory celebrations, leaving the house only to send a telegram. It's been four years since I heard from my father and now, all that is left is to pray he receives my telegram.

My prayers are answered when, two days later, Madame Distel enters my room and hands me a telegram. I finger the black printed letters and by the wild beating of my heart I know it is still inside me.

Dearest Josephine, I am overjoyed to hear that you have survived this terrible time. Sadly, Mama died two years ago. Before she breathed her last, she spoke your name.

I burst into tears with intense longing unable to contain further grief.

I pray you will manage to come to me, I will make all the arrangements to enable you to enter the country,

Papa

"Papa…" I murmur, wiping away my tears. So few words and so much emotion. I haven't lost my capacity to feel, and I have no doubt that he is exactly the medicine I need.

"You're fortunate."

Turning my head I see that Madame Distel is leaning against the door frame.

"This old whore knows people who know people…" She laughs and sits down beside me on the bed.

"The Americans want to send their wounded home."

Pressing the telegram to my heart, I look at her expectantly.

"On the ship, there will also be nurses to take care of the wounded. If we can bribe one of the port officials, we can get you on board in a nurse's uniform."

"Are you serious?"

"Have you ever seen me make a joke?"

"You really are a magician!" I hug her and she laughs.

"We haven't resolved the matter of a bribe."

"The earrings perhaps?" I turn them in my ears.

"We'll also need the ring." Lifting my hand, she examines it closely.

"Not that." I pull away my hand and rub my forehead. "It doesn't belong to me. It belongs to him."

"If you really want to go, you'll need to give it up."

I shake my head, grimacing with frustration. Suddenly, my eyes fall on my bag, which Frederique, the delivery boy, also saved from the cellars of the Gestapo. I hadn't needed it until now and so hadn't looked inside even once. Going to the dresser, I hug it, closing my eyes and praying I will find what I need.

My fingers play with the buckle, and I thrust my hand inside and take out the diamond bracelet. It is still here!

The astonished expression on my face mirrors Madame Distel's.

"Is this enough?" I give it to her with a trembling hand.

She gasps. "I believe this will certainly be enough."

"If so, when would I have to leave?"

"This evening." She points to the earrings and, without hesitation, I remove them and hand them to her.

"I have a small errand to run before the journey." I twist my wedding ring on my finger and thump my chest when the anguish returns.

"I will also go out to make arrangements." She winks at me and leaves the room.

Sitting on the bed, I take a sheet of paper and a pen from the dresser and write the hardest letter I've ever had to write in my life.

CHAPTER FORTY

I'm standing at the entrance to the building, stroking the massive stones around the entrance door. The stones are still gray but now they seem to be bleeding. I entered here frenzied and confused and left battered and unconscious. But no-one can ever make me forget the moments of joy I've experienced here. Pure joy. The raw joy of a man and a woman who loved with enough intensity to last a lifetime.

I walk slowly upstairs. One step after another. With every step, my breathing becomes heavier and this time it isn't because of the effort. I stop in front of Marion's door. The apartment is quiet. For a moment I consider knocking to say goodbye to her, but can't find the strength for another parting.

I continue up the stairs and stand in front of the apartment door. I feel emotionally drained but am determined to finish what I have started.

Knocking twice, I press down the handle. The door opens and I suffocate when I see Marie sitting in the armchair. She seems to have aged a decade within a few months.

"Josephine..." She stands, her eyes widening in shock as if seeing a ghost. "Josephine!" She bursts into tears.

I hurry towards her and hug her tightly, and she weeps. It's the first time I've seen this strong woman really weep, and my heart breaks.

"I thought..." She mumbles, disengaging from me. "I thought I'd never see you again." Her gaze sweeps my body.

"I thought those bastards had…"

"I'm all right." My hand strokes my belly and then holds my crooked elbow. "I was rescued."

"I am overjoyed." She bursts into tears again and starts pacing up and down the room in agitation. "Now everything will be all right. I'll make you lunch and take care of you and…"

"Marie, I'm not staying."

"What do you mean, you're not staying?" She stops and looks at me in confusion. "Your room is clean and ready, I've changed the linen on the bed, it will only take me a few minutes to make you a special meal."

"Marie, please stop pacing." Leaning against the armchair, I try and take a deep breath. My heart is distraught. If I don't find the strength to do what I have to do, I will never forgive myself.

I draw off my glove and look at my wedding ring. "I've come to say goodbye." I take off the ring, gritting my teeth to stop my lips from trembling. "I'm moving to New York to live with my father."

"New York?" She shakes her head, drumming her fingers on her mouth. "But what about Gabriel? He'll come back and look for you. And we're your family."

"Marie, *Cherie*, you do know it was just an act." I swallow the suffocation in my throat and go over to the fireplace.

"You're not making any sense." She continues to shake her head. "They hurt you, made you forget, perhaps, but it was never ever an act."

I place the letter I'd written on the mantelpiece, on it the papers identifying me as his wife. I wipe away the cold sweat covering my forehead and, with the last of my strength, manage to place the ring on top of the papers.

"Have you heard from him?" I ask the question I promised myself I wouldn't ask.

"No, *Cherie*, but you know he thinks you went away with Vincent. He told me he wouldn't ring so as not to endanger me, but now that Paris is liberated, I expect to hear from him at any moment." She grimaces when she notices the ring, and goes over to the telephone table. "Please wait with me. He'll call, or surprise us, maybe, and return. It can only be a few days now."

Looking down, I stroke my belly.

"The baby…" She looks questioningly at me. "Did you lose the baby?" Hugging me she sobs.

"Don't cry. I lost something I didn't have time to love, in order to save the one who taught me what love is."

"So how can you leave him?" She raises her voice and pushes me away. "How can you lie to yourself and say it was just an act, when you know you have become his entire world."

"I didn't only lose the baby." I bite my lip. "I lost the ability to get pregnant in the future. I'm no longer the woman he loved. I'm a broken woman, and he deserves to be released so he can have a family."

"You're mad!" She shouts. "Do you think that will make a difference to him? Do you think he'll stop loving you?"

"No." I smile sadly at her. "I think he will do anything to make me happy. But it's because of that, because I love him more than anything, that I must release him and enable him to realize his dream which I know he can with someone else."

"Don't do this." She falls on her knees, her hands coming up in prayer. "Please, Josephine. It will break him. He will never forgive me for letting you go."

Running over, I pull her up. I hug her, struggling against the enormous pain overwhelming me.

"I've explained everything in my letter." I sniff. "He will understand. He will have to understand that I am doing this for him." I cough as weeping suffocates me, and kiss her head. "During the darkest time I've ever known, I was happy here. Thanks to you and to him. I will always be grateful."

Disengaging from her, I run out. I burst into tears and weep from the depths of my soul. I am parting from everything I have loved. Country. City. The people and my man.

My husband.

CHAPTER FORTY-ONE

Leaning against the rail on the upper deck, I look out, amazed, at the most impressive statue I've ever seen. No picture could ever portray its power as it stands there in front of me in all its splendor.

"You gave us that statue," the soldier standing next to me, says playfully.

Frowning, I look at him uncomprehendingly. My English has improved wonderfully in the three months I've spent on the ship, but I still have difficulty expressing myself confidently.

"Mademoiselle Josephine," he uses the title of an unmarried woman as I'd asked the soldiers on the ship to do, "that's the Statue of Liberty. France gave it to us."

I nod and continue to gaze at the impressive statue.

"It's the Goddess of Liberty," he explains further. "Do you see the seven rays emerging from her tiara?"

I nod.

"They radiate liberty to the seven continents." He notices that I don't understand his words. "They symbolize our sending out liberty to each of the continents," he explains, "which is why we joined the war in Europe."

I nod in thanks.

"And do you see how she flings out her right arm, the one holding the torch? Contrary to the salute of the Germans that symbolizes darkness, she throws her spear to illuminate the way for those who wish to come here."

"So beautiful…" I murmur.

"You're also beautiful." He smiles at me, moving away when he notices my embarrassment. "The war was hard for everyone, Mademoiselle. I hope you find peace here." Diffidently, he strokes my shoulder and walks away.

During the long period I spent with hundreds of soldiers on the ship, I learned to deal with their directness, which I sometimes perceived as rudeness. Nobody imagined that the quiet French nurse had boarded the ship illegally. I was their most devoted caregiver, not shying away from even the worst wounds. On the contrary, I spent all my time with them. I listened to their stories, prayed with them, comforted them and held the hands of those I knew did not have long to live.

I knew the nature of pain. I knew the nature of loss. I knew that if there was some way to ease a wounded soul, I would do it unhesitatingly. In exchange, I gained their respect. The wounded passed their time teaching me English, and some of them even made me their special project. I know the best places to enjoy oneself in New York, the recommended restaurants, and even the means of transport.

Some mistook their feelings for me, imagining that their gratitude was in fact love. In the course of three months I managed to receive two marriage proposals. One of them proposing with his last breath.

The tumult increases on deck as we approach the port, and several soldiers wave and burst into tears. Their country is still at war, with one small and significant difference, the Nazis aren't here.

The ship moors and I see an enormous crowd gathering on the dock. Ambulances, nurses, doctors and, of course excited family members.

Waiting patiently until all the wounded are removed on stretchers, I disembark, one small suitcase in hand. All my worldly possessions are in this shabby suitcase that Madame Distel gave me as a parting gift. Apart from two dresses I was given, there is nothing in it. I have left it all behind me.

"Josephine! Josie, darling!" The excited cry came from a distance, and I raise my head and look at the old man running towards me.

"Papa!" I run to him, dropping the suitcase and falling into his arms in tears.

"I can't believe you're really here." He embraces me and steps back to look at me.

"You've changed so much. My little girl has become a woman. If only your mother could see you now."

"I wish I could see her," I answer painfully. "Papa, you've also changed." I touch the lines at his eyes. Until now, I hadn't realized how much I'd missed him.

"My hair has whitened a little, but your Papa is still young at heart." He laughs and embraces me again. "I have so many questions, I can't wait to hear everything you've been through since we left." He picks up the suitcase and walks towards two men in uniform.

"Do you have your papers?"

I take my old papers out of my bag and hand them to him.

"Au revoir, Mademoiselle Josephine," shouts one of the soldiers who had been on the ship with me, waving his hand.

I bow my head and smile at him.

My father gives my papers to the men, adding one more document he'd brought with him. The men examine my photograph and stamp the documents. "Welcome to America," says one of them. The documents are returned to me and I sigh with relief.

My father leads me out of the port, and I look up and my mouth opens.

"*Ciel…*"

"That was my reaction too when we arrived here." My father laughs. "All these extraordinary buildings. As if the Americans had decided to take over the skies as well."

We sit down in the back seat of a taxi that threads its way through the sea of cars and people. Pressing my head to the window, I look at the new sights in astonishment. Tall, imposing buildings, stores, stalls, soldiers in uniform and men and women hurrying to their destinations. The city is lit up and full of life.

"Papa are you sure this country is still at war?'

"On several fronts," he answers, and when I turn to him, I see he is not looking at the view, but at me.

"It's so different here." I smile sadly at him. "War hasn't taken the colors from the city. It's so colorful and lit up. I'm glad you haven't had to see how gray our city has become."

"Paris will regain her colors." He caresses my shoulders. "Now that she's been liberated from those cursed Germans, she will again become the most beautiful city in the world."

"No-one can erase the black stains that tarnish her." I look down.

"I'm sure you had a hard time. We received terrible reports of what they did to the Jews…"

"I'd rather not talk about it yet."

"Forgive me. You're right." He shakes his head. "We'll let you recover, there will be enough time to listen and tell everything we've been through since we parted."

I nod and look out the window. The scenes change like a fast movie, and everyone looks so energetic. Where are they hurrying to? And how come none of them look scared?

The taxi turns onto an inter-urban road and the crowdedness is replaced by a pastoral scenery. A few minutes later it turns at an interchange and I continue to look out.

"We'll be home in a few minutes," my father says and I shrink. I'd had a home. In the darkest city in the world I'd had a home full of light. I will never feel at home in a place without my man. I bite my lips. The day will come when he'll realize I did it for him, and he'll forgive me and, in the future, even thank me.

"Are you ready to see the room I've prepared for you?" My father asks excitedly when the taxi stops in front of a double-story house surrounded by green lawns.

"Of course." I hold my crooked elbow and put a smile on my face.

"What happened to your arm?" My father asks when I get out of the taxi and walk along the pathway to the house.

"A painful and unnecessary fall," I lie.

"Maybe a doctor should take a look?"

"No, no. No doctors." I laugh irritably. "I'm as healthy as an ox. It will heal."

"All right." He opens the door and waves his arms. "So what do you have to say about our kingdom?"

"Charming!" I pretend enthusiasm. The lobby leads into a wide living room furnished with brown leather sofas and several wood dressers. There are no pictures on the walls or curtains on the windows. The design is masculine and minimalist. I walk inside and immediately go over to the glass door leading out to an enormous yard.

"In summer, we'll have barbeques." My father stands beside me. "I've learned to enjoy their barbaric meals, you will also learn." He laughs, and my eyes fix on the massive tiles of the tiled area in the garden. The universe seems to pull me back by force to Claude's garden. I'm willing to swear that these are the very tiles I stood on at my first meeting with the man who set my world spinning.

"Well, are you ready to see the room I've prepared for you?"

"Yes, of course."

We go up to the second floor, and he points to a room on the right. I open the door and put my hand over my mouth.

"Do you like it?"

"Pink?" I look in horror at the pink walls, pink bedspread and pink curtains.

"I remembered you liked this color," he says, disconcerted.

"When I was six." I burst out laughing and hug him. I don't remember the last time I laughed. Really laughed. And now I can't stop.

"You can decorate it any way you choose." He scratches his head and chuckles. "I apologize, I must have forgotten that you're no longer a little girl."

"Papa, I wasn't a little girl when you left, but it's charming and I don't want to change a thing."

"Well, get ready for dinner. Suzie is a great cook."

I raise an eyebrow and he blushes.

"I haven't had a chance to tell you. A few months ago, I began a romantic attachment with a very nice woman. She doesn't live here, and I hope it won't bother you that I invited her to meet you. She was so excited when I told her you were coming and…"

"Papa, it's fine." I kiss his cheek. "I'm glad you are building a good life for yourself here. I'm sure Mama would have wanted you to find happiness."

"Josephine!" He becomes grave. "Your Mama always was and always will be the great love of my life."

"I know." I put my hand over my heart. "You took such devoted care of her all those years. Maybe if she'd had the chance to release you beforehand, she'd have chosen to do so."

"Release me?" He frowns. "I wouldn't have given up a single day, hour, or even one minute with your mother. We don't choose who will capture our hearts, and not even her illness could diminish the intensity of my love for her."

I nod and turn away my head so he won't see my tears.

"She gave me the greatest gift of my life." He enters the room and pulls back the curtain. "She gave me you. What is life worth without children? After all, they remind us that unconditional love exists."

I choke and put my hand on my belly.

"You have your own bathroom." He puts the suitcase on the bed, not noticing my distress. "Tomorrow I'll take you shopping for everything you need."

I want to cry out that what my broken heart needs he cannot buy me, but I carefully wipe my tears and smile at him in gratitude.

He leaves and I lie on the bed and look at the ceiling. I've gained my life back several times. My body is managing to recover contrary to expectations, and now I'm safe and surrounded by love. I won't let myself wither away from heartbreak. This too shall pass. Pain will become longing, and in the end, I will be able to forget.

If he'd only stay out of my dreams, I'd manage to forget him.

After all, time heals everything.

CHAPTER FORTY-TWO

Sounds of laughter from the ground floor make me smile. I put on the blue dress I brought with me, and fix my hair with clips. The time has come to start my new life, and I should be happy I'm able to do so with my father.

Going downstairs, I see him standing dressed in tailored pants and a black sweater. He seems so comfortable and happy as he looks at the woman sitting opposite him on the sofa.

"Josephine." His face lights up when he notices me, and the woman stands up and smiles at me.

"Gilbert, you didn't tell me your daughter is a beauty." She approaches me, and when I hold out my hand, she waves it away and embraces me tightly. "You're simply breathtaking, darling." Holding my chin, she examines my face. "We'll need a few watch dogs to keep away your suitors." She laughs.

"Thank you, Madame Susie." I respond shyly.

"Madame?" Again she waves her hand and laughs. "Call me Susie. Here, we don't stand on ceremony among friends." She is tiny, like me, but rounder. She is wearing a simple, checked dress and her black hair is streaked with gray. Her smile seems stuck to her face, and I can understand why my father has chosen to spend time with her. Her face radiates purity and happiness, and although she doesn't have a drop of European elegance, her joy is catching.

"Susie, let the girl breathe," my father scolds her affectionately.

"Shhh…Gilbert." Linking her arm in mine, she leads me into the dining room. "She's not a little girl anymore and doesn't need you to protect her."

The table is laid and the food is arranged on it. She sits down without waiting for my father to move her chair for her, and when she notices my expression, she shrugs and laughs.

"It took me time to get used to her," he explains, pulling out my chair. "But you'll learn to like her."

"She already likes me." Susie gives him a cross look. "And she'll like me even more after she's tasted my cooking." She piles food onto my plate, and I nod in thanks. My father pours wine and sits down next to her. She doesn't ask what he wants to eat, filling his plate generously with all there is. He leans back and seems comfortable and pleased she's taking care of him.

"I wish to raise a glass to our family reunion." He raises his glass and both of us do the same. "This is the first night in five years I'll be able to sleep well. The anxiety for my princess was unbearable, not being able to be in contact and know how you were, gave me no rest, but I knew I'd left you in the devoted care of my good friends Claude and Brigitte. That did comfort me a little."

The glass fell from my hand and shattered on the floor.

"What's wrong, sweetheart?" Susie stood up, looking at me with concern.

The realization that he didn't know what had happened to his friends, pulls me back into terrible grief. I breathe heavily.

"Josie, what's wrong?" Standing up, my father gives me a glass of water.

"I apologize for breaking the glass."

"Nonsense. Don't let it worry you." Susie goes into the kitchen and returns with a broom and dustpan. "I'll clean it up."

"Sit down!" My father orders quietly, continuing to look at me.

"But..."

"I asked you to sit down." He pulls her chair back and she sits down. She looks from him to me and back to him, and I sip the water, bowing my head.

"Josephine, please tell me what happened." He sits down. I put the glass on the table and hold my elbow.

"Papa, they didn't survive," I say in French, and when he opens his eyes in alarm and holds his forehead, Susie presses his arm for him to translate for her.

"I don't understand…" he murmurs in French. "What do you mean, they didn't survive? We heard rumors but mainly about Jews."

"Speak in English," Susie raises her voice in frustration.

"Papa, they caught him." I ignore her request, feeling this to be too intimate a conversation to have in front of a stranger. "He spied for the Allies and they caught him." My eyes fill with tears.

"A spy? Claude? It must have been a mistake. Nobody protested? All his friends remained silent?"

I sip the water and tell him everything in a single breath, censoring the marriage proposal and the great love I won. When I am silent, he looks at me in shock.

He finishes the wine in one long sip, and goes to the glass cupboard behind him. "I need something stronger," he says, taking out a bottle of brandy and two glasses. He sets one in front of me.

"Please tell me what happened," Susie pleads. He pours us two glasses and rubs his forehead. When he finishes translating for her, she puts her hand to her mouth and looks at me in horror.

"Why did this man save you?" She asks. "And what happened to Claude's wife and daughter? And where did you live after they took their home?"

So many questions. I nod painfully and look at my father again.

"If I'd known, I would never have jeopardized you in that way," My father continues in French, his eyes distraught. "I was certain you were safe there. Now I realize you went through hell."

"No, Papa." I burst into tears. "I managed. I learned to survive without them, and I had help from a special angel. It's thanks to him and several other angels who helped me along the way, that I'm sitting here now."

"I have to know if you were hurt. I have to know if anyone hurt my little girl while I was here in the illusion that you were safe."

Hugging myself, I sniff. "No, Papa. Nobody hurt me." I choose to lie to him, maybe that way I'll see him smile again. But he appears eaten up with guilt. "They were caught and I managed to survive. I came here to get away from that dark time, and I hope you will allow me to start a new life here," I say the last sentence in English.

"But I have so many questions," my father murmurs.

"This is not the time." Susie puts a soothing hand on his shoulder. "Let her recover and gain strength. When she feels ready to tell you, she will. Until then we'll respect her request and make sure she starts a new and a good life here."

I smile at her and she nods with understanding.

"But…" My father says, falling silent when she presses his shoulder.

"With your permission, I'll go to bed now." I stand up and sip my brandy. "The voyage was long and difficult. I just need to sleep so I can wake to a new day. A new life."

"Of course." My father stands up and I go over to hug him.

He remains standing until I have left the room, and then my heart breaks when I hear my strong, heroic father burst into tears.

Entering my room, I close my eyes. Pray for one night of dreamless sleep.

I open my eyes and the darkness makes my heart miss a beat.

Where am I?

I touch the sheets, breathing a sigh of relief when I remember that I'm in my bedroom, in my father's house.

Like every night, this time too, I wake to the sound of children's laughter and the sight of the special eyes looking at me with love.

"Get out of my dreams!" I shrink into a fetal position. "Gabriel, please, get out of my dreams!"

I sit up when I think I hear voices from the ground floor, remembering that I'm no longer in Paris. The Nazis are not wandering the streets and nobody is knocking at the door in the middle of the night.

But now I'm certain I'm not imagining things. I hear steps.

Putting on a robe, I leave the room. The steps stop, and I tiptoe downstairs.

My father is sitting at a small table looking at a chess board in front of him.

"Did I wake you?" He stands up. "I'm sorry, I couldn't sleep and was tired of tossing and turning in bed."

"It's fine. I couldn't sleep either." I smile at him.

"Sit with me a while." He motions to a chair in front of him. "Do you want something to eat or drink?"

"No." I smile at him and sit down.

"Want to play?" He raises an eyebrow in anticipation.

"You know how bad I am at this game." I move my pawn forwards and he bursts out laughing.

"I hoped in time you'd learn the game." He returns my pawn. "But maybe this game isn't for everyone."

"No, it isn't." I sigh. "It requires concentration, strategic thinking and an ability to predict the moves of your opponent."

"And think at least two…"

"Steps ahead." I laugh, hugging myself. " A few months ago, I met a little boy, about seven or eight." Leaning back I smile sadly. "Papa, if you'd seen him play, your heart would have burst with pride."

"Did you play with him?"

"I played for him." Standing up, I sigh heavily. Caressing my father's head, I kiss his cheek and turn to the stairs. "Maybe the day will come when my father will be able to explain to me how the world has broken." Weeping suffocates me. "Until then, I will go on hoping someone will be able to fix it."

CHAPTER FORTY-THREE

I sit in a taxi rubbing my knees. Susie had taken me on such a one day shopping spree that would have taken me three days in Paris. She rushed me from one boutique to another, not resting until we both collapsed under the weight of the bags.

"You have great taste," she says, handing the driver the address. "But why did you insist on buying fabrics and a sewing machine? We bought so many beautiful clothes."

"It's a hobby." I yawn. "Until I decide what to do with my life, I must keep myself busy with good soothing things."

"You can always work in your father's office." She suggests cautiously. "This war has hurt a lot of businesses, but for a talented engineer like your father, it's a very busy time. He has a lot of projects and I heard that one of the secretaries has left."

"I'll think about it."

She bursts out laughing and I look at her, disconcerted.

"That's exactly your father's answer when I suggest something which he doesn't want to refuse and be dragged into an argument."

"He's always been a man of compromise." I smile at her. "But I'm glad he hasn't compromised and found someone who really makes him happy."

Her smile widens. "Thank you for saying that." She presses my hand. "It was so important to me that you like me. That we get on. For him."

"As long as you make him happy, I will always like you."

The taxi stops in front of the house, and Susie orders the driver to help with the bags. I wonder if I'll ever get used to the blunt behavior of the people in this country where I'm a guest.

We go straight up to my room and she helps me hang the clothes in the closet.

"Have a rest, now." She pats the pillow. "We've been invited by friends to a cocktail party this evening, and your father will be very disappointed if you won't join us because I've exhausted you today."

"Am I also invited to this cocktail party?"

"Of course you're invited. All our friends are looking forward to meet Gilbert's daughter."

"I hope there won't be a lot of people there." I yawn and go into the bathroom.

"Only a few close friends," she shouts and I hear the door closing.

I wash my face and lie down on the bed. Life is so fast here. As if someone is running after people with a stopwatch, counting the seconds needed to carry out each task. Even the shopping, which is supposed to be a pleasant experience, becomes a race after time.

Covering myself with the blanket, I close my eyes. I'm on the Champs-Élysées with Odette. Arm in arm we go into a corner boutique where I sit down and drink coffee, while she tries on dresses. The saleswomen circle around her, and I laugh when she scolds them for choosing her a dress that doesn't meet her expectations.

"Josephine, explain to them." She stands in front of the mirror, arranging her hair. "I need a dress that won't leave a single man indifferent to me. Actually, why am I wasting my time here? Let's go and select some fabrics and, perhaps, you can sew me a dress like that?"

"We don't have time for that." I look at the clock. "The cocktail party starts in less than an hour."

"What cocktail party?" She wrinkles her nose.

"Josephine…" Her voice becomes deeper, and she shakes me. "You need to get up, the cocktail party starts in less than an hour."

"What?" I sit up in alarm and wipe the perspiration off my forehead.

My father looks at me with concern.

"You were talking in your sleep." He says apologetically. "I'd have let you go on sleeping but we're invited to a…"

"A cocktail party." I rub my eyes and get out of bed. "I'll get ready quickly and join you."

"Take your time." He leaves the room, closing the door.

I splash water on my face and yawn aloud. Now Odette is also taking over my dreams. I can escape my city, my country, even the continent, but I can't escape from the people I left behind. The living and the dead haunt me, and I have no way of fighting it, they are deep in my heart.

I finish getting ready and go down to the ground floor. Susie is fixing my father's tie and he kisses her forehead.

He smiles proudly when he sees me. "You look wonderful."

"You can tell me I look wonderful," Susie scolds him. "Josephine looks much more than wonderful." Coming over to me, she smooths the folds of my skirt. The need to make my father proud and satisfied made me put far more into my appearance than I felt like doing.

"My daughter has always been a beauty." He helps me on with my wool coat, and when we go out to the pathway, a taxi is waiting.

"In Paris, you had a car," I say in French.

"Only the brave drive here," he responds in English and laughs.

The taxi leaves the quiet, residential neighborhood and after a few minutes we are in the center of Manhattan. The hooting is deafening. I can't understand why our driver doesn't stop hooting. When he stops at the entrance to a high-rise, I get out of the taxi and stand against the wall. The sights, the noise, and even the smells are unpleasant. Everything here is too fast for me.

"You look like a frightened kitten," Susie comments.

We enter the building and I breathe a sigh of relief when the tumult of the street is left behind. My father summons the elevator and presses the button for the top floor.

"It's a business friend's cocktail party," he explains without my asking. "Everyone there is a close friend of ours, feel free to tell me if anyone overwhelms you with questions."

"Why would anyone do that?" I ask in alarm.

"Sweetheart, it isn't every day that someone arrives here from occupied Paris." Susie answers for him. "People are naturally curious, and that's why they'll ask you questions. If they go overboard, signal to me and I'll rescue you."

I'm already regretting having agreed to join them.

We leave the elevator and my father knocks once on the door and opens it. Not exactly an intimate event…I look in alarm at scores of men and women filling the elegant space. I'm drawn inside and from that moment shake the hand of every man and woman in the room. Smile, nod, smile again and try to remember all the names tossed at me. It's hopeless.

A glass of wine is put in my hand and Susie leads me forward. She stops at a table of appetizers and we are no longer surrounded by the curious. I breathe deeply and nod in gratitude when she hands me a tiny sandwich.

"I'll do my rounds and come back to look after you." She winks at me, and approaches a group of women. It isn't that bad being in the company of ordinary people. The war looks completely different here.

"Good evening, ma'am," a man with a mustache and a bow tie holds out his hand. I put down my glass of wine to shake it. The woman clinging to his arm looks at me strangely, but shakes my hand as well. "My wife would like to ask you a question," the man says with discomfort. "You're the first French woman we've met since war broke out and…"

"I have to know if you are acquainted with the Stern family," the woman interrupts. "They live in Paris."

I shake my head. "I'm sorry, the chances that I'll know this particular family are slim."

"We've heard rumors that…" she clings to her husband. "That the Jews were taken away from Paris to labor camps, but I know they took only foreigners. Only those who came from other countries after the occupation.

The Stern family, my sister's family, are long term residents. So surely they'd be safe?" I look down and without waiting for my response, she continues. "I've sent scores of telegrams. I didn't receive even one reply."

"Ah…you're right." I don't have the courage to look into her eyes. "At first, they did take only foreigners."

"What do you mean 'at first'?" She disengages from her husband and grasps my elbow. "What do you mean? Did they take them too?"

"I'm sorry." The blood drains from my face, and I try to release my elbow from her strong grasp.

"That's impossible!" She shrieks and quiet prevails around us. "They're French. Nobody would have allowed that to happen. The French are a proud people. They take care of their own."

"I think that some of them have forgotten their pride in this case." I cover my face with my hands in a desperate attempt to hide the shame.

"And the rumors?" She bursts into tears. "The terrible rumors of the extermination of the Jews in these camps in Europe?"

"I'm sorry, Madame."

The shriek that emerges from her throat makes me stumble back, and I'm caught in my father's protective arms.

"Rachel, I'm sorry that the news reaching us isn't good." He moves in front of me, blocking me from the distressed couple. "My daughter has come to us after terrible years under Nazi occupation. She isn't authorized to give you reliable information, so let's wait for good news and allow her to enjoy a quiet evening without interrogation."

"We apologize," the man says, embracing his weeping wife. "We won't trouble her further." He leads her away while everyone looks at me silently.

"Go back to your gossip." My father rebukes the group of women, and they turn around and continue talking. The others do the same. "Josie, do you want to go home?" My father asks worriedly.

I long to escape all the looks and curiosity but by the same token I'm determined to get through this ordeal.

"No, papa." I raise my glass of wine. "I understand their pain and sorrow.

It's all right. You can go back to your friends."

"Gilbert, off you go, I'll take care of her." A smiling young woman with dancing curls waves to him, and he smiles at her and nods but still looks at me with concern.

"She'll look after me." I fake a calming smile, and he kisses my cheek and returns to the men.

"I've heard that French women are chatty." She nudges my shoulder. "But I thought that at least on your first evening here you wouldn't talk so much."

"I apologize. They asked and I only..."

"I'm teasing you." She pats my arm and chuckles. "From the moment you came in, I gambled on who would be the first to attack you with questions. Curiosity will kill them in the end."

"I wish I had happier news," I respond with pain.

"Did you play a senior role in the French army?" She asks with a meaningful expression.

"No...I wasn't recruited. Women don't..."

"Then why do you look as if you are carrying this damned war on your shoulders?" She bursts out laughing.

I smile and examine her. She looks about my age. Her face is round and bright and her body lacks feminine curves, but she is graceful and pleasant and her light-heartedness reminds me of my best friend.

"My name is Anne." She holds out her hand. "And I have a feeling we are going to be good friends."

"I'd be glad of a friend." I smile at her, and see her eyes narrow as she examines something behind my back.

"Don't look now," she whispers. "The hostess's sons are here tonight, and I've fantasized for years about Edward, the younger brother."

I turn my head and encounter two pairs of eyes fixed on me. Both are wearing uniforms. One smiles whereas the other, a patch on his right eye, looks coldly at me. His pain passes through to me, making me flinch, and I turn back to Anne.

"I told you not to look." She scolds me and giggles. "I think the older brother, Benjamin, came on the same boat with you from France."

I don't recall him from the months at sea, but it isn't impossible. I was in the makeshift clinic, and all my attention was given to the badly wounded.

"Perhaps you'd like to join me for a drink?" I hear the male voice behind me and go pale. Even his voice carries pain.

"I'm already drinking." I raise my glass of wine without turning my head.

"Nonetheless, I'd be glad of a few moments of your time." I feel his hand grasping my arm.

"Anne, you're invited to join me for a drink," an amused male voice addresses her, and when she nods enthusiastically I realize it would be better to avoid additional drama and accept.

We cross the drawing room and continues into the passage.

"Where are you taking me?" I stop.

"To the kitchen. I'd be glad to talk to you in private."

Placing his hand on my lower back, he leads me forwards into the kitchen. I have no idea what privacy he was talking about. Two women are busy arranging trays, and waiters come and go all the time.

He takes me to a table along the wall and gestures to me to sit. He takes a bottle of cognac and two glasses from a shelf and, sitting down opposite me, he pours cognac into both glasses and then touches the patch on his eye. His brown hair is short, his face good-looking and he looks like a man who has grown older before his time.

"My name is Benjamin. I didn't mean my invitation to a drink to sound like a demand." He apologizes. "I had to sit down for a moment with someone who is able to understand my pain and frustration."

"And that's me?"

"Only someone who experiences pain can identify with a soulmate." He grins sadly. "I arrived yesterday, and I feel I've been thrown into a parallel reality. Everyone talks about the war here, about losses, about the difficulties and the pain, but none of them have personally experienced it." He sips his drink. "Sitting here with you now enables me to breathe. I don't know how to explain it, but from the moment you entered our house, I felt a connection with you."

"I don't think I experienced the war as you did. You fought and were wounded." I smile wretchedly.

"The rumors of what you went through there reached me too."

I open my mouth in surprise and he pours himself a second drink.

"Your heroic escape from the Gestapo…"

"There was no heroic escape." I look fearfully at the kitchen door. "The boy who rescued me was the real hero. But I beg you, I beg you, don't say a word. I don't want my father to know."

"I would never do such a thing." He puts his hand over mine in a way that is too intimate, and I pull away. "I only want someone in my life who will understand what I'm going through, without judging or pitying me."

"If you intend to court me, it's important you know I'm not looking for a relationship." My face hardens.

"Mademoiselle Josephine, emotional involvement is the last thing I am looking for now. I've returned physically and mentally wounded, and even my younger brother, who was recruited to intelligence, is unable to understand me. I merely wish to spend a little time with someone who is not deterred by my pain."

"Your pain doesn't deter me." I close my eyes when I feel his sadness penetrate me. "My pain has become an inseparable part of me, and I no longer fight it. I've accepted it so that I can start again."

"I still hope I won't have to live with it. That in time I will stop feeling it."

I'm no longer anxious about being close to him and put my hand on his.

"The sights I saw there." He sighs. "The wounded, the dead, the civilians who paid such a high price. I still see them every time I close my eyes."

"So this is where you're hiding?" Susie's amused voice makes us jump, and I remove my hand. "Come sweetheart, your father has decided it's time for us all to go home."

I stand up and Benjamin accompanies me to the door.

"I'd be glad if you'd allow me to invite you to a movie or a restaurant," he says, ignoring my father and Susie's looks of surprise.

"Only if you agree that we only go out as friends." I link arms with my father.

"Agreed." He puts his hand over his heart and I nod in agreement.

. In the taxi Susie bursts out laughing.

"I told you we'd need watch dogs to keep off her suitors."

"He isn't my suitor!" I answer firmly, and she stops laughing. "I don't want a suitor, not now and not in the future. I don't want or need a man in my life."

I notice the looks they exchange, but say nothing more. My hand smooths my belly and I lean my head against the window.

I had a man. The most perfect man on earth. My heart will remain his forever.

CHAPTER FORTY-FOUR

Ann is lying on my bed and looking in astonishment at the dresses I am showing her. Tonight we are going out to the Jazz club with the two brothers, and I'd suggested she choose a dress from my new collection.

"Did you really sew them yourself?" She asks, bending to examine one up close.

"Of course."

"But where did you get the design? It's so elegant and innovative."

"I designed them all myself." I proudly show her wide pants that look like a skirt.

"You are wasted here." She strips off her clothes and tries on the green dress. "Now that the war has ended, the economy is flourishing! You must open a boutique on Fifth Avenue."

Shaking my head, I reflect on her declaration. The war has ended on all fronts. The borders are open, immigrants are flowing into the country and only my heart is still held hostage by the man I haven't seen for over a year. It was the right decision, I persuade myself when my heart burns.

"I sew for my soul. I didn't finish my studies and don't have the right qualifications."

"You have a natural talent." She turns in front of the mirror, smiling at the sight of the flying fabric. "I choose this one. What are you going to wear?"

I take out an elegant black dress and hold it against my body.

"Benjamin will pass out when he sees you in that dress." She giggles.

"Why would he pass out?" I sit down in the armchair and light a cigarette. "We're just good friends."

"He may be blind in one eye, but you are blind in both of yours." She sits down at the dressing table and powders her nose. "The man is as in love with you as a puppy in heat."

"You're talking nonsense. We go out at least twice a week, he always behaves like a gentleman and has never hinted that he sees me as more than a friend."

"You really don't see it." She grabs the cigarette from me and opens the window. "Josephine, contrary to his brother who screws any girl who smiles at him, he doesn't see anyone except you."

"Don't swear," I scold her and take back the cigarette.

"Dick. Fuck. Screw." She laughs and I shudder. "Of course he's head over heels in love with you. You are unlike all the vulgar girls around him, like me." She points to herself. "You behave like a queen with all your European manners. Like an ice queen."

"He isn't in love with me," I raise my voice in annoyance. "I explained to him at our first meeting that I'm not looking for a relationship and he promised to respect that."

"It isn't possible to make promises about feelings." Her expression grows sad. "I also promised myself I wouldn't fall in love with his brother, and see how I'm always there to pick up the crumbs he throws at me every time no other girl happens to be around."

"You don't need Edward." I put on the dress and hold my elbow. "You need someone who will love you for yourself. See your inner beauty. Want to make you happy…" I fall silent when my heart burns again, but this time more strongly.

"Josephine, that's exactly what I see in Benjamin's eyes when he looks at you. He's a good man, why don't you let him come closer?"

I turn my head so she won't see the tears.

"Nobody will ever succeed in making me feel like that again." I say the last word soundlessly and stroke my belly.

"We're already a pair of old spinsters." Her tone is lighthearted again, and I'm grateful for her ability to change the mood in a split second. "It's time we found ourselves men who want to marry us, give us some kids and turn us into bitter, married ladies."

"I don't need a man." I fix slides in my hair. "And our taxi has arrived." I roll my eyes at the loud hooting from the street. I will never get used to the noise people make in this country.

We go down together and Susie flutters around us with an uncontrollable onslaught of questions. Anne answers her impatiently, and I smile at my father sitting on the sofa, smoking a cigar.

It's normal. This situation now and all those preceding it during the past few months since my arrival, are completely normal. Everything is so normal, I sometimes wonder if I ever experienced anything else. If it was all just a nightmare. Except that my man had been in that nightmare. My perfect man who infused the grayness with a shining light, who still makes my heart beat fiercely in my chest every time his image pops up before my eyes.

The hooting from the street wakes me out of my daydream. I blow my father a kiss and leave the house.

Benjamin is waiting for us at the entrance to the club. He smiles broadly when he sees me. It's only a friendly smile, I reassure myself.

He kisses Anne's cheek and, when he approaches me, I allow him to kiss me lightly on the cheek before stepping away. He is still smiling, but his eyes darken. Opening the door for us, he doesn't move from my side even when we walk between the tables towards Edward, who waves his hand.

"I'll be getting crumbs again this evening," Anne whispers with annoyance. When we reach the table, she sits down beside him and flirts endlessly with him.

The club is full. The band plays rhythmic music and the dance floor is packed with couples dancing and enjoying themselves. I can't hear the conversation taking place next to me and stare dreamily at two women fighting for the attention of a man standing in front of them.

"I asked if you want a drink," Benjamin strokes my shoulder and I move it at once. He bites his lip in frustration, but smiles again and raises a questioning eyebrow.

"Uh…a martini. Thank you."

Standing up, he approaches the bar, and I go back to watching the figures hopping about the dance floor, remembering the little Jazz club in Paris, Natalie's bothersome questions and the difficult days of loneliness that followed. Terrible days that I wasted by distancing from my man, instead of drawing him to me and thanking him for every minute, every second I could have felt his pure love for me. My gaze wanders to the bar. For a moment, I can imagine him standing there, confident and at ease in his white sweater, turning to me, his eyes burning with love that makes my heart tremble.

Time will heal the pain. It will also heal the longing.

"May I invite you to dance?" A dark-skinned young man blocks my view, and the image of my man vanishes.

"No, thank you."

"She's with me." I hear Benjamin's angry voice behind me, and the young man shrugs and returns to the dance floor.

He places the martini in front of me and I encounter Anne's look of rebuke.

"You don't have to lie to rescue me from an unwelcome invitation." I say the moment he sits down and sips his drink.

"I didn't think I was lying." He taps on his glance looking stressed.

"We're here together as friends." I insist on proving to Anne and to myself that he is wrong.

Benjamin nods and lights a cigarette. He closes his jaws tightly and fixes his glance on the center of the table.

"Shall we go out for a breath of fresh air?" I suggest in an attempt to soothe him. In the past months he'd become a good and valued friend, and in time I discovered that it wasn't only he who needed me in his life. I also needed him. A lost and confused soul who found a real connection with mine and the possibility of losing him stresses me.

"Good idea." He settles the patch over his eye and pulls my chair back.

We leave the club. Even at this late hour, the street is full of pedestrians.

"Josephine, I think we should talk." He says hesitatingly, and I turn to look at him.

"You know that…" He touches his patch and I remain quiet. "You know that you are very important to me."

"You are also important to me."

"Yes, but…I don't think we can continue being friends."

"Benjamin. Why do you say such a thing?" I put my hand on his arm, withdrawing it when I see him look at it with pain in his face. "We enjoy each other, we understand each other and I don't want to lose one of my only two friends here."

"That is exactly the problem." He lights a cigarette and avoids my glance. "I don't want to be one of two friends, I want to be more than that."

"But we agreed. I haven't deceived you. I told you from the beginning that…"

"What you said doesn't matter." He throws away the cigarette and grasps my arms. "I've fallen in love with you. I didn't plan it, it just happened, and now I want more!"

I shake my head.

"Why aren't you willing to try and love me?" His voice trembles. "I'll make sure you have a good life. I'll build you a beautiful home, spoil you, buy you whatever you want and you'll never be short of money."

Closing my eyes I bite my lips.

"Josephine, we are no longer children. I want to have a family with you, bring children into the world with you, and love you. Make you happy."

I shake my head without opening my eyes.

"If you aren't able to be with me because of my disability then you should know that I've seen a doctor who says there's new surgery that can…"

"It isn't because of your disability." I open my eyes and sink into his pain. "I've never seen you as disabled. You are an amazing, good-hearted man. The woman who wins you will be happy, but it won't be me."

"Why not?" He shakes his head. "If it isn't my disability, then what's the problem?"

"It's me who isn't good enough." I stroke his cheek and stand up. "I'm broken. In heart, body and mind."

"I'm willing to accept you exactly as you are." He stands opposite me. "In time we can heal everything. I'm not stupid. I know someone broke your heart, but I'm willing to wait until it is healed. I'll help you forget him. I'll build you a home, raise a family with you and make you happy."

"Benjamin, I cannot fall pregnant," I speak aloud my greatest nightmare, and see his eye open in shock. "Not now and not in the future. Not ever."

"It…doesn't matter to me." He mumbles, rubbing his forehead. "Don't worry. I'll take you to the best doctors," he murmurs confusedly. "We'll try and fix it."

"And if it can't be fixed?" I smile at him. "How long will you be able to compromise on a woman who can't give you children?"

He opens and closes his mouth. His expression reflects pity and I don't want it.

"It's fine." I approach and kiss his cheek. "I've come to terms with it." I wave my hand and a taxi screeches to a stop. "In any case, it wouldn't have mattered. You were right when you said I'd left my heart with another man. It is locked in a safe, and I left the key in the city that was once my home." I get into the taxi. "Goodbye, Benjamin."

When the door closes, I put my hand on my belly and lean back. I've mourned lost friends enough in my short life. I won't mourn any longer.

CHAPTER FORTY-FIVE

A Christmas tree stands next to the fireplace in the living room covered with decorations and colorful, sparkling lights. It's my second Christmas here. The first was three months after uniting with my father. Then I felt like an outsider in a country of happy people.

It's a special night. The first festival after the terrible war years, and the world is celebrating its liberty.

I, however, don't feel free. I feel imprisoned in a fake reality. A year and a half since I parted from my man. A year and a half since the last time I saw his small, magnetic smile, and the immeasurable love that burned in his eyes. A year and a half without him, and he still appears in my dreams.

"Would you like a drink before all the guests come to bother us?" My father stands next to me, looking at the tree with enjoyment.

"I've already taken care of myself." I point to a glass of wine on the mantelpiece.

"We have many reasons to celebrate this evening." He pours himself a drink and opens the curtains. "The war is over. You are here with me. I have a woman who loves me even if I don't understand why." He laughs and taps on the glass door leading into the garden. "I hope that next Christmas we will celebrate your love for a man who will make you happy."

I raise my glass and take a long sip.

"I just want to see you happy." He sighs and kisses my cheek. Knocks at the door make him turn around and go to open it.

Susie comes out of the kitchen bearing trays of pastries. I've done all I can to prove to him that I am happy here. I make sure to keep a fake smile on my face and since Benjamin disappeared from my life, I go out with Anne and her ever-changing partners. I never refuse to join him and Susie for their boring cocktail evenings, and I've never hinted that I might miss something. But, nonetheless, my father knows I'm play-acting.

Guests come over to wish me a merry Christmas and I smile politely. Some exchange a few sentences with me but, clearly, since that embarrassing incident at my first cocktail party, I've been marked as a bearer of bad news, and they choose to celebrate only victories.

Anne waves to me from the entrance and, for a few moments my smile is real. She pushes through the guests and throws her coat onto an armchair near the fireplace.

"Josephine, darling," she imitates my accent. "For 'ow long must we spend time wiz our parents' old friends?" She takes a glass of champagne from a waiter and gulps it down.

"I'm sick of seeing their pitying expressions. Even Kathleen, your father's pitiful secretary, is in a relationship."

"Really? Who with?"

"Her typewriter." Anne bursts out laughing and pretends to type at an impossible speed. "It will be the end of us if we don't find a man soon."

I laugh as she continues to move her fingers and complain.

"I wish I could find a man who excites me." She turns to the glass door and, together, we look out at the dark garden. "It's been so long since I met a man who excited me. And I so need to be excited." She turns back to the living room and I put my hand on the glass and breathe in confusion. *Déjà vu?*

"Wow..." She murmurs. "It seems I've just seen a man who excites me."

The air in the room grows thick and I can't breathe. I can't be imagining the lightning that electrifies my back.

Perspiration washes over my body. I rest my forehead on the glass.

Don't turn around. Don't turn around. Don't turn around.

Turning my head, I choke.

There is only one figure I can see clearly. He is tall, broad shouldered, his long eyelashes shade his eyes, and his lips curve in a small magnetic smile.

The green light in his eyes flashes into mine, and my hearts spins uncontrollably. My knees tremble and drained, I collapse against the glass.

Anne seems to be standing beside me and asking me something. I have to escape from my hallucination. Another second and my heart will stop and I won't be able to save myself.

Managing to turn and open the door, I run along the rough tiles. Standing next to the supporting pole of the pergola I hold onto it.

You're imagining things. You're imagining things!

But the steps behind me are real, and when the large figure approaches I close my eyes and breathe in his scent.

"Josephine, open your eyes." The voice I'd heard whispering words of love in my dreams, is loud in my ears.

I shake my head.

"Open your eyes!"

I groan and open them. There is a yellow rose in front of me. I cover my mouth with my hand and shake my head.

"I promised you that the next time we meet I myself would bring you your rose." His body is close to mine and I breathe without being able to say a word. "I've so missed you…" His breaths caress my cheek and I take the rose and place it on my breast. My heart is beating wildly. "I've missed my wife." Stepping back in alarm I shake my head.

"I…I'm no longer…"

His body moves closer and I can't say a word, just continue shaking my head.

"A married woman shouldn't be without her wedding ring." He raises my hand and kisses my ring finger.

"Gabriel…" I hear myself speak his name and my body trembles. "I left you a letter. I asked you to end our marriage. I explained why." I move back and stroke my belly. His gaze is fixed on my face and his upper lip quivers.

He puts his hand in his trouser pocket and takes out my diamond ring, but doesn't put it on. My fingers are trembling uncontrollably and my breaths sound like groans.

"Have you yourself done anything to end our marriage?"

"No…but…"

"Then put your ring back on your finger."

I shake my head, but cannot release myself from his distraught eyes.

"Didn't you read the letter? Didn't you understand that I can no longer be your wife? Didn't you think that…"

"Josephine, I made a vow to wed you for eternity." He looks gravely at me, and I blink once to prove to myself that I'm not dreaming. "I vowed to you that I am yours and you are mine. You are my wife since then, today and forever, so put the ring on your finger unless you want me to do it by force."

I feel my ring finger rising and the ring slips on. He gives a sigh of relief.

"And now may I kiss my wife."

I stare into his perfect face approaching mine and, the moment his lips cling to mine, I grasp his head and kiss him fiercely. I suck all the air out of him, his safety, comfort, and the love enveloping my heart in layers of protectiveness.

My body is lifted and our chests cling to each other. My fingers intertwine with his hair and move to clasp his neck. His hand caresses my back and arm, and neither of us is able to disengage.

I hear a cough from the door and then another and look round. Confused, I look at my father and his friends who have gathered around him. I'm held in Gabriel's arms, refuse to disengage and he doesn't seem to have any intention of releasing me.

Licking my lips, I look at him again. The small, mesmerizing smile that desolated my nights with anguished longing, now brings an embarrassed smile to my face.

"Josephine, would you like to introduce your friend?" My father insists on throwing me right back into reality.

"I apologize, Monsieur Portiere," Gabriel addresses him in French. He sets me down but continues to hold my hand. "I should have introduced myself a long time ago. To tell the truth, I was supposed to have a man-to-man conversation with you and ask for your daughter's hand in marriage."

"Speak in English," Susie and Anne cry in unison.

Gabriel ignores them and draws me towards my father. "The war prevented me from asking for her hand like a gentleman, but I promise you that I did all I could to make sure she was safe and happy."

"Josephine, what in God's name is he talking about?" My father asks in shock.

"Uh..."

Gabriel raises my hand and kisses my ring finger. Susie cries out in surprise and my father goes pale.

"I'm pleased to meet you, Monsieur," He drops my hand and raises his towards my father. "Gabriel Augustine, Josephine's husband."

CHAPTER FORTY-SIX

The commotion around me transports me back to the restaurant on the night he proposed to me. I close my eyes tightly and when I open them there are still no loathsome Germans in their gray and black uniforms, but only surprised and excited glances of men and women who'd welcomed me to their country with open arms. And among all these glances is the glance of one man who seems astonished and troubled.

"Papa," I go over to him and hug him. "I should have told you, but I was afraid that my story would sadden you."

"I don't understand why you didn't tell me something so important." He doesn't hug me in return. "This man hurt you, is that why you left Paris? Are you afraid of him?"

"No. No." I hug him more tightly. "This man saved me. I love him more than my heart can hold. That's why I left. Because I wanted to release him from my burden."

I feel my father's arms close around me.

Gabriel's upper lip is trembling. "With your permission, Monsieur, that's a conversation I must have with my wife in private."

My father still looks confused, but he nods and moves aside and all the others do the same and make way for us.

Gabriel's arm encircles my waist and I can't think of anything but the heat passing through his arm.

"We can talk in the kitchen," I murmur.

"We're going to my hotel."

Impatiently, he surveys the pile of coats and gestures to me to show him which one is mine. I point at the black wool coat and he helps me on with it.

"I need to bring…"

"You don't need anything." He opens the door and pulls me with him out to the street.

A taxi is waiting at the sidewalk. We get in and he holds my hand and doesn't let go.

The storm of my emotions doesn't allow me to think logically. I turn my head to the window and look at the house fading away behind me. Should I have protested and had the conversation in my father's house? A place I could ask him to leave, after insisting that I'd made the right decision for both of us.

I glance at him and see his eyes are fixed on me. I turn my head quickly to the window and bite my lip. His influence over me is too strong, and I remind myself that I must be strong for both of us. But now, as he holds my hand, confusion blurs my mind. I feel his touch mesmerize me. I feel I belong to him. I haven't felt I belonged for so long.

He doesn't say a word, and as time passes, my courage and determination fade. I put my hand on my belly and rebuke myself. I must fight for him, fight for the realization of his dream.

The taxi stops at the entrance to the hotel and Gabriel doesn't wait for the driver to open the door for me but does it himself. Again he takes my hand and nods to the concierge.

When we enter the prestigious lobby he goes directly to the elevator and when the door closes, he pulls me to him and closes me in his arms. I can't breathe, can't think and can't absorb the fact that he is real. That I am here in his arms.

"I can't believe that you're here with me," he whispers as if reading my thoughts.

"I can't believe you actually came here." I rest my cheek on his chest and listen to his heartbeat.

"For three months I was on the boat on my way here. Three months, praying I'd find you safe and sound."

"You shouldn't have wasted your time." I put my nose in his neck to smell his intoxicating scent once more. "I parted from you in Paris, and now you are making things so hard for me."

I hear his growl of annoyance.

The elevator stops and we enter a large suite. He takes my coat and goes to the bar, gestures to an armchair, and hands me a glass. I'm afraid that if I sit down I won't be able to escape from him, and glance in the direction of the door, and continue to stand.

He sits down, rubs his upper lip and looks quietly at me, examining me from head to toe. "To tell the truth, I'm glad you've come." My voice trembles but I force myself to go on.

"I prayed I could see you one more time. But I came to the decision that our marriage is over, and I ask you to respect that."

He sips his drink then puts it on the table. His lip is still quivering. "Have I done anything to make you lose faith in me?" His voice is quiet and chilling.

"No."

"Have I done anything to make you think I wouldn't honor my obligation to look after you and protect you?"

"No."

"Have I done anything to make you think I don't love you?"

"No." My eyes fill with tears.

"Then why for heaven's sake do you think I can live without you?"

"You'll learn!" I burst into tears and approach him. "You'll learn to live without me as I've learned to live without you." I fall to my knees in front of him and put my head on his thigh. "You might think our love is enough, but it isn't. You love me now, and maybe through the coming years, but how can you continue to love me when you realize I've taken away your dream?"

"Josephine," he grasps my shoulders, forcing me to raise my head and look into his anguished eyes. "What is my dream?"

"I can recite it by heart." I sniff. "I've read it a thousand times."

"What is my dream?" He wipes the tears from my cheek.

"To wake beside your wife in the morning and hear the sound of children's laughter." I look down and stroke my belly.

"That's not my dream." He raises his voice and pulls me up between his legs. I lower my head to look into his distressed eyes. "My dream is to wake **beside you** in the morning." He takes my hands and kisses them. "To wake beside my beautiful wife and feel that I'm the luckiest man in the world."

"But Gabriel." I try to pull my hands away but he refuses to let go. "That's only the first part of your dream. I can never give you the second part."

"The first part is an entire world." He stands and cups my cheeks with his hands. "Nothing else interests me. You aren't the only one who has lost the ability to fall pregnant. We're together in this story. I will never give you up and I won't allow you to give me up."

He bends his head and gently kisses my lips. I feel the power of his love flowing through my veins, and my heart pleads to heal.

"You will hate me because of it," I whisper, closing my eyes. "And how can I live with the knowledge that you hate me?"

"After everything we've been through together..." He steps away from me and shakes his head in disappointment. "You still don't understand that my love for you doesn't depend on anything. I was crushed when I realized that you'd left me, and when I saw you in your father's house I didn't know if I wanted to embrace you or shake you." Taking off his jacket, he loosens his tie. "I could only hate you if you do one thing. Leave me."

He walks past me into the bathroom, and my heart pounds in my chest. The confidence I feel in my decision shatters inside me. And now I don't know what to do.

"Gabriel, we haven't finished talking," I say desperately, walking up and down.

"So I suggest you join your husband in the bath," his loud voice sounds from behind the door and I approach and lean against the door frame.

Run. Run. Run.

Opening the door, I gaze at his perfect back. His skin is tanned and the muscles in his shoulders stretch as he bends to take off his trousers. For so many nights, I fantasized about those arms holding me and his chest sheltering me. I swallow and push myself inside before the voice of reason overcomes my ferocious need for him.

He sits down in the tub and his small smile makes me blush. No man has touched me for a year and a half. For a year and a half **he** hasn't touched me, and now I feel unworthy.

"Don't think so much." He continues to smile. "My wife is known for her impulsiveness, don't spoil it with all those confusing thoughts."

I laugh briefly and remove my dress before the thoughts return. I stand in front of him only in my underwear, hugging myself in shyness.

"My perfect wife," he murmurs, his eyes traveling over my body.

Just two words, which for one rare moment, make me see what he sees in me, drive away the shyness. I remove my clothing, get in and sit down opposite him, the foam hiding my naked body. Leaning my head back, I close my eyes and sigh.

"Tell me what happened to you from the moment I parted from you in the street," he asks tenderly, pulling my foot towards him.

I open my eyes and look at him in horror.

"Josephine, as you have already understood, I have no intention of allowing you to escape from me again." He massages my foot, his eyes shining with love for me. "I suggest you tell me everything without omitting a single detail so that your story won't be a dark cloud over our relationship."

"I'm not sure you understand the implications of your decision to stay with me." Holding my elbow, I contort my face.

"I'm still not sure you understand the implications of running away from me again," he responds expressionlessly. "We won't continue to discuss it because, first of all, we need to get rid of that fog hanging over your beautiful head. It's time for me to hear your story."

"I don't believe you haven't heard it." I rub my elbow, trying to understand how he could still want me. Why for heaven's sake is he so determined to stay with me?

"I've heard it." He caresses my calves then massages my foot again. "But it took me time to gather all the pieces of the puzzle and it's important to me to hear the full story from you."

"I'd rather not. I'm trying to forget, trying to suppress…"

"I need to hear it. And more important, **you** need to tell me!"

I bite my lips again and again. "All that happened was that I went upstairs to get your album and then it all went wrong." I rub my forehead and he doesn't say a word. "When I went to the door I heard the loud steps on the staircase, and then orders and shouts in German. There was nowhere to run."

"I don't understand why you went back for the album."

"Because it was yours. When you weren't with me I found it comforting. I read and reread your declarations of love and that's what kept me sane."

"But I explained you had to go," he insisted.

"It was foolish and childish. But it was too important to me."

Pulling me towards him, he sat me between his legs. His arms envelope me and his warm body clings to me like a human shield.

"Go on." He kisses my head.

"They burst in and I realized that it was too late for me but maybe not for you."

"Why didn't you tell them I'd escaped? That you knew nothing about my treachery? You could have tried to save yourself."

"It didn't cross my mind even once." I put my head on his shoulder and sigh. "If I'd said anything like that they'd have gone in pursuit."

"I'd have managed," he sounds distressed. "I'd prepared for it all my life."

"You needed two hours, and I chose to give them to you." I give him the details of the sequence of events. "And then time ran out. Two hours passed." I tremble as I recall the hard blows. "But I knew in my heart that you were safe, so I didn't care what would happen later on."

"How did you get out of the building?" His body hardens.

"I was unconscious." I press his arm, "but proud. Because, for the first time in my life, I understood the game and thought two steps ahead."

He is silent for a long time and then he growls faintly and holds me tightly.

"You sacrificed yourself to save me."

"Sometimes you have to sacrifice the queen to save the king. You taught me that." I cough to fight off the tears.

"The king would have left the game if he'd known that would be the result."

"I know, and that's why it was so important to me to do it."

"Go on." He clears his throat and I realize that it is more difficult for him to hear than it is for me to relate.

"When I regained consciousness I saw I was in the Gestapo cellars. It isn't really a cellar, you know? Just a musty room stinking of decay."

"What did they ask you during the interrogation?" The tension is evident in his voice.

"What I knew about you."

"And what did you say?"

"That you're a diamond dealer from Switzerland." Laughter mixed with tears. "But they assumed I knew more than that and, ultimately, I did tell them all I knew."

"About my father? About Vincent? About…"

"Certainly not." I rub my elbow. "I told them all I knew about my husband. Your favorite taste, smell, flower, your dream…"

"*Mon Dieu*, Josephine," he shouts, and his fierce embraces suffocates me. "You don't play games with people like that."

"Yes." My face contorts when the memory becomes unbearable. "They didn't behave like gentlemen, and the broken result is now sitting between your legs."

"Broken?" He strokes my elbow. "Even if they twisted the petals of the Fleur-de-Lis, it would still resemble the white lily."

"That lily is not really white anymore." I allow my tears to flow freely. "But I received another rose. I lay on that filthy floor, broken, damaged and hopeless, and then a little angel appeared."

"Frederique…"

"I still don't know how he managed to lift me, evade the patrol and get down to the cellar. I remember only flashes of his calming smile. But he managed to haul me through a small window where his friend was waiting. I owe them my life."

"Although I didn't offer them your life in exchange for their heroism, believe me, I made sure they won't have to work another day in their lives." Gabriel massages my shoulders, and I begin to come to terms with the fact that he has captured me again, and there is now no chance that I will get away from him. I'm anchored to him and no force in the world will make me disengage.

"They left me at Madame Distel's brothel and the rest you already know." I fall silent, praying this will suffice.

"Tell me about the doctor."

I shake my head, refusing to return to that cursed night, the shattering of my hopes and with them, my dreams.

"Josephine, tell me about the doctor!"

"I was unconscious!"

"I know you remember." He kisses my head. "Please, tell me."

I can't believe he is making me relive my nightmare. "I was hemorrhaging badly and he had to carry out a D&C. I don't know if I lost the ability to fall pregnant because of the blows I received or because of his treatment. What is certain is that I'm barren." I raise my knees to get up, but his arms won't let me and I burst into tears.

"Gabriel, why would you want to live with a woman like me? I released you, why don't you pursue your dream? You are my perfect man. The love of my life. I beg you to understand my decision and find happiness elsewhere."

Moving my arms aside, he puts his hand on my belly and the sobs shake my body.

"You're my perfect woman. The love of my life. And I beg you to let me continue to be happy with you."

His beautiful words rip out my heart. "Why did it take you so long to come to me?" I ask in a small voice, wiping my tears.

"I managed to make contact with Vincent only a few months after Paris was liberated." He sighed. "The war continued and each of us was on a different front. Until then I was calm because a week after our parting I got a telegram from him saying that you were safe in a village in Belgium."

"He lied to you?"

"He thought it was the right thing to do." His fingers smooth my belly. "He knew that if I found out the truth, I'd immediately return to Paris."

"But they'd have caught and hanged you." I suffocate.

"That wouldn't have stopped me from coming."

I link my fingers in his. "And Marie? Didn't she tell you?"

"I tried to call her many times. She apparently refused to be the one to tell me."

"So how did you find out?"

"When the war in Europe ended, I returned to our home, and there I found Marie and your letter. I felt as if the ground was swept from under my feet. My world collapsed. And there was nothing I could do to fix it. I was there and you were here."

"I'm sorry…" His pain distresses me.

"I knew it was only a matter of time before I could leave Europe and return you to me. But every day that passed seemed like eternity, until I feared I'd lose my mind."

"I felt like that, too." Splashing water on my face, I stand up. "But I believed I was doing it for you." Covering myself with a towel, I go to the door.

Don't turn around. Don't turn around. Don't turn around.

Turning my head, I'm drawn to the electricity that connects the fragments and unites them.

My heart expands and expands, and when I feel my lips curving in a smile, he leaps from the bath, lifts me in his arms and carries me into the bedroom.

He sets me gently down on the mattress and his enormous chest shelters me.

"What can I do to make you happy?" His eyes are burning with passion, and I accept my defeat. My body shivers from the onslaught of a surge of heat. I need him as I need air to breathe.

"Compensate me for the time I missed you."

"Your wish is my command." Leaning forward, he kisses my lips.

I take his head and press it to me, drinking in his lips, devouring them, panting in the fierce need for his touch. For the first time since they broke me I feel whole.

"We'll do it differently this time." He pulls his head back and smiles his small, mesmerizing smile. "I will compensate each part of your body for the time I lost with you." Putting his head in my neck, he kisses the top of it. His lips cling to my burning skin and he gently sucks at it. His lips pass over my chin, return to my neck and from there to my collar bone. His tongue flutters over it and his teeth bite my shoulder.

Leaning on his elbow, he lifts my hand. Kisses each one of my fingers and goes up to my elbow. He kisses the prominent bone once and then returns to gaze at me. "You're much more beautiful now." He kisses it again, and I try unsuccessfully to fight the tears.

His lips return to my neck and then descend to my chest. My body surrenders to him completely.

He raises his head, closes his eyes and leaning over, his lips cling to my belly.

"Not there," I cry out in frustration, trying to move his head.

He presses my palms to the mattress and rains a shower of tiny kisses on my belly. "I love every part of you." He says, licking my navel. My eyes burn from the salt of the tears, and I no longer try to fight him. Each of his kisses seems to penetrate my belly, uniting all the fractures, enveloping everything I felt was broken, with layers of protectiveness. I manage to feel womanly, healthy. "For me you will always be perfect." He releases my hands and spreads my legs. "I'm in my favorite place." He tenderly kisses me. "I smell my favorite scent." Sinking his nose into my neck, he gently takes me.

"Now I'm living my dream." He smiles at me, and I gaze at the features of his perfect face. Putting my hands on his chest, I feel the fast beatings of his heart. I can't even blink. I'm mesmerized.

He closes his eyes and enters me again. Harder and faster. The muscles in his arms swell from the effort and his groans sound like a melody to me.

Suddenly, his eyes open and I feel him tremble.

"My Josephine, I love you."

CHAPTER FORTY-SEVEN

I'm sitting in the taxi and, this time, instead of gazing at the view, I gaze at my man. He seems so at ease in his tailored suit and his hand doesn't leave mine.

"I'm a little tense."

"I thought I'd managed to relax you several times in the course of the day." Gabriel winks at me and I laugh, glancing at the driver in embarrassment.

"Gabriel, my father is old. I think he needs me."

"I need you more."

"But…we haven't decided what we're going to do. He will probably want to know what our plans are."

"He understands that a woman needs to live with her husband." He responds drily.

"And where will that be?" I ask tensely as the taxi stops in front of the house,

"In our home."

"At home in Paris? In Switzerland? In England?"

"Wherever you choose." He holds my chin and kisses my lips.

"My home is wherever you are."

His answer makes me smile broadly, but when he opens the door of the taxi for me I realize I am even more confused now.

We stand at the door and I knock. It's the first time I do that. Nobody knocks on the door of his home, but now I no longer feel it is my home.

Susie opens the door and hugs me. She holds out her hand to Gabriel and when he kisses it, she rolls her eyes with pleasure.

"The moment I saw you I knew you wouldn't find a man who would excite you here." She chuckles. "Our guys here are good and kind but they lack the magic of European gentlemen. Gilbert, they're here!" She shouts and my father comes into the hallway. He looks troubled.

I fall upon him in an embrace and only after his arms close around me do I sigh with relief and step back.

"Monsieur Portiere." Gabriel shakes his hand.

"Monsieur Augustine." My father nods and examines him.

"I think we can dispense with the formality, call me Gabriel."

My father doesn't suggest the same. He turns into the living room, goes over to the fireplace and pours himself a drink.

I'm not used to seeing my father so lost in thought and I've never encountered impolite behavior on his part.

Tension eats away at me and I look helplessly at Susie.

"Gabriel, I'm so happy you've come." She gives me a soothing look. "I've prepared an excellent meal and I have no doubt that Gilbert is annoyed because I wouldn't allow him to taste the food."

I laugh nervously and she beckons us to join her.

My father puts his glass down on the counter and moves with us into the dining room. Before he can pull out my chair, Gabriel does so and I murmur words of gratitude and sit down.

I know that my father would prefer to hear the story in private, face to face from me,. but Gabriel insisted on being present. And now it seems I'm about to witness a head on collision and have no idea of how to prevent it.

"Let's wet our appetites with a drink." Susie pours wine for everyone and sits down. "I never used to enjoy alcohol, you know, but since I met your father, I…"

"What in God's name is going on here?" My father bangs on the table and she falls silent. My hands close in fists under the table and I look down. Gabriel takes my hand and puts it on his thigh.

"I understand that you're upset," Gabriel says with his usual ease. "But I promise you that your daughter is in good hands."

"She's in good hands because she's in my hands," says my father irritably. "You haven't yet received my blessing."

"I think it's a little late for that." Susie chuckles, and turns pale when my father stares at her.

"She's right," Gabriel says drily. "We've been married for two years. I'd have been glad to ask permission, but while you were resting here, I was busy saving her from the Nazis."

Raising my head I give him a hard look. My father's behavior doesn't justify Gabriel's diminishing him. I have difficulty understanding Gabriel's rudeness.

"My young friend, I wasn't resting here, I came here to take care of…"

"Your wife," Gabriel finishes his sentence. "You indeed did what you had to do, but without intending it, you left your daughter with your good friends, and they planned to sacrifice her in order to save themselves."

My father's eyes open in shock.

"Papa, it wasn't exactly like that." I burst out. "Claude was a hero. He spied for the British and gave his life for France."

"So what did he mean?" My father taps on his glass, without taking his eyes off me.

"In a war one has to make concessions." I insist on protecting the honor of the people I loved. "It was one in exchange for three. There is logic in that, it…" I try to work out how to explain myself.

"There is a great deal of logic in it," Gabriel continues. "Claude was indeed a hero and he did what he was told to do, but you have no idea of the degree to which he jeopardized your daughter."

My father continues to tap on the glass, looking incredulous. Susie sips her wine, looking at him with pain.

"I asked her to marry me to save her, but neither of us expected what happened later on."

"You fell in love." Susie puts her hand on her heart and sighs.

"No." Gabriel caresses my hand under the table, and we all look at him in astonishment. "Fell in love isn't strong enough. That describes a momentary emotion, something that passes, and I love Josephine more that I love myself. She has become my life, my home and my entire world. I hope you bless our marriage, but even if you don't, I will never give her up."

Susie sighs again, and I smile lovingly at him.

"So why the hell did you run away from him?" My father stands up and his chair falls noisily to the floor. "If this is such a great love, explain why you ran away from him. And why didn't you tell me you were married?"

I stroke my belly and bite my lip.

"I think you should leave that to us," Gabriel says firmly.

"I wasn't talking to you!"

"Papa, I wanted to save him," I cry out, standing up. "I wanted to release him because I believed I wasn't worthy of him. I still think so." I collapse onto the chair and cover my face with my hands, trying desperately to hide my tears.

"Why wouldn't you be worthy of him?" My father cries, coming to sit down on my other side. "What could a noble soul like yours do to hurt him?"

"Nothing." Gabriel presses my thigh and I hear the pain in his voice. "There is nothing in this world that she could do to hurt me. It seems I failed. I should have protected and kept her safe, I should have saved her again."

"Papa," I dry my tears. I hear Susie's sobs and continue to look at my father's anguished face. "I still don't understand why he chooses to stay with me, and I hope that one day I will learn to forgive myself for my weakness with him. Because now I cannot let him go."

"What did they do to you?" My father's eyes are moist and I shake my head.

"They did nothing to her that could make her less than perfect." Gabriel turns to me and holds my head. "You are my perfect wife."

My father stands staring at me. His gaze passes to Gabriel and then back to me. I smile a small smile and nod my head once. He closes his eyes, and when he opens them he nods back.

"Well, I think it's time to raise a glass." My father wipes his eyes on a serviette. "I've heard everything I need to hear to understand that this man is exactly what my daughter needs."

Holding the glass of wine, he looks dreamily at the red liquid. "If you ever wish to tell me what happened, you know I'm here for you."

I let out a sigh of pain and relief and nod vigorously.

"Your husband is right. Some things should remain between husband and wife." He raises his glass and we join him. "I would like to raise a glass to Gabriel, my new son."

I burst into tears and Gabriel puts his arm around me and kisses my head.

My father taps on the glass, signaling that he isn't finished. "And I wish to raise a glass to my beautiful, married daughter and pray…" He raises his head. "That their love will conquer any challenge."

The glasses clink against each other and I take a sip of wine and sigh exhaustedly.

"With your permission, I would like to make a toast." My eyes meet Gabriel's and my heart misses a beat.

"I would like to thank you for this wonderful evening and to thank you personally, Monsieur, for managing to create a masterpiece." He kisses the end of my nose. "I promise you that I will do all I can to make her happy, and fulfill her every wish. And so, I will ask her here, too, in your presence. Josephine, my lovely wife, is there anything I can do to make you happy?"

My heart spins and a sweet sense of completion envelopes me.

"I think the time has come for us to build a home." I caress his cheek.

"Your wish is my command." He winks at me and I smile broadly. "You just have to tell me where to set the foundation stones."

"Paris. It has always been Paris."

EPILOGUE

I peep from behind the curtain and see the last model walk out before the audience. The storm of applause makes me smile with relief, and I wait tensely to be called to the stage.

In the first rows I recognize my father and Susie, Maurice and Natalie with the infant, Nita, in her arms, and Madame Distel who is wearing a cloak and waving a fan. Even Marie is sitting there in the elegant gown I sewed for her, looking especially excited.

Where is my husband?

The organizer calls my name and I continue to look around for him.

"I'm always here, looking out for you." The deep voice comes from behind me, and his arms encircle me. He kisses my shoulder and turns me to him. "You look beautiful." He brushes my hair aside and examines my face. "But one thing is missing to make you look perfect."

I look at him in confusion and peep in the mirror.

He puts his hand in his trouser pocket and takes out a small velvet box. When he opens it my eyes open in astonishment.

"It took me a while to find them." He laughs and hands me the box. I touch the diamond earrings with trembling fingers, and can't find the right words to thank him. "There is no doubt that these are the diamonds that have cost me the most money." He shrugs and I take them out of the box and put them in my ears.

"I have the perfect husband." Holding his cheeks in my hands, I kiss him fiercely.

The organizer calls my name again and I take a deep breath, hold my elbow and go out to the stage.

The applause makes my heart tremble and I smile shyly. The organizer hands me the microphone and the audience falls silent. I survey the elegant venue. The boutique looks wonderful. A score of vases with yellow roses are arranged on tables along the walls, but the most beautiful decorations are the smiles of those I love.

I clear my throat and stand erect.

"I would like to thank all the honored guests who have come to share this evening with me." I fall silent as tears choke me and I hear steps in the direction of the door. My handsome husband is leaning against the door frame looking lovingly at me. "I hope you like my new collection."

The applause and cries of enthusiasm from the audience make my smile broaden.

"This boutique has opened today so that I may share my creations with you, but, for me, it also symbolizes something greater." I don't try to wipe away the tears running down my cheeks. "It symbolizes freedom, love and hope and, more than anything else, it symbolizes my need to remember." I lick my lips and taste the salt of my tears. "Remember that our freedom is not to be taken for granted. Remember all those, brutally taken from us and remember the path. The right path that even in the darkest of times, makes us maintain our humanity."

I wave my hand to quieten the applause.

"We are unable to express our dream until it is taken from us." I briefly stroke my belly and sink into the calming eyes of my husband. "Tonight I am fulfilling the dream of a friend who wasn't able to fulfil it herself." My glance passes over the first row and Natalie smiles painfully at me and wipes her tears. "There is, I believe, one dream that I will probably never fulfil but it doesn't cloud my joy or the wholeness of my family. The spotlight illuminated our path and we were blessed with a miracle." I shift my gaze to the last chair in the first row and my heart spins with pride. "Each of us deserves at least one miracle." I blow a kiss to Leon, and his black, deer-like eyes shine with love for me.

Gabriel comes on stage. He takes a rose from one of the vases, hands it to me and lifts me up. "You're mistaken. Our miracle happened during the war." He kisses me fiercely and the audiences claps. "A year ago we received another miracle."

I stroke his cheek and burst into tears. He didn't give up, he gave me the right to be the mother of a rare treasure and my boundless love has healed my soul. We fought to be a family.

This time we won.

I place the rose on my heart and turn my head towards the inner wall. I nod to Frederique, he is standing next to the curtain hiding the sign with the boutique's name.

Frederique winks at me and tugs at the fabric. The audience stands and I lean against Gabriel and look at the sign with pride.

I promised myself I would never forget, and today everyone remembers.

Fleur-de-Lis.

Made in the USA
Columbia, SC
16 July 2023